I0768553

perfect pairing

AMANDA CHAPERON

before you read

Perfect Pairing is a steamy small town romance full of explicit language and sexual content. To avoid—or locate—the open door chapters, please flip to the Dicktionary I've provided in the back. For the complete list of content warnings, please visit my website at www.achaperonauthor.com.

Part One

I knew I was playing with fire when we met,
so I couldn't blame you when I got burned.

— BRIDGETT DEVOUE

chapter 1
Ezra

I DRANK WAY TOO much last night for someone about to enter a job interview.

My head pounded in time with my heart, and I could practically feel the bourbon oozing from my pores.

I just had to hope my future employers couldn't smell it on me—or were willing to overlook it, given the hellscape my life had become in the last six months.

This "interview" was more of a formality anyway. The couple in question had been trying to poach me for years, but I'd never had any desire to leave New York City.

Now, I wanted to run as far away from this godforsaken place as I could get.

"Mr. Wendt?" a voice inquired softly, and I looked up to find a hostess staring expectantly at me. "Let me take you to your table. The rest of your party is already here."

"Oh," I said, hopping to my feet. "Thank you."

As we wove through the tables to one near the windows, Manhattan sprawled below our perch on the fifteenth floor of the hotel, sweat prickled along my forehead, my gut churning. The last thing I wanted was to eat, but I needed something in my stomach before I purged bile all over the ugly blue carpet.

"Ezra, my boy!" Leon Delatou boomed, both he and his wife, Lena, rising to greet me.

I met Leon and Lena about three years ago. They'd been in New York on business and came into my restaurant. When they'd opted for the tasting menu, which consisted of courses I'd carefully curated and paired with different wines and cocktails, I'd emerged from my cave in the kitchen to greet them. The tasting menu wasn't cheap, and I figured I owed it to them to show my face and thank them for trusting me.

Both had fawned over me and my food, endlessly singing my praises. It had done wonders for my ego, and when I found out they owned a winery in Michigan, I'd sat down to learn more. We wound up chatting for hours.

After all, food and wine went hand-in-hand.

We'd stayed in touch since then, and every time I saw them, Leon asked if I was ready to join the Delatou family and work at the winery.

That day had finally arrived.

Hopefully, given my less-than-composed state, the offer wasn't off the table. They knew what I'd been going through, though. I'd explained as much when I reached out a few weeks ago to express my interest in finally making the jump, and they'd been sympathetic and understanding.

Leon heartily shook my hand, practically giving me motion sickness, and Lena pressed a kiss to my cheek. When she pulled away, her golden eyes narrowed.

Yeah, I knew I had bourbon seeping from my pores. I hadn't even bothered to shower this morning after I dragged myself off the couch where I'd passed out the night before. I'd just popped some Advil, splashed cold water on my face, changed my clothes, put on deodorant, and brushed my teeth.

Honestly, the shower wouldn't have helped. The bourbon in question, which had been full last night, sat nearly empty on my table in the light of day.

God, the thought made me want to gag.

I really needed to get my shit together—if not for my sake, then at the very least for Hansen.

Hence this meeting. I was *trying*.

"Are you okay?" Lena asked softly.

I simply shook my head. I wasn't, and I didn't know if I ever would be again.

But again...I was trying.

A moment after we'd taken our seats, a waiter appeared and passed out menus.

"Can I get you guys started with anything to drink?" he asked, his peppy tone doing nothing to quell my roiling gut.

"Wa—" I started, but Lena cut me off with a glare.

"We'll each have a Bloody Mary," she ordered, closing her menu with a *snap*. "Fully loaded. And the full appetizer spread." She glanced at me sympathetically and added, "Plus a pitcher of ice water."

The waiter winked at her. "You got it, ma'am. I'll be right back with those."

"I'm not sure—"

Lena once again stopped me mid-sentence. "I can smell the liquor from here, Mr. Wendt. A little hair of the dog won't hurt. Frankly, you look—"

"Like shit," her husband finished for her.

I choked on a laugh. "I'm sorry," I murmured.

"Don't be," Leon said amiably, waving his hand. "You've been going through a lot, which is, I'm assuming, what prompted this meeting."

"I need a change of scenery, and I can't think of anywhere better to start over than Michigan."

Leon cleared his throat. "We're not a last resort, Ezra."

"No, no," I said placatingly, holding up my hands. "I know that. I just..." I trailed off, searching for the best way to say it without completely losing my shit. "I want Hansen to grow up happy and away from all this." I twirled a finger in the air to encompass the city and our lives inside it, which had taken a steep dive into the gutter in recent months. "You're parents," I implored. "You have to understand that."

The couple shared a look, Leon placing his broad palm atop Lena's slender one on the table. Surely, they were thinking of their five daughters.

"We do," Lena said, meeting my gaze. "And we don't begrudge you wanting to protect Hansen. Life on the peninsula is a lot slower, though. Quiet. Are you sure you're ready for that?"

"Yes," I answered vehemently. "Slow and quiet is exactly what we need."

"Well," Leon said slowly, "as it turns out, our current chef is ready to move onto...greener pastures." He practically spat the last two words, and I sensed some bad blood there.

"I don't want greener pastures. I've had a charmed life, as far as my career goes, and look where it landed me. What I want is Chateau Delatou."

The Delatous shared a look again before Leon looked at me

with a broad smile. "Then welcome to the family."

The lead weight on my shoulders lifted a fraction, and I returned his grin.

"There's just one more thing," Leon added, his expression quickly sobering.

There it was: the other shoe. I should've known it wouldn't be so simple.

"Yes?"

"Stay away from my daughters." I let out a surprised snort, but he plowed ahead. "You're young, you're...attractive, and so are they. But they aren't available to you. Understood?"

I chuckled, the tension in my body easing. "Trust me, sir—that will *not* be a problem."

After my marriage—a relationship in name only, our lives bound by a goddamn piece of paper and, of course, our son—and subsequent messy-as-fuck divorce, the last thing I wanted or needed was a new woman in my life, least of all one of my new bosses' daughters. No, from now on, all my focus was on Hansen and pulling us out of this blackhole we'd found ourselves in.

"I've heard that before," he grumbled, but his serious expression quickly morphed into a grin as he shook my hand over the table.

"You'll just love Apple Blossom Bay," Lena gushed, ignoring her husband's thinly veiled threats. "It's the most picturesque little town, and there are a lot of kids Hansen's age who go to school in Traverse City. There's a carpool system since the buses don't run up there. I can put you in touch with the organizers."

My shoulders lowered further. It had been a long time since I'd had anyone mother me, and in that moment, I was more thankful for Lena Delatou than I could ever say. Don't get me wrong, I loved my dad, but he didn't exactly have a woman's touch. The man was gruffer than I was, which was saying something, considering my staff had routinely called me "Chef Cranky" behind my back.

I never called them on it because...they weren't wrong.

A loveless marriage and growing up without a mother would do that to a guy.

Leon shifted around and withdrew a sheaf of papers from the inside of his sport coat. "And I've taken the liberty of printing some real estate listings for you. Are you interested in renting or buying?"

"Buying," I answered quickly. "Something with a yard and three bedrooms."

"And a large kitchen, of course," Lena said knowingly.

"Well, that's a given," I told her with a grin.

Hell, it felt good to smile. Until that moment, I hadn't been sure I remembered how.

"Three bedrooms?" Leon asked suspiciously.

"I'm hoping my dad will want to come with us," I said. "I haven't asked yet, but..."

"But he's your father," Lena said softly. "I'm sure he'll jump at the chance."

I smiled at her, hoping she was right. When everything with Shannon had gone down, Dad moved in to help with Hansen, and the transition had been seamless. After all, he'd been a single dad most of my life. He knew how it was. We had a nanny for when one or both of us had to work, but typically, at least one of us was always home with Hansen. My dad loved that little boy, and Hansen adored his Papa.

"How soon do you think you can get packed up and moved?" Leon asked.

"Well...I know it was presumptuous of me, but I've already put my two weeks in at work. My last day is Friday."

Leon chuckled and softly shook his head. "Bold."

I shrugged, knowing I had nothing to lose. Whether or not the Delatous had given me a job, I still planned on leaving New York. "I was hoping you'd take pity on a man down on his luck."

Lena reached across the table and settled her warm palm over my hand. "I'm sorry, you know," she said quietly.

Swallowing hard around the lump in my throat, I could do nothing but nod and offer her a grim smile.

Leon barreled ahead. "If you're done here in a week, can we get you started at the winery the last week of June? If that's not too soon."

"That's perfect," I said quickly. "We'll need some time to get settled, and if you have any ideas on childcare, I'd be happy to hear them."

"We can help with that too," Lena said. "In fact, I'd happily take him during the week until you and your father get settled and figure something else out."

Already, I was opening my mouth to protest. "Absolutely not. You're already doing too much for me. I can't take advantage of you that way."

"I'm a parent too, remember?" Lena said. "We had a lot of help with the girls while they were growing up and we were busy at the winery. Trust me, I don't mind doing this for you."

"But—"

"You'd be wise to be quiet and accept her help, son," Leon said. "She's not going to take no for an answer."

I snapped my mouth shut, heeding Leon's warning. The whole thing was...overwhelming. Having a matronly figure in my corner, and having people who weren't related to me genuinely care what happened to me and my son? It had been me and my dad against the world for so long, and then I'd gotten married, and my priorities had shifted to encompass my wife and Hansen.

And now, Shannon was no longer in the picture, but the Delatous stepping up to take some of the edge off that loss was enough to make me cry.

But I'd cried and raged and despaired enough over the last six months.

It was time to move on.

When I pushed through the door of our condo on the Upper West Side a few hours later, I found my dad and Hansen in the kitchen. Hansen was bellied up to the island in his highchair, a half-eaten stack of French toast in front of him. His face, hands, and bare chest were covered in syrup. My dad was at the stove, spatula in hand, also shirtless, a towel tossed over his shoulder.

Dad raised a brow at me in question, and I couldn't help but grin in response. Still, I didn't speak as I crossed the room to my son and dropped a kiss atop Hansen's messy curls. The poor kid had gotten my genes, his head a deep brown mop perpetually in dire need of a cut.

"Well?" my dad prompted.

"Hey, Hansen?" I asked my little boy, ignoring my dad.

"Yeah, Daddy?"

"How would you feel about moving?"

Around a mouthful of bread, Hansen asked in that little boy voice of his, "Where?"

"I was thinking Michigan."

"What's that?" He never took his attention away from where he swiped his plastic fork through the remnants of syrup on his highchair tray.

"Somewhere far away from here."

Hansen, who was barely two and thus perpetually unperturbed by the world around him unless it directly affected his sleeping and eating schedule, shrugged and said, "Okay."

And that was that.

"When do we leave?" Dad asked.

I whirled on him, surprise raising my brows.

"You want to come? I mean, I planned on asking, but..."

"You guys are the only things keeping me here, Ez," he assured me, settling a hand on my shoulder. My mother left him a long time ago, when I was barely Hansen's age, content to sow her wild oats instead of staying to raise her son. To this day, I had no idea where she was, nor did I want to know. Since then, it had been me and Dad against the world. He'd always known what to do and say to bring me back to Earth when I spiraled, and that he was willing to uproot his life to follow me and Hansen across the country meant more than I could ever say. Still, my eyes watered, and I sniffed loudly.

"Are you sure?"

"More sure than I've ever been about anything. Besides, I'm not getting any younger. It's about time I retire, don't you think? I can spend my free time taking care of our little rascal."

I shrugged. "You don't have to do that, Dad. I'm sure there are construction companies in Michigan."

My dad had been a construction foreman for my entire life, getting his start as a day laborer when he was barely in his mid-twenties and working his way up. Now, at sixty, he more than deserved to retire and relax.

Apparently, his idea of relaxing was helping me raise my child, who, like me and through no fault of his own, was motherless.

"I want to," he promised. "Plus, Michigan sounds like an awfully big adventure."

"Like *Peter Pan*!" Hansen crowed.

My dad shot his grandson a wink. "Exactly."

"Well..." I said slowly, eyes darting between the two. "How quickly do you think we can pack?"

Hansen cheered loudly, shooting upward in his chair so quickly, he nearly toppled out of it. After a scare when he was younger when he nearly choked because I couldn't get him un-buckled fast enough, I was loath to strap him in. I caught him at the last moment and swung him around in my arms, joining in on his chant of, "Mich-i-gan!"

Even the *thought* of getting the fuck out of New York had my spirits lifting.

Michigan, here we come.

"Dada, I have to potty."

From the passenger seat, my dad groaned, and I echoed the sentiment.

Obviously, I was all for Hansen learning how to use the toilet. He was nearly two and a half, and I was getting sick of changing diapers. I'd started potty training him about four months ago, shortly after he turned two, and to say it had been a struggle thus far would've been a gross understatement.

So when my boy told me he had to potty, I was scanning the interstate for signs indicating the next exit—even though we stopped not thirty minutes ago.

"You should've put him in a Pull-Up this morning," my dad said.

"Shh," I hissed. "That's a dirty word in this family now. I'm not going to undo all the progress he's made just because you don't feel like stopping every ten seconds."

"You don't feel like stopping either!" he said through clenched teeth.

"Whatever," I grumbled as I navigated us onto the off-ramp.

We were in some tiny town in the middle of nowhere Michigan, maybe twenty miles outside of Traverse City, and the drive had taken significantly longer thanks to my son's tiny bladder and penchant for draining his water cup within thirty seconds every time we filled it.

On the way here, we'd spent a few nights in Niagara Falls. I'd lived in New York all my life and had never been. Before we'd left, Dad and I agreed some sort of family excursions beyond endless hours in the car would be good for us and Hansen. Once we'd crossed into Michigan, we also spent some time in Detroit, taking Hansen to the zoo. He was obsessed with the animals, particularly when it came to feeding the giraffes, and the photos would be memories I'd cherish for the rest of my life.

And yes, while the frequent stops were annoying, I wasn't about to tell my kid he couldn't have water, for fuck's sake. What kind of monster would do that?

"If we stop now, do you think you can last the rest of the way without going potty again?" I asked Hansen.

He shrugged. "Sure."

My dad snorted, and I couldn't help but grin. I had no doubt the kid was only telling me what I wanted to hear, but we were in the home stretch of our trip to our new life in Michigan. A moving company was bringing all of our belongings to our new home, and all we'd have to do when we arrived was unpack.

Following the signs, I turned left at the end of the exit and immediately pulled into a gas station parking lot, easing to a stop in a space alongside the building.

"You want to take him?" I asked my dad.

"Hell no," he said. "I love that kid, but you're on piss duty. I'll keep an eye on the car."

I rolled my eyes but got out and went around the back to free Hansen from his car seat.

"I gonna go potty," he said as I grabbed his hand and walked us inside.

"Yeah, bud. You're gonna go potty."

"Are you gonna go too?"

I shook my head as we stepped inside the dimly lit restroom and locked the door before I bent to help him with his pants and underwear.

"Nope. This one is all you, kid."

The problem with traveling and potty training a boy, I'd quickly come to learn, was that Hansen was too short to reach the toilet, which meant I had to hold him up and let him do his business.

Yeah, I had to hold him over the toilet so he could direct his little stream into the bowl instead of all over himself and the ground.

And who said parenthood wasn't glamorous?

Once he finished, I helped him dress again then withdrew the bottle of hand sanitizer from my pocket and squirted some into his hands, which he enthusiastically rubbed together and said, "All clean!"

I laughed and grabbed his hand again, leading us back outside.

Five minutes later, we were back on the road.

We'd barely left our old life behind, but the more miles I put between my family and the city made the weight I'd been carrying lessen significantly.

My life may have been in shambles, the events of six months ago dragging me deep into a pit of despair I hadn't been sure I'd ever find my way out of. But taking the first step into this new chapter was my way of digging myself out of that hole.

And for some reason, when we pulled up outside of our new home—a one-story Craftsman style on the edge of Apple Blossom Bay that had great bones and just needed some updating—I could already see the light.

"I CAN'T BELIEVE YOU'RE leaving me," my sister Delia whined, throwing herself backward onto my bed.

I made a squeak of protest when she disrupted the carefully folded stacks of clothes I'd set out to pack.

"Excuse you," Chloe protested. "You're not the only one she's leaving."

I rolled my eyes. "At least you three will still have each other," I said, gesturing to Chloe, Delia, and our other sister, Ella.

"Yeah, but it won't be the same," Ella murmured.

"It hasn't been the same since Amara left," I shrugged. "C'mon, you guys. Let's not get all sappy here. It's not like I'm moving to Europe like Mar did. I'm just going to Chicago."

"Might as well be the other side of the world," Delia pouted.

I picked up a sock ball and tossed it at her head. "God, you're dramatic."

Delia yelped, then lifted a rolled-up tee and whipped it at me.

"You're mean," she pouted. "You need to get laid. Get rid of some of that aggression. When was the last time you had sex, anyway? Wait...have you ever even done it?"

"Of course I have."

"Yeah, Lia," Ella piped up. "Don't forget about Brad on prom night."

While I wanted to be embarrassed, I couldn't help but grin as my sisters devolved into laughter.

In the most cliché moment of all time, I'd given my virginity to my senior prom date in the back seat of the limo. We'd thrown an after party at the Villa, and I'd used the parent-free opportunity to take care of that little problem. I hadn't wanted to move to New York with it hanging over my head. It hadn't been romantic or particularly comfortable, and it had lasted all of five minutes—both because he'd also been a virgin and because my parents had decided to stop by and check up on us.

Someone had told my dad where we were, and he'd unceremoniously wrenched open the limo door, brandishing a baseball bat and threatening Brad within an inch of his life until he ran away crying.

To this day, I still had no clue where he'd even gotten that bat.

Also, I was pretty sure I was the reason he'd enacted the no-messing-around-with-employees rule he happily bandied about when hiring some new guy. Brad had worked at the winery in various roles for years growing up.

I settled my hands on my hips and stared Delia down, but I softened immediately at the sadness lining her face.

Having sisters so close in age—barely four and a half years separated Chloe, the oldest, and me, the youngest—was both a blessing and a curse. Growing up, we'd been at each other's throats and joined at the hips in equal measure. But now that the drama of high school and our formative years was mostly behind us, they were my best friends, and I didn't really have too many girl friends outside of them. Sure, I'd made a few in college, but even in the few months since graduation, when we'd all flung ourselves to the four corners of the world to start our new lives, we'd lost touch. And I had *tried*, sending semi-regular texts in those early weeks just to check in and see how everyone was settling. But with different time zones and schedules, it became easier to just...let it go.

Maybe Chicago would be different.

Then again, I wasn't going there to play. I was going there to *work*, to cut my teeth at a patisserie under the tutelage of one of the most talented and world-renowned pastry chefs of our generation.

Bryce Newsome was a badass and kind of my idol. I still couldn't believe that out of the thousands of people who applied and the fifty she personally interviewed, she selected *me* to serve as her apprentice for the next year.

I was really looking forward to the opportunities the next twelve months would bring and to better honing my craft so I could return to Apple Blossom Bay and realize my dream of opening my own bakery.

Was the apprenticeship necessary to accomplish that goal? No. But when the application went live, I filled one out on a lark, including a video submission and recipe for my dad's favorite baklava. I'd taken it from my grandmother's old recipe book and tweaked it to make it my own, and it wound up being one of my favorite creations to date.

Bryce was equally as impressed as my dad, both by the recipe and my personality in front of the camera. Remembering my one-on-one interview with her still felt like floating through a dream—her kindness, how enthusiastic she'd been about my submission and my career potential. I still hadn't figured out what exactly had set me apart from all the other applicants, but I wasn't complaining. Chances like these didn't come around every day, and I wasn't taking a single second of it for granted.

"It really is a shame you're leaving, though," Chloe said, pulling me from my reverie. "I've been looking forward to you baking us those fucking delicious spiced apple cupcakes with those apples."

She pointed out the window to the grounds surrounding Mom and Dad's new house, which they'd finally completed construction on and moved into only a month ago. It was strange, finishing my culinary arts programs in New York and moving back to this house instead of the Villa or the one at the edge of Traverse City where we'd grown up. But the weirdness quickly dissipated when I settled in this new room and remembered home was wherever my family was.

At the edge of the property was a small apple orchard, filled with trees that had been planted there ages ago—well before any of us existed—and stood the test of time against the sometimes-harsh Michigan winters. The Granny Smiths were the same variety of apple that could be found closer to the winery as well as all over Apple Blossom Bay. In fact, the Bay was named because of the way those trees flowered in the springtime, their pretty soft pink and white blooms bursting from the trees and scenting the air with their incredible natural perfume. And when the petals started to fall? It was like nature's confetti littering the streets.

The variety was also ironic, given that my paternal grandmother's maiden name was Smith—so we referred to her as

Granny Smith.

She loved to cook, and though I was barely a year old when she passed, I loved that our mutual obsession with baked goods was something that connected us, even beyond death.

"You know what?" I said, an idea striking with Chloe's comment.

"Hmm?" Ella asked from where she stood at my floor-to-ceiling bookshelves, absently running her fingers over the spines.

"All of this can wait. What do you say we spend the afternoon with a little baking demonstration? I'll teach you how to make those *fucking delicious spiced apple cupcakes*."

Ella's head whipped in my direction so fast, I heard her neck crack. Chloe's mouth dropped open, and Delia gave me a wicked grin.

"Bee," Ella said quietly. "You just swore."

After a beat, I burst out laughing, and my sisters and I tangled our arms together to head down to the kitchen.

While I orchestrated the construction of the cupcakes, my sisters and I chatted about everything and nothing, alternating between reminiscing on our childhoods and making plans for the future.

There wasn't anywhere else I wanted to be in that moment, and my heart squeezed painfully at the thought of leaving in two days.

I knew I'd be back before long, but it didn't make it any easier to stomach the time we'd be apart.

After my sisters and I spent the previous evening first making cupcakes and then having a movie marathon, studiously ignoring the fact that I was gearing up to leave, we spent the morning packing. For all our cheerfulness the night before, it was a somber affair, where we only spoke when one of them asked if I was bringing something or where I wanted them to put another.

The squeezing discomfort in my chest, the band around my heart, only grew tighter as the day wore on. I had no idea how Amara made the decision to put an ocean between us.

At last, it was time to start loading the car because I'd be leaving the next day.

Naturally, when it involved heavy lifting, my sisters couldn't get away from Mom and Dad's house fast enough.

"If you stay and help, I'll treat you to lunch at the winery!" I shouted after them.

Ella and Chloe only laughed, but Delia turned and shot me a wink as they hopped into her ragtop Jeep. "Fat chance, baby Brie. You know we eat there for free."

"Those girls are awful," Mom said as she followed me out of the house.

"Truly. Who in the hell raised them?" my dad quipped.

I couldn't help but giggle, understanding my sisters not wanting to be here. Saying goodbye was tough.

"Are you sure you have to go now?" Mom asked as she loaded a basket of linens into the backseat of my car. "Why can't you stay until after the Fourth?"

"Because I want to get down there and get settled before my apprenticeship starts," I gently reminded her, like I had every day for the past several weeks.

"But it won't be the same without you," she pouted, looking so much like Delia from the day before that I nearly laughed.

If anyone ever wondered where we got our dramatics, I'd just point them in Lena Delatou's direction.

"That's what everyone keeps saying," I told her. "But I doubt you'll even notice I'm gone."

"Oh, we'll notice, all right," my dad said as he walked out of the house carrying two of my suitcases. "No offense, honey"—he looked at Mom—"but you can't cook for shit."

My mom pressed a hand to her chest, mouth dropping open in what I knew was mock outrage. "That's a bit like the pot calling the kettle black, don't you think, *honey*?"

Dad chuckled as he hefted the luggage into the car then turned and pressed a kiss to Mom's brow. "You know I love you. I didn't marry you for your skills in the kitchen."

"Then why did you?" she asked.

My dad's eyes darted in my direction, and he leaned in, whispering something in her ear that had my mom giggling like a schoolgirl.

"Gross," I said, though I couldn't help but grin. Their love was my favorite, the benchmark against which I measured my own relationships.

Then again, I'd never actually had a serious boyfriend. I'd had situationships in high school that fizzled out before they ever really started, and I'd had a few flings during culinary school, but no one had ever really caught my eye in a way that made me want to push for more.

I was starting to wonder what was wrong with me, and my only saving grace from a deep shame spiral was the fact that each of my sisters were also single.

And the reminder that I was only twenty-one. I wasn't exactly an old crone.

"I don't know why you're so worried about cooking," I said as we trudged back inside for another load of my stuff. "You spend all of your time at the winery anyway, and there's a perfectly good restaurant right there."

In fact, it was more than perfectly good. Arguably, it was one of the top restaurants in the entire state of Michigan. Our head chef had overseen kitchens in places like Rome and Paris, New York, Los Angeles, Miami. The fact that my dad had been able to coax him into working for our small-town winery was nothing short of a miracle.

"Speaking of which," my mom said to my dad conversationally. "Did the Wendts get settled?"

"Yes!" Dad said, his lips tipping up into a wide grin. "They arrived last week, and I spent a few hours at the new house helping them unpack."

"Why didn't you call me?" Mom asked. "I would've driven down to help."

My dad waved her off. "It's alright, honey. There will be plenty of time for you to help them out."

"Wait wait wait," I said, holding up a hand. "Who are the Wendts?"

"New chef and his family."

"*New chef*?" I asked, stalling in the middle of the foyer. "What the hell happened to Roscoe?"

My dad huffed an irritated sigh through his nose, the muscles in his jaw twitching as his teeth ground together. "He wanted out, so we let him go."

I gaped. Roscoe had been working for our family for *years*, since my sisters and I were toddlers running rampant through the vineyards. He used to feed us grilled peanut butter and jelly sandwiches and hand-squeezed lemonade for lunch, and he brought us his homemade chicken noodle soup when we weren't feeling well. Essentially, he'd been another father to us.

"What happened?" I asked softly.

Mom settled a hand on my arm. "He wanted to spend what was left of his career back in Europe."

There was more to it than that, but it said enough. We weren't where he wanted to spend his twilight years, and that was fine. Clearly, Dad didn't think so, but I knew he'd get over it. He and Mom hadn't wasted any time replacing him, after all.

I was included in the family business to an extent. Each of us girls owned shares of the company. Chloe was supposed to take over when Dad retired, and Amara had recently finished her MBA and stayed in Europe to expand the winery's international distribution. We'd all gone over to London to celebrate her graduation a couple months ago, and I couldn't be prouder of her. She and Chloe were built for their roles. On the flip side, my passions lay elsewhere. I preferred to be involved more in name only.

"So tell me more about this new chef," I said as we resumed packing my car.

"Oh, he's wonderful," Mom gushed as she loaded a box labeled *fantasy books*. "We met him a few years ago when we ate at his restaurant in New York City, and he's just such an amazing man, especially given everything he has been through."

"His food is quite honestly the best I've ever had," my dad confirmed before he ruffled my hair. "Next to yours, of course."

"Don't lie to me, old man," I said, wagging my finger at him. "Just because I *can* cook doesn't mean I'm the best. I'll stick to pastries."

"Fine, fine," Dad said. "You're...passable." I chuckled—he wasn't wrong. "Chef Wendt is...exceptional."

My curiosity was sufficiently piqued for a number of reasons. First, while my mother routinely fawned over any and every one—that was the kind of woman she was; she never met a stranger—my father was far more reserved with his praise. Not to mention, he had personally hired Roscoe back in the day and had not only been good friends with the man but also a big fan of his food.

To hear him speak so highly of this new guy was equal parts disconcerting and intriguing.

And that said nothing of the fact that this Chef Wendt had come from the city I spent the last four years in. I wondered if we'd ever crossed paths...then shook off the idea. There was no possible way.

"Well, what do you say?" I asked a few hours later, planting my hands on my hips and surveying the hatch of my SUV, which was packed floor to ceiling with boxes and suitcases. "Want to go grab lunch at the winery?"

"Yes!" Mom said, excitedly clapping her hands. "Today happens to be Ezra's first day, so it'll give you guys the chance to meet before you take off."

Ezra Wendt, I thought. The name tickled something in my brain, but I couldn't latch onto what.

"Great!" I said, genuinely looking forward to meeting him.

We piled into Dad's Suburban and headed down the peninsula. Mom and I chatted idly about them coming down to see me next winter when things at the winery slowed down for the season, and we discussed my plans to come home for Christmas. Soon, we pulled up to Chateau Delatou, and I found myself eager to get inside. I loved eating at the winery restaurant when Roscoe was running the show, and I couldn't wait to see how the new guy measured up.

We were shown to a table in the center of the dining room, and the hostess tried to give us menus before my dad waved her off.

"Tell Ezra three of the Delatous are here, and that we'll eat whatever he feels like making us," he said. The girl simply nodded and scurried off.

While we waited, my mom chatted animatedly about how well her flower garden was doing, the gossip she'd picked up at the diner the other day, and their plans for the Fourth of July—all of which she discussed like I'd be present.

My stomach growled, and I rocked side-to-side in my chair simply for something to do, my eyes scanning the room. Nearly all the tables were full, wine flowing, food disappearing quickly from plates as our guests enjoyed their afternoon. Ezra had really been thrown into the fire for his first day, and I admired the man's bravery for agreeing to start a new job in a new kitchen in the middle of our busiest season.

I swept my gaze over the heads of customers, and it snagged

on a tall, dark-haired man coming down the short hall from the kitchen, three plates balanced in his hands.

Inexplicably drawn to him, I couldn't tear my eyes away. I started my perusal at his feet, which were encased in a scuffed pair of white Chuck Taylors. Then, I dragged my gaze up—and up and up—over long, lean legs, a trim torso covered by a white button up shirt rolled to the elbows, exposing strong forearms dusted with dark hair. Higher still, my eyes roamed to the strong column of the man's throat, over his chiseled jaw shaded by stubble, and a long, straight nose. At last, I connected with his brown eyes, the same color as the burnt sugar crust atop a crème brulée.

The second our gazes collided, something shifted in me. It reminded me of that moment in romantic comedy movies when the lead and love interest meet for the first time, and everything around them fades away. The whole world narrowed to that point of contact. I didn't know how or why, but my *body* knew.

This man belonged to me, and I belonged to him.

His strides were confident as he crossed the dining room toward us, and though he shot smiles and words of greeting to every guest he passed, his eyes never wavered from mine.

Damn, was it hot in here, or was it just him?

"Ezra, my boy!"

I jerked like I'd been shocked, tearing my eyes from his and dropping them to the table, taking deep, steady breaths, attempting to calm my suddenly racing heart.

Holy shit. This *was Ezra?*

Almost instantly, I recognized him, but not because I'd never officially met the man. I'd never forget that chiseled face or the dark, unruly hair. I'd spent three hours ogling him from afar while he guest-lectured in one of my culinary arts classes, teaching us how to prepare a roast chicken, which was, according to him, a "staple in the repertoire of any chef worth their salt."

I silently thanked the universe for bringing him back into my life.

Did I have a little crush? Absolutely. Maybe I'd finally get my chance to act on it.

Even though we hadn't spoken a word and he'd barely spared a glance in my direction over the course of his instruction that day, something shimmered in the air between us. I doubt he felt it too, but now that he'd returned to my orbit, that thing was back, settling in my chest and pulling me in his direction.

It was the strangest sensation, giving crazy-boy-obsessed energy, but...I desperately wanted to see where it would go, if he would reciprocate.

Once Ezra set the plates on the table—loaded with sandwiches, bread lightly toasted and layered with meat, cheese, and vegetables—my dad stood and hauled him into one of those one-armed bro hugs, and I blinked in surprise.

Who was this man to make my father act twenty years younger than he was?

Mom rose and gave Ezra a kiss on the cheek before pulling away and smiling at him. "It's good to see you. How was the trip?"

"Great," he said. "Hansen loved Niagara Falls and the Detroit Zoo, and I'm just happy to be out of the city."

Mom and Dad nodded knowingly, and I wondered what his story was. I'd loved living in New York, being surrounded by all the amazing restaurants and bakeries, but nothing beat Apple Blossom Bay. For someone like Ezra, though, who had presumably grown up in the city, this change of pace and lifestyle had to have been...jarring.

Ezra's eyes landed on me again, and, as if remembering I sat there, my dad smacked himself on the forehead.

"I'm sorry, sweets," he said to me. Then, to Ezra: "This is our youngest, Brie."

Inhaling a deep, fortifying breath, I rose from my chair and extended my arm for a handshake. The moment Ezra's palm settled against mine and those eyes held my stare, my entire body electrified, like his hand was a live wire.

"So you're the infamous Baker Brie," he said, smiling. "It's nice to finally put a face to the name."

I groaned. "Please don't call me that."

"Why not?" Ezra asked, his smile taking on a hint of mischief. "I think it's cute."

Internally, I scoffed. *Cute.* Exactly how every woman wanted to be described by the hottest man she'd ever laid eyes on.

I shrugged. "I'm not a little girl anymore."

"No," he said, eyes sweeping me from head to toe in a way that made me want to squirm, lowering his voice so only I could hear, "you're not."

I dipped my head to hide my blush. "Right. So it's just Brie."

From behind me, my mother said, "I knew you two would hit it off."

"As *friends*," my dad growled.

Yeah, as friends, I thought wryly. Because heat *wasn't* settling low in my core from exchanging only a few words with this man, from the way his gaze scorched my skin.

Dad's rule about not fraternizing with company employees hadn't mattered much when we were younger. We'd been too worried about high school boys, parties, the latest fashion, and teenage drama to be worried about Dad's stuffy old colleagues.

But now...well, if he kept hiring men who looked like Ezra, my sisters and I were in trouble.

Ezra's gaze never strayed from my face as he grinned widely, and my eyes flicked to his mouth. His canines were slightly elongated, giving him a wolfish air, and I couldn't stop myself from envisioning him eating me alive.

I'd willingly let him consume me. Hell, I'd *thank* him for it.

"Well, *Just Brie*," Ezra said, "I've been dying to meet you. I hear you're a whiz in the kitchen, and I was wondering if you'd like to bake for me sometime."

They were such innocent words, but the sensual way they caressed my body held such promise.

I practically choked on my own tongue in my haste to answer. "Yes."

I didn't even have to think about it, and somehow, Ezra's smile only widened.

"That easy, huh?"

Attempting to cover the eagerness that had nothing to do with baking and everything to do with wanting to be near him, I said, "I love being in the kitchen," punctuating my words with a one-shoulder shrug.

"We have that in common, then."

"Somehow, I don't think that's our only similarity."

Wait, what? Where had *that* come from? I wasn't the brazen, take-life-by-the-balls sister. That title belonged to Delia, the wild middle child, and, on occasion, Amara, the second oldest. But *never* me.

"How about sometime next week?" Ezra asked.

"Oh, I'd love to, but—"

"But she's moving," Dad finished for me, dropping a heavy hand onto my shoulder, reminding Ezra exactly who I was in a silent threat to stay away.

"Moving where?" Ezra asked.

"Chicago," I said quickly before my dad could cut in again. "I'm doing an apprenticeship with a pastry chef there for the next year."

"Congratulations!" Ezra said, and it sounded like he meant it. "Well, next time you're home, we'll figure something out."

I grinned, unable to stop myself as I said, "It's a date."

chapter 3
Ezra

"Okay, buddy," I said, helping Hansen slip on his coat. "Papa is going to take you to play group, and Miss Lena is going to pick you up this afternoon and take you to her house until he gets off work. How does that sound?"

"Great!" Hansen cheered. "I love Miss Lena. She lets me go to the water."

He dragged out the word 'water' in an awestruck, little boy manner, and I couldn't help but grin. It eased my dad guilt that he so happily and easily rolled with the changes in our lives the last year.

They said it took a village to raise kids, and while I had absolutely no one on my side save my dad when we were in New York, moving to Michigan gave us the community we'd so desperately needed—the kind of family I'd longed for growing up.

Working at the winery was a breath of fresh air. The entire staff, from the corporate workers to the bus boys, the groundskeepers and the Delatou family themselves, welcomed me, Dad, and Hansen into the fold with open arms. I'd never be able to properly thank Leon and Lena for all they'd given me, so I simply made it my mission to be the best goddamn employee they'd ever seen.

Not to mention, my personal staff was a dream compared to the shit I'd dealt with in New York. Everyone deferred to my expertise and treated me with respect, which drastically cut down on my stress. I didn't leave work each night with the desire to drown myself in a bottle of bourbon simply to take the edge off.

I went home, read Hansen a story and tucked him into bed, then headed either to the living room to catch up with Dad or my room for a shower and an hour or two of *Criminal Minds.*

Life on the peninsula was exactly what my family needed. I breathed easier watching Hansen flourish, and my dad slipped easily into his new role with a local construction company the Delatous had connected him with.

In short, we were living the dream.

I dropped a kiss on Hansen's head then nudged him toward my dad, who grinned at me before extending his hand and tugging him out the door.

This morning, I had a meeting with Leon and Lena to discuss the winery's contribution to the Apple Blossom Bay Fall Festival, an event Hansen was greatly looking forward to. Apparently, they'd been discussing it all week at his play group—which was really a fancy term for pre-K—and he couldn't wait to walk through the corn maze and sample all the treats.

It was mid-September, and this far north, the leaves on the trees were already changing. There was a bite to the air each morning that dissipated before lunch, a promise of colder weather the next several months would bring.

The drive from our house to the winery took me down a winding, two-lane road surrounded by autumnal trees on all sides, shading me in a canopy of oranges and yellows, reds and pinks and browns. I'd only experienced the peninsula for two seasons now, but each new one was equally as stunning as the last, and I couldn't wait to see what winter and spring would bring. Hansen, for one, was excited about the prospect of snow and playing in the yard.

Neither my dad nor I were looking forward to keeping our driveway clear, however. I was a city boy to my bones; I'd never needed to learn how to use a snow blower, and I wasn't entirely sure what I'd do when the winery closed from January through March. Since I finished my culinary arts program and became a full-time chef, I'd never had much down time, and I had even less as a father.

Maybe Dad and I would tackle some house projects...

The gravel of the lot crunched satisfyingly under my tires as I pulled in and parked near the front door, then my shoes as I made my way inside. Leon and Lena waited for me, glasses of red wine resting on the table in front of them.

Leon shook my hand when I reached the table, and I dropped a kiss to Lena's cheek.

"Would you like some wine?" she asked as I sat.

"I have to work later," I reminded her.

She shot her husband a wink and said, "I don't think your boss will mind."

On cue, my boss raised his own glass and tilted it toward me in toast. Lena poured me a healthy serving, and I lifted it to my nose, inhaling the cherry and chocolate notes of Chateau Delatou's signature Pinot Noir. When I sipped, aromatic liquid hit my tongue, spreading over my taste buds. I savored the flavors before I swallowed, sighing when warmth instantly hit my stomach and coated my limbs.

"So good," I said when I returned my glass to the table.

"The best," Leon agreed. "Lena worked hard perfecting all our recipes."

I quirked a brow. "You mean these aren't the ones your family started with?"

Leon boomed out a laugh as Lena chuckled indulgently beside him. "Hell no," he said. "I loved my grandfather, but that swill they produced back then is nothing compared to the stuff we make now."

"I'm sure technology has a lot to do with it."

"That and...well, I'm a certified sommelier, so I like to think I know my way around a wine blend," Lena said.

I blinked, surprised. These people were truly fascinating, and I loved simple meetings like this, when we got to sit and converse. I learned more about them each time, and it amazed me how poised they both seemed while running a wildly successful business and raising five daughters. Some days, I could barely keep my head above water with one kid. I'd spent time traveling after culinary school, and I could honestly say I hadn't met anyone as worldly as Leon and Lena Delatou.

"How do you do it all?" I blurted.

The skin between Leon's brows puckered, but Lena gave me a soft, understanding smile.

"We had help," she said, reaching out to place her hand over mine. "A lot of it."

I nodded and swallowed thickly. "Thank you for being that for us. I know we've only been here a few months, but I have no idea how we'd survive without you."

"Anytime," she said. "We never got the chance to raise a boy, and now that our babies are grown, well…it's nice to have that energy back around the house. Hansen is a wonderful kid, far too smart for a two-year-old," she added with a chuckle.

I snorted. "Don't I know it."

"But really, we don't mind."

I took Lena at her word. This winery and the enterprise it represented was their livelihood, sure, but their daughters were their entire world. Since moving to town, I'd met all but one. Chloe was the oldest, the one Leon hoped to pass the mantle to one day. Delia, the classic middle child, practically burst with restless energy and had a wild streak. I could admit, though—the girl was a hell of a social media strategist. Ella, the quiet second youngest with dainty, fine line tattoos lining her arms, had a love for flowers and nature.

And, of course, there was Brie.

The baby.

The baker.

The girl I hadn't been able to get out of my head for nearly three months.

I didn't know how to explain it other than to say something electrified the air between us that day, and I'd been shocked by my reaction to her. After Shannon, I was sure I'd never feel that way about anyone ever again. Hell, I'd never really felt it for her. But Brie Delatou called to some basic part of me, and learning she was moving away for a year had settled like a lead weight in my stomach.

She'd felt it too, right? The spark? She hadn't been able to take her eyes off me, and she'd agreed so quickly when I asked if she wanted to bake for me sometime.

No, she definitely felt it—as had her parents. It was why Leon had made that comment about us only being friends.

I found myself counting down the days until Christmas time, when, thanks to her parents, I knew she'd be returning to our small town.

"Now, how about we get down to business?" Leon asked, clearing his throat and snapping me out of my thoughts.

Damn, this man would murder me and bury my body in the vineyard if he knew I was romantically interested in his daughter.

Then again...was I really? Or was it some weird, flukey physical attraction that would wear off with distance?

Given that had yet to happen, I was betting not.

"Obviously, I've never participated in this event," I started, forcing myself to focus on the here and now, "so I'm not sure what's expected of me."

"Finger foods," Lena said, twisting to reach into the bag slung over the back of her chair and withdrawing a piece of paper.

She passed it to me, and I scanned the list of ideas in her elegant scrawl.

"Turkey legs?" I asked, huffing a laugh.

"There's just something very...*fall* about people walking around gnawing on massive turkey legs, don't you think?"

I didn't, but I wasn't about to tell her that. At least, not with her husband sitting nearby.

I liked my head attached to my body, thank you very much.

"Otherwise," Lena continued, "I was thinking mozzarella sticks, corn dogs, hot dogs and burgers, pepperoni pizza rolls—"

"Oh, I actually have an amazing recipe for those," I said, perking up for the first time. There wasn't anything wrong with the items Lena had listed, but they were all things you could buy at the store and cook at home. Until she mentioned pizza rolls, I was having difficulty imagining why my services were necessary. "I make them like a pinwheel shape instead of the traditional pizza roll style. Hansen loves them."

"Then they'll be perfect for the festival."

"I have some other ideas as well…"

"Such as?" Leon asked, tone warning me to tread carefully.

"I like corn dogs because, I must admit, my beer batter recipe is top-notch. But for the rest of it, I think we can get a little more creative. Do you have a pen?"

Lena dove back into her purse and withdrew one of the winery branded pens, handing it to me. I flipped her list over and began to scribble.

"Walking tacos, bacon-wrapped corn, stuffed potato pancakes, deep fried pickles," I listed as I wrote. "Deep fried macaroni and cheese bites, fried green tomatoes, and some of my famous Swedish meatballs."

When I looked up at the Delatous after finishing my brainstorm, they had their brows raised in question.

"Are you sure you want to put that much work into it?" Lena asked.

"Positive," I assured her. "Things like mozzarella sticks and hot dogs and burgers are great, but they're all things people could easily go out, buy, and make at home. This stuff"—I gestured to my list—"isn't as complicated as you think, and I think the festival goers will really appreciate the variety."

"If you're sure…"

"I am. But I hope you're putting someone else on sweets," I said with a chuckle. "I can't be held accountable for that. I'd burn everything."

"Oh, I'm sure you're not that bad, but we've got someone in Traverse City handling all that." She turned to her husband. "It's a shame Brie isn't home, though. She always loved the festival growing up."

"Where did she learn to bake?" I blurted, desperate for more intel on this girl. "Neither of you can cook."

They were both still for a beat before Leon tipped his head back and laughed loud enough that the girl carrying our appetizers jumped and nearly dumped them on the ground. I leapt to my feet, steadying her with my hands on her upper arms. She looked up at me gratefully, though I didn't miss the pink tinge to her cheeks.

Quickly, she set down our food and scurried away. When I returned my attention to the Delatous, they wore matching bemused expressions.

"What?" I asked, lifting a piece of grilled bread and spreading some of the whipped ricotta.

"That girl has a crush on you," Leon said.

I scoffed. "She does not."

"Oh, honey," Lena said, placing her hand over mine on the table. "She absolutely does."

"Well…" I trailed off, unsure how to navigate this shift in conversation. At last, I settled on, "She's too young for me."

"Have you given any thought to…romance lately?" Lena asked.

I inhaled so sharply, a piece of bread lodged in my throat, and I coughed roughly, trying to clear it from my windpipe. My eyes watered as I fought to regain my composure, and I lifted my glass to wash it away with some wine.

Not ideal, but it did the job.

"Why are you asking me about romance?"

Lena lifted a slender shoulder, attempting not to make a big deal of her trying to pry into my private life.

Had I somehow broadcasted my curiosity about Brie to her? Was this mother's intuition at work?

"You've been single for an awfully long time, Ezra. Long before your marriage truly ended."

"And?"

"And...we all need that companionship. Hansen could use a mother figure in his life."

"He has you."

Lena's entire demeanor shifted, sadness clouding her peculiar golden eyes. "I don't count."

I averted my gaze as blood rushed to my cheeks. This conversation was so fucking uncomfortable for a number of reasons, and it took every ounce of self-control I had not to fly off the handle. I knew Lena's concerns came from a good place, from that deep-seated maternal instinct that drove her to mother everyone around her.

But my romantic life—or lack thereof—wasn't up for discussion.

"We're doing just fine on our own," I told her, leaving no room for argument.

I chanced a glance in her direction, and though she looked like she had more to say, she nodded curtly before returning to our discussion.

We spent a few tense hours going over everything we would need for the little popup food stand we'd put in the old Delatou family barn, and then I headed into work. The afternoon and evening passed in a flurry, and by nine p.m., I was home, sagging against the door in relief.

"Long day?" Dad asked from the living room as I strode through. His glasses were perched on the end of his nose, an old Harlan Coben novel clasped in his hands.

"You could say that," I told him, continuing toward the fridge.

I withdrew a bottle of beer, twisted the top off, and guzzled as much as I could before pulling it away and gasping for air.

"What's going on?"

I startled, not having heard him approach. "Just..." I turned to him, and he waited me out while I marshaled my thoughts. "How come you never moved on after Mom left?"

Surprise flicked across his face before his expression settled into determination and acceptance, as though he'd been waiting for the day I'd want to have this conversation. It was impossible not to draw the parallels between our situations, and after my earlier conversation with Lena, I was curious how alike we truly were.

"At first, between keeping a roof over our heads and keeping you alive, I just didn't have time. But the longer I went without having a person to share my life with in that way, the more I realized I just...didn't need it. I was content with just me and you."

"Weren't you angry?"

I was angry. Angry that Shannon had chosen drink and drugs over her son. Angry that we'd never loved each other to begin with. Angry that, like me, Hansen had to grow up without a mom.

"I was, but I got over it."

"Well, clearly, it hasn't been that easy for me."

"I think you're holding onto your anger as an excuse because you think it's better than admitting nothing that happened with Shannon was your fault."

I opened my mouth to protest, but Dad cut me off. "You've always been a martyr, walking around your whole childhood thinking you were the reason your mother left. In reality, the woman was as easy to nail down as the wind. She was never meant for motherhood. You're here because I *begged* her to keep you, to give the family thing a shot. And she tried, but in the end...well, you know the rest. The point is, Shannon was never meant for motherhood either. It's not your fault she stepped out on you and had substance abuse problems. Those issues existed long before you came into the picture. I know you love your son, Ezra, just like I love you, but to be the best father you can be, you have to be happy. And right now, you're so far from that, I'm not even sure you know what it looks like anymore."

I scowled. "And how do you propose I find it?"

"Moving us to Michigan was a good start."

"And what about you?" I asked quietly. "Are you happy?"

Suddenly, the answer meant more to me than I could express. If he wasn't happy...it was yet another thing I'd carry on my shoulders. I'd uprooted him from the only life he'd ever known so I could run away from my problems. But maybe...maybe I hadn't actually been running from them. Maybe I was simply running toward a solution.

Dad clapped a hand on my shoulder. "Yeah, kid. I am."

"But haven't you been lonely all these years?"

"I haven't been lonely," he protested. "I had you."

I groaned. "You know what I mean, Dad."

He sighed, scrubbing a hand through his salt and pepper hair. "Some days were harder than others, but at the time, I had other priorities."

Me, I reminded myself.

"And now?" I asked. "I'm grown, Dad. Taking care of myself."

He squinted at me briefly, his eyes hazing over, as though a veil had dropped between now and the past. Then he said, "Come with me."

Confused but curious, I followed down the hall toward Hansen's room. He pushed open the door, both of us wincing as it creaked on its hinges, hoping it didn't wake my sleeping boy. Thankfully, Hansen could sleep through a hurricane. Everything in me softened as I watched the delicate rise and fall of his chest, at his blanket twisted around his legs, arms flung wide, his face slack and peaceful. That was my whole world right there.

"He has to be the most important thing to you," my dad whispered, glancing over at me. "But just because he and his happiness have to be the *most* important doesn't mean they have to be the *only* important thing in your life."

"You're important to me," I protested.

He grinned. "Obviously, but...I made a lot of mistakes, Ez. With you, with your mother, with my life. And things turned out okay. Just...don't make the same ones."

With a squeeze of my shoulder, he padded away, in the direction of his own room, leaving me there to watch my son sleep and mull over his words.

To question if, maybe, I was more ready than I thought to not make his mistakes.

chapter 4
Brie

I'D BARELY ROUNDED THE corner into the kitchen at my parents' house, shouting, "I'm home!" before I was engulfed in a tangle of limbs, the voices of my sisters floating around me.

I sank into them, a grin on my face.

God, it was good to be back.

"My baby!" my mom wailed over the heads of my sisters, who all backed away to let her through. I loved my mom more than anything, but every time one of us left, it was like the end of the world, our return practically a national holiday.

But I could admit, the enthusiastic greeting did wonders for my ego.

After wrapping me in a Burberry-scented hug, my mother held me at arm's length.

"You're not eating enough," she said matter-of-factly.

I groaned. "Mom, I'm a chef. I'm eating plenty."

I'd recently finished the first stint of my culinary internship, and I was eating more than ever. Only my good genes and morning jogs along Navy Pier and Lakeshore saved me from gaining weight.

Now that I was home for a brief Christmas break, my mother was intent on smothering me with her unnecessary worries, as usual.

"Well, all that sugar can't be good for you," she said, locking her slender hand around my upper arm and dragging me into the kitchen. "Leon!" she shouted for my dad. "Come make Brie something to eat!"

"Why can't you?" my dad shouted back. "I'm busy!"

My mother turned a conspiratorial smile on me. "Busy watching fishing videos, no doubt," she said. "I swear, now that he's thinking about retirement, all he does is dream about the day he can buy a boat and spend his days on the water."

She sighed dramatically to punctuate her statement, and I giggled.

"Neither of you can cook anyway."

"Brie Anne Delatou!" my mother scolded me, her grip on my arm releasing into a slap.

"What?" I shrugged. "It's true."

"Fine," she pouted. "You can fend for yourself then."

My sisters, who were already gathered in the kitchen, broke apart when we walked in, turning innocent looks on my mother.

Mom stopped dead in the center of the room, hands coming to rest on her hips, and said, "What were you four gossiping about this time?"

My sisters shared a look then broke into laughter. "Just discussing plans for the week now that baby Brie is home," Ella said, waving a hand dismissively.

I narrowed my eyes at them, but Mom simply said, "Whatever" before she turned on her heel and headed down the long hallway off the kitchen, presumably toward Dad's man cave at the opposite end of the house.

I moved deeper into the kitchen, aiming for the industrial-sized refrigerator along the outer wall—an appliance I knew they purchased for this house when they started construction on it two years ago solely because of me.

I wasn't mad about it. The exterior was a sleek, shiny black with golden handles, and I pulled them both open to reveal shelves fully stocked with everything I could want and need. In truth, it was about as well equipped as the fridge back in our kitchen in Chicago. Without a word to anyone else, I started pulling ingredients free, and soon, the counter was piled high with the necessary components of my favorite stuffed French toast. It was a recipe I'd been working to perfect for years and finally recently nailed thanks to the help of my mentor.

"God," Amara said, dropping herself onto one of the stools at the island. "I haven't had good stuffed French toast in ages."

My eldest sister, Chloe, slid onto the seat next to her, Delia and Ella bookending them. "Weren't you just in Paris like…last week?"

"I was *working*," Amara said. "And in France, they're all about crêpes. Sometimes, I just need a thick slice of white bread stuffed with good old American cream cheese and a ridiculous amount of Brie's blueberry compote."

The rest of my sisters hummed in agreement, and I grinned as I set to work preparing our meal.

Conversation flowed easily even though it had been nearly a year—since the previous Christmas—since we'd all been in a room together. Picking up and leaving London while she'd been working on her MBA had been difficult for Amara, but since graduation, she had more free time. My other sisters lived locally, but the holidays wouldn't have been the same without Amara, so I was grateful she'd been able to come home.

The kitchen with my family around me truly was my happy place. I lost myself in the frozen blueberries, locally sourced maple syrup, lemon, and vanilla simmering in a saucepan. I moved onto dredging the bread in the egg, milk, and vanilla mixture before placing them on the griddle in the center of Mom and Dad's stove. The scents twined in the air around my head, soothing me in a way nothing else did. My sister's voices were distant murmurs, but they didn't try to pull me into the conversation.

"So what *is* the plan for this week?" I asked later as I plated everyone's food. My sisters dove into their meals with gusto, moaning happily around forkfuls of fluffy toast topped with smooth cream cheese and a healthy pour of blueberry compote.

"The usual," Chloe said with a shrug. "Kicking ass and taking names."

We all broke into a fit of giggles, but I sobered quickly. "No, seriously. I've only got nine days, and Mar has even less. I want to pack in as much as I can."

"Well," Amara began. "There's a school production in Traverse City tonight of *The Nutcracker* that we thought we'd check out. Maybe grab dinner and drinks in the city?"

"Birdie's?" I asked hopefully.

Amara groaned, but my other sisters perked up at the mention of the relatively new restaurant in Traverse City. Amara's reticence had nothing to do with the place itself—which served the best food in Traverse City—and everything to do with the fact that she used to hook up with the owner, Owen Lawless.

"Do we have to?" Amara asked.

Delia quirked a brow. "I thought you and Owen were friends."

"We *are*," Amara assured us. "But I haven't seen him since I moved to Europe. We text on occasion, but what if things are weird?"

"Do you still have feelings for him?" Chloe asked.

"Hell no," my second oldest sister said, shaking her head. "We're just friends."

"Then I don't see a problem," Delia said with a shrug. "Plus, what're the chances he'll be at the restaurant tonight anyway?"

"Probably pretty slim..." Amara conceded.

"Exactly," Ella said, joining the conversation for the first time. "So Birdie's it is. I could really go for a giant bowl of that house ricotta and toast points."

My stomach grumbled in agreement despite the fact that I was shoving French toast in my mouth.

I may have dedicated my career to the art of pastries, but I had a culinary arts certification from the Institute of Culinary Education in New York. I knew good food when I tasted it, and Birdie's had some of the best around. I supposed it helped that Owen was filthy rich and could afford to pay a top chef handsomely.

In fact, I think the only place that may have rivaled Birdie's for culinary excellence was our very own winery restaurant.

My dad had deep pockets too.

Before we could plan any further excursions for the week, Mom breezed back into the room, my dad hot on her heels. His eyes swept over his daughters before landing on me, and he hustled to where I stood at the island.

A moment later, his arms were around me, pulling me into my favorite bear hug.

"Hi, Daddy," I mumbled into his chest.

"Hi, sweets," he responded before he pulled back to study me, exactly as my mom had. "You look good. Work treating you well?"

"Work is great," I said, emphatically shaking my head. "The patisserie is amazing, and I'm learning so much from Bryce."

I'd been with Bryce for just over five months, and I'd already honed my craft beyond my wildest dreams. According to her, when I ultimately left her employ next summer, I could have my pick of jobs; she'd even offered me one herself. She never hesitated to sing my praises, always reminding me I could be as well-known and respected as her one day.

But I didn't want all that—the fame, the fortune, the accolades. I simply wanted to learn from the best of the best then move back to Apple Blossom Bay and open my own bakery.

Finding the perfect space was high on my agenda while I was home, and I already had my eyes on a particular storefront.

"I'm so happy to hear that." Dad smiled brightly, pulling me in for one more squeeze before letting go. "What else is new? Seeing anyone?"

Ignoring his questions, I said, "There's actually something I wanted to talk to you about."

Leaving my sisters and Mom chattering away in the kitchen, I pulled Dad down to his study, closing the door behind us.

All my life, I'd never asked for anything from my parents. I was the dutiful youngest daughter, keeping mostly to myself, making myself scarce. It wasn't difficult to do when my three eldest sisters had all-consuming personalities that demanded attention. The second youngest of us, Ella, was more like me, quiet and steady.

But when we were born, we'd each been granted a trust fund we would gain access to when we turned twenty-five. So far, only Chloe and Amara were old enough. Amara hadn't touched it, but Chloe had dipped into hers to build a house a few miles down the road.

As the youngest, I wouldn't see a penny of that money for another three years, but...I needed some now.

"What's going on, honey?" my dad asked as he dropped into one of the armchairs in front of his desk. "You're kind of freaking me out."

"It's no secret I want to move home when my apprenticeship is up," I started.

"No, it's not," he agreed. "And we'll welcome you back with open arms. But if you decide you want to do something else—"

I cut him off before he could continue. "No, that's not what this is about. I *want* to come home. You know it has always been my dream to open my own bakery. It just so happens I've found the perfect spot."

One of my father's dark brows rose. "Okay..." he said slowly, urging me to continue.

"It's right on Main Street in town," I said quickly. "I haven't set foot inside yet, and it's going to need a lot of work, but I just know this is the place."

"Where on Main?"

"Three doors up from Blossom's," I said, naming the flower shop Ella worked at since she finished college.

His eyes narrowed. "The old Brubaker place?"

I nodded. "That's the one."

"That place was closed down because they continued to violate health code regulations!"

"I told you it would need a lot of work," I pointed out. "Please don't say no yet. Just come look at it with me."

"Why do I need to be involved anyway?"

"Because I want to use my trust fund to buy and renovate it."

"Absolutely not," he said quickly, and my heart sank into my butt. Noticing the forlorn expression on my face, he backtracked. "I mean, I'll go look at it with you, but you're not sinking your own money into it."

"Technically, it's *your* money," I mumbled under my breath.

"Brie," he warned.

"Sorry. I just don't know of any other way. I don't have that kind of money right now, and you know there's always developers sniffing around up here, looking for their next payday. I don't want some greedy, big city asshole to get his hands on it before I do."

My father blinked slowly, clearly surprised by my vehemence. I wasn't blind to the fact that the building—both inside and out—would need a lot of work, but the location was perfect, and given that it had previously operated as a mom and pop cafe, the infrastructure was already there. I had a vision, and I needed my dad to see it too.

"By saying no to accessing your trust fund before you're twenty-five," he started, "I wasn't saying no to purchasing the building. I'm only saying let me handle that stuff for now."

"But..."

His hand reached out to grab mine. "I know you want your

own place, honey. And it will be yours. Your name will be on the door and everything. But you're not even living here right now. Once we look at it and I decide if the building is worth the investment, I want to handle renovations for you."

"You'd do that?"

"You're my baby," my dad said softly. "I'd do anything for you and your sisters. Plus, if this pans out, it'll keep me out of your mother's hair while the winery is closed for the winter."

"As long as I get to be fully involved."

"Of course," he promised. "Whatever you want."

"I want to go look at it on Saturday."

"Then that's what we'll do."

After giving him one more hug, we returned to the kitchen, where my mom and sisters gave us various looks of wariness, confusion, and curiosity. But I wasn't about to spill the beans, not until we scoped out the place and decided if it was worthwhile. Already, my hopes were through the roof, and I'd be devastated if my dad deemed the property a money pit. I wanted my own place so badly, with a *Brie's Bakery* sign hanging in the window and a pale orange and cream striped awning over the door.

chapter 5

Ezra

I awoke Christmas morning when a small mass collided with my stomach.

"Mewwy Chwistmas, Daddy!"

I blinked my eyes open slowly to find my son hovering over me, his face shining with joy, lips stretched into a wide grin.

Snaking my hands out from under the comforter, I settled them on his tiny torso—and dug my fingers into that ticklish spot at his hips. A moment later, he rewarded me with loud giggles, flopping sideways on the bed to get away from my torture.

"Daaaaaad!" he shouted as I rolled over and continued my assault.

At last, I stopped, chuckling as his laughter faded.

"Merry Christmas, my boy."

Hansen was on his feet in a flash, jumping up and down on my bed as he chanted, "Pwes-ents! Pwes-ents!"

My heart grew about ten sizes at the sight of my son's smiling face.

Without argument or a sound of protest, I rose from the bed, tossing on a white cotton tee and a pair of pajama pants—yes, they matched Hansen's—and padded out to the living room.

Though I was the chef in the family, I'd learned a lot from

my dad over the years, and he was in the kitchen, the scents of bacon and Swedish pancakes floating through the air. Beyond the windows of our house, the sun was barely lighting the sky.

Being awake so early may not have been my first choice, but the upside was, I wasn't hungover. Still, I needed coffee if I was going to survive, so I shuffled into the kitchen, mumbling good morning to my dad.

"How're you doing?" he asked softly. Across the great room, past the demarcation line between the kitchen and living room, Hansen sat near his mountain of presents, practically vibrating with excitement. He waited patiently for me and Dad to join him and give him the go ahead to tear into his gifts.

Today was a hard day for both of us, and I may have gone a little overboard.

"I'm fine," I grumbled as I filled a mug to the brim and took a large swallow, the scalding liquid burning a path down my throat.

"It's okay if you're not," Dad said. "It's the first big holiday—"

"Thanksgiving was the first big holiday," I said, cutting him off. "And we survived that just fine."

My dad gave me a disappointed look at my tone, but I didn't want to talk about it. Shannon was gone, and talking about my feelings wasn't going to change that.

Besides, where she was concerned, my feelings trended more toward anger than despair.

Thankfully, Dad didn't press and, after removing the last batch of pancakes from the pan, he washed his hands and joined me and Hansen in the living room.

Watching my son open his gifts did wonders for lifting my

spirits, and after he finished and we ate breakfast, we spent the remainder of the day taking his new toys from the packaging and playing with them. Later that afternoon before the sun went down, we headed outside to make snowmen and sled down the hill near our house. Though he was nearly three, Hansen had never seen snow like that. We'd taken a few trips up north to Vermont when he was a baby, before life had gone to shit, but this was the first chance he'd gotten to truly enjoy the season and be the toddler he was.

When he started to complain about the cold—he lasted far longer than I'd expected—we returned to the warmth of our home, and I set to preparing our Christmas dinner.

Next to Hansen's smile and laughter, cooking was the one thing in the world that soothed me. With a knife in my hand, chopping potatoes or fileting salmon, my jagged edges smoothed. Food was my happy place, the arena where I was confident. Where everything made sense, and the worst thing that could happen was accidentally over or undercooking a dish.

I'd been formally trained, but my earliest memories featured me and Dad in the kitchen, experimenting and bonding. I hoped that when Hansen was bigger, we could have those times together too.

A few hours later, we were gathered at the dining room table, an impressive array of food spread out before us.

Yes, impressive even to me, the man who cooked it all. I may have gone a bit overboard.

There was the aforementioned salmon, which I'd filleted and broiled with garlic butter and lemon slices. I'd made a mountain of garlic parmesan Hasselback potatoes, a huge salad topped with thick chunks of tomato and black olives, and my grand-mother's turkey stuffing. I'd never met the woman, but my dad had her cookbooks hanging around, and I'd attempted a number of her recipes over the years. That would always be one of my favorites, my lone traditional Christmas offering to our dinner table. My cooking style tended more toward blending Swedish cuisine and American, and I typically balked at anything status quo.

But damn, that stuffing. I could never pass it up, and I loved feeling connected to the woman responsible for raising my father.

Yeah, I came from a *long* line of single parents.

Dessert was not my forte, but I still managed to whip up a decent-looking array of Hallongrotta, butter cookies topped with raspberry filling. I even added some shaved coconut because I knew it was Hansen's favorite.

"So what's your plan for the next week?" Dad asked when we'd finished our meal. He reclined in his chair and settled a palm on his stomach, which he pushed out comically far for Hansen's benefit. My dad was wiry, even in his fifties.

"In terms of…"

"Work," he said. "What's your schedule look like?"

Even though it was slow season, Leon and Lena had asked if I wouldn't mind opening the kitchen for a few days for locals to come in and enjoy a meal with their out-of-town families during the holidays. I'd jumped at the chance. I loved my dad and my son, but it was better than sitting around this house wallowing.

Plus, the Delatou family was coming in for dinner in a few days, and I knew Brie was going to be there. It'd be the first time I saw her in nearly six months, and my skin tingled with anticipation.

"We're open on the thirtieth, and then we're shut down until April first."

My dad raised a brow. "And what are you going to do with all that free time?"

I shrugged. "I was thinking maybe we could get started on some of the projects around here."

The house was by no means a dump, but it was woefully outdated. For the time being, it worked, but we needed to re-configure a few things, like add another bathroom—particularly one with a tub—and gut the entire kitchen.

"I want a blue woom," Hansen said.

That was another thing. If we were going to put down roots here—which I had every intention of doing—this house needed to become a home.

And if my boy wanted to paint his bedroom blue, we'd paint it blue.

"Of course, bud," I said, reaching out to ruffle his hair. "You can paint it whatever color you want."

"I want it blue like the sky," he said matter-of-factly, though it took some mental gymnastics to translate his little boy speak. "And staws on the ceiling."

"Done," I said. "We'll even go shopping together and you can pick it all out yourself."

"Weally?" he asked excitedly.

"Of course," I told him. "It's your room. It should be the way you want it."

Hansen was out of his chair and throwing himself into my

arms a heartbeat later. "You the best daddy eva."

My heart melted into my ass, and I caught my dad's gaze over Hansen's little brunette head. He was smiling wistfully at us, as though remembering the days when I thanked him for something as simple as a fresh coat of paint.

I vowed in that moment to be better. Hell, the man had uprooted his entire life—which, admittedly, largely revolved around his grandson—to move with us. Instead of acting like an asshole and making him carry my emotional baggage, I should've been doing everything in my power to make sure he stuck around. I wouldn't have survived the last six months without him around to help with Hansen while I put in long hours at my new job, and it wouldn't kill me to remind him I was grateful every now and then.

"So what do you say?" I asked Dad when Hansen had run off to his room to play with his new toys. "Do you want to help me fix this old place up?"

My dad studied me for long moments, and I resisted the urge to squirm. Thirty years old, and the man still made me feel like a little kid sometimes.

"On one condition," he said finally.

"What's that?"

"We get rid of all the wood paneling in this entire fucking house. It's too goddamn dark this time of year to be living in a cave. Plus, it's just fucking ugly."

I barked out a laugh, the tension in my shoulders easing instantly.

"Sure, Dad. We'll get rid of the paneling."

He grinned, clapping his hands together. "When do we start?"

chapter 6
Brie

"WELL?" I ASKED MY dad. He stood in the center of the main space, hands on his hips, turning a slow circle.

Honestly, it wasn't pretty. Thanks to nearly a year of inoccupancy, grime coated every surface. The kitchen and corners of the dining space had clearly played host to numerous rodents, if the detritus and feces were any indication. The windows were boarded up, forcing us to illuminate the space with the flashlights on our phones. The appliances were outdated, the layout was all wrong, and the bathrooms weren't handicap accessible.

But the bones were good, and if I closed my eyes—and didn't inhale too deeply; the smell was absolutely awful, even through the N95 mask my dad insisted I wear—I could see it all so clearly.

I'd been keeping a secret Pinterest board of ideas since I was eighteen, honing my recipes for even longer than that, and I was ready to make my dreams a reality.

"You weren't joking about it needing work," he said at last.

"Daddy," I sighed.

"Honestly, sweets?"

"Yeah, *honestly*. What do you think?"

"I think once Jay works his magic, it'll be perfect. I know we don't have a lot of time before you leave, but maybe we can—"

I held up a hand to stop him. "No. It's the holiday season, and I'm sure all his kids are home to celebrate. We'll bother him after the first of the year."

"But you'll be back in Chicago by then."

"I know you're old and everything, but even you've heard of cell phones and email."

My dad hooked his arm around my neck and hauled me into his side, ruffling my hair. "You little shit," he said.

"A little shit with a storefront for her bakery?" I quipped hopefully.

My dad held me at arm's length, his pine green eyes, so like my own, darting across my face. "You sure this is what you want?"

I nodded emphatically. "It's exactly what I want."

"Then it's yours."

❧ ❦

When we returned home, Mom and my sisters were in the great room, reruns of *The Real Housewives of Beverly Hills* serving as background noise while they gossiped.

"Where have you two been?" Mom asked when we came in.

"Just went for a drive," Dad shrugged, crossing to drop a kiss to Mom's cheek. "What's for dinner?"

"Well, since it's Amara's last night in town for too long," she sniffed back tears at the thought of her daughter leaving so soon, "I wanted to do something special."

"We've got something else to celebrate too." Dad's eyes sparkled with delight as he yielded the floor to me.

Mom glanced suspiciously at us. "Oh?"

"You know that vacant storefront on Main?"

"The one a few doors up from Blossom's?" Ella asked.

"That's the one." I grinned at Dad then gestured between us. "You're looking at the new owners."

Mom's brows slammed together in confusion. "You bought a building without asking me?"

"Lena," my father groaned. "It's not for me or for us. It's for Brie."

Suddenly, six pairs of eyes landed on me. "We bought it for my bakery," I said proudly.

The room exploded, the voices of my five favorite women twisting together and rising in volume as they tried to speak over one another. Finally, my dad took pity on me and shouted, "Hey!"

The riot ceased immediately, and my mom and sisters grinned at me sheepishly.

"Sorry, honey," Mom said.

"It's okay," I assured her. "But yes, we bought the building for my bakery. Dad is going to hire Jay Daniels to renovate it while I'm finishing up my apprenticeship. Then, next summer, I'll move home and officially open the shop."

"Oh, that's just the best news!" Mom crowed, coming over to wrap me in a tight hug. My sisters joined in, and soon, the entire Delatou family stood in the middle of the great room, our limbs tangled together as they congratulated me.

"Well then," Mom amaid when she pulled away. "Even more reason to head down to the winery for dinner."

"You know I'll never turn down a meal at the winery," I said with a broad smile, and my sisters nodded their agreements.

"Speaking of, how's that new chef working out? Should I actually be looking forward to this? Is he even still around?"

I hadn't been home since I'd left for Chicago at the end of June, and while I'd secretly been dying every day to ask about Ezra, I knew if I showed even a modicum of interest, my sisters would latch onto the knowledge like I was about to marry the guy.

We'd only met once, and while it had certainly left its mark on me, I doubted the same could be said for Ezra. I needed to temper my expectations.

"Oh, no, he's still around," Chloe said pointedly then glanced at my sisters, and they all shared a giggle.

My brows pinched together. "Okay? So how is he?"

"He's..." Ella started, pushing her sleeves up to her elbows, revealing her forearms, which held more tattoos than the last time I saw her. There was a blue butterfly right below the crook of her left arm and a random scrawl of words across her right that I couldn't read from across the room.

She trailed off, once again looking at Chloe and Delia.

"He's what?" I asked, tone laced with annoyance. This beating around the bush was really starting to irk me. I hated being left out of the loop. It happened all too frequently, and though we were close in age, it didn't negate my insecurities over being the baby and the odd man out.

Delia closed her eyes and sighed then popped them open and leveled that whiskey gaze on me. Mischief glinted in their depths, and I already had a bad feeling about where this was headed. "You'll see."

The realization struck me then.

I'd never told them, and Mom and Dad must not have either.

My sisters had no idea I'd already met the infamous Chef Ezra Wendt.

And honestly? That was for the best.

❧❧❧❧❧ ❧❧❧❧❧

By the time we were seated at dinner, my skin hummed with anticipation. I couldn't wait to see what all the fuss for this man was about. Was he the second coming of Gordon Ramsay or something? The next Bobby Flay?

I knew filling Roscoe's shoes would be difficult but, according to Dad, Ezra Wendt had more than stepped up to the plate. He made a mean turkey club, but anyone could put together a sandwich. I guess I didn't know him well enough to be falling at his feet like the rest of my family.

I only wanted to know him in...other ways.

And it was those sorts of thoughts that would get me in trouble.

The moment the appetizer round appeared at the table and I popped one of his stuffed mushrooms into my mouth, I was intrigued—okay, more than intrigued. It was different than I expected, somehow light despite the heavier flavor of the mushroom, complexly layered in a way that made it difficult for me to tease each ingredient of the filling out.

Cheese, obviously. Pecorino, if I had to guess, and I was rarely wrong. An interesting choice, given most people would've used Parmesan, but one I thoroughly appreciated. Bacon bits, sun-dried tomatoes, parsley, and...

I held the half-eaten mushroom in front of my face, squinting at it.

"Are there...pine nuts in here?" I asked my dad.

Dad let out a hearty laugh and clapped his hands together. "I've been trying to guess that for *months*," he explained. "I can't wait to brag to Ez that my brilliant pastry chef daughter figured it out on the first try."

I preened under Dad's praise. This man may have made himself into some sort of legend around here, especially with my family, but I knew my stuff.

The main course was a religious experience. The moment the first bite of chicken ramen—a special seasonal offering Dad and Ezra had apparently decided to test out for the holidays—hit my taste buds, I moaned around my chopsticks.

Okay...this guy was good. Better than good, actually. I'd never been to Asia but had eaten at enough authentic Asian restaurants in my life to know the difference between someone who knew how to handle the ingredients and someone who didn't.

Ezra Wendt fell into the former category.

Every bite was packed with flavor. The chicken was breaded and baked to perfection, juicy and expertly seasoned. The noodles were soft and hearty, the broth so heavenly, I wanted to swim in it. He'd also included a perfectly soft-boiled, teriyaki-marinated egg, shoots of baby bok choy, thinly sliced cabbage, and thick strips of brown sugar bacon. The entire production was a masterpiece, and I damn near cried when I slurped down the final spoonful of broth.

"My god," I breathed as I set my chopsticks down and leaned back in my chair. "That was..."

"Just wait until you try his grilled cheese," Dad said. "Absolutely life changing. The best I've ever had. Cal and I come here for lunch all the time just for that."

Cal, also known as Calvin Ryder, was our Chief Financial Officer and my dad's right-hand man. He'd come to work for us about two years ago and had quickly made himself indispensable.

"I haven't had ramen that good since I lived in New York."

"Sissy, we gotta get you to Asia to try the real thing," Amara, the world-traveler of the family, said.

"Just say the word and I'm there, Mar," I told her with a wink.

"We should all go!" Chloe chimed in.

"*Road trip!*" Delia shouted, emulating Margot, Elle Woods' blonde friend in *Legally Blonde*.

My sisters and I doubled over in laughter, a highly unattractive snort leaving my lips the harder I laughed. I was bent at the waist and tilted to the side, and when I straightened, I found my gaze inexplicably drawn across the room, my attention locked on the man who had just appeared.

Somehow, the six months since I'd last seen him had done Ezra Wendt *good*. I'd found him attractive before, but now? The man was sex on a stick, like a piece of really good chocolate I wanted to unwrap and savor.

There was something different about him, and it only took me a moment to realize his eyes were brighter, less haunted than they had been the first time I'd met him.

I hated that I'd been paying close enough attention to recognize it now. My infatuation with the man was a recipe for disaster.

"Delatou family," Ezra greeted us when he reached our table, his voice like a glass of ice water on a hot day the way it rolled over my body. "It's good to see you all, though I believe there's one of you I haven't met?"

Amara stood and leaned over the table, extending her hand. "Amara," she said, tone practically a purr. "Second oldest."

"The one who lives in Europe, right?"

"That's right," Amara preened. "You've been paying attention."

"Your parents are so proud of all five of you," he said noncommittally. "Naturally, they talk about you a lot."

Then, his eyes met mine. Something passed between us, and I suddenly wished to be anywhere but in front of my family for this little reunion.

"Brie," Ezra said. "Good to see you again."

"Wait," Delia hissed. "You two have met?"

Ignoring her, I said to Ezra, "You as well."

"You ready to bake for me?"

"Not wasting any time, huh?"

Ezra shook his head, neither his stare nor his words wavering as he said, "I've been waiting for months."

A shiver raced across my skin at the promise in that statement, and I found myself ready to clear my entire schedule to make time for him.

"How long are you in town?"

"Until the end of the week."

"Can you come back tomorrow?"

Tomorrow was the day before New Year's Eve, and I didn't see any reason why I couldn't spend the afternoon here, holed up in the kitchen with this gorgeous, insanely talented man.

"Tell you what," I said, "I'll come by tomorrow and bake for you if you promise to make me your signature dish."

"Deal," Ezra said quickly, and we grinned stupidly at each other for several beats too long before my father pulled him away with a question about a menu item.

Yeah, a menu question, even though the winery was about to close for the next three months. Dad couldn't have been more obvious in wanting to get him away from me.

When I dropped into my seat again, I found all five sets of eyes belonging to Delatou women on me. Chloe leaned over and said, "What the hell just happened?"

Still mesmerized by the turn the evening had taken, I said quietly to my sister, "I have no idea, but I'm really looking forward to finding out."

Chapter 7
Brie

"And just where do you think you're off to, missy?"

I cursed under my breath before turning around. I'd almost made it out the door, but leave it to one of my sisters—Amara, in this case—to halt my progress and make it into a thing.

"Just heading to the winery. Wanted to get some baking done."

"What's wrong with Mom and Dad's kitchen?" she asked.

"Nothing…" I trailed off, mentally concocting an excuse to quickly get me out of this interrogation.

Naturally, I was too slow. In truth, I'd never been good at lying anyway.

"It's cute that you still haven't figured out how to lie," Amara said, stepping closer to me, her golden eyes narrowed. "We all heard you and that hot chef make plans to cook together today."

"He's not hot," I said, rolling my eyes.

Amara barked out a laugh. "Please, sissy. You've been drooling over the man since you laid eyes on him yesterday. Now, you're not leaving until you tell me what's going on."

Damn my sisters and their persistence and stubbornness. Short of attempting to make a break for the door, there was no getting out of this.

Plus, she was faster than me.

Dragging my feet, I followed her into the kitchen and toward the not-so-little breakfast nook tucked into the bay window overlooking the water off the point of Old Mission.

Up until this past summer, Mom and Dad had lived much closer to the winery, in the home we affectionately referred to as the Villa. My sisters and I had spent a lot of time in that house growing up, especially the summers, when we'd close up the house in Traverse City to spend our time on the peninsula, running around and wreaking havoc. Now, my parents lived in this monstrosity—honestly, what did two near-retirees with five children who no longer lived at home need so much space for? But it worked well when all of us were here, when there was a guest room for each of us, a massive dining room where we had holiday meals, and a living room with soaring ceilings currently decorated within an inch of its life, the tree the sort of thing you'd find at Campus Martius in Detroit.

While I was still getting used to the change of scenery, I couldn't deny the view was breathtaking. I'd never tire of living on the water, and I loved this slice of paradise so much, it really was a no-brainer for me to come home once my apprenticeship was done.

By the time Amara set a steaming mug of hot chocolate in front of me, the rest of our sisters had padded into the room and joined me at the table.

"Why do you look like someone pissed in your Cheerios?" Delia asked me.

"I was on my way out, but Mar forced me into this little family bonding moment."

Each of my sisters scoffed. "Please, little one," Chloe said, tapping my nose. "You love us."

I sighed heavily. I hated being called 'little one' about as much as I hated being called 'Baker Brie.' Those were childhood nicknames, and I was a grown woman now.

"What I love," I said sharply, giving myself over to the temper that rarely plagued me but could be destructive nonetheless, "is being treated like an adult." I narrowed my gaze on Amara. "And that means leaving the house without having to sit down and spill my guts all over the table. I don't owe any of you an explanation."

I rose quickly, stalking out of the room and out of the house, not stopping until I reached my car. The late-December air cooled the fire licking at my veins, and by the time I pulled out of the driveway onto the main road to the winery, I'd calmed significantly.

Had I overreacted? Absolutely.

But...my god. I was twenty-two. I wasn't a child, and I hated when my sisters ganged up on me like that, acting like I was some helpless little girl who couldn't live without their guidance.

I rarely allowed my temper to get the better of me, but things had been shifting for me lately. First was finishing my culinary arts programs. Graduating college was a rite of passage for a lot of people, and it was certainly a crowning achievement of mine to that point. Then, being selected to apprentice with Bryce was a major eye-opening moment for me. It was proof I *could* do things on my own, that I was fully capable of living my own life and being my own person without my family looking over my shoulder, directing my every move.

I wanted to return to Apple Blossom Bay when my time in Chicago ended, but not if my family couldn't treat me like the woman I was instead of the little girl I'd been.

Though my temper had mostly fizzled out, I was worked up for a whole new reason by the time I pulled into the lot of the Chateau and turned off my car. A midsize SUV I had to assume belonged to Ezra was the only other vehicle in the lot. We hadn't set a specific time, and I'd been hoping to beat him here, if only to have the upper hand. With that out the window, I took a fortifying breath and shuffled inside.

Snow was beginning to fall, dusting the ground under my feet with a layer of delicate flakes. They caught on my hair and my eyelashes, and I paused for a moment to tip my head to the sky, sticking my tongue out to catch a few like I did when I was a child.

When I unlocked the lobby door and pushed into the foyer, music greeted my ears.

Def Leppard blasted as loud as the sound system would go, and I couldn't help grinning. With "Rock of Ages" practically rattling the mortar that set the bricks of the foundation, Ezra didn't hear me approach, so I took a moment to stand in the doorway and study him. His long sleeve thermal shirt was rolled up to his elbows, showing off sinewy forearms. A towel was slung over his shoulder, and he occasionally wiped his hands as he moved between the island and the stove. The scent of tomatoes wafted through the air, and a deeper inhale had me identifying other ingredients. Basil and freshly baked bread were the strongest, but something else I couldn't quite name lingered as well.

Moving deeper into the room, I grabbed the remote that controlled the speakers and lowered the volume.

Ezra whirled on me, hand to his chest.

"My god, Brie," he said, breathing heavily. "You can't sneak up on an old man like that."

I raised a brow. "Old man? You can't be more than thirty."

He dropped his hand and grinned. "You're good."

I shrugged. "Sorry I scared you. Maybe if you weren't destroying your eardrums with the best of the eighties hair bands, you would've heard me arrive."

He inclined his head to the speakers. "You like Def Leppard?"

"Doesn't everyone?"

"My kinda girl," he said, and I preened, toying with the end of my braid and turning my attention to the stove to avoid looking at him.

"What're you making?"

"Grilled cheese and tomato soup."

My forehead scrunched in confusion. "*That's* your signature dish?"

Ezra chuckled. "Nah. My signature dish is Swedish meatballs with glazed dill butter potatoes and roasted veggies, but grilled cheese sounded more fun. Plus, it's my son's favorite."

I blinked, blindsided by the off-handed comment. *He has a son.*

"What's his name?" I asked, surprising myself with the steadiness of my voice.

"Hansen," Ezra said proudly. "He's nearly three and the light of my life."

I couldn't stop myself from asking, "And his mother?"

He wasn't wearing a ring, a fact I noted about him almost immediately when we'd met back in June, but that didn't mean there wasn't a woman in the picture.

"She's...gone." A dark, haunted look passed over his eyes, and I'd do anything to return him to the brighter version of himself from a moment before.

As it turned out, I didn't need to do anything, because a moment later, little feet pattered across the tile floor, and something small collided with my legs.

"Oof!" the small something exhaled sharply, and I whirled to find a little boy staring up at me.

It was easy to see who he belonged to, with his hair both naturally messy and the same chocolate shade as his eyes, both of which he shared with the man standing across from me.

"Be careful, bud!" Ezra said, moving toward us and crouching so he was eye level with his son. "You've gotta watch where you're going."

"Sowwy," he said, though his gaze never strayed from me. "You pwetty."

I flushed warmly as I knelt next to Ezra.

"Thank you," I said, then extended my hand. "I'm Brie. I'm a baker. Who are you?"

"I'm Hansen, and I'm a boy."

I laughed, delighted, as Ezra chuckled lowly next to me. "Hansen, this is my friend Brie. She's going to bake some treats for us today. How does that sound?"

"I wuv tweats!" the little boy shouted, driving a tiny fist into the air.

"How about you help me while your dad makes our lunch?"

I asked, then straightened to my full height and reached for his hand. "I was thinking we'd make cupcakes."

"I wuv cuhcakes!"

I shot Ezra a wink as I led his son to the other side of the counter and retrieved a stool for him to stand on.

Then, we got dirty.

More of the ingredients landed on the counter than anywhere else, but Hansen was having the time of his life, and I was thoroughly enjoying teaching him. Across the way, Ezra continued to construct our sandwiches.

I'd just slid the tray into the oven when Ezra announced the food was ready, so while he got Hansen settled at the workspace with a highchair from the dining room, I put away any perishable ingredients before joining them.

"So good," Hansen groaned happily around a mouthful of food from where he sat between me and Ezra, and I barked out a laugh.

"He's quite the kid," I told Ezra, who practically had hearts in his eyes as he watched his son enjoy his meal.

"He's definitely something," Ezra said softly, ruffling Hansen's hair before diving into his own soup and sandwich.

Before I took my first bite, I remembered what my dad had said about Ezra's grilled cheese being life changing.

I held the triangle of sandwich out in front of me, inspecting it closely as I said to Ezra, "You know, my dad speaks very highly of this particular dish."

Ezra chuckled. "He and Cal do order it a lot."

"How much is a lot? I feel like that much cheese can't be good for my dad's arteries."

"At least three times a week."

"Dang, that's impressive."

Ezra shrugged. "It's only impressive if you think so."

I could tell there was a lot he *wasn't* saying with that statement, and it warmed me to realize my opinion mattered to him.

So, with his eyes on mine, I dipped the sandwich into the tomato soup, lifted it to my mouth, and took a bite.

Flavors exploded across my tongue, and I closed my eyes to savor them all. The slightly acidic bite of the tomato balanced the heavier flavors of the cheese perfectly. The bread was expertly toasted, the crunch providing a nice contrast to the soft cheese.

Ezra watched me closely, his gaze lingering on my mouth. I couldn't resist tracing the tip of my tongue across my bottom lip and watching his chocolate eyes shift from milk to dark.

That spark between us once again electrified the air, and I was grateful for the presence of Ezra's son. Otherwise, who knew what I'd be liable to do?

I'd never felt this way about a man, never experienced any sort of compulsion to rip his clothes off. I wasn't a virgin, but my dalliances were few and far between.

And I'd only been with boys.

Ezra Wendt was all man, and I wanted to sink my teeth into him, to savor him like I was his food.

Hansen noisily slurping his soup pulled me out of my daze, and I snapped my attention back to my own meal, my cheeks surely turning as red as the soup thanks to my rising embarrassment.

God, who did I think I was, salivating over Ezra? He'd lost his wife somehow, and I was sure the last thing he needed was some girl going moony-eyed over him. Especially not when that girl was his boss's daughter—and eight years younger than him.

The tugging sensation in my chest urging me toward Ezra was nearly impossible to ignore, but I'd try my best.

We consumed the rest of our meal in a fraught silence that was ultimately broken by a voice shouting for Ezra from the dining room at the same time the oven timer went off. I rose to turn it off and take out my cupcakes.

"Ez?" the voice asked as it came closer. "You here?"

"In the kitchen, Dad!" he hollered back, and a moment later, a man who bore a striking resemblance to his son appeared in the entryway.

"Papa!" Hansen shouted, throwing his hands out for a hug from where he was strapped into his highchair.

"Hi, *älskling*," the man said, crossing the room to drop a kiss to his grandson's head.

"What're you doing here?" Ezra asked.

"You weren't answering your phone, and I wanted to make sure Hansen was with you."

"I'm wight here," Hansen said, pointing a finger at the center of his chest.

I couldn't help but chuckle. I didn't get to spend much time around kids, but dang, he was cute.

As if noticing me for the first time, Ezra's father blinked slowly, eyes darting between me and his son.

"Fredrik Wendt," he said, extending a hand for me to shake. "You can call me Rik."

The Wendt genes were strong, given that Ezra was a near carbon copy of his dad. Same height, nose, milk chocolate eyes, strong jaw, and messy hair—though Rik's was threaded with silver. And when he smiled, it was the exact same as Ezra's, down to those slightly elongated canines and the way it tilted higher on one side.

"Nice to meet you, Rik. I'm Brie Delatou."

"Delatou, huh?"

"Yep," I said proudly. "My family owns this place."

"Well, in that case…" He leaned conspiratorially closer and, in a stage whisper, said, "Thanks for getting us out of New York."

Behind him, Ezra groaned, and I giggled.

"My pleasure," I said. "Although you really should be thanking my parents."

"Don't worry," Rik said as he straightened. "We have, multiple times. Things were bad for a while, and I'm grateful Leon and Lena took a chance on my boy."

Things had been bad? I mean, I'd seen the shadows cross Ezra's eyes when I'd asked about Hansen's mom, but *bad* could mean any number of things. Oh god, what if she'd died? I was over here thirsting after a man who was obviously in mourning.

God, I was such an idiot.

Unaware of my internal struggles, Ezra and Rik carried on a conversation that I only managed to process snatches of. Finally, Rik clapped his hands, jolting me from my trance.

"Well, I'm gonna take the little guy home," he said pointedly, glancing between me and Ezra. Then, he asked his son, "When will you be back?"

"As soon as I clean up," he said, dropping a kiss to Hansen's head. "See you in a bit, bud."

"Bye, Dada!" he shouted, waving so hard, his entire body

shook as Rik led him out of the kitchen.

"So...that's my family," Ezra said sheepishly when they'd gone.

"I like them. Hansen is a great kid, and I love that your dad is so helpful. Hansen clearly adores him."

The tips of his ears turned pink. "I'd be lost without them both. But I'll admit, some days, it's hard when he doesn't have a mom."

I couldn't imagine what that must be like, and my heart squeezed painfully for both of them. God, we were so different. I grew up with this big, loud family around me, with more sisters than I knew what to do with most days and two parents who loved each other and us beyond reason. My heart ached for the hand Ezra and Hansen had been dealt.

"I'm sorry," I said, knowing it was woefully inadequate.

Ezra only grimaced and mumbled his thanks before he turned from me to busy himself with clearing up our dishes.

I moved to the rack of cupcakes. They had cooled enough to frost, so I piped the hot chocolate icing on top of them, setting a few into a container and bringing it to Ezra.

"For you, Rik, and Hansen."

"Thank you," he said quietly. "Hansen will love them, I'm sure."

I only nodded before trekking back across the room to clean up my own station before heading back to Mom and Dad's. The air in the kitchen had become suffocating in the last five minutes, and I needed to get out. I needed to regain my composure and remind myself that, as much as I liked to delude myself into thinking otherwise, Ezra Wendt and I were not meant for anything more than...this. Cooking together. Maybe becoming friends who bonded over our mutual love of food.

Hurriedly, I rinsed my dishes and placed them in the industrial dishwasher alongside Ezra's then turned it on and wiped down the counters.

At last, the kitchen was spotless. We had a cleaning crew that would come in while it was closed for the next three months to ensure there weren't any issues, but one thing I'd learned in culinary school was to always keep my station clean. A messy work environment made for messy foods, and we couldn't have that.

Cooking, after all, was as much about presentation as flavor.

After sweeping my gaze across the room a final time, I sighed and headed for the hooks on the far wall, hanging my apron and replacing it with my puffy winter coat. When I turned to say goodbye to Ezra, I found him only a few feet away.

"Would you want to do this again before you leave?" he asked, eyes darting everywhere but my face, his hands shoved deep in his pockets, shoulders curved forward, as though bracing for my response.

"You...want to?"

"Of course," he said instantly, looking at me at last. "Why? Do you not want to?"

"No, I definitely do. I just...I thought I put my foot in it by bringing up the family stuff."

"No, Brie," Ezra said, his hand reaching, seemingly of its own free will, to toy with the end of my braid draped over my shoulder. We sucked in matching breaths as his fingertips brushed the skin of my neck, sending a current down my spine. "I was the one who brought that shit up. You didn't do anything wrong. If you're interested, I'd like to see you again."

"Yes." It was the easiest answer I'd ever given. I hadn't been able to stop thinking about him for months, and the idea that he'd been thinking about me too had warmth and pleasure suffusing my limbs. "Tomorrow?"

"Can't tomorrow," he said, grinning sheepishly. "It's New Year's Eve, and we've got this whole movie marathon family tradition. I can't miss it."

"Which movies?" I asked.

"The *Marvel* ones," he said. "It was a thing my dad and I started when I was in high school, and now, there are just so many that it's fun to see which new ones we can add year after year. We make homemade popcorn and a ton of other fried foods throughout the day and just...rot on the couch."

"That sounds a lot like what my family does," I said with a laugh. "Except my sisters and I watch as many episodes of whatever teen drama as we can manage."

"How do you decide?"

"We rotate. This year," I said, rubbing my hands together excitedly, "I get to pick."

"And?"

"We'll be spending our day binging *The O.C.*"

Ezra laughed. "So how about the day after, then? Do you have plans for New Year's Day?"

I shook my head. "I'm all yours."

chapter 8
Brie

"WHAT'RE WE MAKING TODAY?" I asked Ezra when we returned to the winery two days later. The time away from him had felt like years instead of hours, and I wasn't ready to examine *why* too closely.

"I was thinking pizza," Ezra said. "And you could show me your favorite bakery treat."

I snorted. "No offense, Ez," I started. "I know you're talented and everything, but we really don't have time for me to teach you how to make baklava."

"We've got all day," he said lowly, words full of promise.

I fought off a blush, though willing my body not to give in to its natural response to this man was no easy task. "Let's just start with something simple, like danishes."

"I love danishes," he assured me.

"And I love pizza," I promised. "But one day, you *will* feed me your meatballs."

Ezra stilled, and I realized a beat later the undertones of the words that had just left my mouth. I hadn't meant them that way, but they certainly had sexual connotations. The way Ezra's entire body froze told me that was exactly how he took them.

"I'm sorry," I said quickly, my hands coming up to hide my

flaming cheeks. "I didn't mean it like that."

Or...maybe I did. But it was far too early in our acquaintance to be letting my inner vixen run the show.

Ezra cleared his throat and returned his attention to the pizza dough in front of him. "No, I know," he said. "You just...continue to surprise me."

I tilted my head questioningly, and he continued. "Your family portrayed you as this innocent, helpless little girl," he said with a wince. "I wasn't expecting someone so..."

"So what?" I prompted when he trailed off.

"Well, you're certainly not a little girl," he said, his gaze darting to me quickly before returning to his task. "And you're not as quiet as I expected you to be."

I scoffed. "My sisters only think I'm quiet because I can never get a word in around them. Ella is the quiet one, not me."

One side of Ezra's mouth kicked up. "Noted."

"What else?"

His eyes met mine, and in a rush, he asked, "How old are you?"

"Twenty-two."

Ezra's throat bobbed as he swallowed. Quietly, he said, "You don't look twenty-two."

"I–I don't?" I stammered, unsure how else to respond.

Ezra only shook his head, eyes trained on the ladle of sauce he spread over the pizza dough.

Knowing it was unwise to press the issue, I let the conversation drop and moved around to the other side of the kitchen. The silence in the room was deafening, and I hated the awkwardness. Ezra and I hardly knew each other, so how had we found ourselves in this situation so quickly?

Across the room, Ezra cleared his throat and looked up at me. "So what kind of danishes are you going to make?"

"Cheese and apple," I said, smiling, grateful for the change in subject.

Food was safe territory. Food would force me to keep my hands—and errant thoughts—to myself.

This recipe was one I'd recently added to my repertoire. I hadn't yet given it a try, but I had found an apple danish recipe in my grandmother's old cookbook. My personal favorite was cheese, so I wanted to see if I could marry the two.

"You mean like...two different kinds? Or cheese and apple in one?" Ezra asked, sidling closer.

"Cheese and apple in one," I clarified as I moved around the kitchen, pulling out ingredients and lining them up on the counter. I could feel Ezra's eyes on me as I moved.

"You really know your way around this place, don't you?"

I glanced at him briefly over my shoulder then moved to the fridge. "I've been cooking here since I was a kid," I said as I opened the doors and reached inside for butter and milk. "I'm sure you've learned by now that neither of my parents can cook."

Ezra choked on a laugh. "I let your dad attempt to cook me eggs during that first week I was here. I can assure you, I won't make that mistake again."

I chuckled along with him, easily able to imagine my dad turning something as simple as scrambled eggs into charred lumps better suited for use as grill charcoal. "We've all accepted that their talents lie elsewhere. But as I got older and grew more interested in making a career out of food, they came to realize that simply supervising me in the kitchen to make sure I didn't burn the house down wasn't enough. So, I started spending a lot of time here with Roscoe, your predecessor."

"Heard great things about the man's food," Ezra said solemnly. "Not so much about how he parted ways with the family."

"He was Dad's best friend in a lot of ways," I said, now moving toward the cupboards to pull out bowls and mixing utensils. I even hauled the stand mixer over to the island and plugged it in. On the other side, Ezra had dropped into a chair while the pizza baked, elbow resting on the counter, chin propped on a palm, listening intently to me. "Bringing Roscoe in was the first big hire Dad made after he took over the company, and I know him wanting to leave really messed with him. But I learned so much from that man, and however he left things, I'll forever be grateful he helped me hone my craft and recognize my calling at such a young age."

Ezra raised a brow, that sensual mouth hitching up on one side. "Your calling, huh? I think I'll be the judge of that."

With a sly grin, I said, "I can't wait to make you eat your words."

A full-on grin bloomed across his face, and I returned it before diving into my task.

While I worked, we talked about everything and nothing. How he was settling into Apple Blossom Bay, if he liked working for my parents. How my internship was going and if I felt like I was learning a lot. He told me surface-level stories about his dad and son, and I shared random, inconsequential things, like my favorite color and what songs I had on repeat.

We were scratching the surface, exploring whatever this weird hum of energy between us was, clearly both deciding if it was something worth digging deeper into.

I could admit—I was absolutely smitten. I could've spent days in that kitchen with him, listening to him talk about the most random things or watching him prepare our meal.

At last, the danishes were done, and when I set them up on a rack to cool, Ezra presented me with a massive pizza, the cheese still bubbling, the crust a crispy brown. He slid it onto a pizza stone and immediately cut it. The stringy cheese clinging to the blade had my mouth watering.

"The trick to making a good pizza," Ezra started as he pulled up a stool next to me and lifted a piece off the plate, "is both in the crust and the sauce. Toppings are the same no matter what you put them on, but if your dough is too soft, the pizza will fall apart. And if you add too much sauce, it'll overshadow all the toppings. I'll let you in on a secret, though." He leaned closer to me, his breath tickling the side of my face. "I like to put shredded cheese in my crust too."

"Like stuffed crust?"

Ezra made a face like I'd said something blasphemous. "Absolutely not. Stuffed crust is for hacks."

"What about deep dish?" I asked. Having spent the last five months in Chicago, I had my opinions, but I was curious where Ezra stood.

"What did I just tell you about sauce?"

I giggled. "I think it's disgusting too."

"I'd never yuck anyone else's yum, but I don't understand the obsession. Give me New York style any day."

"Now that," I said, lifting my own slice at the crust and folding it in half, "is how you make a pizza."

"I knew I liked you."

"I just don't understand how you made it so thin but soft enough to fold without cracking." Lifting it up, I studied the underside, where the golden-brown dough had indeed curved but showed no signs of coming apart.

He nudged me with an elbow before holding his pizza out for a cheers. "Stick with me, kid. I'll teach you all sorts of things."

I quickly averted my eyes as my cheeks heated, willing the lust coursing through me to stand down. Certainly, he hadn't meant those words the way I'd taken them.

Right?

After blowing on it, I lifted the slice to my lips and took a bite. He'd kept the toppings simple, with pepperoni I'd watched him chop himself, diced bella mushrooms, and black olives. He'd also told me that putting down a thin layer of cheese, adding the toppings, then sprinkling more cheese over top was the only way to make a pizza.

"It prevents the toppings from sliding off while still giving you a generous amount of cheese," he'd said.

Ezra watched me closely as I chewed, his eyes darting around my face while he waited for my reaction. I couldn't help the small moan that slipped free from my throat.

"Good?" Ezra whispered, his voice husky.

My eyes popped open. "Amazing," I breathed. "What the hell do you put in your sauce?"

Ezra's lips tipped up in a satisfied smile. "I'll never tell."

I narrowed my gaze on him, brows drawing low. "What's it going to take for you to change your mind?"

Ezra leaned closer until he was a breath away. "What're you

willing to give me?"

I pulled back enough to tap my chin, feigning contemplation. "A thousand dollars."

He whistled low then tipped his head back and laughed. When he faced me again, his eyes sparkled with mischief. "Is that all I'm worth to you, honey?"

Honey. God, that was so much better than *Baker Brie*, especially when it flowed from his lips like its namesake.

"I'm not sure what you're worth to me yet."

"How badly do you want to find out?"

His eyes widened slightly after that statement slipped free, like he hadn't meant to speak it aloud. His hand rose to my face, fingertips brushing against my cheek as he tucked an errant lock of hair that escaped my braid behind my ear.

Unable to stop myself, I leaned into that touch, closing my eyes and savoring the feeling of his hand on my skin.

What was happening here?

I hadn't realized I'd spoken the words out loud until Ezra replied, "I don't know, but I'm dying to find out."

I slowly lifted my eyelids, wanting to stay lost in the moment for as long as possible. Then, I brought my own hand up to cup his face.

"My dad warned you to stay away from us."

It wasn't a question, and Ezra didn't treat it as such.

"He did."

"You know this is a bad idea."

He shook his head, his rough stubble scratching my palm. "Not from where I'm sitting."

"I don't want you to get in trouble."

"When was the last time you did something reckless, Brie?" His voice had lowered and deepened, and every word caressed my skin promisingly.

"Never."

"Because you're a good girl."

Ezra studied me for long moments while he waited for my response, and his chocolate gaze dug deep beneath my skin, seeming to cut right to my core. Locking on the girl who'd grown up in the shadow of four stunning and talented older sisters, who wanted nothing more than to chart her own path. Who simply wanted...*more*.

Giving in to this inexplicable attraction I felt for Ezra—which he obviously reciprocated—was a recipe for disaster, like burning the soufflé minutes before the dessert course at a fancy dinner party and not having a backup plan.

But damn, did I want to get burned.

"You're right," I said slowly, angling on my stool and shifting further into his space. "I've always been a good girl. But just once...just this time, maybe I want to be bad." I trailed a finger over his chest, along the column of buttons holding his shirt closed. "What do you say, Chef? You wanna be bad with me?"

"Are you asking if you can have my first kiss of the new year?"

I nodded and leaned even closer, lifting my face until I was centimeters away from his lips, until we were sharing breath.

The scant inches between us felt like kindling waiting for a flint to spark it into an inferno.

God, I wanted to feel that fire.

"Take it," he whispered.

So I pressed my mouth to his.

KISSING BRIE DELATOU WAS surely the worst idea I've ever had, and her father's warning from the day he hired me rang in my ears. Still, I couldn't muster an ounce of regret. Not when my entire body lit up like a Christmas tree the second her plush mouth met mine. Not when that point of contact warmed me from the inside out, deep into the marrow of my bones and right through my skin in a way that hadn't happened since...well, *since*.

What started as soft and hesitant quickly became fevered and insistent. Our mouths opened in sync, tongues tangling. I explored every hot inch of her, consuming her, learning what made her tick. Discovering that a slow arc of my tongue across hers elicited a whimper. That sinking my teeth into her full bottom lip drew a moan from deep in her throat. That notching my thumb under her jaw and angling her head where I wanted her had her fisting my shirt, pulling me closer.

My hands skated down her sides, along the gentle swells of her hips to her backside. I dug my fingers in, standing and lifting her onto the counter in one smooth movement. The stools toppled over around us, but I didn't have a fuck to give. Brie's knees spread, her heels digging into the backs of my legs, urging me closer.

I went to her willingly, fitting my hips between her thighs.

Brie gasped as my cock pressed into her stomach.

"What are you doing to me?" I whispered when I pulled away, though only far enough to direct my attention to her throat, nipping and sucking my way down the smooth column.

Brie tipped her head back and said, "I could ask you the same thing."

"Let me touch you."

"You are touching me."

"Brie..." I groaned, dropping my face into her shoulder.

"I don't—I've never..."

She trailed off, and I lifted my head to stare at her, finding color high on her cheeks.

"You've never what? Had sex? Had a guy finger bang you?"

Her blush deepened, but she squared her shoulders and said, "No. I'm not a virgin, and I've been...*finger banged*"—she whispered the last two words—"but it never felt good. I don't think I like it."

I gaped at her for a moment, both appreciative of and blown away by her honesty. Few women would admit to that. Well, no. A lot of women would happily share every single like and dislike they had when it came to sex, but even from a few hours in her company, I knew Brie was more reserved. I understood it wasn't easy for her to share that with me, a man she hardly knew.

"Well, that's a shame," I said slowly, and her gaze snapped up to mine.

"What is?"

"You've only been with boys before, Brie. Boys who clearly had no idea what they were doing." I ducked my head and captured her mouth with mine again. Against her lips, I said, "But I'm a man, and I promise you'll love the way I play with your pretty little pussy." She inhaled sharply, and I chuckled as I withdrew enough to see her eyes fully. "Do you trust me?"

Though her eyes were wide with uncertainty, she nodded.

"Take your apron off," I commanded.

Without hesitation, Brie reached around her back and untied the straps around her waist and neck before she tugged it free and tossed it on the floor.

God, I had plans—plans that involved her entirely naked and spread out on the counter like a fucking Christmas feast—but I couldn't keep my mouth to myself. Once again, I captured her lips, teasing, coaxing them open and sweeping my tongue inside. She opened wider, letting me deeper, letting me show her exactly what my mouth could do to her cunt.

"Your lips taste so good," I murmured. "Like honey. Tell me, Brie." I pulled away to pepper kisses along her jaw. "How do you think your other ones taste? Do they taste as good? Is that pussy as sweet as this mouth?"

Instead of answering, Brie hopped up on the counter and reclined back, lifting her hips, tucking her hands into the waistband of her leggings, shoving them and her panties down her legs. They joined her apron on the floor a moment later.

And then, in a move that shocked me as much as it thrilled me, had my cock turning to granite, harder than I'd ever been before, she hooked her heels on the edge of the counter and spread herself wide.

Showing me every pink, perfect, glistening inch of her sex.

There was no apprehension in her face, no nervousness in the lines of her body as she said, "Why don't you find out?"

Wasting no time, I stepped closer and trailed my hands up her legs, starting at her ankles and working north until they settled in the creases of her thighs. I brushed one thumb over her, and she twitched.

"Sensitive, are we?"

"I'm so turned on, I can barely think straight."

I chuckled. "How about I take care of that for you?"

"*Please*," she breathed.

Leaving her only briefly to haul over a nearby stool, I sat my ass down, pleased to find my face level with her pussy.

"You okay?" I asked her. She was practically vibrating above me, and I wanted to make sure I wasn't forcing her to do something she didn't want.

"I might die if you don't touch me."

Needing no further encouragement, I swiped two fingers through her slit.

I was rewarded with a moan, long and low, as Brie's head dropped back.

"Oh, I don't think so, honey," I said, the nickname falling too easily from my tongue as her gaze snapped up to mine. I'd never be able to call her anything else. "You're going to watch. You're going to see how much getting you off gets *me* off."

"Really?" she asked incredulously.

I removed one of her feet from the counter and brought it to my lap, pushing down on my cock. I hissed at the pressure, needing so much more from her. But I was willing to sit with the discomfort in order to please her.

"I'm painfully hard," I told her when she hummed in appreciation as I returned her foot to the counter. "But this isn't about me. This is about you."

My tone allowed no room for argument, and Brie simply nodded.

"Good girl."

Refocusing my attention between her thighs, I once again brushed my fingers through her arousal, coating them. Her pink tongue dipped out and traced her bottom lip as I brought my hand to my mouth and licked them clean, groaning at her flavor as it coated my taste buds.

"Mm," I hummed. "As sweet as I thought you'd be."

"Ezra," Brie breathed. "It's not nice to play with your food."

The comment forced a bark of laughter from me, but I sobered quickly. "Be careful what you wish for, gorgeous," I said before diving in.

Using two fingers, I spread her lips wide and dragged my flattened tongue from entrance to clit, tracing a path around her bundle of nerves before repeating the process, up and down. Glancing up through my lashes, I could see Brie's eyes were heavily lidded as she struggled to keep them open, to keep watching me.

"Fuck," I groaned. "Your pussy is my new favorite meal."

"*Ez.*"

That single syllable spoken in her desire-laced tone snapped the final tether on my restraint, and I greedily returned my mouth to her sex. I alternated fluttering flicks of my tongue against her clit with long, slow drags. One of her hands came to my hair, digging in and grabbing a handful, the sharp sting at the roots showing me just how much she liked what I was doing.

Wanting to feel her walls clamp around me, I shoved a finger inside her pussy, and she rewarded me with a sharp cry of my name.

God, this girl. Her sounds. Her taste. The eager way her hips rocked to meet every one of my licks.

"You have no idea how sexy you are," I said, pulling my mouth from her flesh to watch my finger pump in and out of her. "And you're so tight. I bet you'd feel like heaven around my cock, wouldn't you, honey?"

"I think we should find out."

I let out a dark laugh. "Not today, my needy girl. Today, you get my hands and my mouth." I punctuated the statement by adding a second finger, and she hissed around the stretch, walls clenching me tighter, but she quickly relaxed. "Fuck, Brie. I knew I'd be eating today, but I didn't think I'd be eating this good."

The oven timer chose that moment to go off, and I pulled away enough to glance between it and her.

"Don't stop," she begged, giving up watching to drop her entire torso back on the counter. A hand came up to cup her breast through the material of her sweater, plucking at her nipples, and I groaned. "I'll die if you stop."

"Never," I promised, the incessant beeping drowned by Brie's sounds as I curled my fingers, massaging that special spot that had her thighs quaking. "Fucking hell, I could lose myself in this cunt all day, every day."

"You eat my pussy so well, Ez," she said breathlessly. "Your tongue...feels like...heaven."

"Nah, honey. This pussy is heaven. Now hold on."

The easiest thing for Brie to grab happened to be my hair, and I wasn't mad when she gripped a handful and forced my face back into her sex.

I was done with the teasing licks and slow rocking of my fingers. I picked up the pace on both, pumping my hand in and out like I'd do with my cock, faster and faster as her moans of pleasure increased in frequency and volume. We were entirely alone here, the winery cocooned in the snow and surrounded on all sides by endless acres of the vineyard. I loved that she was loud, that she wasn't holding back from me, that she trusted me enough to give herself wholly to me in the moment.

And I rewarded that bravery. When her walls clamped tightly around my fingers and her thighs were shaking uncontrollably, I sealed my mouth around her clit and sucked it deep into my mouth, rapidly fluttering my tongue over its silkiness.

Brie detonated with a scream, my name echoing around the kitchen as she spasmed atop the counter. My pace slowed as I worked her through it, loving how her walls pulsed against my fingers, how her release coated my palm.

When the aftershocks ceased, I withdrew my hand and licked myself clean, not wanting to waste a single drop of her honey.

"Fuck, that was hot," I grinned as I stood, bending over her. "How do you feel?"

A blissed-out smile decorated her lips, and she reached out to pull me close, our mouths coming together in a wet, sloppy kiss that did nothing to quell the blood rushing to my cock.

"That was the best orgasm I've ever had."

I winked. "There's more where that came from."

Her chest still rose and fell rapidly, and her face relaxed as she closed her eyes.

"For real, though... Are you okay?" I asked.

Those gorgeous green eyes flew open, though I couldn't read the emotion swirling in their depths. "I..."

Fuck. I pushed too hard, and now she was going to take it all back.

"I am," she promised. "But...we shouldn't have done this."

I jerked like she'd slapped me. How had we gone from the connection of a moment before to this being a mistake?

"What happened to being reckless? What happened to *'best orgasm I've ever had'*?"

I couldn't stop myself from asking. I couldn't explain what had happened between us these last few hours—hell, since I'd first seen her those months ago—and how it felt last night to have her back in my orbit, but it was...well, the only way to describe it was *magical*. As though the snowflakes falling softly outside were fairy dust, turning this normal New Year's Day into something extraordinary.

Damn, Hansen and I had been watching way too many movies on Disney+ lately. That was some *Frozen* level thinking right there.

"You're my dad's employee, Ezra," she said as she sat up and slipped off the counter. I held back a groan as she turned away from me, giving me a full view of her perfect ass as she stepped back into her panties and leggings and hauled them up her delicious, golden-brown stems.

Fuck, I was in a bad way.

I didn't respond as I watched her skirt the island to the stove, where she removed the blackened chunks that should've been her cheese and apple danishes, dumping them right into the trash. The acrid scent of smoke hung in the air, quickly bringing me back to reality.

Still, I tried to hold onto the magic we'd found together a moment longer.

"I'm also thirty years old," I told her. "I make my own choices."

When she looked at me again, the regret in her eyes was obvious, but I couldn't tell if it was from what we'd done or the fact that we couldn't do it again.

If I had to guess? Probably both.

Amazing how quickly pleasure could sour.

She gave me a sad smile and said, "I'm not going to be the reason you lose your job. You have a child to worry about."

And there it was—the only thing that could've stopped me from fighting her. Nothing in the world was more important to me than Hansen, and Brie was right. I had a hefty savings account, so I wasn't entirely reliant on the job to support us, but I needed this job because it kept me sane. Without the ability to escape into the kitchen, I wasn't sure I would've survived the shit life had thrown at me.

And then where would Hansen be? Without both of his parents?

No, that wasn't something I could stand for. His mother was gone, and I was all he had left. I'd do everything to ensure it stayed that way.

I swallowed hard and extended my hand to Brie. "Fine," I said. "Friends?"

Her lips twitched as though she wanted to speak, her eyes

glassy, but she slipped her palm into mine. "Friends."

Or as friendly as we could be after the orgasm I'd just given her and the way, in a single day, she flipped my entire world upside down.

JANUARY

"Hello?"

God, his voice.

I hadn't heard it in nearly a month, but it still undid me exactly as it had that first time.

"Ez, I need help," I said without preamble, not giving myself the chance to back out. When we'd exchanged numbers after our…tryst, it felt like more of a formality than anything.

I never expected to use it.

But there I was. Calling him. Asking for help.

"What's wrong?" he asked instantly. "Are you okay?"

"I'm fine," I said quickly. "But I somehow got conned into hosting a dinner party tonight for some fancy restauranteurs in Chicago, and I have no idea what I'm doing."

"Why not just get it catered?"

"Because that's the coward's way out," I said, exasperated.

"So why are you calling me?"

"Because you're the best chef I know, and…"

"And what?"

"We're friends, right? That was the deal."

Ezra's sigh echoed through the speaker, and I bit back a grin.

"Are we really friends?" he asked.

"You tell me. Do you usually eat your friends' pussies?"

"Brie!"

"Yes, Chef?"

"Who are you and what have you done with my Brie?"

My Brie. I shouldn't love that so much, but I wanted to belong to him in whatever way he'd have me.

A few hours with the man had turned me inside out. I'd done my best to stay away from him, to never tap the screen when I was three glasses of wine deep and my finger hovered over his contact in my phone. I always avoided bringing him—and our hookup—into conversations with my sisters, not wanting to discuss it. In hindsight, the whole thing felt like a dream, a moment trapped in a snow globe forever, and I didn't want to risk shattering the glass and destroying the magic.

But he was always there, in the back of my mind. I constantly wondered what he was doing, where he was at. With the winery closed until April, he had a lot of free time on his hands, and I desperately wanted to know how he was filling it.

I wanted to know everything.

"I guess one afternoon with you turned me into the wanton woman I was always meant to be."

Ezra snorted. "There's nothing wanton about you, Brie."

Exasperated, I sighed. "Can we get back to the matter at hand?"

"Right," he said, clearing his throat. "Your dinner party."

"Are you going to help me or not? You're not busy, are you?"

The winery was closed, so I knew he wasn't working right now. A quick flick of my wrist had me clocking the time at just before two p.m. My guests would be here at five, and I'd spent more time freaking out about the fact that I had to entertain these super important people in the culinary landscape of Chicago than I had actually preparing to cook. I was out of time, and calling Ezra, though dangerous—this was, after all, the first time we'd spoken since going our separate ways that day—was my last hope.

"Of course I am. Now, how much time do you have?"

"Three hours."

He cursed softly. "You should've called me sooner."

"I was afraid," I admitted quietly.

"You never have to be afraid of me. I'll never say no to you."

Hope flared in my chest, and I did everything I could to smother it. The words were too sweet, too perfect, too much of everything I wanted to hear from him and the reminder of everything I couldn't have—that he couldn't give me.

Unable to respond without spilling my heart all over the phone, I said, "So what am I making?"

"What do you want to make?"

"I don't know, Ezra! That's why I'm asking you for help!"

I was frazzled, spinning entirely out of control both thanks to him and the mess I'd gotten myself in.

But his voice soothed me when he said, "It's okay, Brie. You're going to kick ass. Just take a deep breath and tell me the first dish that comes to mind."

"Gyros," I blurted.

Ezra laughed. "You want to make gyros for a fancy dinner

party? That's so...Greek of you, honey."

"Well, I am half-Greek," I reminded him.

"Trust me, I'm aware," he said lowly, and my skin tightened at the recollection he conveyed with those words. "How about we fancy it up a bit and do a deconstructed lamb gyro with roasted vegetables?"

"That seems...easy enough."

"I'll talk you through every step," he promised. "Now, get a pen and paper. You need to go shopping, and here's what you need to buy..."

Thirty minutes later, I walked back into my apartment and called Ezra again.

"Okay, I'm home and got everything you said. Now what?"

"First, get the lamb in the marinade. You're going to need lemon juice, oil, paprika, salt, pepper, and minced garlic for that."

I withdrew ingredients from my grocery bags as he listed them off, lining them up on the counter before digging through the cupboards in search of a large glass bowl.

I measured out the ingredients per Ezra's instructions, but otherwise, he was silent. Neither of us felt the need to fill the quiet. It was companionable, the kind of stillness I often craved. I loved my sisters, but...they could be a lot. They were why I hadn't had roommates since my first year of culinary school, when I thought it'd be a great way to make friends.

I'd been wrong, but it taught me some valuable lessons about constructing boundaries for myself.

Once I finished the marinade, added the lamb, covered the bowl with plastic wrap, and put it in the fridge, I asked Ezra, "Now what?"

"Now, you need to prep the toppings. Get the honey and vinegar in a saucepan and bring them to a boil. You'll add the onions to give them a quick pickling. Then, start chopping the cucumbers and tomatoes."

"You know," I said as I pulled more ingredients from my grocery bags, my hands closing around a particular can, "I still have no idea what I'm supposed to do with these chickpeas."

Ezra snorted. "You're going to toss them in lemon juice, dill, and mint. The texture will provide a nice bit of richness to balance the rest of the dish."

"Why am I not just making hummus?"

"Because hummus is too heavy. We're going for lightness. If you want to serve hummus on the side with some chopped fresh veggies, you can, but we didn't plan for that, and it's an added step I'm not sure you have time for."

"You're probably right," I said with a sigh. "Okay. Back to business. What's next?"

"I mean, the hard part is done," he said. Then, his tone more urgent, he added, "Do you have any alcohol?"

"There's a bottle of tequila in my freezer," I said, confused.

"Great. Take it out."

I did as he asked, the bottle clinking loudly against my counter when I set it next to the phone in front of me.

"Now what?"

"Now pour a shot and toss it back."

I choked on a laugh. "Ez! It's barely three in the afternoon, and I have guests coming over!"

"And you need to take the edge off. Everything is going to be fine, but I can tell you're freaking out. Just...be a good girl and do what I tell you."

Be a good girl.

The words dragged me right back to our time together, to him asking me the last time I'd done something reckless.

The truth was, I didn't think I had a reckless bone in my body—at least, not where anything but he was concerned. With him, I wanted to be someone different. Someone new. Sexy, desirable, confident, bold, playful. I wanted to shed my old skin, let the flames of our desire consume me, and rise like a phoenix from the ashes.

Which was why agreeing to be just friends had been such a difficult pill to swallow, even if I'd been the one to pump the brakes. For starters, I lived over three hundred miles away. Long distance wasn't an option for a relationship that would maybe—probably—never move beyond physical chemistry. Secondly, he worked for my father, which was a whole other set of issues. I was long past the point of letting my parents dictate my life, but their opinions *did* matter to me, and I never wanted to disappoint them. Plus, Ezra's job with the winery was important to him, allowing him to provide for his number one priority—Hansen. I would never jeopardize that, no matter how much it hurt my heart.

With a sigh, I retrieved a shot glass from the cupboard and filled it with the silvery liquid. Then, to Ezra, I said, "Cheers," and downed it.

The alcohol scorched a path down my throat, suffusing my limbs with warmth, loosening the tension in my shoulders.

After a beat, Ezra asked, "Better?"

"Much."

"Good. Now get back to work."

"Yes, Chef," I said cheekily, and Ezra barked out a laugh.

"I love when you call me that."

"Maybe I'll have to do it more often."

"Is this going to become a thing?" he asked, and I didn't miss the hopefulness in his tone. "Us...cooking together?"

"It could...if you want it to."

He was silent for a moment before he said, "I definitely do."

"Then it's done," I said happily. "How did you even learn how to cook, anyway?"

I realized then, despite the fact that he knew the exact sounds I made when I came and I knew the exact outline of his cock where it pressed against the fly of his pants, we didn't know a ton about each other on a personal level. Intimacy was funny that way—the details of what made up a person weren't really necessary when it came to exploring that physical connection. But I *wanted* to know those things about him, wanted to know what exactly made him into the man he was.

"My dad," he said. Then, in a rush, he added, "I'm sure you've noticed I don't mention my mom."

"I had picked up on that, yes," I said. But like the absence of his wife, until now, it seemed like a sore spot I didn't have the right to press on. "Is she...dead?"

"In the sense that we haven't seen her since I was three, have no idea where she is, and have no desire to locate her. I suppose, for all I know, she actually could be."

"I'm sorry." My mother was one of my best friends, and I'd be completely lost without her—without both of my parents.

"It's fine," he said, and I believed him. "The point is, my dad taught me how to cook. My dad taught me everything. Growing up, I was a curious child, and I especially loved watching him cook. One day, I asked if I could help, and the rest is history."

"Do you have any formal training?" I asked.

Before he could answer, the timer I'd set to let me know when the lamb was done marinating went off, so I took it out and uncovered it, dumped some oil in my cast iron skillet, and turned the heat on.

When I returned, he said, "I went to the Institute of Culinary Education, actually."

"Shut up," I gasped.

"What?"

"I went there too."

"You're joking," he said with a disbelieving laugh.

"I'm not. Actually..." I trailed off, wondering if it was wise to inform him of our previous, albeit inconsequential, connection. Then, I thought, *screw it*, and did it anyway. The man was already intimately acquainted with my private parts; this little admission wouldn't make a difference.

"You guest-lectured in one of my classes during my own culinary arts program. You probably don't remember, but you were showing us how to properly prepare—"

"A roast chicken," he piped in, cutting me off.

"Yeah. You...remember?"

"Vaguely," he said. "God, that had to be, what, three years ago now? Did you just do the program or get your Associates?"

"I went the Associates route," I said. "I wanted to learn as much as I could, so I did that, followed by getting my Associates in Pastry and Baking Arts, and topped the whole thing off with the Restaurant and Culinary Management program."

Ezra whistled low. "Damn. That's impressive, Brie. I only did the culinary arts program, so I don't have any fancy degrees, but..."

"You don't need them," I assured him. "Some people just have natural talent, and you're one of them."

"I could say the same about you."

My cheeks heated with my blush, and I was grateful he couldn't see me preening at his words.

The oil in the pan began to sizzle, so I moved back to the stove and dumped the lamb in, spreading it out in a single layer so it would cook evenly.

In truth, I probably hadn't needed Ezra's help for this. I could read a recipe just fine, and a quick Google search would've yielded something perfectly simple to prepare for tonight. But I liked talking to him, and for some reason, when my earlier stress was spinning me out of control, he was the first person I thought to call.

We chatted idly about inconsequential things while I prepared the rest of the meal. He told me more about Hansen and his dad. Not that I needed to hear them, because I was well aware how amazing they were, but he sang my parents' praises. I got the feeling there was more to his relocation than he was letting on, but he wasn't saying, and I wasn't about to ask. That wasn't my place.

Even though we'd only spent a few amazing afternoons together, he calmed me. Being around him, or talking on the phone with him, as it were, was so easy. I could imagine days like this, dancing around a kitchen together instead of separated by hundreds of miles.

I wanted that for myself: a simple life with a good man who made me feel things no one ever had. Unfortunately, I had found him—but I wasn't allowed to have him.

chapter 11
Ezra

FEBRUARY

"Hello?"

"Hey, honey," I said, unable to hide the smile in my tone.

Barely two weeks after her dinner party dilemma, we were on the phone again—though this time, I was the one who needed help.

"Hey," she said softly. "Uh...what's up?"

"I need your help."

She chuckled. "Are you experiencing déjà vu, or is it just me?"

"Trust me, the irony of this moment isn't lost on me."

"So what can I do for you?"

"Valentine's Day is on Wednesday."

"I'm aware."

"And instead of doing boxes and paper valentines, Hansen's preschool teacher got a stick up her ass, and each of her students has to bring a treat to pass around. It has to be gluten, dairy, and nut free, and..."

"And sweet treats are not your forte," she said with a giggle. "So you've come to the master."

"Yes," I breathed. "Please, O Wise One, teach me your ways."

"Gluten, dairy, and nut free, you said?" she asked, and I could hear what sounded like the rustle of pages in the background.

"Yes. Basically all the fun shit."

"Desserts can be fun without all the stuff that could potentially make someone sick, Ezra," she scolded.

"Shit, I know, you're right," I said, scrubbing a hand over my face. "It's just...this is two days away. Hansen didn't give me a lot of time to plan, and of course my dad was totally useless."

Then again, we'd been so busy working on home renovations that, for all I knew, Hansen could've told me ages ago, and I'd simply forgotten.

"How's Hansen?" she asked. "And your dad?"

"They're good..." I said slowly. "Hansen is finally enjoying his new school. It seemed like once he came back from Christmas break, he started to really settle in. He's had a few friends over, and I even had a group of boys here for a pizza making party one night."

"Pizza sounds delicious," she said absently, the rustle of paper still evident in the background.

Instantly, I was transported back to that day a month and a half ago, making pizza for her while she made those danishes that burned because we'd been too lost in each other to care. I doubted the dessert could've competed with *her* taste anyway. The tang of her arousal bursting like fireworks on my tongue with each new swipe through her pussy. How easily she'd fallen apart for me—how quickly she'd given me everything I asked for.

Fuck, I'd gotten myself off to memories of her sounds more times than I could count.

I wanted her again, badly, but I couldn't let myself go there, not when there was so much at stake for me. Not when the livelihood of my son rode on me keeping my dick to myself.

And, of course, there was the Shannon of it all—the relationship that wrecked me so thoroughly that, in the end, I wasn't sure I'd ever be able to come back from it.

"What're you flipping through?" I asked in an attempt to distract myself from the situation in my pants.

"My recipe book. Well, not mine exactly. It was my grandma's, but as the only baker in the family, it's mine now."

"Is that where you got your danish recipe from?" I asked, once again bridging the present to the past.

"It is," she said slowly, as though timid about broaching this subject. Surprising, given she was the one who'd brought it up in our previous phone conversation.

"Is that when you got serious about baking?" I asked. "When you discovered that recipe book?"

"Oh, no," Brie said with a laugh. "I've been obsessed with baking for as long as I can remember. I used to have an Easy-Bake Oven I'd routinely use to make the family grossly raw little treats. As I got older, with Mom and Dad's supervision, I started experimenting in an actual kitchen. It was..." She trailed off, clearly searching for the right words. "It was quite the learning curve at first, but we figured it out, especially with Roscoe's help."

"Plus, they reaped the benefits."

She chuckled again. "I'm not sure any of us would've said that in those early days, but they certainly do now. But no, I actually didn't get Granny's cookbook until I graduated high school. Tanya, who owns Granny Smith's Tavern, found it when she was cleaning out the attic one day and gave it to me as a graduation present. It's...my prized possession."

A moment after her words, my phone let out the distinct trill of an incoming FaceTime call, and I quickly, greedily accepted.

Brie was...resplendent. Neither my memory nor the grainy phone screen did her justice. Her hair was braided, the end tossed over her shoulder in the way I was coming to recognize as her signature style. I couldn't begrudge her, knowing it was more functional than anything, but I secretly wished I could see it loose and wavy down her back.

At her side, she held the recipe book, which was leather-bound and stamped with a massive S in the center. At the edges, I could see numerous tabs of various colors. The edges were worn, the clasp cracked with age. Clearly, it had been well loved.

"Tell me about her," I said.

"I didn't really know her," she admitted. "She passed when I was a baby, but my dad has shared numerous stories about her with us over the years. Back in the seventies, she decided she was tired of being a housewife—my dad and his siblings, who are now flung across the world, were grown past the stage of needing constant supervision—and asked my grandfather if she could help out at the winery. He knew they'd likely kill each other if they worked together, so he sent her into town with a blank check and told her to buy whatever she wanted to entertain herself."

"That seems...dangerous," I said with a chuckle.

"Oh, it was. Granny Smith ended up buying an entire block's worth of empty storefronts. Apple Blossom Bay had been experiencing a decrease in population at that point, and a lot of those businesses had shuttered as the owners left. So, Granny purchased the buildings on Main Street, opened the Tavern, and leased the other storefronts for pennies to anyone willing to put down roots in town."

I pulled up a mental image of Main Street, orienting myself around Granny Smith's Tavern and trying to imagine a day when the lively area was basically a ghost town.

"So your family used to own the Tavern, Penny's gift shop, that ATV rental place by the bay, the candle shop, *and* Brubaker's place?"

"Yep," she said, popping the *p*. "My dad obviously sold all of it, including the Tavern to Tanya Geralt back in the nineties, before any of us girls were born. Thanks to a lot of sweat equity from him and my mom, the winery was booming, and he just didn't have any interest in being a landlord or running a restaurant outside of the one at the winery."

"That's...crazy. Knowing the history, it must be painful to see the Brubaker place go down the way it did."

When I moved to Apple Blossom Bay the previous spring, the Brubaker Cafe had been thriving. But after the unexpected death of Char, the matriarch of the Brubaker clan, her sons had taken over the business...and quickly ran it into the ground. After violating numerous health and building codes, they were eventually forced to close their doors last fall.

"Yeah," Brie said slowly. "Dad definitely wasn't happy, but...it won't be empty for long."

"What do you mean?"

"Dad and I sort of bought the building..."

"*What?*" I asked, incredulous. "Why are you telling me this now? What are you going to do with the space?"

A thousand more questions whirled through my brain, but one thought stuck out more than the rest, flashing neon—did this mean she was coming back?

"I'm opening a bakery," she said simply.

Fucking hell. She *was* coming back. My skin hummed in anticipation of getting to see her again, and more regularly at that. Maybe...

No.

I firmly shut that thought down, boxed it, locked it up, wrapped it in chains, and tossed it into the proverbial Mariana Trench in my mind. We'd agreed to be nothing more than friends for a reason, and I wasn't going to let my imagination wander with delusions of grandeur where she was concerned.

"When?"

"I'm moving home as soon as my apprenticeship is up. Dad has actually been hard at work on it while I'm in Chicago, so it'll be ready for me to decorate and open once I move home."

"Which will be when?"

"My apprenticeship finishes up at the end of June, so I'm hoping to be open by the middle of July."

I whistled low, impressed and surprised. "I had no idea you wanted to open a bakery."

She grinned. "There's a lot you don't know about me." Then, she resumed flipping through the recipe book but said, "Now, enough about me. Tell me what you've been up to."

"You know, normal stuff. Trying to keep my energetic son alive. Oh, and my dad and I have been renovating the house. We ripped out the kitchen yesterday, so tomorrow, we'll get started on rebuilding now that supplies have started to arrive."

"Wait," she continued, seeming to snap out of whatever task she'd been lost in. "You ripped out your kitchen?"

"Yeah, I just said that..."

"Then where exactly are you planning on baking this treat?"

"The winery," I said with a shrug. "Your dad has been cool about letting me use it when I need to."

"So that's how you've been spending your time off," she said, almost to herself, but I perked up.

"You've been thinking about me?"

"Every day," she admitted, though she seemed reluctant to do so.

"Well, that makes two of us."

The line was silent for several heartbeats, any words quashed under the weight of all the things we *couldn't* say. Then, Brie clapped her hands.

"Okay," she said. "Back to the real reason you called. You're going to make spiced apple cupcakes. Now, get a pen and paper. You need to go shopping, and here's what you need to buy..."

I grinned as she parroted my instructions from our last phone call back to me and did as she asked.

⚘ ⚘

Two days later, my phone rang as I was in the middle of tearing out the old sheet linoleum lining the floor of my kitchen. Grateful for the break, I pulled it from my pocket, my mood picking up further when I saw it was Brie.

"Hey, honey."

"What are these?"

I grinned. "You're going to have to be more specific."

With an exasperated sigh, she said, "I had a massive arrangement of flowers delivered to the bakery today while Bryce and I were working. The note said, 'for my honey Bee.' Know anything about that?"

"I would've had them delivered to your apartment, but I don't know your address. I had to make do with the information I did have."

"You're insane."

"You love it. Plus, I had to thank you for coming to my rescue with that cupcake recipe."

"The kids loved them, I'm assuming?"

I chuckled. *Loved them* was an understatement. They ate and left no crumbs...literally. I'd already been asked by several parents if I could share the recipe. Apparently, Hansen's classmates had gone home and sang my praises, demanding they learn how to make Brie's cupcakes.

"I actually wanted to ask you if it was okay to pass the recipe along. I've had basically all the parents begging for it."

"And I bet you just love all that attention," she said, and I could hear the grin in her tone.

"Well, it's not like I deserve it. That's all you, honey."

"You have my blessing to share the recipe with all those moms thirsting after your...*cupcakes*."

I snorted at her suggestive inflection. "Someone sounds jealous."

Brie scoffed. "I'm not jealous. We're friends, right?"

"Are we?"

She didn't respond right away, but when she did, it was to say, "I love the flowers, Ez. Thank you. But...this doesn't feel very friendly."

I shrugged, though she couldn't see me. In truth, nothing I felt for her *was* friendly, and I couldn't resist the opportunity to make her feel special. "Friends give friends flowers."

"Not the kind of friends we are."

"And exactly what kind of friends are we, Ms. Delatou?"

Across the room, my dad perked up. I hadn't mentioned Brie or our brief dalliance to him before, and I knew I was in trouble if the storm brewing on his face was any indication.

I turned my back on him, not wanting him to draw a cloud over my good mood from hearing Brie's voice.

Her voice was low, barely above a whisper, when she said, "We're the kind of friends who maybe want to be more but recognize it's not a good idea."

Hope bloomed like a flower in my chest, but I quickly closed an imaginary fist around it, quelling the sensation before it could invade my entire being.

"And that's why I sent you the flowers."

Brie sighed. "Maybe it's best if we don't talk anymore."

"No!" I said quickly. "That's the last thing I want."

"Then how are we supposed to play this?"

"We keep doing what we're doing," I said. "If this is the only way I get you, I'm not giving it up."

"This would be so much easier if we'd just never met...or never gave into temptation."

"You're not wrong, but I don't regret what happened." Then, something occurred to me. "Wait, do *you* regret it?"

Brie snorted. "Please. I'm the one who got an orgasm out of the deal, plus the best pizza I've ever had. I definitely don't regret it."

I rolled my eyes. "Aside from all that, I mean."

"No, Ezra," she said softly. "I could never regret you."

MARCH

"When is your birthday?"

I went silent. How could she possibly be asking that today of all days? We'd been conducting these late-night FaceTime calls for weeks now, and it had never once come up.

"Uh..." I trailed off. *Fuck.*

"Are you having a stroke or something?" she asked. "Did you just forget your own birthday?"

"No," I said slowly. "I didn't forget. It's just... It's tomorrow." I faked a cough on the last word, hoping to cover the worst of it, but no dice.

"*Tomorrow*?" Brie shrieked. "And you're just now telling me?"

"I don't want to make a big deal out of it. Hansen's birthday is really the only one that matters to me now."

Brie scoffed. "Birthdays should always be celebrated, Ez."

"Please," I begged her. "Please, just...let it go."

I could tell by her silence that she wasn't happy with me, but that was fine. Her anger was better than learning how fucked up I truly was—so fucked up, in fact, that my birthday had become an anniversary from hell rather than something joyful to celebrate.

I breathed a sigh of relief when she seemed to move on.

"I have another question," she blurted suddenly. "And you absolutely don't have to answer, but...I've been dying to know."

"I'll tell you anything you want to know." For her, I was an open book.

"Where is Hansen's mom? Is she...dead?"

"No," I said quickly, swallowing hard. "Though that might be easier."

Once again, she'd unknowingly pushed on a bruise. She'd given me an out, but this was a story I wanted—no, *needed*—to share with her. Somehow, I knew she'd handle it all with care, take the news in stride, exactly like she'd done with everything else. She was so young, it would've been easy for her to freak out and run away from me.

But she hadn't. She was still here, still wanted whatever we were doing. Hell, she still wanted *more*, even if we knew we couldn't have it.

I hadn't allowed anyone but Dad and Shannon's parents to shoulder this burden with me. Maybe it was time I let someone else help me carry it.

"Then what happened?" she asked softly.

I took a deep breath, craning my neck from side to side. I felt like I was preparing to run a marathon. I knew when I finished telling this story, I'd be emotionally exhausted in a way I hadn't been since everything had gone down.

"She's in prison," I said flatly, giving Brie a beat to digest the statement.

She sucked in a gasp but didn't speak, allowing me space to continue.

"Everything about Shannon had been so glamorous when I met her," I started. "She came from money, like...descended from John Rockefeller kind of money. And somehow, she'd fallen for me, this lower-middle class guy who only wanted to make good food and live a relatively quiet life. I wanted a family one day, but I wasn't sure *her* family or their lifestyle was the one for me.

"And then, she got pregnant, and everything changed."

I remembered that day like it was yesterday, when she'd showed up at the restaurant where I worked at the time, distraught, causing a scene in the middle of the dinner rush in an effort to speak to me. I'd ushered her into the small office at the back of the kitchen and, sobbing so hard I could barely understand her, she told me she was pregnant.

"I'd done what I thought was expected of me," I said, shrugging. "I proposed on the spot, in a dingy, six-square-foot office that may as well have been a cardboard box. I was the product of a single parent household, and while my dad had done everything he could to make sure I never went without, I didn't want that for my own child. I didn't want him or her to have to split their time, to be shuffled back and forth until they graduated high school. Getting married was the logical step. While her family wasn't...thrilled, exactly, they welcomed me as best they could."

"So things were good for a while?" Brie asked softly.

I nodded. "We got married a few weeks later in a small, private ceremony, and life went on as usual. Until Hansen was born."

I hated having to explain the next part, hated having to relive how fucking blinded I'd been. By exhaustion from being a brand-new parent with a baby who rarely slept through the night. By my desire to keep my little family together.

"She started cheating on me not long after she had him," I told Brie, averting my gaze from the camera so she couldn't see exactly how embarrassed I was to admit that.

At first, I genuinely hadn't noticed. She'd pulled away from me—emotionally and physically—and I thought it was her way of dealing with her postpartum body and navigating life as a new mother. I never once thought she'd just been seeking intimacy elsewhere while I'd been drowning, trying to keep myself and our son alive.

When I did find out—thanks to overhearing a phone call between her and her lover when I'd unexpectedly come home early from work one day—I wasn't even surprised. In the year that followed, while I was certain she knew I knew, neither of us discussed it. There was never talk of splitting up and bringing the fate I'd never wanted for him down on Hansen's head.

We became roommates who shared a child, nothing more.

"I don't know how long I would've let it go on before I finally mustered the courage to file for divorce if it hadn't been for the accident."

"Accident? Are you okay?" Brie asked hurriedly then smacked her hand over her face at the absurdity of the question.

"Hansen and I are fine," I said with a chuckle, surprised I could even muster a laugh. "The same cannot be said for Shannon's boyfriend."

Brie gasped again as the pieces clicked into place. "He didn't make it."

I shook my head.

I hadn't known about the prior arrests and substance abuse issues Shannon had until that day, when her addiction to alcohol resulted in the death of someone else. I'd never gotten the whole story—Shannon refused to see me in the aftermath; in fact, she forbade me from attending any of the court proceedings. From what I managed to gather through secondhand accounts—mainly her parents who, once I divorced their daughter while she sat in jail during the trial, cut me and their grandson out of their life with such brutal efficiency, it made my head spin—Shannon and her boyfriend had been running away. She'd told her parents she was leaving me and she was heading to their house in the Hamptons for some time away. During their last phone call, she'd told them the attorneys could handle everything, and she'd come back into the city only if absolutely necessary.

A celebratory dinner had gotten a little too rowdy and, despite two previous DUIs, Shannon had gotten behind the wheel anyway.

They never made it out of the city before she lost control and slammed the car into a concrete divider. Her boyfriend died on impact while she sustained cuts, scrapes, and a fractured right arm.

"The judge threw the book at her," I said. "Her prior arrests and subsequent offenses combined with her history of alcohol abuse and the fact that her addiction resulted in a death...well, he wasn't taking any chances. She's serving a life sentence with the possibility of parole in 2050."

Twenty-seven years from now.

By then, Hansen would be thirty and likely have a family of his own.

But where would I be?

Surely not with this woman on the phone, who had silent tears tracking down her cheeks at the conclusion of my story, but damn, I couldn't stop my mind from conjuring the image anyway. Of me and Brie, having made a family together, a few siblings for Hansen to lord over as the oldest running around. A big old farmhouse with a barn and garden and plenty of room for our babies to run.

I'd lost so much, including the life I'd never have with Brie because I was too destroyed emotionally to give it to her.

But I'd do it all over again as long as I got Hansen out of the deal. My boy was my world.

"I am so sorry," Brie said with a sniffle.

"It's not your fault."

"None of it is yours either," she said emphatically, swiping angrily at the moisture on her face. "Don't for one second think it is. Shannon made her choices, Ez. She chose to cheat on you. She chose the bottle over her son, over her family. There wasn't anything you could've done."

I shook my head. "I wasn't enough. Maybe if I'd—"

"*No*," she cut me off, and I met her eyes in the tiny screen. The fierceness of her gaze had me rearing back, those emerald eyes blazing.

"You are more than enough for m—" She cut herself off and started again. "For anyone lucky enough to have you."

The words she cut herself off from speaking hung there between us anyway.

You are more than enough for me.

"It's okay. Really."

"It's not," she protested. "And I just...god, Ez. I'm so sorry you and Hansen went through that."

And I knew she was. She'd carry this with her, feeling my pain. She was empathetic like that.

"That's why I don't want to celebrate my birthday," I said. "Last year, I spent it in court finalizing my divorce from a woman who sat across from me in handcuffs and prison orange."

Brie gasped. "That's not a reason not to celebrate," she said. "In fact, I think that's all the more reason *for* a celebration. To create new memories to replace those bad ones."

"You're far too pure for this world, honey."

I hoped she would always stay that way, intent on seeing the bright side of everything instead of the darkness like I did.

"I'm just speaking the truth, Ez," she said. "If I was there, I'd force you to do something fun."

"Like what?" I asked suggestively. "Like eating you for dessert?"

"That probably could've been arranged," she said with a smirk. "I was thinking more like baking some sweet treat that me, you, Hansen, and Rik could enjoy."

"Something from Granny's cookbook?" I asked, perking up. The idea of spending a day with her lifted my spirits considerably, even knowing it wouldn't happen.

"Mhm," she hummed, rising from her bed to move through her apartment. A moment later, she rested me against something on her kitchen counter and pulled said recipe book toward her. She had that juicy bottom lip trapped between her teeth as she flipped through it, and I bit back a groan. I wanted to be the one sucking and nibbling on her like that.

"What's your favorite dessert?" she asked, pulling me from my lust-fueled haze.

Truthfully, it had been too goddamn long since I'd last gotten laid, and I could definitely use an encounter that didn't involve my hand.

Unfortunately, I didn't want anyone but the woman before me. Maybe I'd grow out of it one day, but for now, it meant a lot of nights with my cock in my fist for the foreseeable future.

"I don't know if I have one," I answered honestly. "Dad and I were never really about sweets when I was growing up, and as a chef, you're well aware that's not exactly my area of expertise."

"You should learn," she said, still paging through the book. "For Hansen's sake. You can't be calling me every time there's a cupcake emergency."

"And why the hell not?"

Brie paused, eyes flicking up to mine. "I don't know. Just seems like something you should do."

"And I disagree. Why would I when I have the best pastry chef I know on speed-dial?"

Even from over three hundred miles away and through a tiny phone screen, I easily saw the flush creep up her neck and spread across her cheeks. God, I loved that blush. I wanted to press my lips to her fevered skin and warm her for entirely different reasons.

Fucking hell, Ez. Get your shit together.

"You worked at restaurants in New York City," she said with an eye roll. "I'm hardly the best pastry chef you know."

I only smiled serenely at her, letting her think whatever she wanted. I remembered being that young and just embarking on my career, how it felt to have people praise me and think they couldn't possibly mean it. She'd grow into her confidence, and I hoped I was around to witness it.

The next evening—my thirty-first birthday—I had my hands buried in a bowl of ground beef and seasonings—Hansen requested meatballs for dinner—when our doorbell rang.

"Dad, will you grab that?" I hollered, hoping he'd hear me wherever he was in the house. If he was outside in the garage, I was fucked.

"Sure thing!" he shouted back, and I listened as his heavy footfalls approached the door. "Oh, hello," he said to whoever was there. The response was too low for me to hear. "Okay, sure. Thanks."

When he entered the kitchen, a box in his hands, my forehead scrunched in confusion.

"What is that?"

Dad shrugged. "For you."

"Who delivered it?"

"FedEx driver. Seemed like a nice kid, though awfully young to have that job."

"Can you please just open it and tell me what's in it?" I said, nodding at my meal prep. "I'm kinda busy."

Dad moved around the kitchen, absently pulling open drawers until he located the scissors, and I couldn't help but laugh.

We'd finished renovations on the space a few weeks ago, and both of us were still navigating the new configuration. Sometimes, it took me several tries to remember where I'd decided to store the measuring cups.

I knew we'd get used to it eventually, and it was satisfying to walk in and see the manifestation of our hard work. It was my dream kitchen, perfectly functional and, according to Brie, very pretty.

I scoffed at the memory, and my dad shot me a questioning look. Just because it was bright white, with grey-veined marble for countertops, top-of-the-line, stainless steel appliances, and pale wood cabinets that my dad had spent nearly the entire months of January and February custom building didn't mean it was *pretty*.

To my male eyes, it was simply a kitchen. Functional. The perfect place to feed our three-man family.

As if my dad could read my mind, he withdrew a card from the box first and held it out. "It's from Brie."

I cursed low, quickly rinsing my hands and drying them. "That little shit."

Dad reached both hands into the box and lifted a squat Styrofoam carton out as I opened the card. Before he even pried the lid off, I knew what we'd find inside.

"She didn't."

"Who didn't what?" Dad asked.

I nodded at the box. "There are cupcakes inside."

Dad quirked a brow then opened the box. From this angle, I couldn't see inside, but the way he glanced between it and me in question told me I was right. He picked it up and moved it around to my side of the island, and I gasped as I took in what rested inside.

A dozen cupcakes, each decorated differently.

I turned to the card I had yet to open and read aloud.

"Since you apparently don't have a favorite dessert, I gave you twelve options. Maybe now you'll figure it out. Happy birthday, Chef. XO, Brie."

My dad barked out a laugh, and I glared at him. "What's so funny?"

He shrugged. "She's got you pegged. What's going on there?"

I sighed, lifting a hand to scrub it over my face. "I don't know, Dad," I said, exasperated. "There's something there. That day we cooked together at the winery, we—"

He cut me off with a raised hand before I could go further. "I don't need the details of your sex life, Ez. Just...be smart." I resisted the urge to squirm under that dark gaze, hating how easily he'd guessed what happened. He glanced pointedly between me and my son. "There's more at stake here than just your heart."

"We're just friends," I replied lamely.

Dad hummed like he didn't quite believe me then walked into the living room and scooped Hansen up. "Come on, bud. Let's go play in your room so your dad can make a phone call."

The truth was, telling myself Brie and I were just friends was getting old and losing all its luster. I wanted so much more from her, but so many things held me back.

How did I tell her that after she'd been the one to pump the brakes on New Year's Day? Could I shuffle my priorities to include her? Was I capable of giving my heart away to someone again, knowing they could break it? Despite how angry I was with her, I *had* loved Shannon. Falling out of that love happened so slowly but so completely. I often wondered, in those days and weeks and months before the accident, when I felt things fraying between us, if it was ever real. But I knew it was—the devastation I'd experienced in the wake of her infidelity proved that.

Brie was Shannon's complete opposite in every way. Yes, her family had money, but you'd never know it by looking at or interacting with her. Leon and Lena had raised those girls right, to work hard for the things they wanted. Each of them was humble and dedicated to carving their own path.

Brie was loyal, unfailingly kind, funny, sweet, and incredibly sexy. Conversation between us flowed so easily, it wasn't uncommon for three or more hours to pass in the blink of an eye. But if I couldn't keep a woman like Shannon around—worldly, yes, but someone my age and who, I thought, wanted the same things out of life—what could I possibly offer Brie? How did I know she wouldn't change her mind in a few years when she'd settled back into Apple Blossom Bay, was running her business, and simply had more life experience?

I didn't think Brie was the kind of girl who'd be so wishy-washy, but I also had never been a twenty-two-year-old girl. I didn't know how their minds worked, and I didn't think I could risk Brie growing out of her feelings for me.

I heaved a world-weary sigh and called her.

"You little minx," I said when she answered. "How'd you even get my address?"

"My dad is your boss," she reminded me. "I called his assistant."

"You didn't have to do this. In fact, I wish you hadn't. I told you I don't care about my birthday."

"Well *I* do," she protested. "You deserve to be celebrated, Ez. Today and every day. I'll happily stay up into the early hours of the morning every night and pay an ungodly amount in express shipping every day if that's what it takes to remind you."

"I don't deserve you," I said quietly.

Brie scoffed. "No, Ez. You deserve *everything*."

APRIL

THE WINERY OPENED BACK up at the beginning of April, which meant my and Ezra's constant contact waned significantly as he got back into a working routine while also caring for Hansen. I knew they weren't busy yet, but those days were coming. I supposed I'd better get used to it.

And it wasn't like I wasn't busy with my own stuff. My apprenticeship took a lot of my time, particularly early morning hours when Bryce and I went into her bakery to prep for the day, usually until late into the afternoon. Ezra and I worked opposite shifts, and I hated it.

I was learning a lot from Bryce, and I was so grateful to be under her tutelage, but...I was ready to go home. Less than three months stood between me and my return to Apple Blossom Bay, and they couldn't pass fast enough.

One night in late April, I found myself on the phone with Ezra yet again. After the distance earlier in the month, he'd taken to calling me after putting Hansen to bed each night. Sometimes, we'd get on FaceTime and cook together, or we'd chat while we wound down before going to sleep.

Other times, like tonight, I was in bed, exhausted from a day on my feet in front of the ovens as Bryce and I made desserts for a Chicago Fire Department fundraiser.

"If you could be anywhere in the world right now," he asked me suddenly, breaking the comfortable silence we'd found ourselves in, "where would it be?"

With you.

"Paris or Rome," I said. "Somewhere with really good treats."

I could practically hear Ezra's eye roll as he said, "You and your sweets."

"You love my sweets," I quipped.

The silence that greeted me from the other end of the line was so complete, I swore he'd hung up on me. I even went so far as to pull the phone away from my ear to check.

"I do," he croaked at last.

I knew we weren't talking about actual food anymore, but I also knew it was dangerous territory.

"Have you traveled overseas?" I asked, steering the conversation into safer territory.

"I have," he said slowly, as though reluctant to let his previous words go, but then he seemed to perk up. "I've been to all the culinary hotspots, of course, though I really think you could argue anywhere in the world is a culinary hotspot. I traveled some in my early twenties after I finished my culinary program for some more life experience. Dad and I scraped together every penny we could to make it happen, and I'll forever be grateful for everything he gave up to give me that opportunity."

Knowing Rik had raised Ezra by himself, I could guess that

wasn't the only time he'd sacrificed in the name of making his son's dreams a reality.

I loved hearing about Ezra's life, loved the soothing sound of his voice. My entire body sank deeper into my bed, my body relaxing as his words washed over me. It wasn't only his voice I loved, though. I enjoyed listening to Ezra's stories because his life experience was so vastly different from mine—mainly the fact that he *had* life experience.

Sure, I'd gone to culinary school far away from home and chosen to take on this apprenticeship, but it wasn't the same. I'd left the country as a child, been to Macedonia where my father's ancestors hailed from and visited all the other Grecian tourist traps, but I'd never done anything like what Ezra had.

I'd never been totally alone. The first time I felt like I'd made that leap of independence was moving to Chicago. I hadn't known anyone here, and I still mostly kept to myself, thanks to endless hours in the kitchen at Bryce's bakery.

Ezra told me about learning the proper pasta techniques in Italy, how to prepare the perfect macaron in Paris, and all about making paella in Spain. I couldn't see him, but his words were animated, and I could hear the smile in them as he extolled all his adventures.

"Do you miss it?"

He sighed heavily. "Sometimes. I miss leaving my flat in the morning and not knowing what the day would bring. I miss waking up in Germany and being able to fall asleep in Hungary or Poland or Austria. Life was slower, and being on my own, making my way through all that foreign territory by myself, really changed me as a person. But I'm content with where my life ended up, and I'd give up all memories of that trip for Hansen a million times over."

"Bold claim," I mused, though I wasn't surprised. That little boy was the light of his father's life, and anyone who spent even a few minutes in Ezra's presence knew it.

"I mean...you've met him," Ezra said with a chuckle. "You know he's the best."

I grinned at the memory of that day. I hadn't been around kids much in my life, but I could agree there was something special about that one.

Maybe I was biased because of how attracted I was to his dad.

"Maybe we can cook together sometime," I said softly. "When I'm home from Chicago."

"We've already cooked together," he reminded me.

My cheeks heated as memories flashed through my mind—the cool countertop under my bare bottom, Ezra's hot mouth on my slick flesh, the snow falling outside and the smoke from my danishes filling the air around us.

The way he'd licked me clean while whispering the filthiest of words.

"Do you think about that day?" I asked abruptly, emboldened by those memories. He'd been there too, after all, and finding my pleasure wasn't anything to be ashamed about. This man knew me on an intimate level, not only physically, but through all the things I'd shared with him these past few months. I was safe with him in a way I'd never experienced with anyone else.

I hoped it was the same for him.

"All the time."

"I'm sorry," I whispered. It was my fault we were here, that we had to content ourselves with long-distance phone calls and *friendship*.

But I'd never forgive myself if Hansen suffered because of me. I knew what Ezra's priorities were, and I'd never delude myself into thinking I could shift them. I also couldn't allow myself to be wounded by his choice, so I'd made it for us.

"Don't apologize, honey," he said. "It was the right call. But..."

"But what?" I asked, sitting up quickly in bed. I could tell from his tone that an idea was sparking in that beautiful brain of his, and if it was some sort of loophole to our agreement, I was all ears.

"Have you ever had phone sex?"

I snorted, though my skin heated with the promise in his seemingly-random question. "Please. I'm twenty-two. Most guys I've interacted with are barely imaginative enough to have *real* sex."

"Well...phone sex isn't breaking any rules, is it? We're still keeping our hands to ourselves."

"No one has to know but us..." I whispered, catching his drift and rolling with it.

"Exactly. So what do you say? You wanna touch that gorgeous cunt and tell me how much you wish it was me?"

My blood heated, and my pajama shorts and panties floated to the floor at the side of my bed a moment later.

I gasped when I slid my fingers slowly through my slit, surprised at how wet I already was, how worked up only a few filthy words from Ezra made me.

"Are you wet, honey?"

"Soaked," I replied.

"I wish I was there to clean you up," he said. "But I'm going to stroke my cock while you touch yourself and pretend."

"Do you…" I trailed off, and Ezra waited me out, gave me the moment to gather my courage. "Do you want to FaceTime?"

He didn't even respond, just clicked the button that had my phone ringing with the incoming call a second later.

My cheeks were bright red when I answered, but Ezra smiled softly when he saw me. "Hi, beautiful."

I grinned in response. "Hey."

"So we're going full send on the phone sex, huh?" he asked, but I barely heard him, transfixed by his bicep flexing and relaxing as he worked his hand over his dick out of frame. "My eyes are up here, honey."

I snapped my gaze to his face in the small screen, grinning sheepishly. "Yes," I said in answer to his question. "Full send." I extended my arm and angled the phone as I boldly spread my pussy open, giving him a full view. "Besides, it's nothing you haven't seen before."

"Prettiest pussy I've ever laid eyes on." His voice was low and rumbling through my speakers as he praised me. "Show me how you pleasure yourself, Brie."

"Slow to start," I said, mirroring my words by lazily circling my clit. "Sometimes, I like to watch porn first."

"What kind?" he asked, his hand on his cock moving in tandem with mine.

"I'm not picky," I answered honestly, biting my lip as I held myself back from increasing the pressure.

"Girl on girl?"

"Sometimes."

"You into that?"

I shook my head. "For the record, I think sexuality is fluid, even in people who claim to be straight. I wouldn't consider myself bi, but...maybe I'm a little curious."

"Curiosity is hot," Ezra said. "But you should know I don't like to share."

"Neither do I." I choked on a laugh as I pressed the pads of three fingers right against that bundle of nerves, my pulse thumping against my flesh, begging to be set free. "At least, I have no interest in sharing you with anyone."

Ezra's groan emanated from deep in his chest. "If I had my way, I'd lock us in a cabin deep in the woods for a week and fuck you until you couldn't walk. I'd fuck you until you forgot every name but mine for how many times I'd make you scream it."

"Ez," I breathed. "I need more."

"Fuck yourself with your fingers, honey. Fill yourself up and imagine it's my fingers right back where they belong, stuffed deep inside that tight cunt."

I did as he asked, cursing low as I curled two fingers inside myself. "I wanna see you."

Ezra shifted the phone above his body. That day in the winery kitchen, I hadn't seen enough of him, hadn't seen anything beyond his forearms and the strong, sexy column of his neck. The rest of him was lean but not skinny. He wasn't stacked like an athlete, but he was muscular, like he exercised regularly—not in a showy way, but in a way that told me he was a different type of strong. His biceps bulged deliciously as he flexed his hand against his shaft. His pecs and abs shadowed the skin of his torso. I traced my eyes over the idents at his hips, the faint V drawing my eye to his cock, where he worked himself.

My mouth dried out.

"You're...awfully big," I said awkwardly, and Ezra chuckled in response.

"I promise, honey, you could take it."

God, I wanted to try.

"I wish I'd gotten to taste you," I told him.

"If that was all we got, that one day, that single moment...I'm glad it was you who got off and not me."

"Why?"

"Because every night when I've found myself just like this"—he gestured to his engorged cock—"it's been the memory of your taste on my tongue, your sounds in my ears, and your name on my lips as I came."

"I've thought about you too," I admitted, my heart rate kicking up. I knew it wouldn't take much to set me off. My skin was too tight for my bones, my head light from my labored breaths. While I wanted to believe I could get myself there with a simple touch, my fingers were no match for the way Ezra had undone me with his. So, I dropped my phone onto my bed—which Ezra protested loudly—and reached into my nightstand for my vibrator.

When my phone was back in my hand, I brandished the sex toy in front of the camera. "I pretend this is you," I said, moving my phone and toy at the same time, giving Ezra a close up as I worked the silicone around my clit before slowly pushing it inside my sex.

"I bet it doesn't fill you as well as I would," he grumbled. "Bet it doesn't fuck you as good either."

"Ez," I groaned when the toy was fully seated then flicked it on. The vibration sang through my entire body, and my back arched into it.

"Fuck, honey," he whispered reverently. "That's the hottest thing I've ever seen."

"Keep talking. Please," I begged as I began to work the toy in and out.

Through my heavily lidded eyes, I watched as Ezra increased his pace, his hand flying over his cock. Even in my lust-induced haze, I couldn't help but marvel at his size and thickness, at the vein snaking along the underside and the broad, blunt tip that steadily leaked beads of precum. I wanted to swipe my tongue over that slit, to become as intimate with his unique flavor as he was with mine.

"I bet you'd take my cock so well. So perfectly. You'd fit me like a glove. And you'd let me fuck you bare, wouldn't you?"

"I'm on birth control," I managed to gasp out as my orgasm crested higher.

"That's my girl. I'd fill that pussy with my cum until it was dripping out of you. God, I'd kill to see that, to see my cum slipping down your thighs after I fucked you."

"I'm close," I said, though it came out as more of a whisper, the edges of my vision darkening with my impending release. The pressure at my clit was nearly unbearable, and I pumped the vibrator faster, imagining Ezra's hips slamming into me, driving his cock deep inside me over and over, fucking me recklessly.

I wanted him to fall apart for me, to be as consumed by me as I was by him.

"Get there, honey. Come for me. Come all over that toy you

wish was my fat cock."

"Ez!" I shouted as I crashed, the wave of my climax pulling me under. My body spasmed so hard, I barely managed to keep my phone upright, to let Ezra coach me through it, murmuring praises as I lost all sense of time and space.

I came back to my body in time to watch Ezra barrel toward his release, his hand flying over his shaft as he gritted his teeth.

"Come for me," I whispered as I struggled to catch my breath. The three words he'd given me repeated back to him triggered his undoing.

I watched, enraptured, as he came in great, long spurts, that milky liquid coating his fist, his balls, his thighs, his stomach. His chest rose and fell rapidly as his hand slowed then left his cock to swipe across his abdomen, marveling at his cum covering his hand.

With a blissed-out smile, he met my eyes in the phone and said, "You've made a mess of me."

That makes two of us.

chapter 14
Ezra

MAY

"YOU'LL NEVER GUESS WHAT happened today," Brie said in lieu of a proper greeting when she connected our FaceTime call an evening in the middle of May.

"Considering I'm over three hundred miles away and not a mind reader, you're probably right."

Brie rolled her eyes, and I chuckled. I loved riling her up.

"Okay, smartass," she said, grinning. "So you know how my apprenticeship ends next month?"

"Yes."

I was, in fact, well aware of the end of her time in Chicago. Despite our agreement to remain friends, I didn't think either of us could deny that something more was cooking between us these last few months. I wanted her to come home, wanted the opportunity to see where it could lead.

So maybe I had the date she was moving back marked down on the calendar in my phone, and I might have been counting down the days.

Yeah, I was down bad. Fucking sue me.

"Well, apparently, Bryce wants to test me one final time before I move on from her instruction, so she's setting up this sort of *Iron Chef*-inspired competition for me to participate in."

"Holy shit," I breathed. "She's not messing around."

"No, she's not. I'm really nervous, actually."

"Don't be. You're going to kick your opponent's ass."

"Oh, Ez," she said with a soft giggle. "I'm going up against Bryce."

"*What*?" I shouted then winced, my ears perking up to listen for any sounds from the other bedrooms. When the house beyond my walls remained still, I returned my attention to Brie.

"Yeah..." she trailed off. "Even if I don't beat her, it's not the end of the world. It's just a friendly competition to see how I perform under pressure and to test how well I've retained everything she's taught me, but..."

"But you want to win."

"Of course, I want to win," she said. "Wouldn't you? Could you imagine being able to say you beat Bryce Newsome in a head-to-head pastry bake-off?"

"Well, no," I said, grinning when she made a noise of protest. "But I'd never be in that position. We both know pastries are not my forte."

She rolled her eyes. "You're no help."

"You're going to be amazing, Brie. It's only for bragging rights, so there's no pressure other than what you put on yourself. Just have fun with it."

"'Have fun with it'?" she asked. "That's your best advice?"

I shrugged. "I don't know what else you want me to say. I can only believe in you so much. At some point, you have to pick up the slack."

Her mouth popped open, eyes widening in surprise. "I can't believe you just said that to me."

"I'm not going to sugarcoat things for you, Brie. You've got two parents and four sisters who will do that for you plenty. If you wanted someone to blow smoke up your ass, you would've called one of them. But personally, I don't think you want or need that. You *are* talented, more than anyone else I've ever met, but you have to believe it too, or the whole thing will be a total wash."

Brie sighed, her entire body deflating as she threw herself backward onto the mountain of pillows lining the head of her bed. "You're right, obviously."

I smirked. "I usually am."

"That's something I've always struggled with, you know. Self-confidence."

"Which I find insane, personally."

This girl was thoughtful, intelligent, loyal, and, as previously mentioned, ridiculously talented. The fact that she was worried about going up against this Bryce woman—who, by the way, I'd personally never heard of until Brie came into my life—was comical. I'd bet all the money to my name that Brie could stack up against the most notable pastry chefs from across the *world* and come out on top.

It killed me that she doubted it.

But I secretly loved being the one to remind her.

"Imposter syndrome is a very real thing," she said petulantly. "Haven't you ever experienced it?"

"Can't say I have."

"Well, you're a man *and* an only child, so I suppose you wouldn't."

"What's that supposed to mean? I didn't choose to be born this way, nor did I ask my mother to run off to god knows where before she and Dad could give me a sibling. I didn't ask for my dad to be so busy raising me while also trying to keep a roof over our heads and food on the table that he never even considered remarrying. I didn't ask for any of it, Brie. Believe me, I would've loved to have grown up in a two-parent household with a bunch of siblings running around, but that wasn't in the cards for me."

I heaved a deep breath at the end of my tirade, surprised I'd allowed myself to get that worked up.

Brie apparently hadn't taken too kindly to it, because the line between us went dead a moment later.

Fuck.

My first instinct was to call her back and keep doing so until she answered and let me apologize, but something stopped me.

The truth was, I'd meant every word I said. My childhood hadn't been the easiest. I'd been made fun of in school for not having a mom, for my second-hand clothes, for never being able to attend school functions because I didn't have anyone to drop me off or pick me up. In fact, I'd learned how to use the NYC subway system by the time I was twelve simply to take some of the pressure off my dad. The second I was old enough, I'd gotten a job at a restaurant to help with bills. It wasn't until I graduated high school and he handed me an envelope full of cash that I realized he'd been saving it the whole time, waiting for the moment when I was ready to go off on my own. In turn, I asked him to keep it safe until I finished my culinary arts program and was ready to take that trip to Europe. I hadn't lied when I told Brie we'd scraped together every penny we could to send me on that once-in-a-lifetime adventure.

I'd spent every moment I could since trying to repay him—an impossible task, given he was now helping me raise my own son.

Brie and I came from vastly different backgrounds. Neither the fact that I was a man nor that I was an only child had nothing to do with whether I'd experienced hardship or whether I doubted my abilities. Every day was a battle. My child was motherless, and every time I looked at him, I had to attempt to rectify the fact that I loved him beyond reason—more than my own life—with the fact that the woman who birthed him couldn't be bothered to love him more than her addiction...or love him more than she hated her life with me.

I failed frequently. I'd known I would, but there were days when the feeling was overwhelming, when all I wanted to do was drown myself in a bottle of bourbon.

But that sort of thinking was the exact thing that had taken Hansen's mother away from him, and I refused to cost him another parent.

I still drank but sparingly, and never simply to get drunk, alone in my room at night.

Brie had been way off base with her comments, and while I already missed her like I'd miss a limb, I wasn't going to be the one to come crawling back.

She had to be the one to fix this.

It took her three days.

Three long, seemingly interminable days, during which I picked up my phone, my finger poised over her contact info more times than I could count.

My entire body sagged in relief when it rang that night, her contact picture—a silly little selfie she'd sent me a few months ago—filling my screen.

"I'm sorry," she blurted the second it connected.

While I was grateful we were speaking again, I wasn't going to make this easy on her.

"You should be."

Chastened, she dropped her gaze from mine. "I shouldn't have said that. I know growing up the way you had couldn't have been easy, and it wasn't fair of me to make stupid comments about it."

"You're right, but..." I trailed off, and her demeanor perked up. "I'll admit I could've responded better, so I'm sorry for that."

"You have nothing to apologize for," she said, waving me off. "I know how different we grew up, Ez. I know you would've given anything to have a normal family unit like I do. I'm sorry you never got that chance, and I'm sorry for making you feel like shit about it."

I sighed heavily. "I spent a long time letting a lot of people make me feel exactly like you had," I told her. "I just... It sent me back to a bad place."

"I'm sorry," she said again.

"I forgive you."

"Really?"

"Of course," I said with a laugh. "I've been dying to call you for days."

"Well, I'm glad your stubborn streak won out. This was my screw up to fix."

I wanted to remind her that she was only twenty-two and still young enough to be making mistakes—especially given the fact that she had yet to experience any real hardship in her life—but now that we were back on solid ground, I wasn't about to rock our proverbial boat. Not to mention, it wasn't my place to call her out on stuff like that.

After all, who was I to her but a friend?

A friend who desperately wanted to get her naked and writhing under me, screaming my name, but a friend, nonetheless.

"It's okay, honey," I said. "Really."

Brie hummed happily in response. "Did we just survive our first fight?"

A laugh burst free from my throat, the last of my anxieties from the past few days dissipating along with it.

"Yeah, I think we did."

JUNE

"FUCKING HELL, BRIE," I gasped as I bent over my bathroom sink.

"You are so sexy when you come," she said, her voice tinny through the phone speaker.

I choked on a laugh. We were a far cry from that day in the winery kitchen, but I loved how comfortable she continued to feel with me.

I supposed that's what happened when you watched each other work toward multiple orgasms through the phone a few nights a week.

It was almost like I couldn't get off anymore without her watching me, like a reverse voyeur situation. Ever since our fight—and especially long makeup phone sex after the fact—my desire for her constantly scratched and clawed at my skin. I took my hand to myself more frequently during the day, the ever-fading memory of her scent in my mind, those sounds she made as she climaxed on a loop as I found my own.

So now, nearly every night after Hansen was fast asleep and

Dad was holed up in his room with the latest in an impressive stack of crime and thriller novels, I locked myself away and called Brie.

This thing with her...it wasn't only about the scorching hot phone sex. We talked too, a lot, about everything. I remained shocked I managed to find so much in common with a woman so much younger than me when we were at very different places in our lives.

"You think I'm sexy period," I quipped at last as my breathing returned to normal and I pulled my sweatpants back up.

"True," she said with a giggle.

"So how did today go?" I asked when I reclined on my bed and nestled into my mountain of pillows.

Yeah, I'd chosen to get off before we even had a conversation. I'd had a shitty day, and I needed that release. Brie hadn't complained. I loved how her sparkling emerald eyes darkened to pine green when she was turned on, and I loved her soft, sexy words of encouragement while I worked myself over. She'd been happy to let me, whispered how good she knew my cock would feel inside her. How my hands would feel on her body. How badly she wanted to taste me.

I was spilling all over my bathroom sink in minutes.

But today was a big day for her. She'd been so nervous the past few weeks as the date of her competition with Bryce neared. I had to remind her frequently that she was talented, capable, and was going to wow the judges. If she didn't come out on top, that was okay. The experience alone, having industry professionals give honest critiques of her work, would only make her a better baker.

But her worth wasn't tied up in some contest that wouldn't

mean anything in the long run, and I hoped however today had gone, she remembered that.

Secretly, I'd been making it my personal mission to ensure she did.

"Amazing!" she breathed. "I blew everyone away."

"Gonna need a bit more than 'amazing,' honey," I said.

"Ez..." she trailed off. Then, tone full of awe and wonder, she added, "I won."

My heart expanded so quickly and widely in my chest, it felt like it was going to burst. With pride. With excitement. With a whole slew of other emotions I wasn't prepared to name.

"Fuck yeah, you did!" I whisper-yelled. "I'm so fucking proud of you!"

She was practically preening for me now, her head held high, the most satisfied grin I'd ever seen her wear dancing on her lips—which was saying something, given how many times I'd dirty talked her through an orgasm.

"Guess all those nights spent coaching a helpless chef through pastry baking really paid off."

"Watch it," I growled, and Brie laughed. "I'm not helpless. My area of expertise is just elsewhere."

"You have turned me into a much better chef," she conceded.

"You're damn right."

"And...you've helped me become more confident too."

The pride coursing through my veins morphed to something softer and sweeter in an instant. All I wanted in that moment was to hug her.

Kiss her.

Maybe fuck her.

Okay, *definitely* fuck her.

But the distance had been good for us. It had given us the opportunity to explore this thing without the stakes being too high. We could seek our pleasure together from over three hundred miles away, and no one would be the wiser. While we texted almost all day, every day between work and other duties, it hadn't affected our daily lives in any negative way.

In fact, my life was richer for having Brie in it, even if it was unorthodox.

But she was moving home in less than two weeks, and while I knew she'd be busy getting her bakery up and running and I was in the middle of the summer season at the winery, I wondered how we'd navigate that new terrain. Would the pull I felt to her be stronger, knowing she was only a few miles away? Would we be able to resist, or would we damn the consequences and give in?

Six months ago, none of this would've bothered me. I had been so focused on settling into our new life and keeping Hansen happy and cared for that I hadn't balked when Brie pumped the brakes. We had, after all, only spent a handful of hours together. That wasn't enough to go turning my—and my son's—entire world upside down.

But that was six months ago.

Now, confronted with Brie's impending return to Apple Blossom Bay, a date that was no longer some shimmering mirage in the distance but sharply in focus right in front of us, it was time to take a good, hard look at what our relationship would look like going forward.

I wanted her in ways I'd never wanted a woman before, but her dad was my boss, which, according to him, made her off limits. We'd gotten away with it so far because it was easy to keep these nightly phone calls a secret. If her father found out what I was doing with his youngest daughter—and how badly I wanted to move things from cyberspace to a physical one—he wouldn't hesitate to kick my ass out the winery door. I couldn't let that happen. I couldn't piss on my life and set it on fire.

"What're we going to do, Brie?" I asked quietly.

"About?"

"About us."

"Is there an us?"

Fucking hell, I wished and wanted and hoped and dreamed.

But it was all a fantasy.

"You don't know how badly I wish I could say yes," I told her honestly.

"I wish you could too," she said quietly. "I wish...so many things were different."

"Me too, honey." I scrubbed my hand over my face and through my hair, settling it on the back of my neck and rubbing circles, as if that would make this all okay, as if I could massage into my scalp that the idea of "us" was a bad one when nothing else in my life had ever felt more right.

"What are we going to do?" I asked again.

I needed her to make this choice for me. Exactly like that day six months ago, I wasn't sure I was strong enough to do it for us.

She inhaled deeply, her chest rising and falling. "The second I get back...this has to be over. It's the only way."

I swallowed hard, my throat thickening with emotion at the thought of letting this easy intimacy I'd found with her go. Still,

I knew she was right.

"Friends?" I asked.

"Always."

JULY

ALL MY WORRIES WENT away the second I drove back into Apple Blossom Bay. Nothing settled me quite like being back on home soil. There was an added prickle of anticipation against my skin this time, knowing that I was coming home for good and that I was only a few weeks away from opening my very first bakery—a dream I'd had since I was a little girl.

In the seven months since I'd last been home, I'd spent countless hours on the phone with my dad and Jay Daniels, our contractor, going over every detail to make sure it was perfect.

They'd started off by gutting the space, addressing all structural issues and potential health hazards, then rebuilding it all. All the important pieces were in place—my counter and POS system, topped with a large bakery display case. Tables and chairs were ordered for the open space, and booths had been constructed along the walls. The kitchen was honestly a wet dream, with top-of-the-line appliances and a massive island workspace where I could prepare all my confections.

My dad had spared no expense, and while having the family

company retain ownership of my baby wasn't ideal, I had to admit, it wound up being for the best.

When I pulled up to my parents' house, I barely remembered to shut my car off as I sprinted inside, shouting for my dad as I burst through the door.

He met me with a wide grin in the hall halfway between the kitchen and foyer.

"Well, hello to you too, sweets," he said when I threw myself at him, letting him sweep me up in a big hug. "This is quite the greeting."

Once I landed back on my feet, I grabbed his hand and tugged him toward the door. "Enough with the pleasantries. I want to see my bakery."

My dad chuckled but let me lead him back out the door, shouting to my mom that he'd be back later.

We wound up taking his Tahoe instead of my car, mostly because my dad's six-foot-three-inch frame couldn't squeeze into my RAV-4 when it was packed full of everything I owned.

"So...I've got a surprise for you," he said as he navigated us down the peninsula toward town.

"Okay..." I said slowly.

"You absolutely don't have to accept it. We're... Well, I'll explain more when I show you."

I rolled my lips between my teeth, resisting the urge to press him for more information.

I found out soon enough.

Instead of parking on the street and taking me in through the front door, my dad parked around back. Our building was one of the wider ones on the block, about double the size of the slimmer storefronts on either side. There were two doors here: one to the bakery and one that led upstairs.

When we got out of the car, Dad withdrew a keyring from his pocket and moved toward the upstairs door.

"Where are we going?" I asked.

"You'll see," he said, unlocking and holding it open for me.

The stairwell smelled of fresh paint, the walls coated in a creamy white, the stairs themselves sturdy, sealed oak. At the top was a landing with hooks along one wall and a door on another. Once again, Dad selected another key, unlocked it, and swung it open.

I gasped when I took in what lay beyond.

I'd known there was an apartment up here—or at least, the infrastructure for one—but with all the excitement of getting the renovations done, I hadn't really given it a second thought.

To the left sat a kitchen with white tile floors and a small island lined with two stools. The spaces for a refrigerator and stove were empty, but the hookups for the appliances were there. To the right was a living room, the entire back wall consisting of windows that looked out over Main Street. Down a short hall was a bathroom, in-unit washer and dryer, and a bedroom.

After taking a minute to scope the place out, I returned to the center of the living room, hand to my mouth in awe as I stared at my father.

Who held the keys out to me.

"It's yours if you want it."

"I...what?"

"Look... You're an adult. While your mother and I would love to have you living with us again, we understand that you need your own space. So while we spruced up downstairs, your sisters and mom combined efforts to renovate this space for you as well. This way, you're close to work too."

Once again, I spun in a circle, taking in the light grey walls and digging my feet into the thick carpet. The apartment was a blank slate I could put my own mark on. I could easily imagine a plush sofa in the center of the living room, my entertainment center and TV setup along the right wall, flanked by my modest but prized collection of books. In the kitchen, they'd been wise not to purchase any appliances for me, knowing I'd want a say in that selection. The spaces were big enough so I could easily fit a French door fridge with the freezer on the bottom and a five-burner gas range with the included oven.

The bedroom wasn't all that large, but seeing as it was just me, I could still fit a full-sized mattress in there, and the bathroom had a tub that would be perfect for soaking with a glass of wine at the end of long days.

"So what do you say?" my dad asked carefully.

For the second time that day, I threw myself into his arms. "It's perfect," I said, tears springing to my eyes as I squeezed him tightly. "Thank you."

***

Despite coming back to Apple Blossom Bay and immediately becoming a building owner—with a "rent" that was disgustingly low—I didn't have time to focus on getting myself settled in my new apartment when all my energy needed to go into getting the bakery ready for my opening the first week of August.

Two weeks. That was all I had.

I was starting to regret pushing so hard to open so quickly.

Especially when I'd been so busy finishing my apprenticeship that I hadn't had time to iron out my recipes.

I'd attempted nearly every recipe Granny Smith had left behind in her cookbook. Some I'd mastered easily, while others had taken a bit longer to perfect—and some, I still hadn't quite figured out.

All I knew was I wanted Granny and her creations to serve as the centerpiece of my menu. So, between running around like a chicken with its head cut off at the bakery, hanging decor, unpacking and organizing supplies, and familiarizing myself and my lone employee with the point-of-sale system, I spent every waking second in the kitchen at Mom and Dad's.

"I don't understand why you've taken over my kitchen for this little project," Mom said one night about a week before I opened. "You have a brand new, state-of-the-art kitchen in town."

"Because I need a taste-tester," I explained, brushing the back of my hand over my forehead to push a wisp of hair that had escaped my braid out of my eyes. "And Dad graciously volunteered."

Mom snorted. "*Graciously*. He's got the biggest sweet tooth out of anyone we know. Plus, you're making his mom's recipes. It makes him...nostalgic."

I looked up at my mom and grinned. As the owner of a sweet tooth myself, I loved that this was something Dad and I could share, this bond with his late mother for just the two of us.

"If it bothers you that much, I'll head into town," I said, though I couldn't just walk away with the lemon poppy seed muffins I had in the oven.

"It doesn't bother me, sweetheart," she said, moving to my side and wrapping an arm around my shoulders to pull me into a hug. "I just thought you might like to get the lay of the land before you open."

I could admit when she was right, and this was one of those instances. I'd been so focused on keeping everything perfect before I opened the doors, I hadn't considered that, one day, I would have to mess things up a little bit. The kitchen needed to be broken in.

"I'll head down there tomorrow," I said.

"Wonderful!" She clapped, pulling away from me. "And when are you planning on moving into your apartment? Not that we don't love having you here, but your sisters and I didn't slave over remodeling that space for nothing."

"Moooooom," I groaned.

"Just wondering," she said, shrugging in forced nonchalance.

"I need furniture. I'm too old to be sleeping on the floor."

"So let's run into Traverse City on Saturday and get everything you need."

I perked up at the idea of making a girls' day of it, of getting away from the stress of getting the bakery open to focus on getting settled in my apartment.

"Can we invite my sisters too?"

"Duh," Mom said, sounding more like one of them than my parent. "You think they'd let us go without them?"

I laughed. "No, they definitely wouldn't."

By the following Monday, four days before my grand opening, I was sleeping in my apartment. I had the essentials: bed, sofa, television. My books were unpacked, and the storage closet was stocked with towels, toiletries, and cleaning products. The only appliance I had was a coffee pot. While we waited for my new fridge and stove to arrive next week, I'd be eating out at Granny's or Sydney's Diner—a reality I wasn't complaining about. After spending all day baking, the last thing I felt like doing was cooking for myself.

And baking was exactly where I found myself on Tuesday evening. The giant workspace in my kitchen was laden with sweet and savory scones, croissants, turnovers, danishes, and muffins. I thought I'd finally nailed down the menu, but I couldn't help feeling like I needed one final second opinion.

I'd studiously avoided thinking about Ezra since I'd returned home—truthfully, I hadn't had time—but now that I was staring down opening my doors, I wanted him here, wanted his culinary expertise assessing my menu offerings and giving me the green light.

"Hey, honey," he said when he picked up.

"Hi, Ez," I replied, unable to hide the grin in my voice. "You busy right now?"

"Surprisingly no. I have the day off, so Hansen and I are just chilling at home."

"How about spending some time with me instead?" I said suggestively.

"What kind of time?"

"I want you to taste my—"

"Yes," he said hurriedly, not letting me finish.

I barked out a laugh. "Ezra! Get your mind out of the gutter. I want you to come sample my bakery menu."

He scoffed. "I've already sampled your...other goods anyway."

I rolled my eyes with a grin. "Get your fine ass down here."

"Give me a bit to figure out a playdate for Hansen...unless you want him to come?"

I should've said yes, should've agreed to using Hansen as a buffer between us. Unfortunately for the little guy, I wanted his dad all to myself.

"Just you," I whispered. "Please."

"I'll text you when I'm on my way."

God, inviting him here was dangerous; I knew that. But I trusted his opinion more than just about anyone else in the world, and I knew he wouldn't hold back his feelings on my baking. I wanted honesty, not my family blowing smoke to make me feel good about myself.

I had no delusions about what would happen when he got here. We'd agreed to be friends and nothing more. I wasn't expecting him to rush in and sweep me off my feet, consuming me in a kiss worthy of the silver screen.

This was simply a man and a woman who had once been intimate and now weren't. We were adults. We could get through this without things being weird...or so I thought.

chapter 17
Ezra

I HADN'T BEEN ABLE to answer fast enough when Brie's name popped up on my phone screen. I knew she'd been back in town, but we were keeping our distance, so I hadn't sought her out. In fact, our only communication since she'd moved home was a text from me the day she arrived, asking if she made it safely. Her response had been polite but distant.

I did. Thanks for checking, and thanks for all your help these last few months.

Like I said...polite, but lacking all the intimacy we'd found together.

Fuck, I'd found myself in a real mess, hadn't I?

Either way, when she asked me to come down to the bakery to taste test her menu, I jumped at the chance. I didn't want to miss out on a single opportunity to spend time with her.

"Okay, buddy," I said to Hansen as I walked him up to the front door of his friend's house, where he was going for a play-date since my dad was at work. "I'll be back to pick you up in a few hours. You have fun with Gerard!"

Gerard's mom, a pale blonde woman who was so soft-spoken, I barely heard her most of the time, opened the door and grinned widely at my son.

"Is that Hansen Wendt I see?"

"Yes, Miss Penny!"

"Well, come on in then." She stepped to the side and ushered Hansen in. He was off and running to greet Gerard the moment he crossed the threshold, his old man entirely forgotten.

"Thanks for taking him on such short notice," I told Penny.

She waved me off. "No problem at all. How long do you think you'll be?"

"Only a few hours, I'm sure." It couldn't possibly take more than that to sample a few menu items, could it?

Penny nodded in agreement. "Great. We'll see you then."

I offered her a grateful smile and said, "Thanks again" as I turned to leave.

As instructed, when I reached the bakery, I parked at the back of the building and entered through the door off the kitchen. The second I laid eyes on Brie, my whole world narrowed to that point. Nothing outside of those walls mattered. There was only her.

My honey.

"Hey stranger."

She looked up with a gasp, her hand flying to her chest. "My god, Ez. You scared me."

"Sorry," I said sheepishly. "I should've knocked or something."

"No, it's okay." She waved me off then stilled to look at me—really look at me. Her emerald gaze swept my body, setting my skin on fire.

"What're you doing?"

"Looking at you," she said with a shrug.

"Why?"

She met my eyes again, the green blazing even in the dim lights of her kitchen. "Making sure you're real."

I fisted my hands at my sides, doing everything I could to remain rooted in place, to not go to her, sweep her into my arms, and kiss her soundly. Every fiber of my being craved her—but that wasn't who we were to each other. We had to remain friends, which meant I needed to keep, at the very least, the massive island between us.

I wanted her so badly, in every single way she'd have me, but platonically was the only way I'd get to keep her, and I wasn't about to fuck that up.

Was it rude to blatantly ignore her comment? Probably, but she had to know she was toeing a fine line. I was a red-blooded male with a finite amount of restraint, and the bulk of it had gone out the window the second I laid eyes on her. She couldn't fault me for skirting around my desire and diving right into the reason she asked me here.

"So what am I sampling today?"

Brie blinked slowly, like an owl, before she seemed to come back to herself. With a quick shake of her head, she tore her gaze from me and moved to one side of the island, gesturing to the five trays she had spread across its surface.

"I've decided on five categories: scones, muffins, croissants, danishes, and turnovers. Each category has three offerings. I didn't want to go too crazy to start, especially since I know I'm going to be busy the second I open thanks to the season. I went with recipes that are easy to prepare the night before and bake fresh first thing in the morning. We'll also be offering standard coffee drinks. Black, decaf, chai, and a small selection of hot or cold herbal teas."

She pushed a piece of paper toward me, a rudimentary menu she'd scribbled on and doodled all over. "I still need to get these printed, but I just haven't had time."

"Will you have some sort of menu board up behind the counter?"

Nodding, she said, "You want to go check it out?"

I perked up at that, desperate to escape the confines of this kitchen. Over the months, she'd shared progress photos with me, which had been sent to her secondhand from her dad or contractor. I could admit—I'd been skeptical at first. It needed more work than I probably would've wanted to put into it, but when I stepped out onto the main floor, I quickly discovered her father had spared no expense.

The space was utterly transformed; nothing of the dark, dirty business that had been here before remained.

One wall was papered in a mural of white, pastel pink, yellow, and orange flowers, lined with booths wrapped in dark green faux-leather. Tables filled the rest of the room, the seats of the chairs matching the booths. The floors were what appeared to be light laminate planks, but upon closer inspection, I found they were actually tile that looked like wood. The entire front wall was nothing but windows, letting in a ton of natural light and facing out onto Main Street. The counter was to the left, topped with white faux-marble and faced with what looked like pieces of reclaimed wood.

It was funky, fresh, a little girlie, and a whole lot of stunning.

"It's gorgeous," I said.

"You think so?" she asked, chewing on her bottom lip.

"Absolutely," I assured her. "It's going to be a hit. People will come inside because it looks cute and eye-catching, but they'll stay because your food is incredible."

"You haven't even tasted it yet."

"Then maybe we should fix that."

With a small smile, Brie inclined her head, and I followed her back into the kitchen. She gestured to a stool she'd hidden under the counter, and I sat as she put the first plate in front of me.

This close, her scent stuffed itself up my nose—butter, sugar, and honey. It wasn't a traditional floral or spicy scent you'd usually find in women's perfumes because it wasn't something you could bottle. No, that blend was all Brie.

"First, we have a selection of scones." Reaching out, she pointed to each in turn as she named them. "Cranberry orange, triple chocolate, and ham and cheese."

"Ham and cheese?" I asked with a quirked brow.

"I wanted to offer something savory, and when I came across that recipe in my grandma's old cookbook, I couldn't resist trying it."

She damn near glowed when she spoke about her grandma and that collection of recipes, so that was the one I went for first.

"Fuuuuuuck," I moaned as the first bite hit my tongue. Wide-eyed, I turned to her. "Are you joking with this?"

Brie's brow furrowed, her cheeks turning dark pink. "It's just a ham and cheese scone, Ezra."

"Well, it's the best damn ham and cheese scone I've ever tasted."

"You mean that?" she asked skeptically.

"I would never lie to you."

And I meant *that*. I didn't have a reason to lie to her. This girl—she knew my secrets, the darkest parts of me, and none of it phased her.

And this scone...

When I thought of scones, I thought of heaviness, of dense carbs that overshadowed the flavor of whatever other ingredients the baker used.

Brie's was none of those things.

It was airy but substantial. The sharp cheddar with honey ham created the most delicious explosion of savory and sweet on my tongue, and the inclusion of chives rounded out the flavor profile nicely. It was something I could imagine being served in some high-end New York City bakery.

Instead, this gorgeous, talented, small-town woman had created it all on her own with the help of her late grandmother's cookbook—and that right there made all the difference.

As corny as it sounded, all the best food was made with love, and this scone was no exception.

"You're never getting rid of me now," I said around a mouthful. "I'm coming to visit every day just for one of these."

A broad grin spread across her lips, and she met my eyes head on, allowing me to witness the flush creeping up her neck and over her face, showing me how deeply my comment pleased her.

"I never wanted to get rid of you anyway," she said.

Time slowed in that moment, like a movie scene where the whole world around the main characters ceased to exist. World War III could've been happening outside, and I wouldn't have noticed. It was the kind of moment the old me would've taken advantage of—that version of me who hadn't had his heart ripped out by the woman who vowed to love him, who hadn't spent the last year and a half raising his son alone.

The man who hadn't already been pushed away by *this* woman.

All sense returned with that reminder, and I blinked, swallowing hard and awkwardly clearing my throat. I set the remainder of the scone to the side and said, "What's next?"

Brie gave her head a little shake and turned her back on me, heading to the opposite counter, where the rest of her confections were laid out. She carried the tray back and set it in front of me.

Slowly, I worked through each one, offering my honest opinions. Unsurprisingly, I had nothing but rave reviews to give. This woman knew her way around a pastry, and I knew without a doubt that the bakery would be a resounding success when she finally opened the doors.

Brie was all business after the *almost* moment, though, and kept things between us strictly professional. I knew it was for the best, but it didn't ease the vise squeezing my chest.

I was at war with myself, wanting to stay close but also needing to get away so I could breathe a lungful of air that wasn't laced with the scents of butter and sugar—that wasn't laced with *her*.

When I'd consumed every last morsel of her menu, I moved to the sink and washed my hands while Brie tidied the kitchen behind me. I turned to face her again, but neither of us moved. We just...looked at each other.

I let my eyes rake over her face, along the weave of the dark braid she had perpetually draped over her shoulder. Down the sage-colored apron, the sleeves of her white shirt that ended at her biceps and along the slender lengths of her arms. Down her legs to the tips of her toes, stuffed in sensible tennis shoes.

Slowly, I dragged my gaze back up. Brie's chest rose and fell more rapidly than before, and she wrung her hands in front of her, clearly anxious.

That made two of us. I was walking a fine line between the desire to run for the hills or run into her arms.

"Well, thank you for coming down," Brie said at last, ending our staring contest by averting her gaze. "I really appreciate your help."

"You're amazing," I breathed. "You didn't need it."

She looked at me again, eyes wide with something I couldn't name. It wasn't *surprise*, exactly. It was something deeper—something like...longing?

"Maybe I didn't need it," she said. "But I'll always want it."

I heard what she wasn't saying.

I'll always want you.

I sucked in a breath; to say what, I didn't know, but it seemed my body made up my mind for me, the switch between fight or flight finally flipped in a single direction.

When I exhaled, the only words that left me were, "Fuck it," before I closed the distance between us and crashed my mouth down on hers.

chapter 18
Brie

BEING KISSED BY EZRA again was like inhaling a deep lungful of air after being underwater a bit too long. My entire body relaxed the second his lips touched mine, only to tighten again as desire coursed through my veins. Everything between my thighs went hot and wet in the span of a heartbeat.

He paused to ask against my lips, "Is this okay?"

"More than," I assured him. It was everything. *He* was everything.

"Fuck, I missed you," he breathed, pulling away from my mouth to nip at my jaw, trailing kisses toward my ear. He nibbled on the lobe, and a whimper escaped me, goosebumps rising across my skin. "I've thought about having you in my arms again every day, Brie."

"That makes two of us," I assured him, lacing my fingers through his silky, dark locks and moving him where I wanted him—with his mouth on mine, our tongues tangling in a way that reminded me exactly what he'd done to my clit all those months ago.

I fisted his shirt but pulled back, giving us room to breathe while I stared into his eyes. The skin between them pinched slightly, and his shoulders tensed, as though preparing for me to shoot him down, to remind him why we couldn't do this—to once again pump the brakes on our out-of-control attraction.

But I was done fighting it, done pretending I didn't want him, hadn't missed him, wasn't ready to cross every line and break every rule with him.

What my dad didn't know wouldn't hurt him.

"I—" I started, the syllable coming out on a croak. I cleared my throat and tried again. "I live upstairs."

The creases between his eyes deepened. "Are you saying what I think you're saying?"

"I want you in all the ways you'll let me have you," I told him. "I missed you too, and I've thought about this every day. I want real orgasms with you, not the inadequate ones we've been giving ourselves over the phone. The next time you come with my name on your lips, I want it to be inside me."

Ezra was still for a beat longer before he hauled me off the counter and over his shoulder. I squealed, laughing as he moved out of the kitchen and down the short hall to the back.

Thankfully, I hadn't locked the lower door when I'd come down earlier, so he pushed inside, his footfalls heavy as he ascended the stairs, carrying me like a sack of flour. The door at the top required fingerprint access—my dad wasn't taking any chances with my safety, he'd said—so Ezra spun me, and I let us in.

Once inside, he didn't pause to look around, didn't set me on my feet. He just made a beeline down the hallway, pushed into my bedroom, and dropped me on the bed.

"Fuck, Brie," he said, leaning over me, running his hands up the length of my torso, from hips to breasts, until he cupped the mounds, his thumbs teasing over my nipples, which had pebbled beneath the fabric of my bra and shirt. "Are you sure about this?"

"More sure than I've ever been about anything," I promised.

Ezra took his time stripping himself out of his clothes. His long, thick fingers worked nimbly as they unfastened each button on the front of his shirt. When he shrugged it off, I was surprised to find his skin had turned a golden brown in the months since I'd last seen him in the flesh. Not to mention, he'd packed on some more muscle, and as he stepped out of his pants, my eyes dragged over his entire body.

"God," I groaned, throwing myself backward onto my mattress and tossing an arm over my face dramatically. "How did you get even hotter the last seven months?"

Ezra chuckled, the end of my bed dipping as he knelt between my thighs. I moved my arm and opened my eyes, finding him fully naked, his cock heavy and engorged, jutting out from his body.

My mouth suddenly went dry.

Ezra reached for the waistband of my leggings, peeling them and my panties down. I sat up and made quick work of my apron, top, and bra, groaning when he knelt again and hauled me up against him. Each of my nerve endings sparked to life when we connected, and I bent to capture his mouth with mine. I wanted to consume him, to let him climb inside my body and stay with me forever, but for his sake, I needed to make something clear before we went any further.

"I know this is a one-time thing, Ez," I whispered against his lips. "I'm not asking you for anything but this—this single night. I just...needed you to know that."

Ezra stared at me, the only sounds in the room the twin thumping of our hearts. Then, he jerked his head once in the approximation of a nod before tipping me backward and covering my body with his.

"Just once," he agreed softly before he claimed my mouth again, his groan reverberating through his chest and mine as my tongue swept against his. I circled my legs around his hips, bringing him closer.

His tip bumped against my entrance, and a shiver passed through me.

He was so big. I knew this from nights on FaceTime, but seeing it on my tiny iPhone screen and being confronted with it in real life were two very different things. It was one of those "objects in mirror may be closer than they appear" moments, only Ezra's dick was much thicker and longer than I'd anticipated.

"You gonna let me fuck you bare?" he asked through gritted teeth, his grip on my hips just shy of painful as he held himself back from sinking into me. "I can't—if this is the only night I get you, I don't have it in me for foreplay right now." He reached between us and brushed his fingers through my slit. They came away coated in my arousal, and he grinned. "So fucking wet. All this sweet honey, just for me. I could slide inside you so easily."

I nodded, not needing to think about it. "If this is all we get, I want to be as close to you as possible."

"Fuck, honey," he said, dropping his face to my neck and shifting closer. "Put it in."

I reached down and gripped his length, giving him a few experimental tugs that had him making that delicious groaning sound against my skin. Then, I notched his head at my core, and he pushed inside.

"Slow," I gasped as he began to stretch me. "It's been...a while."

Over a year, to be exact, but I wasn't about to admit that to him.

Ezra heeded my warning, angling himself deeper inside me with a slowness that took my breath away. I'd never had a man take care of me in bed before, never had one care about my pleasure, making sure what we were doing felt as good for me as it did for him.

But the entire time Ezra worked to seat himself fully inside me with shallow advances and retreats, he murmured words of praise, telling me how sexy I was, how good I felt, how perfect my pussy was. He pressed kisses to my temple and forehead, eyelids and cheeks.

When he slid all the way in at last, he captured my mouth in a sweet, slow kiss that did wonders for distracting me from the slight burn as I acclimated to him.

"You okay?" he asked.

At last, I relaxed fully, and I hooked my legs around his waist, digging my heels into his ass. "Yes. Now move."

Bracing himself on his palms over me, Ezra watched the space between us as he pulled all the way out and slammed back in with one forceful stroke that stole a cry from my lungs.

Ezra shifted his weight so he could grip my chin in one hand. "You tell me if it's too much. I...fuck, Brie. I'm so gone for you, it's not even funny, but I want this to be good for you too. I *need* this to be good."

"It's already the best I've ever had," I promised him.

"You're ruining me," he said as he began to move again, his thrusts steady but unhurried.

I thought it would take more, that I'd need him to take me hard and fast to get me there, but already, my insides wound, the pressure in my core increasing each time he buried himself to the hilt, his broad head stroking some deep spot only he'd ever been able to reach.

I angled my hips and met him thrust for thrust, anchoring myself to him with my legs around his middle and my nails gouging lines down his shoulders and back as I clung to him.

"More, Ez," I breathed. I was so close, I thought I'd die if I didn't get there immediately. My climax shimmered before me, almost within reach.

Knowing exactly what I needed, Ezra pressed his thumb to my clit, circling in time with the drive of his hips, and I shattered.

A scream tore from my throat, a sound I'd never heard myself make, as I came apart at the seams. My vision danced as I quaked in Ezra's arms while he slammed recklessly into me, chasing his own release and prolonging mine. At last, he came with a roar, bowing his back and shouting my name at the ceiling, pulsing and spilling hot and long inside me.

I'd be damned if it wasn't the hottest thing I'd ever witnessed.

He pulled free from me a beat later and sat back on his heels, my legs still draped over his thighs.

My lips and clit were swollen and sensitive, and I twitched as Ezra swiped a finger through my slit. Lifting it, he showed me our mingled desires then brought it to my mouth.

"Open up. Tell me how good we are together."

I did as he asked, closing my lips around his finger and sucking it clean, swirling my tongue over the tip, calloused from years of wielding kitchen instruments.

I moaned around him as our combined releases exploded on my tongue.

I met his eyes as he pulled his finger free. "A perfect pairing."

I WOKE IN AN unfamiliar place, wrapped around a warm body that was far too long and feminine to be my son. Some sort of floral freshener hung in the air and clung to the sheets, but it was the woman in my arms who stole my breath. I wanted to stay here forever, wrapped in her warmth and sugar and butter scent.

I blinked open my eyes, and the night before came flooding back.

Brie.

Sex.

Holy fuck, I had *sex* with *Brie*.

Before I could spiral too deep into my freak out, an insistent buzzing filled the room. The vibration of a phone.

Carefully extricating my limbs from Brie's—no easy task when we were wound together on her narrow full mattress—I sifted through our discarded clothing on the floor until I came across my pants, and thus, my phone.

I stepped out of the room and quietly closed the door behind me.

"Dad?"

"Ezra!" he shouted, and I hissed at him to keep it down. "Where the fuck have you been? You didn't call, didn't text. You never picked Hansen up from his play date, so his friend's mom called me in a panic. I had to leave the jobsite to do it. What the fuck, kid?"

"Shit," I said, scrubbing my hand over my face. "I'm so sorry. I was helping Brie with some bakery stuff and...the day got away from me," I finished lamely.

There was no good way to spin this, nothing I could say that wouldn't alert my dad to exactly what *my boss's youngest daughter* and I had been up to last night.

My dad's sigh of disappointment was audible. "I'm all for you having fun and blowing off some steam, Ez," he said softly. "But really? Brie Delatou? I thought we talked about this. What the fuck were you thinking?"

"Clearly, I wasn't," I said with a wince. "Actually, I had been, just with the wrong head. Desire overrode sense."

"Well, figure your shit out and get home," he grumbled. "Your son is worried sick."

I grimaced. "I'll be home in ten."

"Make it five," he said then hung up.

"Ezra?"

I spun toward the quiet voice to find Brie standing at the mouth of the hallway, an oversized Chateau Delatou winery tee draped across her torso, her long legs bare beneath.

I had to look away, lest my smaller head get ideas—the kind that involved giving my father and son the middle finger and taking her back to bed for the foreseeable future.

"Is everything okay?"

"Yeah." I reached up to scrub the back of my neck, avoiding her gaze. This whole thing was so goddamn awkward, from my nakedness to the fact that I couldn't get out of here fast enough but didn't want to hurt her feelings. "Just...forgot to check in with my dad. He and Hansen have been worried sick. I need to get home."

"Right," she said slowly. "Bedroom's all yours."

She moved into the kitchen, seemingly oblivious to the state her legs and that tee that barely covered her ass had me in. My entire body was rebelling against my brain. I wanted to take her again—even though I'd had my cock buried deep inside her three times last night and made her come on my tongue twice more. But I needed to protect myself and my son from letting another woman who could hurt us into our lives.

Brie... She wasn't Shannon. I knew that. But after only one night together, I was already shirking my duties as a single parent. The moment I'd stepped foot in the bakery last night, all thoughts about anything but Brie left my head. I couldn't afford that kind of distraction from Hansen. Not now. Not ever.

I shuffled past her and dressed at warp speed. When I emerged, she was still in the kitchen, her back to me, the scent of coffee wafting through the space. What I wouldn't give to be able to stay for breakfast, to share stories over mugs of caffeine and some of her delicious pastries, to pretend for a little bit longer that we were different people who could enjoy slow mornings together.

"Well...see ya," I said, moving toward the door.

"Wait," she said just as my hand touched the knob.

I spun toward her, finally looking at her face for the first time since we'd woken up. Brie had the kind of natural beauty that didn't require makeup—not that I thought there was anything wrong with women who did wear the stuff. With full lips a rosy shade of pink, flawless olive skin, and those striking green eyes lined in sooty lashes and topped with thick, perfectly sculpted dark brows, she was a showstopper.

And too fucking young and pure for the likes of me. After all, only a fucked-up asshole walked away from a woman like her—and I was seconds away from doing it.

"Yeah?" I asked, doing everything I could not to bounce on the balls of my feet, demonstrating how desperate I was to escape.

"I was thinking that maybe we could do this ag—"

I cut her off before she could fully speak that thought into existence, shaking my head vigorously. "We agreed on one time."

"But I thought—"

"I neglected my child yesterday, Brie. I dropped him off at a playdate on my way here, and I was supposed to pick him up when I went home. Only, I didn't. Never told my dad where I was going to be.

"Being with you...I lose all sense. Ignore the things I need to focus on. My entire perspective narrows until there's only you, and I can't—" I choked on what I needed to say, clearing my throat and trying again. *God, this was going to fucking hurt.* "I can't let you be a part of my life. It's too hard. After Shannon, I just...can't."

I didn't wait for a response. I simply turned on my heel and ran away like the fucking coward I was.

chapter 20
Brie

THE SECOND THE DOOR shut behind him—not an echoing, slamming boom, but the quiet *snick* of the lock catching, which was honestly so much worse—I collapsed to the floor, a sob tearing free from my throat.

Seeing as I was crying too hard to speak, I didn't know what I was thinking as I crawled to my room and grappled around on the floor for my phone. When I located it, I called the sister who could get to me fastest.

"El," I choked out when she answered.

"Brie?" The alarm was evident in my sister's tone. "What happened?"

"Can't—"

I didn't know what I was trying to say, but it was cut off by a sob anyway.

"I'll be right there," Ella said softly. "Whatever it is, Brie, we'll figure it out. It's going to be okay."

Though she couldn't see me, I nodded, and barely a minute later, footsteps echoed in the stairwell outside my apartment. The only other people who could get past the fingerprint scanner on my door were my sisters and parents, and Ella stepped inside after a faint beeping.

Then she was gathering me in her arms, and I was sobbing uncontrollably against her chest.

When my tears slowed and cries quieted enough that Ella could speak, she asked, "Do you want me to call in the cavalry?"

I shoved back to look at her and shouted, "No!" a bit too loudly. "Sorry. I just... I don't need them going all big sisters on me right now."

"But I'm your big sister too," Ella said softly.

I rolled my eyes and moved to stand, extending a hand to help her to her feet as well. "It's not the same and you know it."

Ella only nodded. Since she'd been born in September and I arrived in August of the following year, we were Irish twins and had always been close growing up. I loved each of my sisters equally and for different reasons, but the thing I appreciated most about Ella—and why she'd been the one I'd called the moment my heart shattered with the door slamming shut behind Ezra—was her stillness. Despite the tattoos and pink streaks in her dark hair, she was quiet and free-spirited. She didn't speak simply because she couldn't stand the silence. Everything about her was intentional and carefully considered.

It was why we were all so flabbergasted that she'd started dating Alfie, who was the opposite of everything she was and stood for. My parents especially hoped it was only a phase she'd grow out of.

"What do you want to do then?" she asked.

"Don't you have to work?"

Ella shook her head. "I have Wednesdays off."

I quirked a brow. "Since when?"

"Since the beginning of summer," she said with a shrug.

I lifted the hem of my shirt to my face and wiped away the tears, mopping myself up as best as I could, grateful I thought to put underwear on before Ezra left.

"I have so much work to do for the bakery," I said, sniffing loudly to clear my nose. "I don't have time to wallow."

I think I was trying to convince myself more than her, and Ella simply nodded.

"I think there's always time for wallowing."

I looked at my sister, who came running when I'd called, who'd given up her only day off to help me work through the pain I was experiencing—pain she didn't understand because I hadn't yet explained.

"As badly as I want to sink into the couch and have an Anne Hathaway marathon, there's just too much work to do downstairs. Plus, keeping busy will keep me distracted."

Ella didn't press, didn't beg for more information or dig her fingers into the sore spot on my chest, right over my heart. She only moved closer and settled her hands on my shoulders.

"What can I do to help?"

God, I hated myself in that moment. I'd been so wrapped up in my own stuff, between finishing my apprenticeship, prepping for the bakery opening, and...*him* that I hadn't bothered to check in with my sisters. But here Ella was, doing whatever she could to help me—to make me feel better.

Some days, I wasn't sure I deserved my sisters, least of all this one.

"I'm sorry," I told her. "I've been so..."

"Busy," she finished for me, hitching up a shoulder. "I get it."

"It's not an excuse."

"It is when you're falling in love. Ezra, right? I saw him drive past on my way here."

"I'm not..." I choked on my words before I could finish the sentence. "I just really like—*liked* him."

Ella pursed her lips as if to say *get real*, knowing full well I couldn't turn it off that quickly. After all, she'd witnessed my emotional breakdown only minutes before.

And the truth was...I more than liked Ezra. But how was it possible to fall in love with someone after spending only a handful of real, physical, tangible moments together? Then again, I'd learned more about him over the course of our late-night phone calls than I ever had anyone else. The distance and darkness had given us a safe space to spill our secrets.

Maybe, in sharing all my truths with him, I'd also been handing over pieces of my heart all along.

It gutted me that I'd never get them back.

Part Two

I'll love you.
But just this twice.

— ATTICUS

chapter 21
Brie

TWO YEARS, TWO MONTHS LATER

"CAN I RUN SOMETHING by you?" Ezra asked me and my sister, pulling me up short.

I was halfway out of my seat, desperate for some clean, Ezra-free air after he, Delia, and I spent the past few hours discussing the winery's contribution to the Apple Blossom Bay Fall Festival, which started in two weeks. Every year, we set up booths inside the barn near the corn maze and pumpkin patch to serve snacks and treats. As Ezra was the winery's head chef and I was the resident pastry girlie, we'd been forced to work together on it for the last two seasons since I moved home from Chicago and opened the bakery.

Truthfully, I wanted to be anywhere else.

I'd done my level best to maintain a professional and amicable relationship with Ezra since *that night*. I didn't go out of my way to avoid him, but I also wasn't making it a point to spend any extra time in his presence. He'd made it clear what he wanted from me when he left my apartment that morning—which was *nothing*, for the record—and I'd been a foolish, naive girl to think one night of incredible passion, a connection I hadn't found with anyone else before or since, would be enough to change his mind.

The worst part was, I couldn't even fault him for it. Hansen had to be his top priority. I'd done what I could to move on and make our working relationship as smooth and tension-free as possible.

"What's up, Ez?" I asked, dropping back onto my chair.

My gaze darted across the table to Delia, who also sank back into her seat. She gave me a reassuring smile, and I resisted the urge to reach for her hand, to ground myself when my heart was beating out of my chest.

Call it woman's intuition, but I had a feeling I wasn't going to like whatever happened next.

"I want to get more involved in the community, beyond all of this," he said, gesturing to the winery. "So I was thinking about ways I could give back, and I thought perhaps hosting a fall dinner of sorts at the community center would be fun. I'm thinking a ticketed event with five to seven courses, each cooked by me and paired with a Chateau Delatou wine. I could do fall-inspired dishes with a Swedish flair."

Instantly, I perked up. In all my years of living here, I could say with confidence that neither the community nor the winery had ever hosted anything remotely similar. I gaped slightly at Ezra. For the last few years, he'd been...withdrawn. The bags under his eyes had practically been designer, and everything about him had seemed haunted. Maybe I was delusional, but I couldn't help thinking it had something to do with me. But now, he was present. His eyes were bright, dancing with excitement, and his normally flattened mouth was tipped up into a heart stopping smile.

I'd missed that smile—missed being the one who put it there.

"And Brie," Ezra continued, startling me into closing my mouth and relaxing my posture, forcing myself into pretending I wasn't hanging on his every word. "I was hoping you'd contribute to the dessert course. Maybe you could come up with something to pair with the CD ice wine?"

"I—" I started, choking on that single letter, then cleared my throat. "That sounds wonderful, Ez. Count me in."

After all, this was *my* community too. I was more than happy to participate.

I tuned out Delia and Ezra discussing marketing logistics and running through ideas of where to donate the proceeds. Already, my mind swirled with ideas, and I couldn't wait to get home and consult Granny's recipe book for some more inspiration. I'd definitely be doing something with apples, but maybe I could also whip up some sort of sweetened pumpkin concoction...

Distantly, I clocked Ezra mentioning needing to figure out where he'd cook everything, but I was still lost in my head.

Until my sister quipped, "You should use the bakery's kitchen! It's only a few storefronts up from the community center, and there's plenty of workspace and storage."

I gritted my teeth and said, "Storage I use for my shop."

My sister had a habit of doing stuff like this. I was no stranger to what she referred to as her "inner chaos demon," I'd just never been on the receiving end of the shit-stirring until now.

Unperturbed, she shrugged and pressed on. "You can use that industrial sized fridge that takes up ninety percent of the kitchen in your apartment. After the hell you put Dad and Logan through to get it up there, it's really the least you could do." Her eyes twinkled with mischief as she added, "Unless you want Ezra using that one instead."

I glared daggers at my sister, wishing I had the ability to nuke people with a simple look. Over my dead body would Ezra Wendt step foot in my apartment ever again, and Delia knew that.

I'd never gone into specifics with my sisters about what happened between me and him. They knew about the first hook up at the winery, but nothing else. The phone calls—those were too precious to me. Meant to be kept safe in that moment of time for only him and I to remember, preserved like a dragonfly in amber.

Ella had been there in the aftermath, holding me together enough to pick up the pieces and get the bakery open, but even she wasn't privy to the full story.

That was between me, Ezra, and the past. I preferred it stayed there.

I definitely hadn't told them I'd had sex with him. I loved them dearly, but Chloe, Amara, and Delia all had huge mouths. My parents would know right away because they'd never be able to keep it to themselves, and I hadn't wanted Ezra to get fired. That would've only made a bad situation worse.

Although now that Amara was his boss, I supposed it didn't matter so much.

"I really wouldn't want to impose..." Ezra said slowly, pulling me from plotting all the ways I could get back at Delia for this.

Both of them stared at me expectantly, clearly anticipating my rejection. Ezra had curled his shoulders inward, as though protecting himself from the blow he thought I'd deal.

But that wasn't my style. The only one of us who handed out rejections was him.

Unfortunately, Delia knew me better than that, knew I'd never turn down someone in need—even if they were my ex…*whatever* who had broken my heart.

"No, no," I said at last, waving my hand. "It's fine. You're more than welcome to use the bakery."

Ezra's eyes widened, a smile halfway unfurling before he bit down on it, offering me a closed-lipped one instead.

"Thank you, Brie. I'll…text you to sort out the details."

I blinked in surprise, shocked he hadn't immediately deleted my number in the aftermath of our ill-fated fling. I wondered if he'd held onto our text thread as well. I had, and in my weakest moments—usually several glasses of wine deep—I'd scroll through them. Torturing myself with how happy I'd been during those months.

Before I could say anything else, my sister was saying goodbye and rising out of her chair, power walking into the winery and down the hall toward the parking lot.

She had another thing coming if she thought I was letting her get away that easily.

After a quick apology to Ezra for running off, I raced behind her.

"Delia!"

She stopped quickly and turned to me, her arms folded over her chest, feigning innocence.

"Yes, baby sister?" she asked, tone saccharine.

"What the fuck is wrong with you?"

Delia stepped back, eyes widening in shock. I *rarely* swore, and the fact that I did now showed how upset I was.

Quickly regaining her composure, Delia said, "Do you want the short answer or..."

I huffed out a laugh, equal parts amused and irritated. "What were you playing at back there?"

"Remember last Memorial Day when I forced Amara and Cal into making out in front of all of us with that dare?"

"Yes..."

She shrugged. "This is your dare."

Dumbstruck, I watched in silence as she pushed outside. Fuming, I returned to the patio to gather my things, grateful Ezra had already disappeared.

If Delia thought her meddling would accomplish the same for me as it had for Amara and Cal, she was delusional.

I stewed the whole way back into town, though my mood lightened significantly when I stepped foot inside my bakery and wrapped myself in the soothing scents of pastries.

"Hey, Bee!" Celia said brightly as I walked through the door, instantly putting a smile on my face.

Celia was one of three Brie's Bakery employees in addition to myself. The operation wasn't that big, so during the slower months, I tended to either run the shop alone or have one other helper. Celia was a student at Northwestern Michigan College in Traverse City, and she'd been working for me since she began there three years before. I honestly wasn't sure what I'd do in the spring when she graduated and inevitably left me, but that was a problem for Future Brie.

"Hey, Cee!" I parroted back, and we devolved into a fit of

giggles like we normally did. "How has the morning been?"

"Steady," she said, gesturing to the empty shelves behind the counter. "But you're going to have to make more take-and-bake mixes, because, as you can see, we sold out."

Internally, I lit up like the Fourth of July, but outwardly, I only gave Celia a broad smile.

The take-and-bake mixes had been one of my more ingenious ideas, aided by Delia and some social media strategies we were working on one night in the early days of the bakery. The first two months had been nothing short of madness as the summer traffic to the area kept me so busy, I barely had time to leave the building. But once fall rolled around and things cooled off—both figuratively and literally—I began thinking of ways I could keep the lights on in the cold winter months. As the marketing whiz kid in the family, Delia had been helping me with my Instagram, TikTok, and Pinterest accounts. When she pointed out that people frequently commented about their desires to live closer so they could try my treats—particularly my scones—I pitched the idea of creating premade dry mixes customers could purchase and make at home.

A month later, and with the help of Amara this time, I had an online store up and running. As soon as I announced it on my socials, the orders began pouring in, and I quickly realized I didn't have enough product on hand to satisfy them all. My sisters, Mom, and I spent an entire weekend filling as many orders as we could.

Since then, it had been a steady revenue stream. I loved getting tagged in daily videos of people and their families enjoying my creations, and I continued to ship my muffin and scone mixes all over the globe.

I'd never expected my small-town bakery to gain me recognition on an international scale, but a few weeks ago, I'd received an email from a very popular—as in over two million combined TikTok and Instagram followers—food blogger about doing a segment on me, my bakery, and Apple Blossom Bay. Naturally, I'd jumped at the chance, both to celebrate myself and help promote the town that had given me and my family so much over the years.

The blogger, a guy named Damian, had been in and out of the shop all week, trying something new from the menu each time, asking me questions as we worked through my process and interviewing my customers. The exposure was going to do wonders for me and the town, and I couldn't wait to see it all come to fruition.

As though I'd conjured him, a bright blond head appeared over the sign hanging on the door, the bell tinkling as Damian pushed inside.

Today, he wore an aqua blue Polo that turned up the vibrancy of his similarly colored eyes and tan Chinos, a crease perfectly pleating the front, a pair of loafers on his feet. He wasn't anything like I expected. In his videos, he gave off a laid back but enthusiastic vibe, so his country club style came as a bit of a shock.

Still, he was a nice guy who seemed genuinely interested in learning about my business and the town.

"Oh, look," Celia said dreamily as he approached, though low enough he wouldn't hear. "Your new boyfriend is here."

"He's not my new boyfriend," I hissed, playfully smacking her arm. I straightened and offered Damian a large smile when he approached the counter.

"Good afternoon, Damian," Celia said. "What can we get started for you?"

Damian's eyes never strayed from mine as he ordered a turnover and strawberry lemonade. Celia rang him up quickly, and Damian still didn't look away as he paid. When Celia moved away to prepare his meal, he leaned his elbows on the counter, propping his chin up in a palm.

"I hope you love the turnover as much as you've enjoyed everything else," I said with a smile. Then I hooked my thumb over my shoulder, in the direction of the kitchen, and added as I turned away, "I should get started on prep for tomorrow."

As I turned to leave, he blurted, "Go out with me."

I stopped so fast, my shoe squeaked against the floor.

Damian wore a soft smile when I faced him again, and from the corner of my eye, I clocked Celia frozen at the counter, pretending to be preparing his drink when I knew she was eavesdropping.

"Are you sure?"

Damian chuckled lightly. "Of course I'm sure. I've been wanting to ask you out since I met you, but it felt like a bit of a conflict of interest. Now that my videos are all shot and with my producer, my job here is done. I'm ready to...play. And my first order of business is taking you out."

His blue eyes twinkled with promise at his last statement, and I couldn't help grinning in response.

It had been a long time since a man had pursued me, and even longer since I'd been asked on a date. The last few years had been spent building my business, leaving me little time for a personal life. I was fine with that. I was, after all, only twenty-five.

Of course, there was also the Ezra of it all.

But I didn't want to think about him right now, not with this gorgeous, sunkissed man in front of me giving me the attention I'd spent the last three years so desperately craving from the one man who refused to give it to me.

Ezra had tried to satisfy me with crumbs.

I deserved the whole damn meal.

"So what do you say?" Damian prompted, flashing his perfect white teeth in a wide grin.

"I'd love to go on a date with you."

"Great!" Damian said excitedly, straightening to his full height. "Since I've been staying in the city, there's one place up here I haven't had the chance to visit, and it's so highly rated that I thought we could check it out together. Have you been to the winery restaurant? Chateau Delatou?"

Behind me, Celia made a choking sound, and I cut her a glare.

For the sake of my safety—not that it was something I concerned myself with too much, given I lived in the smallest town in America—I kept my personal details, including my last name, close to the vest when it came to what I shared with my social media followers. To the public, I was simply Baker Brie. Given how much I'd come to dislike the nickname, the irony wasn't lost on me. Damian not knowing who I was wasn't entirely surprising, but it was refreshing.

In the area, I'd spent my entire life as "one of the Delatou girls" or "a Delatou daughter." I loved my family legacy, and I wouldn't begrudge my parents or my ancestors any of their success when it provided me the life I had today. Still, I wanted to be something more than just "that Delatou girl" or "Leon and Lena's youngest."

Who I was to my core was a woman who liked making people happy, and the way I accomplished that happened to be through pastries and sweets. *That* was how I wanted to be known.

Damian getting to know me without my family legacy shaping his opinion was a breath of fresh air, and I wasn't above taking advantage of it.

"Chateau Delatou sounds perfect," I assured him.

"Great. How about tonight?"

I gave him a sly grin. "Eager, are we?"

"To be seen with you? Absolutely."

"In that case, tonight is great."

"Perfect," he said with a wide smile, accepting his order from Celia. "Where do you live? I'll pick you up."

I pointed toward the ceiling. "Upstairs."

"Then I already know where to find you," he said. "See you at seven."

With a wink, he was gone.

chapter 22
Brie

DELIA CAME TO MY apartment ahead of my date under the guise of helping me pick out something to wear.

But I saw it for what it was: nosiness.

Thankfully, I called in Ella for reinforcements, and she was doing her level best to run interference—not an easy task, considering Delia was a bulldozer.

"Lia, you are aware that I've been dressing myself for years," I said as I flicked through the hangers in my closet. "I can get ready for a date alone."

"No, you need us, baby sister," Delia cooed, walking over to pat my head despite the fact that we were the same height. I swatted at her, and she leapt away from me with a cackle.

"God, you're annoying," I told her, though I couldn't help but grin when I turned away.

"You love me," she quipped, throwing herself onto my bed. The cheap mattress folded dangerously under her frame, and she grumbled, "I don't know why you don't move into a bigger place so you can get a bigger bed."

"I like it here," I said. "And how come you guys don't bug Ella about her shoebox apartment?"

"Hey!" Ella exclaimed. "Don't drag me into this."

"I'm just saying," I sighed. "Ella's place is actually smaller than mine, but no one tells her to move to a bigger one."

"Maybe we should," Delia said, turning her gaze on Ella. "It's not like you guys can't afford it."

"I like being close to the shop," Ella and I said in unison, then both broke into a fit of giggles that had Delia pouting.

"Just because you bought a huge farmhouse with enough rooms for our entire family doesn't mean we have to do the same," I told Delia when I settled.

Delia shrugged. "I'm just saying. A little more space for sleep-overs wouldn't kill you. And how can you stand sleeping in that tiny ass bed?"

"I like my bed," I said, though from the looks my sisters gave me, they saw it for the lie it was.

Okay, so I didn't love it. I'd much rather starfish on a large mattress than be stuck within the confines of my full one, but it was all I could fit. And it's not like I had anyone to share it with.

I refused to let myself remember the one and only time I'd had a guest stay here with me. Those three years had passed in a blink but painfully slow at the same time. It was the first and last time I'd let a man I wasn't related to into this space. As much as I tried to forget, there was no scrubbing my memory of the way Ezra had wrapped his long, lean body around mine, both to avoid falling off the bed and to keep me close—not that I would've gone anywhere. I'd learned that night that his arms were my favorite place to be, and I hadn't felt that way about anyone since.

This date was the first step in moving on. I was finally letting go of that tiny spark of hope in my chest that said Ezra would come back.

"Can we get back to the matter at hand?" I asked, blowing my hair out of my face. I was grateful the building's central A/C serviced the shop and my apartment, because it was unseasonably warm out, and I would've been sweating otherwise—both from nerves and the temp. I opted to wear my hair down—something I rarely did. The thick, heavy curtain was usually more of a nuisance than it was worth, and I secretly wished I was as brave as Ella, who had long ago chopped hers to her collarbones. If she wanted length, she added clip-in extensions.

Braids were my go-to, my signature hairstyle, typically a single one, the tail hanging between my shoulder blades or draped over my shoulder. Sometimes, if I was feeling spunky, I'd do two.

But this was a date, which meant stepping out of my comfort zone and putting some effort into my appearance. I even applied makeup, another thing I rarely did.

Delia resumed her flicking through my closet, gasping when she came upon something she liked. She pulled the hanger off the rod and turned toward us, and I couldn't help but grin.

"I forgot I had this," I said, moving across the room to take it from her, letting the fabric glide through my fingers.

"It's perfect," Ella agreed.

The mini dress had a tight bodice that flared out at my ribs into a flouncy little skirt. It had sheer sleeves, a deep V-neck, and adorable crochet detailing along the collar and around the band below my breasts. The caramel color was perfect for fall, looked amazing with my olive coloring and dark hair, and made the few specks of gold in my eyes pop. My sisters nodded approvingly when I put it on, and after further rummaging through my closet, Delia passed me a pair of light tan ankle booties. With gold dangly earrings and my favorite rings, the look was complete.

And not a moment too soon.

Promptly at seven, Damian texted to let me know he'd arrived. After blowing kisses to both of my sisters, I headed outside to meet him. He was leaning against the side of his car, arms crossed over his chest, admittedly delicious biceps stretching the black material of his shirt—another Polo—to its limits. A pair of Ray Bans shaded his eyes, but the soft smile on his lips bloomed into a full-on grin when I stepped onto the sidewalk.

He approached me, taking my hands in his and studying me head to toe. "You are breathtaking."

Heat rose to my cheeks as I squeaked out, "Thank you."

"Ready to go?"

"Yes, please. I'm starving."

He chuckled lowly as he led me around to the passenger side and opened the door for me. "I appreciate a girl who can eat."

After I settled in the car—a fancy silver Tesla that would never survive a winter in Michigan—and he was behind the wheel, steering us through the streets of Apple Blossom Bay, I said, "Of course I can eat. I own a bakery, after all."

His eyes flicked to me quickly before returning to the road. "You definitely don't look like it."

I resisted the urge to roll my eyes. What exactly was a pastry chef supposed to look like? The Pillsbury Doughboy? And even if I didn't look the way I did, there wasn't anything wrong with that. It wasn't Damian's place to make comments about my body, and I couldn't help but make a mental strike against him.

"So what is there to do for fun around here?" he asked conversationally as we wound up the peninsula toward the winery.

"We usually go into the city," I admitted. "But there's also Granny Smith's Tavern here in town, which is a fun place to grab casual drinks."

"Sounds...quaint," he said, his lips twitching.

I pursed my own but didn't speak. Small town life wasn't for everyone, but I didn't appreciate the insinuation in his tone. *Sigh, another strike.* Maybe I wasn't meant for dating after all. Maybe I should've learned my lesson with Ezra.

Oh, wait.

Ezra.

The man who would be cooking dinner for me and Damian.

My heart rate kicked up to cardiac arrest levels as we pulled into the winery lot. The gravel crunching under the Tesla's tires seemed comically loud, and I scrambled for a way to get out of this before it even started.

At this point, I was prepared to consider the whole evening a wash.

But, oblivious to my internal strife, Damian hummed happily as he parked the car, got out, and came around to help me out and lead me inside. My eyes darted across the space as we moved into the lobby and toward the hostess stand. Of course, the girl working recognized me immediately, but I shot her a pleading glance, willing her to keep her mouth shut. Damian had begun to show me his true colors, and the last thing I needed was him laying it on even thicker when he found out my name was on the walls, my family's fingerprints all over this place.

"Reservation for two," Damian said. "Under Damian Fellowes." He shot the hostess a smarmy smile, and I choked back a groan.

Why hadn't I seen it before?

Well, I knew why.

I'd been so desperate for some attention, I'd accepted a date with the first guy who batted his eyelashes at me instead of taking the time to think things through. Damian's presentation was gorgeous, with his classic, all-American good looks and charm, but as a chef, I knew that wasn't everything. The flavor—or in this case, personality—was what mattered, and the more time I spent with him, the more I found Damian's lacking.

And I wasn't even getting a free meal out of it, because it's not like I paid for my food at the winery anyway.

Mentally, I shook myself, dropping my shoulders away from my ears. I was here, Damian was nice enough, if a bit pretentious, and I was obviously a huge fan of Ezra's cooking and CD wines. I could find a way to enjoy myself.

Once we were seated—and I was once again forced to make sweeping cutting motions across my throat at our waitress behind Damian's back as she approached our table—he took the liberty of ordering us a bottle of wine to share.

"I'm a bit of a wine-o," he said, giving me a sheepish grin. "I hope you don't mind."

I shook my head. "Go for it."

Our waitress stood idly by while Damian perused the menu, and I was annoyed on her behalf. He could have asked her to come back, but he held up a finger when she said she'd give us a moment to decide...then proceeded to ask questions about every wine on the menu.

The poor girl's eyes kept darting to me, knowing I could answer them all better than she could, but I was just along for the ride, and what a bumpy one it was proving to be.

At last, Damian said, "We'll take a bottle of the 2000 Cabernet." He grinned at me as he handed the wine menu back to the waitress, who scurried away quickly.

When she returned with our bottle, Damian poured us each healthy servings, swirling his around and holding it up to his nose.

"Great bouquet," he said absentmindedly then took a small sip, smacking his lips together as he let the liquid coat his tongue.

God, I needed to get out of here.

Desperate to take the edge of my annoyance, I swallowed a large mouthful despite my dislike of Cab, and Damian narrowed his eyes on me.

"You're supposed to savor it."

I plastered a phony smile on my face and shrugged. "Sorry."

"I will say, though, I've sampled wine all over the world, and this"—he brandished his glass, the deep red liquid sloshing up the sides, dangerously close to the rim—"is really good liquid for this being such a small operation."

I'd lifted my water glass to my mouth to wash away that dry mouth feel the Cab left on my tongue, and I was grateful that pretending to choke on the water covered the sound I made over his comment.

There was nothing small about the Chateau Delatou operation. This winery was the flagship business, where everything was made, bottled, and shipped from, yes. But our wines were in restaurants, bars, and clubs across the entire globe. We'd won numerous awards for quality, taste, and packaging, going toe-to-toe with other big-name wineries in the world and beating them.

But I wasn't going to waste my breath explaining that to him. Instead, I nodded and drank my wine as quickly as I could, grateful when the waitress returned to take our orders.

"I'll have the ribeye," Damian said. "Medium rare, with Hasselback potatoes and a garden salad."

"Dressing?"

"Whatever you've got for vinaigrette," he said. "On the side, please.

The waitress nodded then turned her attention to me. "And for you?"

"I'll have the whitefish cakes with a Caesar salad on the side." I lifted my empty wine glass. "And could I also get a glass of Lena's Best Sangria."

The waitress grinned as she punched my order into her tablet. "Sure thing. I'll be right back with that."

When she disappeared again, Damian turned a disappointed frown on me. "You don't like the wine?"

"I'm not really a Cab girl," I said with a shrug.

"That's okay," he said, reaching across the table to pat my hand condescendingly. "Not everyone can have a palate as refined as mine."

God, what was wrong with this guy? What happened to the sweet man I'd spent the last week around? The one who seemed genuinely interested when I told him about the businesses lining Main Street alongside the bakery? Who raved about my food and the slice of paradise in a small town I'd carved out for myself?

Conversation was stilted—and mostly one-sided—after that, and I heaved a sigh of relief when our food arrived, saving me from having to make any more small talk about his travels or stupid TikTok follower count.

For the record, Delia had more followers than him, and she rarely ever talked about it. But Delia and Damian were clearly very different people. One was someone I loved deeply, who was loyal and funny and would literally give anyone the shirt off her back if they needed it.

The other was...a douche.

I eagerly dug into my meal, my mood lightening for the first time since we walked into the building as the first bite of the whitefish cake hit my tongue. The smoked fish, combined with the spices and bright cheese, was heaven in my mouth. I hadn't let myself enjoy Ezra's food in too long, but in that moment, I happily let his expertise distract me from my disastrous date.

Well, I tried. But then Damian muttered "what the fuck" after cutting into his steak, and my good mood popped like a balloon.

"What's wrong?" I asked, though, to be honest, I didn't particularly care.

"My steak is undercooked," he grumbled. When he lifted his head to signal our waitress, his cheeks had gone ruddy, a vein appearing in his forehead.

I leaned forward to get a better look, finding the meat...perfectly cooked to medium rare.

"You asked for medium rare," I said calmly. "That's exactly what that is."

"I didn't ask for it to still be practically bleeding," he hissed at me. "What'd the chef do, cut it off a live cow?"

"I can assure you, he didn't."

Damian made a disgusted sound in the back of his throat, raising his arm over his head and waving at the waitress. I couldn't begrudge the girl the fear in her eyes as she approached.

"Can I get something for you?" she asked politely, sparing me a glance. I gave her what I hoped was a reassuring smile in return.

Damian gestured to his plate. "This is undercooked. Take it back and have the chef prepare it correctly this time."

It took everything in me not to come to Ezra's defense—hell, not to defend my family's establishment. I bit my tongue hard enough that the coppery tang of blood coated my mouth.

As the waitress apologized to Damian and retreated to the kitchen with his plate, I couldn't help but think I was sitting there waiting for a train, unable to stop, about to barrel into a car parked on the tracks.

chapter 23
Ezra

"Chef, we have a problem," a waitress—whose name I couldn't remember for the life of me—said as she came back into the kitchen, carrying a plate with a beautiful ribeye she'd just brought out to one of her tables.

"And what's that?" I asked, barely sparing her a glance as I worked on plating a mushroom and Swiss topped with a healthy helping of fragrant grilled onions.

My mouth watered, and with a low curse, I realized we'd been so busy, I hadn't eaten in hours. My stomach let out a grumble of protest, and I mentally told it to shut the fuck up.

I didn't have time to be hungry.

"The customer said this steak was undercooked."

I froze in place, right in the middle of sprinkling bread and butter pickles on the side to help balance the heavier flavors and textures of the burger.

I straightened and stalked over to her, grabbing the plate and whirling to the prep counter. I grabbed a fork and prodded at the ribeye. The customer had already cut a slice off, and I was greeted by the sight of the perfectly pink inside.

"Can you pull up that order?" I asked the waitress. "Tell me exactly how he wanted it prepared."

"No need," she said. "I distinctly remember him ordering it medium rare. His date even confirmed it."

"Then what the fuck is the problem?" I shouted, whipping the towel from my shoulder and throwing it on the floor. I felt bad when the girl flinched, and I mumbled an apology. "What table?"

"Seventeen."

With a curt nod, I headed out onto the floor to track down the fucker who got exactly what he'd asked for and still found something to complain about.

I was thirty-three years old and had been cooking since I was old enough to see over the counter. There was nothing fucking wrong with that steak. The customer had asked for medium rare, and that was exactly what I'd given him. I'd never under or overcooked a steak in my life, and today was no different.

When I pushed out of the kitchen and approached the mouth of the dining room at the end of the short hall, my eyes swept the space, mentally counting until I landed on table seventeen.

The man was on the taller side, probably around my height, wearing a black Polo shirt at least two sizes too small for him, clearly purchased purposely to make his biceps and pecs look larger than they were. I couldn't see his lower half, but if I was a betting man, I'd put money on the fact he had on some form of khaki pants and loafers.

But the woman—my heart stopped dead in my chest despite the fact that I could only see the back of her head and the gentle slope of one, olive-skinned shoulder.

I'd recognize her anywhere, my body in tune with hers even when I didn't want to be.

If Brie wasn't mad at me before, she was about to be after I handed her date his ass.

I willed myself to remain semi-calm as I approached the table, barely sparing Brie a glance. Her eyes flicked briefly in my general direction before focusing on something across the room.

That was good. Eye contact between us had always been dangerous.

"Hello, sir. Ma'am. I'm Chef Ezra. Can I ask what exactly was wrong with the steak you sent back?"

"It was far too rare."

"You asked for medium rare," I reminded him in a tone I hoped was gentle but I was afraid came out more condescending than I wanted. "That's going to come with pink meat and some juices."

"I wanted it more medium than rare."

Then you should've ordered it fucking medium, *you asshat.*

Outwardly, I grinned, which I knew was really more of a grimace. "Apologies, sir. I'll make you a new one."

As I stalked back to the kitchen, I willed myself to chill the fuck out. I'd spent my career in New York dealing with assholes far worse, and far richer, than this guy. There was no reason for me to be so pissed off.

Then again, my fury had nothing to do with the fact that this guy didn't know how to order a fucking steak, and everything to do with the fact that he was on a date with *my* girl.

I had no intention of cooking him an entirely new steak. When I re-entered the kitchen, I picked up the now cold piece of meat and dropped that sucker back on the griddle in the center of my stove. My eyes glazed over as I watched the flames lick at it, and though my sous chefs asked me what I was doing, I didn't move again until the fat along one side was charred to a crisp.

Then I stabbed it with a two-prong meat fork, turned and grinned at my staff—a bit maniacally—before stomping back into the dining room and dropping it unceremoniously on the prick's plate.

"There you are, sir," I said happily with a sarcastic bow. "A medium rare steak."

The idiot sputtered as he stared at the hunk of blackened meat, and Brie gasped. I wanted to apologize to her for causing a scene in her family's place, but someone need to knock this guy off whatever fucking high horse he fancied himself on.

I grinned when he turned rage-filled eyes on me.

"What the fuck is this?"

"Your steak, sir. No pink in sight."

"You burned the shit out of it!" he boomed, rising to his feet and throwing his napkin onto the table. Only Brie's quickness saved it from being caught on fire by the candle.

I shrugged. "Maybe next time, you'll think twice before sending back a perfectly prepared steak."

"I'm the customer, you imbecile. I'm always right."

"Not in my restaurant, you're not."

"Oh, so you own this place?" he asked with a derisive snort.

"No," I said, cutting a look at Brie. "But she—"

With a shake of her head, she cut me off, and I clamped my mouth shut. She rose to her feet, glaring at her date. It took all my willpower not to drag my gaze along the length of her body, knowing now was not the time. Her emerald eyes flamed with anger, and it was nice to, for once, not be on the receiving end of her ire.

"He doesn't," she said, nodding at me, "but *I* do."

The guy rolled his eyes. "The boys are talking, sweetie. You don't need to come to this poor excuse for a chef's defense."

"He's the best chef I've ever known," Brie said, stepping closer to him. I was pleased equally by the knowledge that this putz was only about an inch taller than her, so she looked him dead in the eye with her heels on, and that she thought I was such a great chef. It had been a long time since she'd last complimented me on anything.

"And don't call me sweetie."

The guy gestured to his plate and the ruined ribeye. I cringed, knowing I'd pay for that lost revenue and ruined inventory out of my own pocket. While the prick deserved what he got, I was mad at myself for destroying such a beautiful cut of meat.

"He can't even properly prepare a steak!" he protested to Brie.

"He prepared it perfectly," she countered. "You're just an asshole who thinks he's better than everyone else because he's got over a million TikTok followers. Now get the fuck out of my winery. And while you're at it, get a life too."

"*Your* winery?" He laughed disdainfully. "You own a little *bakery*. That you live above."

Brie returned to her chair, though she continued to speak as she grabbed her purse and rifled through it.

"I live above my bakery because I like being close to my business. I own a forty-acre plot of land on this peninsula, about two miles from here, and a massive trust fund I could use to build on it whenever I want. A trust fund I gained access to last month but haven't had to touch because my *little bakery* provides me more than enough." At last, she withdrew her wallet and slipped a card free, then stepped back into Dumbass's face and slapped it against his chest. "The name on the building is Delatou, right?"

The man studied what I realized was her ID, eyes darting comically from me to Brie to the ID to the Chateau Delatou sign on the wall and back.

"Get out."

Brie's tone left no room for argument, despite its low volume and evenness.

"Fuck you," he hissed, and I stepped toward him, ready to slam my fist into his face if he made a move in her direction. But Brie held up a hand, and the asshat went on. "You can forget all about getting a feature on my social channels."

Brie snorted. "I don't need your help anyway."

The guy's face was tomato red, the vein pulsing dangerously in his forehead. Though he looked poised to explode, he only tossed Brie's ID back in her face and stormed from the restaurant.

As he did, cheers and applause erupted in his wake, and I couldn't help but grin.

But my good mood died quickly when Brie turned a glare on me.

"You. Offices. Now."

Swallowing hard, I nodded and trotted after her as she stomped into the foyer. Off to the right was a doorway that accessed the Delatou, Inc. corporate offices, and Brie punched in the code, swinging the door open and breezing through.

It nearly smoked me in the face before I could follow behind her, but I caught it just in time. Our footsteps were painfully loud as we traversed the long hall. It was late enough that everyone, even the CEO, Brie's workaholic older sister, Amara, had gone home for the day.

We could have this showdown in peace, though I had no doubt everyone in town would hear about the show we'd put on in the dining room before the end of the night.

I loved small town life for its familiarity and the tight knit community, but I hated it sometimes for the same reason.

At last, Brie stopped in the middle of the lobby-type area, where a number of secretarial and other support staff desks sat, and whirled on me, resting her fists on the gentle swells of her hips.

God, she looked fucking stunning tonight, and I couldn't keep my eyes to myself as they dragged up and down her body—that dark orange dress with lace details that accentuated all my favorite parts of her body, her tan booties, showcasing her lean arms and miles-long legs. *Fuck*. Being in this building and seeing so much of her flawless skin only served to remind me about the first time.

The day she'd first let me taste her.

The day I'd first felt her come around my fingers.

The day she tilted my world on its axis.

"What the hell is wrong with you?" she asked, pulling me from my fantasies. Her expression had grown impossibly darker, those eyes the color of winter pines telling me she hadn't missed my perusal of her body.

Then again, I hadn't exactly been trying to hide it.

"That guy was a prick," I said simply.

"You're jealous." It wasn't a question. It was a simple statement of fact from this woman I hadn't been able to get out of my head since I met her over three years ago.

And I wasn't about to deny it.

Well, maybe I was, if only so I wasn't lying my bleeding heart at her feet, giving her the opportunity to stomp on it.

I snorted, an ugly sound entirely at odds with the emotions swirling inside me. "No, I'm not."

"You have no right," she pressed, stepping forward and driving her finger into my chest.

"How could you bring him *here* of all places?" I asked quietly.

Brie deflated a bit. "I didn't have a choice."

I scoffed. "You always have a choice. Your name is on the door, Brie."

"He...he didn't know who I was. You saw. It was nice to be wanted for me and not what he thought I could give him. That guy..."

"Who the hell was he, anyway? I've never seen him around here."

"A really popular TikTok food blogger who wanted to do a segment on the bakery. And he was great when it came to work. Seemed to genuinely care about me and the shop, as well as the town. But I saw a different side of him tonight, and I hated every second. Still, by the time I realized you'd be working, we were already walking inside."

I resisted the urge to roll my eyes. I took nights off here and there, but they were few and far between. Brie knew that, so it was a weak excuse.

"I think you wanted me to see you with someone else," I said. "I think you wanted to make me jealous."

"In case you forgot," she started, backing up a bit, "I'm not the one who ended things. That was *all* you."

"I did what I did because of Hansen," I argued.

"That's a cop out. I know you love him, and I don't begrudge you that, especially with Shannon gone, but it didn't have to be one or the other. I know Shannon hurt you, but...God, Ez. *You* hurt *me*. And now you don't get to go all caveman and have some pissing contest with another guy because he asked me on a date. That's not how this works."

"It's not the same as it was with Shannon, and you know it. I spent nearly three years with her, knowing she didn't love me or our child, nor did she particularly even want anything to do with either of us. Our marriage was over long before the accident, and Hansen was without a mother long before she got sent away. But then you waltzed into my life and...fuck, honey." The old nickname slipped out unbidden, but being here in the place where I'd first used it had the veil between past and present blurring until it seemed like every iteration of us and our relationship stood in the room with the people we were now. "I've been trying so hard, but I'm so fucking tired."

"Tired of what?"

"Of fighting this."

And then, I did the dumbest thing—or maybe the smartest.

I closed the distance between us and crashed my mouth to hers.

God, kissing her again was like coming home. Everything in me settled then ratcheted up again as she met every greedy swipe of my tongue with equal fervor. I wanted to consume her, to mold our bodies together until we didn't know where I ended and she began.

She fisted her hands in my chef's coat, I thought to pull me closer.

But she tore her mouth away and shoved me backward. I was caught so off guard, I stumbled a step. Brie's hand flew to her mouth, eyes wide with shock as she stared at me.

A whole slew of emotions crossed those emerald depths, and I waited for one to settle in place, bracing myself for whatever came next.

But they shuttered quickly, and with lethal calm, she said, "Don't *ever* do that again."

And then, she disappeared, and I was left wondering why I couldn't seem to stop fucking up where Brie Delatou was concerned.

chapter 24
Ezra

IN HINDSIGHT, I RECOGNIZED my tantrum at work was less about the steak and the jackass who didn't know how to order and more about the fact that said jackass had been on a date with my girl. And the kiss after—another dumbass move on my part, but I couldn't bring myself to regret it. The way Brie had clung to me before ultimately pushing me away only stoked the fire of my desire to win her back. I'd made a lot of mistakes where she was concerned, but I was determined to rectify each and every one. I'd worship at her feet every day if she'd let me.

Which is how I found myself at Birdie's the following week, surrounded by her entire family after inviting myself along to their weekly dinner.

I'd been to plenty of events hosted by the Delatou family before, but the pressure hadn't felt as suffocating on those occasions as it had tonight. The stakes were so much higher, especially with Brie covertly glaring daggers at me.

I'd also brought along my dad and Hansen, and Delia hadn't batted an eye. Secretly, I thought she was rooting for me and Brie to find our way back to each other. I didn't know what the youngest Delatou had told her big sisters about us, but I could guess they were aware that *something* had gone down. It was the only explanation I had for Delia offering up Brie's bakery kitchen to me and the silent death threats Brie conveyed to her sister in the aftermath.

Delia was stirring the pot, and if I hadn't spent the last three years absolutely wild about her sister, I could kiss her for it.

That, and Owen would probably break me in half if I even tried. Being ripped apart by an ex-NFL quarterback wasn't high on my bucket list. He and Delia were still figuring their own shit out, but it was obvious how much they cared for one another, and I figured it was only a matter of time.

On the flip side, it was clear Brie didn't want me anywhere near the sanctuary of her kitchen—or *her*, for that matter—and I couldn't blame her.

The morning after we slept together...I had handled everything so poorly, deciding to cut the ties between us before we could inextricably weave them together. I'd only been attempting to be the best father possible. Hansen had to come first always, but I wish I'd gone about everything with Brie differently. I wish I'd sat down and had a real conversation with her instead of a rushed, half-assed explanation while I made my escape.

Maybe then we wouldn't have spent the last two years apart.

I deeply regretted my cowardice. I was an adult capable of compromising and juggling multiple priorities. The fact that I'd turned away the most impressive and stunning woman I'd ever known because I was afraid of how it would affect my ability to parent wasn't something I could ever forgive myself for. I'd spent every waking minute of the last three years hating myself for it.

Brie deserved better than that—better than me.

But...I was reaching the point where living without her was

doing me more harm than good. The what-ifs were eating me alive, keeping me up at night, wondering how different my life would look if I had her by my side.

Anytime I found myself in her vicinity was pure torture, especially when all I wanted to do was wrap her in my arms and claim her once again. The fucking cake batter scent of her skin drove me insane, had my stomach hollowing out like I hadn't eaten in days and the only thing that would satisfy me was her body on mine.

I'd royally fucked up, and it was about damn time I did something about it.

Leon left it up to me to order wine for the table, so I requested the Chateau Delatou Cabernet, which was my personal favorite of the winery's offerings. When the waiter reappeared with several bottles, they were passed around the table. Glasses filled as chatter filtered through the air. Across from me, Alfie and Leon got into an argument when he made some annoying comment about ordering a bottle produced by another winery. Leon quickly put him in his place, only for Alfie to turn and have Owen ready to chew him a new ass both for complaining and for making some comment to Delia I missed in the commotion.

I hadn't spent much time around Alfie, but I knew one thing with absolute certainty: if Hansen grew up to be anything like him, I'd consider myself a failure as a father.

Another certainty was Owen was so gone for the middle Delatou girl, and as I glanced at Brie out of the corner of my eye, I couldn't help thinking that I knew the feeling all too well.

At least Delia wasn't inclined to hate him like Brie did me.

Next to me, she sipped her wine and made a sound of disgust.

"Too dry," she said, and I held back a chuckle.

"Excuse you, young lady," Leon said. "I worked very hard to perfect that blend."

Under her breath, she said, "Should've tried harder."

Leon's eyes narrowed, and I knew he heard her.

"Watch it, Brie," he said. "Take one more shot at my prized possession and I'll take your bakery away."

Leon Delatou was intimidating as shit and a shrewd businessman. I wouldn't put it past him to make some crazy decision like that if he felt insulted.

But this was his daughter we were talking about—and his baby, no less. Not to mention, the bakery was wildly successful. And surrounded by his five daughters on all sides, as a parent myself, it was easy to recognize a stupid wine recipe was far from his pride and joy. Not with all of the amazing things his girls had accomplished so far in their lives. It had to be nothing but bluster.

When Brie gasped theatrically, I knew I was right.

"You can't do that, Daddy," she said cheekily, sticking her tongue out at her father. I resisted the urge to chuckle. "And you know it."

"I can damn sure try."

"You do, old man," Brie started, pointing her father menacingly at him. Or as menacingly as she could, given we all knew she was far too sweet to ever do any real harm to anyone, least of all someone she loved. "And you'll never taste my baklava again."

Leon pounded his fist against his chest as though he'd been fatally wounded, and I finally released the laugh I'd been holding in.

This family was something else.

"You wouldn't dare," he said.

Brie tipped her nose into the air and shrugged. "Fuck around and find out."

"Brie!" Lena scolded as the rest of the table devolved into a fit of laughter.

Though I joined in, I found myself mesmerized by the woman next to me.

I knew, having heard it directly from her mouth, that she sometimes struggled to find a place in her family. As the youngest, she often felt overshadowed by the bigger personalities and successes of her sisters: Chloe, the writer; Amara, the CEO; Delia, the marketing whiz and influencer who used her time and knowledge to help local businesses expand their social media reach.

I think Ella was the only one she didn't try to measure herself up against. As a free-spirit, Ella was content with her job at the flower shop, brightening people's days through her, admittedly stunning, floral arrangements.

I loved seeing her like this, with her father deeply pained by the thought of never tasting one of her creations again, with her being vocal about her likes and dislikes. The easy way she slotted into her family that I wasn't sure she recognized.

These people—it was painfully obvious how much they loved her. My honey was pure sunshine, and her family was content to bask in the glow she cast on all of them.

I wanted to be included in that warmth, more than I'd ever wanted anything in my life.

"I never knew you didn't like Cab," I told her once the table had settled. I needed to speak with her, if only superficial things. I wanted to remind her that I was here *for her*, that I wasn't going anywhere.

Brie looked me dead in the eye, not an ounce of fear or hesitation or pain or any of the other things constantly swirling within me present in their emerald depths. "There's a lot you don't know about me."

I snapped my mouth closed. She wasn't wrong and clearly had zero desire to speak with me, so I let my mission drop for the moment.

While my own father chatted easily with Leon and Lena at the head of the table and kept Hansen busy with a piece of paper and crayons one of the staff had procured for him, I was content to soak in the good energy that came from being around this family. Leon and Lena certainly had their hands full, especially when the elder three daughters were so outspoken and firm in their beliefs. It hadn't taken me long to realize all five of them were stubborn as hell, which is the only explanation I had for why Brie had been able to—at least as far as appearances went—move on from our...*thing* so quickly. She simply wouldn't accept anything less, wouldn't let me or her family see her hurting.

I admired her for it but secretly hated it. I wanted her as outwardly torn up as I was inside. Then again, maybe the dissolution of whatever had sparked between us hadn't broken her heart the way it had mine.

But I'd be damned if sitting there next to her wasn't as easy as breathing, if spending time with her, with her family welcoming me and mine with open arms, hadn't felt like two puzzle pieces clicking into place. The Wendts and the Delatous went together like meatballs and mashed potatoes.

Each casual brush of her shirt sleeve against my bare forearm when she reached for her wine glass had my body lighting up like the Fourth of July.

I wanted those sparks with her, wanted to rekindle the flame we'd found on a cold New Year's Day and tended into an inferno on a hot July night.

Simply put, I wanted her. I had her once, and it wasn't enough. I didn't think anything ever would be.

It was about damn time I started fighting for what I wanted.

And I wasn't above fighting dirty.

I leaned close, my breath fanning the wisps of hair around her face as I said against her ear, "Will you pass me the bread?"

Brie sat up straighter, attempting to move away from me without making it obvious she was doing so. She accomplished it for a moment as she leaned across the table to grab the basket of garlic knots, but she was right back in my space a second later, her sweet scent at war with the bread for which was more heavenly to my nose.

Who the fuck was I kidding? It'd always be her.

"Thank you," I said when she handed it to me, purposely brushing my fingers against hers. She gasped at the contact, and I bit back a grin.

It was nice to know she still responded to me the same. Maybe we weren't entirely a lost cause.

"What are you doing?" she hissed.

I shoved a knot into my mouth and chewed, then innocently said, "Eating?"

Brie's eyes narrowed. "That's not what I meant, and you know it."

"I know nothing of the sort," I said.

"You're being...friendly."

"Am I not a friendly guy?"

"No," she said almost immediately, and I would've been hurt by the frankness of her answer had she not been right.

I hadn't been a "friendly guy" in a long ass time.

I lowered my voice to barely above a whisper, ensuring only she could hear me when I said, "That's not what you were saying the night I had my tongue between your thighs, or the one with my cock buried deep inside you."

"Ezra!" Brie yelped.

All conversation at the table stopped, and too many sets of eyes found us.

"Everything okay, sweets?" Leon asked his daughter.

Brie cleared her throat. "Everything is fine, Dad. Ezra just accidentally elbowed me in the side."

I choked on my sip of wine. A terrible excuse, one I was certain no one at the table was buying for a second. Still, I was surprised when they all returned to their separate conversations. Leon seemed the least inclined to move on, narrowing his eyes and flicking them between us, attempting to suss out the issue. I watched Brie give him a reassuring smile, and he nodded once before giving his attention to Logan on the other side of the table.

"What the fuck is wrong with you?" she asked.

"God, I love it when you swear," I groaned. She did it so rarely, I found her loss of control unbearably hot. I did everything I could think of to keep my cock from hardening. The last thing

I needed was to pop a spontaneous boner in front of her entire family.

"Seriously, Ez," she said. "What has gotten into you?"

"I miss you," I blurted, my voice practically a low hiss. "I thought that kiss last week made it obvious. I'm fucking dying here, Brie."

Brie's entire body went still, and she turned to me slowly. We were seated so close, thanks to the number of people crammed at the table, that our noses nearly touched. Each of her exhales became my inhales, and vice versa.

"You don't get to miss me. This is broken because of *you*."

I reared back like she'd slapped me, staring at the side of her face in stunned silence until she angled her body away from mine to chat with Amara on her other side.

Okay then.

The worst part was—she wasn't wrong, but I wasn't giving up that easily.

Brie may have won the battle, but I fully intended to win the war.

chapter 25

Ezra

THE SECOND DELIA AND Brie were on board with the Wine & Dine event, I'd reached out to the community center to get the date booked. The only day they had available was the first Saturday of November, which had given me plenty of time to cobble together a menu. Unfortunately, I was a perfectionist, and it took me ages to settle on the perfect offerings for each course. Four days before, I texted both Delia and Owen to swing by the winery and sample what I'd created.

I might have been giving Delia a taste of her own medicine, and my work was complete when she and Owen had a moment that left him decidedly hot and bothered for the rest of the tasting—and sent him practically running away when we were done.

I understood that feeling all too well.

And now, it was my turn to suffer torture at the hands of a different Delatou woman.

The day before my event, I set my dad and Hansen up with a vat of macaroni and cheese for dinner and headed to Brie's Bakery.

I pulled up to the back door, reversing my Subaru into the space so I could unload my supplies from the hatch. I couldn't help comparing this to the first time I'd come here and recognizing how vastly different the circumstances were.

Though the door was unlocked, Brie was nowhere to be found, and I was a little grateful I'd have the chance to get my bearings before confronted with her and the memories I knew being together in this space again would bring up.

Once everything was spread out on the island and I set to work unpacking the grocery bags, I heard the back door open and close.

A moment later, there she was.

Olive skin free of makeup, hair braided and draped over her right shoulder like always. Black leggings that had flour stains all over them, an oversized *2025 Apple Blossom Bay Fall Festival* tee hanging down to her knees.

It was so like those nights, both at the winery and in this very kitchen. I half expected her to lead me out into the dining room to show me around.

And then take me upstairs and let me reacquaint myself with her cunt.

Things between us were still awkward and stilted after the kiss at the winery and my admission that I missed her at dinner a few weeks before, but I was determined to fix it. I hadn't been able to stop thinking about that kiss. About her sugary sweet scent stuffing its way up my nose again, about how it felt to have her back in my arms. Those soft, full lips against mine, her tongue slipping into my mouth.

Hell, even the moment she shoved me away. All of it turned me on in the worst way. I wanted Brie in all the ways she'd let me have her, and I couldn't lie: her stubbornness was sexy as fuck.

It'd be that much sweeter when she finally gave in and let me have her.

When I finally got to sink back into that beautiful body and claim it as mine forever.

"Hi," I said nervously, shaking off that mental image.

"Hey," she said. "Sorry I wasn't here to greet you. I fell asleep."

"In the middle of the day?"

She flicked her wrist to check her watch. "First of all, it's seven p.m. Second, we were absolutely slammed today, and I've been up since four. The apple cinnamon scones were a huge hit up at the barn during the festival, so everyone has been coming in to buy some of the mix to take home."

I couldn't help but grin at her. God, she'd come such a long way from that fresh faced twenty-two-year-old just about to open this pace. Now, she was an accomplished businesswoman with one of the busiest shops on Main Street.

The addition of take-and-bake mixes for her most popular menu items had really launched her into the stratosphere, so much so that she'd even opened an online store and shipped her confections all over the world.

"I hope you know how proud of you I am," I said softly.

Brie's swallow was audible, though her responding "thank you" barely was. Then she awkwardly cleared her throat and, louder, said, "So what can I do to help?"

"First, there's something I wanted to ask you."

During the tasting with Delia and Owen, Delia had asked me about ticket costs and what I was planning to do with the funds raised. Thanks to her and Owen both pledging to match whatever money came in, I could afford to spread the wealth.

Farms for Folks had always been high on my list, an organization that paired Apple Blossom Bay residents in need with local farmers and locally grown food. As a chef, I'd always been a huge advocate for both living off the land and using locally sourced ingredients whenever possible. The task was far more difficult back in the concrete jungle of New York, but since moving to small town life, I'd really made it my mission to make up for lost time.

The second place I'd be donating was to the volunteer fire department. Those men and women provided necessary emergency services to the entire peninsula, and they were woefully underfunded.

The final item on my list had always been more of a pipe dream than anything, but Delia and Owen were helping make it a reality.

"Shoot," she said.

"So your sister and Owen both agreed to match any funds raised for the event through ticket costs, and since the community center rental is low and the winery is donating all the wine, I'm going to have a lot left over to allocate to some organizations I feel really strongly about."

"Farms for Folks, right?"

I nodded. "And I want some to go to the volunteer fire department."

Brie smiled. "That's great, Ez. They can certainly use it. But what does that have to do with me?"

"I've always wanted to form a scholarship fund to help kids who want to attend culinary school but could use some extra financial support. While in New York, it didn't make sense because…" I trailed off, not really wanting to get into the particulars of how my money—yes, even the money I'd earned myself—had been tied up with all sorts of strings attached.

And Shannon had spent a lot of it. But that was neither here nor there.

Coming back to myself, I said, "I'd like to set up a scholarship at the Traverse City high school, and I was wondering if you'd be interested in helping me fund it."

Brie blinked in surprise, as though she hadn't expected that. But…who else would I ask? Of the two of us, she was the one who had grown up here. Had attended the very high school where I wanted to establish a scholarship. Had roots that went deeper into the ground beneath our feet than most people realized.

At last, she said, "I love that idea, Ez. I'm happy to help."

I grinned, deeply pleased I'd done something right by her for once.

Brie's smile grew to match mine but quickly flattened, the brightness in her eyes dimming slightly, like she couldn't allow herself to express any sort of positive emotion in my presence. I hated myself for making her feel that way.

After awkwardly clearing her throat and looking away from me, she said, "Where do you want me to start?"

I directed her to first get some eggs hard boiling, then asked that she start chopping vegetables.

Working alongside her was easy, like we'd been navigating a kitchen together for years. There was no awkwardness, no stepping on toes or slamming into each other. We moved around in a well-choreographed dance. Once she'd completed the prep tasks and it was my turn to do the heavy lifting, she moved on to getting started on her dessert.

"You never told me what you were making," I said, voice hoarse from disuse over the last few hours.

"Mini apple cobblers with homemade ice cream," she said, not looking up from where she sliced up a handful of juicy Granny Smith apples.

"Do I get a taste?"

The words came out far more suggestive than I intended, and I dipped my head, not wanting to see her reaction. I wasn't exactly batting a thousand where she was concerned, and I was afraid my forwardness at Birdie's that night had done more harm than good.

Especially since it seemed like she'd been avoiding me.

"Yes, Ezra," she said softly. "You can sample the cobbler when I'm done."

With a curt nod, I turned back to the stove, the swirling of the squash soup around my wooden spoon mirroring my spinning thoughts.

I should never have agreed to this, should never have let Delia push Brie into letting me use her kitchen. After my errant comment, Brie was more closed off than ever, and the tension in the room was thick as butter. It seemed I couldn't stop fucking up where she was concerned, and I was beginning to lose hope of ever winning her back.

Unfortunately, food prep wasn't something I could rush. I couldn't decide I was done, tuck my tail between my legs, and run. I had to stay here, feeling every second of the awkwardness like a knife to the heart.

Where the silence before had been...not quite companionable, but easier, now it was painfully loud. I actually breathed a sigh of relief when I finished the last bit of prep I needed for the next day. I moved to the sink to wash my hands, and as I wiped them dry, Brie spoke.

"It's ready if you still want a taste."

My head shot up, and I spun toward her so fast, I nearly tripped over my own two feet.

The words had been soft, barely above a whisper, but they were an olive branch.

I willed myself to cross the room slowly, to not appear too eager and scare the shit out of her. I knew it wouldn't take much for her to disappear upstairs and lock me out of her life again.

In front of her sat two dishes, each laden with a perfectly round apple cobbler, the scent of cinnamon rising into the air, mixing with the fragrant vanilla of the scoop of ice cream and reminding me far too much of the way Brie's skin smelled.

She handed me a spoon and, without another word, dug into her own dessert. I watched raptly as she chewed and savored, eyes closing in bliss.

I loved that she loved her own food so much, that even sampling her own creations elicited this sort of reaction from her.

When her eyes popped open and she caught me staring, I didn't look away.

"Aren't you going to try it?" she asked, tilting her head to the side.

"Sure." I lifted the little plate from the counter and scooped off a spoonful of ice cream with the cobbler. Eyes never straying from hers, I opened my mouth and closed my lips around the bite. Immediately, a riot of sensations exploded on my tongue.

The creaminess of the ice cream next to the rougher, crunchy granola topping. The warm, soft apples juxtaposed against the cold, frozen treat. Cinnamon and sugar and warm vanilla.

It was heaven on a spoon, and I couldn't stop the groan that emanated from deep in my chest.

"Good?" Brie asked, her tone low and husky.

"Fucking amazing, Brie," I said. "But you already knew that."

She shrugged. "You know your opinion matters to me."

"Still?" I asked, incredulous.

Another upward hitch of her shoulder. "Always."

I didn't know how to respond to that. I could only watch her, my eyes darting over her face, tracing every single one of her freckles, sweeping across every lash, searching for the falsity of her words.

All I found was the truth.

Unbidden, my hand reached out and tucked a lock of dark brown hair behind her ear. She leaned into my touch only slightly when my palm cupped her cheek, those emerald eyes tracking my every move. I didn't miss the way her pulse strummed rapidly against the delicate skin of her neck, as though she was waiting.

I'd be an absolute fucking dumbass not to take the opening.

Shuffling forward a step, I closed the distance between us until our bodies almost touched, backing her against the counter. Each inhale had the tips of her breasts ghosting against my chest, and I sighed sharply through my nose, sliding my hand down her throat until it rested where her shoulder curved up to meet it.

She didn't stop me as I leaned in...

But she turned her head at the last second so my lips collided with the soft surface of her cheek.

Eyes bright with an emotion I couldn't name—pain? sadness?—Brie ducked away from me and stalked to the other side of the room, putting the island between us.

"I told you not to do that again."

"You gave me a pretty big opening," I pointed out. Then, softer, I added, "Why are you doing this to us?"

Brie was silent for painful, interminable moments. Did she...not want me? Had I so grossly misread the situation?

"It's not that I don't want you," she said at last, answering the question I hadn't asked aloud as she turned to face me. "I just...I can't, Ez. Nothing has changed."

"*Everything* has changed, honey." A gasp left her, and her hand flew to her mouth with the resurrection of the old nickname. "Your dad is no longer in charge at the winery, and Amara would be pretty hypocritical to fire me for hooking up with you when, for one, you don't even work there, and two, she was sleeping with Calvin when she was still his boss."

"I don't want just a hookup, Ez," she said softly. "You know that's not my style."

"But back then—"

"You knew I was going to ask for more that morning," she protested, pointing a finger at me, her voice rising in volume, the sadness in her eyes flaring into anger. "That's why you cut me off and ran away."

I hung my head, sufficiently chastened. She wasn't wrong.

"Things are different now."

"How? What has changed exactly? Because from where I'm standing, you're still the same man, and I'm still just some girl."

"For starters," I said, taking a tentative step around the island toward her. When she retreated, I stopped and rested my hands on the counter, my gaze locked on hers. "You're not *some girl*. You're a beautiful, talented, intelligent *woman*."

Even back then, at twenty-two, she'd been more woman than girl, her head on straighter than most.

"Okay, fine." She rolled her eyes. "I'm a *beautiful, talented, intelligent woman*. What about everything else? Or are you forgetting you have a son? That little boy who has to take priority over whatever *this*"—she gestured between us—"is?"

"So you're admitting there's something here," I said, unable to contain my grin.

Brie sighed, clearly exasperated. "That's not the point, Ez."

"Of course I'm not forgetting about Hansen," I said. "But he's older now. Five and in school full time. Plus, it's been years since all the bullshit with Shannon. We're both doing better, and he doesn't need me as much."

The realization honestly broke my heart, but my baby boy was becoming more self-sufficient by the day. He obviously wasn't old enough to do things like cook for himself or drive him places, but even though he was only five, I was already dreading those days. The days when I'd have to let him go out into the world on his own and make his own memories and a life that no longer revolved around me.

He'd always be my baby boy, and I'd always be his father, but damn...watching him grow up and become this person who no longer needed me as much was so fucking bittersweet.

"I don't know what you're saying," she murmured, but the way she avoided eye contact with me told me she knew exactly what I was getting at.

We could no longer use Hansen as a buffer between us. My son could no longer serve as the reason we weren't giving into this fucking pull to each other.

"The last two years have given me a lot of perspective on the things I want out of life."

"Which is?"

"You. Just you. *Always* you."

Maybe I was laying it on a little thick, but I didn't know how else to be. I wanted her in ways I never imagined, in ways I never thought I'd be able to feel again after Shannon had slowly dismantled my heart and belief in love and romantic relationships. Since then, the love for my son and my father were the only kind I anticipated ever experiencing again.

And then this woman blew into my life, with her quiet beauty, those emerald green eyes that ensnared me every time I looked into them, how important her family was to her, and her passion and talent for her chosen craft—well, I was a fucking goner from the first moment I looked at her across the winery dining room.

I'd had her once, and I fucked it up.

I wasn't going to make the same mistake twice.

Brie leaned over, propping her elbows on the island and resting her head in her hands. When she spoke, her voice was muffled.

"I just don't know if I can trust you." She looked up at me again, those jewel-toned orbs shining.

"Then at least give me the opportunity to prove you can."

Brie inhaled deeply, holding it in, her eyes closed, as though she was at war with herself about something and debating whether or not to share it.

When they popped open again, she breathed out and said in a rush, "In that case, there's something I need to tell you. Something no one else knows. And you're probably not going to like it."

A test, then. I could handle that.

I gripped the edge of the counter to stop myself from reaching for her, to comfort her while she spilled this secret. "Okay..." I said slowly.

"That first time we slept together, I got pregnant."

Three little words instantly transported me back to nearly seven years ago, when a different woman had come to me in a different kitchen on the other side of the country to tell me she was having my baby.

I willed myself to remain still, to process the words without any sort of reaction. Brie said no one else knew about this, and she clearly had a reason for that. I owed her the chance to explain.

"I—" I croaked out then cleared my throat and started again. "We don't have a child."

She shook her head sadly. "No."

"What happened?" The softness of my tone surprised me, given the dangerous maelstrom of emotions swirling inside me.

Would I have been okay with another baby conceived accidentally and out of wedlock? With Brie, I think I would've been okay with anything, but it was hard to think straight through the blood roaring in my ears.

"I lost it," she said quietly. "I found out that August—on my birthday, actually," she added with a disbelieving chuckle. "I didn't tell anyone. Just made an appointment with my doctor to figure out my options. I didn't want to get anyone's hopes up, least of all my own. But the day I went in for my first appointment and they sent me to the bathroom to pee in a cup...I was bleeding. My doctor confirmed I was miscarrying shortly after.

"It was...mortifying," she continued, her cheeks reddening with the memory. "That I couldn't even hang onto a pregnancy long enough to confirm it really existed. I just never told anyone, because how do you explain that to the people you love? A one-night stand turned accidental pregnancy turned miscarriage in the span of a few months? I couldn't live with the disappointed looks my family would give me."

"It wasn't a one-night stand," I breathed.

She looked up at me, eyes more vibrant thanks to the tears welling in them. "No? Then what was it?"

"God, Brie," I said, at last giving up on holding myself back from her. I crossed the room in three long strides and gathered her into my arms, whispering into her hair, "It was everything."

Her slim shoulders shook with a silent cry, and I clung tighter, holding us both together as best I could.

"It was everything to me too," she whispered, the words pained.

"Why didn't you tell me before?"

Silence reigned for long moments as Brie pulled herself together, and when she spoke again, her words were hoarse.

"I knew what you'd gone through with Shannon. You're a good man, Ezra. One of the best. And I know you would've once again done the thing you thought was expected of you. I never wanted to put you in that position. So while I hadn't exactly made up my mind, I think I knew deep down that I was going to keep it. And when I did finally tell you, I wanted to give you the option to be in our child's life...not make it feel like a requirement, another set of shackles holding you to a woman you didn't want."

Her words hit me like a shot straight to the heart. The situation was so similar to what happened with Shannon, yet vastly different.

She wasn't wrong in assuming I would've done the right thing. My ill-fated marriage was proof of that. But what she failed to realize was that my relationship with Shannon didn't hold a candle to the things I felt for Brie.

"It wouldn't have been shackles, honey. Not with you. With you...it would've been wings."

I pulled away and held Brie at arm's length, reaching up to swipe my thumbs across her cheeks, collecting the moisture slipping down them.

"And I would've been there for you," I vowed. "I'll *always* be here for you."

Brie gave me a watery smile then folded herself back into my arms.

And I couldn't help thinking I'd passed her test.

chapter 26
Brie

Ezra was...different lately. I'd noticed it before, but that haunted expression he often wore previously seemed to have evaporated, replaced with...I wouldn't say happiness. I didn't think he could be truly happy with things between us so up in the air. In fact, he'd made that perfectly clear the night before. But Ezra seemed content, settled in a way I hadn't really witnessed from him before.

Maybe he'd been telling the truth. Maybe everything *had* changed, and I was needlessly keeping us in this holding pattern because I was too afraid of getting my heart broken again.

And really, who could blame me? I didn't fall for people easily. I wasn't like Chloe, who romanticized everything—and had made a career out of the talent as a novelist. Nor was I like Delia, who wore her heart on her sleeve, or the free-spirited Ella. I'd always been more reserved when it came to giving away pieces of myself, more of a pragmatist like Amara.

It figured the first time I truly did, the man had gone and made me regret it.

From the moment I laid eyes on him in the winery dining room, I'd wanted him in ways I couldn't quite explain—ways that didn't make sense—and that desire for him hadn't gone away. It had only tempered, edged in pain and sadness.

I didn't want to put myself back there, didn't want to try again only for it to all fall apart, but I also wanted him so badly, it hurt to look at him. It seemed I'd found myself in a bit of a catch-22.

Ezra had recruited me, Ella, Liam Danvers, who worked as our vintner at the winery, and a number of Owen's waitstaff from Birdie's to help serve at his Wine & Dine event, and I hadn't been looking forward to spending an extensive amount of time with him. I'd barely managed to hold him off the night before—and when he'd kissed me in the CD offices that one day, my body remembering how easily he could light me up and make my nerve endings sing—but I'd been worried for nothing.

Once the appetizer course was passed out and Ezra seemed satisfied everyone was enjoying themselves, he approached me, Ella, and Liam.

"I think we're off to a good start, don't you?" he asked with a wide grin.

"Absolutely," I assured him.

"I still can't believe you sold out of tickets," Ella mused.

"I can," I said without thinking, then resisted the urge to slap my hand over my mouth as I looked at Ezra with wide eyes.

His grin was shit-eating, the chocolate depths of his gaze swirling with satisfaction. "Careful, Brie," he warned. "You start singing my praises, and I might think you actually like me."

I scoffed, mentally grappling for something witty to say in return, but my mind was dreadfully blank. Before I could respond, he shot me a wink and waded back into the dining room.

After that, he was so busy running around answering questions and basking in the glow of a meal well-cooked that we never really crossed paths.

Which was fine. I was content to watch him from afar, to witness the people of Apple Blossom Bay fawn over him and his culinary genius.

Although, a few of the younger women got a little too handsy, and only Ella gripping my arm, holding me in place, stopped me from stomping across the room and staking my claim.

I really needed to get it together, but he hadn't been wrong earlier: I *did* like him. I never stopped, and it was a constant thorn in my side.

His words, which wound up being his parting statement before he gave me a sad smile and disappeared into the dark last night, had wound on an endless loop in my head over the last twenty-four hours.

And would've been there for you. I'll always *be here for you.*

Everything else he'd said was right, of course, and despite my reticence to do so, I trusted him implicitly. Everything *had* changed, and with Dad no longer at the helm of Delatou, Inc., there wasn't anyone standing in our way, no sense of propriety holding us back from each other.

He had broken my heart—though not through any fault of his own. Back then, I'd been a young girl giving way too much of herself to a man who had higher priorities.

And maybe my heart hadn't been broken so much because he'd chosen his son over me, a decision I couldn't begrudge him. In his position, I would've done the same thing. Maybe it was simply leftover trauma from dealing with the highs and lows of finding out I was pregnant to miscarrying not long after that made me so...sad and overwhelmed with grief when I looked at him. I'd been broken when he'd left my apartment that morning, but I would've gotten over it. Compounding it with everything that came in the few months after had only made it that much more difficult to bear—something I'd had to do alone, no less.

Now, it seemed his priorities truly had shifted, and damn, did I want to give him—give *us*—another chance. He'd handled the news so perfectly, exactly as I hoped he would, and it made me fall for him that much more.

That night, after we'd cleaned up the community center, my sisters and I convened at Mom and Dad's. I'd sent an SOS text, and they'd all dropped whatever they had planned to respond.

Now that we were all older and moving on with our own lives—and starting our own families, in the case of Chloe and Amara—I'd come to find my sisters understood me better than when I was younger. While they still got on my nerves on occasion, for the most part, they were the best friends I could ask for.

Which was why I needed them.

I was finally ready to spill my guts about my relationship with Ezra Wendt.

Thankfully, Mom and Dad were gone on their annual fall trip to Greece, which they were extending an extra week now that Dad was fully retired from the winery. I wouldn't have to risk them overhearing as my sisters and I set up camp in their theater room, loaded up on popcorn and sweets, turned on *Legally Blonde* for background noise, and got down to business.

It was Delia who broke the ice. Unsurprising, given she'd always had a sixth sense when it came to these things.

After all, look where Amara and Cal had ended up.

Then again, she was doing a damn good job of fighting her attraction to Owen despite its blatant obviousness, so perhaps her sixth sense was broken.

Or she was ignoring it.

Probably the latter.

"So what's going on, Bee?"

"I hooked up with Ezra."

My sisters made various sounds of annoyance, and Chloe went so far as to chuck a pillow at my head.

"We know that, you goof."

"No…I mean, more than once."

The room stilled, going so quiet, I could've heard a pin drop before the four of them erupted.

Delia: "What the fuck?"

Amara: "You little minx."

Chloe: "I need all the tea. Maybe I'll put this in my next book."

Ella: "How many times is more than once?"

"Chill out!" I shouted above the din, and they all went silent. I looked at Ella. "To answer your question, more than once means exactly twice. Although…we had phone sex pretty regularly for like four months."

"What the fuck?" Delia exclaimed again, and I chuckled.

I walked them through everything. How I'd called him that first time in a panic over what to cook for my dinner party. How I returned the favor the following month by helping him bake for Hansen's preschool. How those two innocent calls had morphed into constant texts that had become nightly calls that eventually culminated in seeking our pleasure together through FaceTime.

I'd shared so much with him, and I truly had been mourning the loss of that friendship, perhaps more than anything else, all these years.

"But that summer when I moved home? Right before I opened the bakery?" They all nodded in understanding. "I invited him down there to sample my menu items. I...trust his opinion when it comes to that stuff more than anyone, even if he isn't a pastry chef, and I wanted honest feedback. One thing led to another, and..."

"And you fucked," Amara said bluntly.

"Yes," I replied, willing my blush away. There wasn't anything to be embarrassed about, not with my sisters, but I'd never been good at talking about this stuff, mainly because I didn't have as much experience to draw on as Amara and Delia, nor had I ever been in long-term committed relationships like Chloe and Ella. "We had sex, and it was honestly the best night of my life."

"How big is his cock?" Delia asked.

"DELIA!" I shrieked.

My older sister tipped her head back and laughed. "God, don't be such a prude." She smirked and added, "I bet he's huge, though. He gives Big Dick Energy."

I shook my head, unable to stifle my laughter at my sister's ridiculousness.

"So why are you telling us now?" Chloe asked.

"Because...I mean, we're not together, so I think it's obvious that things did *not* pan out the way I'd hoped. I was really hurt, but I understood why he did what he did. He has Hansen to worry about, first and foremost. Plus, Daddy was running things at the winery at the time. You know his rule about staying away from us."

"The rule you and Brad are responsible for," Delia quipped.

"Which is why Amara and Cal didn't get together until after he'd signed the company over," Ella reminded us.

We all nodded in agreement, even Amara.

"Precisely. And unlike Amara, I don't even work for the company. The bakery may be a company asset," I said, holding up a hand to stop Amara before she could offer up that little argument, "but I pay all the bills myself and operate outside of the winery grounds. It's not the same."

"So you want to give things another shot?" Delia asked.

I shrugged. "He does. He kissed me at the winery after my date with Douchebag Damian in September and almost did again last night. God, I wanted to give in so bad. I miss him more than I'd like to admit. Before, I wasn't sure I could trust him—"

"Wait," Chloe said, holding up a hand. "Back up. What happened at the winery?"

I stilled, stunned into silence. Surely I'd told them about that. Hadn't I?

Then again, I'd been so wrapped up in other things that maybe I'd...forgotten?

Delia crossed her arms over her chest and said, "Spill, Bee."

I gave them all a sheepish grin and said, "So, you guys obviously remember my date with Damian."

"Yeah. That guy was an asshat. We really should've seen it coming from a mile away," Ella said, and I couldn't help but chuckle as my other sisters nodded in agreement. Ella rarely got worked up about anything but, like the rest of us, she was fiercely protective when any of us was threatened. And while I personally thought Damian was harmless—after all, he'd held true to his word and not given his trip to Apple Blossom Bay a single second of video time on his social accounts, not even in an attempt to give me and the town bad publicity—my sisters weren't as forgiving. In fact, Delia had prepared a smear campaign, ready to launch like the nuclear codes if he ever decided to go scorched earth.

"What I didn't tell you was that Ezra went full on jealous asshole," I said, wincing when my sisters gasped. I didn't want to examine too closely why I hadn't shared this part of that evening with them. Probably because I hadn't thought it mattered.

Now, though...well, it was like Ezra had said the night before. Everything had changed.

"What happened?" Chloe asked.

I quickly explained the events of the evening. Damian's condescending comments and entire air of superiority. The steak he ordered and sent back when it wasn't cooked right, despite being prepared exactly how he'd ordered it. How Ezra came out and confronted him, agreeing to cook him a new one, and then bringing out that blackened hunk of meat.

I couldn't help the laugh that burst from my mouth at remembering Damian's face when Ezra dropped that ribeye on his plate, acrid smoke rising off its surface and scenting the air around us.

"I don't know if I've ever seen a man that angry," I chuckled. "I truly thought Damian was going to have an aneurysm with the way the vein in his forehead pulsed."

"So what'd you do?"

"I finally told Damian who I was and kicked him out. He spewed some hateful things as he left, but I wasn't bothered. From the moment he'd picked me up, I'd known I wouldn't see or speak to him again."

I didn't have much dating experience, but I knew how I deserved to be treated, and Damian's behavior wasn't it.

That and...he wasn't Ezra.

"Anyway," I said, waving a hand. "The point is, after Damian left, I pulled Ezra back to the offices, intent on chewing him a new ass for causing a scene like that, and he kissed me."

"Was it hot?" Delia asked.

I tried to play it cool, but I could feel the blissed-out smile that played on my lips and the heat rising to my cheeks as I remembered that too brief moment. My toes curled against the couch with the memory of how my entire body came to life under his touch.

The physical connection between us had never been the problem, and I said as much to my sisters.

"I don't see the problem," Amara said. "That's half the battle."

I narrowed my gaze and pursed my lips at her. "Says the girl who hated her now-boyfriend and future baby daddy."

Amara rolled her eyes. "I never hated him."

"Bullshit," Delia proclaimed. "You hated him for years. But it's a fine line between love and hate, and you two ended up on the right side eventually."

"The point is," I said, pulling my sisters back to the matter at hand—*me*, "I told him never to kiss me again. Thanks to the event tonight, we've been spending some time together. Before, I wanted him to stay far away from me. It was too painful, and after he'd been so callous that morning he left my apartment, I couldn't handle that sort of disappointment again. But now..."

"But now, what?" Amara asked. "Has he ever been anything but completely honest with you? Even though he hurt you, has he ever lied?"

"I mean, no..." I lifted my hand to my mouth and chewed on the skin around my thumbnail nervously. "Actually, I was the one who wasn't truthful. I kept a huge secret from him—you guys too."

My sisters quieted but stared at me expectantly. They were wholly unprepared for the bomb I was about to drop, but now that Ezra knew, it was time they did too.

"That first time we hooked up," I started slowly, dropping my gaze to my lap, too embarrassed to face any of them directly, "I got pregnant."

The pause was deafening, and then they exploded once again, each of them asking questions over each other, hands reaching for me, offering reassuring squeezes and side hugs.

"What the fuck happened?" Delia asked. "This was like...over two years ago? Why didn't you tell us?"

"I found out on my twenty-third birthday, and I was so scared. I just made the appointment and pretended like it wasn't happening until I knew what my options were. But I miscarried the day I went in. I was so...embarrassed."

"Oh, Brie," Amara said, voice thick as she settled her hand over her stomach and the life growing inside of it. "You should've told us. We never would've judged you. You could've given us the chance to be there for you."

"I know," I said, hanging my head and swiping away the tears springing from my eyes and rolling down my face. "I just...I couldn't tell Ezra, not after everything he went through with his ex, and if I wasn't telling the father, I couldn't in good conscience tell you guys."

"But he knows now," Chloe said, also cupping her own baby bump. God, this news must have been so difficult for her and Amara to hear. They were both mostly out of the danger zone where miscarriages were concerned, but I couldn't imagine that made it any less scary to think about losing the babies they were both so excited about.

"Yeah, he does. I told him last night."

"And how did he take it?" Ella asked.

"Better than I ever could've dreamed. He didn't yell or berate me for not telling him. He just...held me, apologized that I had to go through that alone, and assured me everything was okay."

"And you care about him," she continued. It wasn't a question. "A lot."

I lifted a hand and tapped my chest, right over my heart. "There's an invisible string here," I said. "And it leads right to him."

"Then I don't see what the problem is," Delia said. "You're into each other. He's hot as fuck and an absolute boss in the kitchen. Plus, he's the best dad ever—second to ours, of course. All your cards are on the table. I say go for it."

"That's rich coming from you," Chloe snorted. "Miss I'm Going To Pretend My Business Partner Doesn't Have Hearts In His Eyes Every Time He Looks At Me And That I Don't Feel The Same."

"Please," Delia scoffed. "It is *so* not like that."

Amara snorted. "That man is down so fucking bad for you, and you're a simp for him. How about you stop fighting it?"

Delia rolled her eyes and said, "We're here to talk about Brie."

"I'm just saying," Amara continued, raising her hands in surrender so Delia wouldn't come for her and numerate all the ways she and Cal had been idiots about their own feelings for each other. "The way you two are around each other... There's something there. We all saw it at grape crushing."

Toying with the hem of her sweater, Delia was silent for a beat before she said, "I like him, but...after everything, I'm afraid to go there."

My heart went out to her in that moment. My sister had been through a shitty relationship with an older guy in college and had been reluctant to give her heart to anyone since. Owen wasn't that douchebag, though, and Delia knew it. I had all the confidence in the world she'd find the bravery to take the leap before too long.

I reached out and grabbed her hand, giving it a squeeze. "Now you know how I feel."

Her expression softened, and she shifted over on the mountain of blankets and pillows we'd set up on the massive sectional to pull me into a side hug.

"I guess we'll never know unless we try, huh?" she said quietly to me.

"Giving me and Cal a chance was the scariest thing I've ever done," Amara said. "But I also knew I was ready to take that step because I couldn't imagine a life without him."

I knew where she was coming from, and maybe I was ready to take my own leap of faith at last.

Ezra was finally presenting me with the whole damn meal I'd wanted from him for so long, and it was time I sat down at the table.

chapter 27
Ezra

"Are you sure we're allowed to be here?" Hansen whispered as we stood on Leon and Lena's front porch, waiting for someone to let us in.

"Yes," I said, reaching down to ruffle his hair. "The Delatous invited us, and you're going to be on your best behavior."

"Duh," he said.

I sighed heavily. I wasn't sure where he'd picked up that little expression, but I assumed it was from one of his friends at school.

Five going on fifteen.

In truth, Hansen's question wasn't too far off base, because I'd been having similar internal struggles about coming here all day. But we'd been invited, and I'd happily take any opportunity to be near Brie, even if it meant spending an evening under the watchful gaze of her entire family.

I supposed I shouldn't be feeling too honored, though. After all, the Delatous welcomed the entire staff into their home for Thanksgiving. The winery truly was a family business, and they treated their employees as an extension of that. As their head chef, it was only natural I be included.

At last, a shadow appeared on the other side of the fogged glass door, and it opened to reveal none other than Brie.

The cold had absolutely nothing to do with the fact that all the air vacated my lungs in an instant.

I rarely ever saw her with her hair down or in anything but leggings, an oversized tee, and her signature sage-green apron. Tonight, her long, chocolatey strands hung in waves down her back, one side pulled away from her face with a comb fashioned to look like a butterfly wing. As usual, she wore no makeup, save something shiny on her lips, making them look even more plump and luscious than normal.

I willed my cock to stand down.

Her emerald sweater matched the exact shade of her eyes, and her dark denim pants hugged every curve of her lower body, reminding me of what those legs looked like naked and wrapped around my waist.

Fuck, I needed to get it together.

"Welcome, Wendt family!" she said happily, her gaze lingering on mine as she stepped to the side. "Come on in."

My dad offered her a warm greeting as he crossed the threshold, and Hansen hurried inside after shouting, "Hi, Baker Brie!" and making a beeline toward all the voices deeper in the house. When he reached what I presumed was the kitchen, happy exclamations rang out from the Delatou women at the sight of my little man.

Unfortunately, he had more swag in his pinky than his father did in his entire body.

But I wasn't worried about charming the entire family—not when I only had eyes for the girl standing a few feet away from me.

I had every intention of moving right past her and following my son and father, but the moment that delectable scent of hers filled my senses, my body acted on its own. I leaned in close, inhaling deeply as I pressed a soft, lingering kiss to her cheek.

When I pulled back, I said, "Hey, honey."

"Hey, Chef," Brie choked out, and I chuckled. "Thanks for coming."

"You know I can't say no to your mom," I reminded her. "And I definitely wasn't missing out on the chance to enjoy one of Brie Delatou's world famous desserts."

A blush crept into her cheeks, and she ducked her head. "I'm definitely not world famous."

Brazenly, I tucked a finger under her chin and lifted it so she met my gaze. "You are to me."

She averted her gaze but couldn't hold back the grin that bloomed on her mouth.

God, fuck dessert. I wanted to eat *her* instead.

Clearing my throat and willing my cock not to thicken with that thought—with memories of our one perfect night—I moved out of the way so Brie could shut the door behind me.

I'd been up here a few times in the past couple years for summer holiday gatherings—mainly the Fourth of July—but I'd never been inside the Delatous' sprawling estate. High on a hill, it overlooked the point of Old Mission Peninsula and the waters of Lake Michigan where they fed into Grand Traverse Bay. Even in the darkness of the late fall evening, the moon glinted on the waves, their distant crashing against the shore calming my frayed nerves.

We reached the entryway to the kitchen, and Brie moved into the room, weaving through her sisters in the direction of the oven, which she pulled open to check on whatever baked inside. Awkwardly, I stood on the threshold, watching the Delatou women circle around each other easily, random snippets of conversations that would never make sense to me in a million years floating my way.

At last, Lena looked up and found me watching them, a warm smile stretching across her mouth.

"Ezra!" She hurried toward me to give me a hug then held me at arm's length when she pulled away. "It's so good to see you. Thank you for joining us. I couldn't bear the thought of the three of you celebrating all alone today."

"I really appreciate the invitation," I told her earnestly. I *wanted* to be here, wanted to be in Brie's orbit, to ingratiate myself with her family.

To make her family mine one day, and vice versa.

"We're happy to have you," she assured me.

"Is there anything I can do to help?" I asked, gesturing to the kitchen behind her.

"Absolutely not," she said firmly. "You're a guest in my home—"

"And guests don't cook," Brie finished for her from across the room. With a wink at me, she added, "No matter how good they are."

I grinned at her. "Then what do you expect me to do with myself?"

"Go down to the den," Lena said, pointing to another archway down the hall. "All the guys are in there watching the Mustangs game."

With a shrug and a final imploring look at Brie, who only

offered me a demure smile and shake of her head, I made my way toward the guys, finding both my son and father sprawled out on one part of the large sectional—my dad with a bottle of Molson, Hansen with a juice pouch—watching the game and shooting the shit with the rest of them.

Well, Hansen wasn't shooting the shit so much as he was exclaiming loudly with every hard tackle or big play, peppering Owen with endless questions about how football was played.

My heart swelled in that moment, grateful for these people who had easily welcomed us into the fold and acted like we belonged with them.

Fuck, how badly I wanted to make that a reality.

"Grab yourself a beer, kid," my dad said, gesturing at the fridge cleverly concealed under a bar top along the back wall. I had to chuckle at the sight he presented, manspread across the couch, fingers lightly gripping the neck of his own drink while he watched the game and conversed with Owen, Leon, Logan, Calvin, and Liam like they were all old friends.

I grabbed a bottle of craft IPA and dropped onto the couch next to my son and Liam.

"Hey man," Liam said, lifting his own bottle over Hansen's head in a toast.

"Hey," I said. "Surprised to see you here."

Liam chuckled. "I could say the same."

Liam Danvers was a bit of a wildcard in my opinion. As the winery's vintner, he was directly involved in the growing of the grapes and production of the wine. Early the past summer, he and Amara had even teamed up to create a line of ready-to-drink, wine-based cocktails that hit the market in June and made a major splash. Personally, I was obsessed with the Lena's Best Sangria—named, of course, after the Delatou matriarch—as was everyone else. In addition to his job as the CD vintner, he was also an insanely talented mixologist and had some sort of agricultural engineering degree.

The dude was wicked smart, but you'd never know it by the beard, flannels, and tattoos.

"Figured after three years, I could take Lena up on her invitation," I said noncommittally.

Liam nodded in understanding. "My family lives in Vancouver, and I couldn't take time off to go home."

I blinked, surprised. "I didn't know you were Canadian."

"Really?" he asked, quirking a brow. "Everyone tells me it's obvious by my accent."

"You don't have an accent," Hansen said helpfully, and Liam chuckled, reaching out to ruffle my son's hair.

"I don't?"

"Nah," Hansen said, his eyes never straying from the TV. "You sound normal to me."

I barked out a laugh at my son's confidence and decided it was nice having Liam here, reminding me I wasn't the only odd man out around this family.

Plus, I was happy to see him for a different reason.

"So," I said conversationally, and Liam glanced at me, brows shooting up. "There's actually something I've been wanting to talk to you about. You think maybe after the holiday season, we could set up a meeting with Amara to discuss an idea I've got?"

Liam shrugged, easy-going as ever. "I don't see why not."

"Did I just hear my girl's name?" Cal asked from across the

room.

"Simmer down, Ryder," Liam said. "It's work stuff. None of your concern."

Cal slapped a palm over his heart in mock hurt. "You wound me, Danvers."

"You say that like you didn't get yourself fired from the company for being a jackass," Owen mumbled, and I couldn't help but chuckle.

Cal gasped, and Leon barked out a laugh. "You deserved that one, son," Leon said.

Cal only nodded, hanging his head. "One day, you guys will stop giving me shit for that."

"Not anytime soon," I assured him.

"You stay out of this, Wendt," he said, aiming a finger at me. "You're not even part of the family."

Mutely, I stared at him, knowing he was right, though I desperately wanted to weasel my way in, make Brie a part of my family, make her a permanent fixture in the Wendt household.

We could use more of her feminine influence.

"I'm just glad to have all you guys around now," Leon said to Logan, Cal, and Owen. "This year, you can help me cook for Christmas."

Early on in my tenure, I learned from Leon that the women cooked Thanksgiving dinner while he was in charge of Christmas—which usually ended with him hiring a caterer.

Last year, that caterer had been me, and I wasn't being left out this time either.

"I can help too."

I bit my lips together, as though that would take back the

words. These other guys were father, husband, and brother-in-law, and boyfriends of the Delatou women. I was...the chef at their winery. I had no claim to family time or participating in traditions.

Leon waved a hand dismissively. "Oh, you don't have to do that. If I want you to cook for me, I'll just come down to the winery." Then, as if latching onto some thought, those green eyes narrowed on me—eyes so like Brie's, it was disconcerting and a bit uncomfortable to hold his gaze. "Unless you've got something going on with one of my daughters. You know the rules, Wendt," he said, pointing a finger menacingly at me.

"Oh, give that a rest," Cal said with an eye roll.

"You're only saying that because you're the poster child for breaking the cardinal rule," Logan said, elbowing him in the side.

"What about Lawless?" Cal sputtered.

"Owen never worked for me," Leon pointed out.

"And I wasn't working for you when Amara and I got together either," Cal retorted.

"Children, children," Owen said, waving his arms in a *simmer down* motion. "This is a stupid and useless argument. We all know those girls are going to do whatever the fuck they want, and not a single one of us can tell them otherwise."

"Plus," I said quietly into the silence that followed Owen's proclamation. "Amara is my boss now."

Excited chuckles and exclamations rang out from the other guys, but Leon sucked in a gasp and sat up straighter. "Which one?"

"Which one, what?" I asked innocently.

"My guess is Brie," Cal said, shooting me a wink.

"God, you're such an asshole," Owen said with a disbelieving laugh. "Between you and Delia, I've got my hands full with shit-stirrers."

"You love me," Cal said with a cheesy grin.

Owen threw a pillow at his head, and the room erupted into laughter.

But all was not forgotten, at least not by Leon, because when everyone settled again, he said, "*Is* it Brie?"

I nodded, giving him a sheepish grin. "I'm kind of crazy about her, and I'd like the chance to pursue it."

Leon studied me for long moments, those emerald eyes like laser beams flaying through skin and bone straight to my soul, testing my words for verity.

"You're adults and you don't need it," he said at last, "but you've got my blessing anyway."

chapter 28

Ezra

"WHAT'S ALL THIS?" DAD asked when he padded out to the kitchen late morning three days before Christmas.

"The Delatou family holiday party is tonight. They've got this tradition where the women cook Thanksgiving dinner and the men handle Christmas. For years, it was obviously only Leon fending for himself, but now that he's got a whole group of us, we each agreed to pitch in something for the party."

He raised a brow. "And you're pitching in by making a five-course meal?"

I huffed out an annoyed sigh, which also served to blow the stubborn lock of hair off my forehead. I was in dire need of a cut, but life had been so crazy lately with the holiday season at the winery, as well as all of Hansen's end-of-semester programs, that it had fallen by the wayside.

"This," I said with an eye roll, sweeping my hand over the island, "isn't a five-course meal. I just want to make a good impression."

"You cook for these people every day," my dad said with a snort. "I think you're doing just fine."

I glared daggers at him. "Leave me alone."

"Just saying, kid. You're putting in a lot of effort for a simple holiday party."

"If I'm going to win Brie back, nothing about it is simple."

Dad's eyes narrowed. "About time you pulled your head out of your ass."

I chose to ignore that and added, "Plus, you know food is my love language."

"What's a love language?" Hansen asked from the living room, where he was building some sort of Legos tower.

"It's how you express and experience love," I told him. "Like...you know how you get really happy when someone tells you you've done a good job, so you keep doing things that ensure we do it again and again? That makes me think your love language is words of affirmation. You're happiest and feel the most loved when people are praising you."

"Hmm..." Hansen said, tapping his forefinger to his chin and looking far older than his five and a half years. "Makes sense. So you feel happiest and most loved when you're cooking and feeding people?"

"Exactly," I confirmed, smiling widely.

Honestly, my favorite part of parenthood was watching him grow and learn and discover new things about the world. I knew I was going to fuck up sometimes, but I was thoroughly enjoying this stage. Hansen was so smart and curious, but also silly and playful. In truth, he was the perfect kid, and I counted my blessings every day that he was mine.

"So what exactly are you making?" Dad asked.

"Finger foods," I replied, spinning from the stove to point at each dish on the island. "Deviled eggs, meatballs on skewers, stuffed mushrooms, fig, pecan, and brie bites, and sesame scallops."

My dad, who had never been one to beat around the bush, narrowed his gaze on me and said, "You do realize you're not technically part of the family, right?"

I flipped him off. "Thanks, Dad."

He shrugged. "I'm just saying, kiddo. This is a lot of work for nothing."

"It's not for nothing," I protested. "At the very least, everyone who attends the party will rave about my food, and that right there is enough to make the night a win in my book."

"But you want more than that."

I sighed, wiping my hands on the towel slung over my shoulder and dropping it onto the one bare spot of counter space.

I *did* want more. When it came to Brie, I wanted everything. The crazy extended family. The mass of sisters and their significant others becoming the siblings I never had. The father-in-law who terrified me and the mother-in-law who fawned over me and my son at every opportunity. The people who, when I was down on my luck and desperate for a change, gave me a soft, safe place to land. This little town and all its quirks.

The bakery, Brie's cake batter skin. Her calling me "Chef" and me calling her "honey." I wanted all of it. Forever.

"Do you remember our first Christmas here?" I asked my dad.

"I do," he said slowly.

"It's funny to think how much has changed, isn't it?"

He pondered that for a moment. "I don't think it's funny, exactly. That's what happens in life—time marches on, and the world keeps spinning around us. I think without all the Shannon drama holding you back like it was that first year, you've had the chance to become the man and father you were always meant to be."

"You mean that?" I asked. "You think I'm a good man and father?"

"Hey, Hansen?" Dad asked, ignoring me.

"Yeah, Papa?"

"Do you love your dad?"

"More than anything in the world," my son said without hesitation.

My dad turned his attention back to me, giving me a soft smile when he saw the tears welling in my eyes. "I think that says enough, don't you?"

"What about everything else?" I asked quietly, voice hoarse as I tried to corral my emotions.

"I think only you can answer that, son. But if you want me to tell you how proud of you I am, both of the man you've grown into and the father you are to my favorite grandson—"

"Hey!" Hansen shouted, cutting in. Apparently, he'd been playing closer attention than we thought. "I'm your only grandson."

Dad shrugged. "Doesn't mean you're not my favorite."

"Whatever," Hansen grumbled, though good-naturedly, before returning to his Legos.

"The point I'm trying to make," Dad continued, "is that you got the short end of the stick with your last relationship. Maybe it's time you sought happiness again."

"Brie makes me happy," I said, fighting to get the words out around the stinging in my nose and eyes. "After Shannon, I didn't think I'd ever be able to feel this way again. It's scary, but...I need that woman in my life in whatever way she'll have me."

"Then do what you gotta do, kid."

I smiled, knowing I had his blessing. He knew this pursuit of Brie wasn't something I took lightly, not when I'd spent the last nearly six years of my life making decisions with only one person in mind—my son. But I was ready to do what I'd been too fucking scared and broken to do before.

This time, I wasn't going down without a fight.

✦✦✦✦✦ ✦✦✦✦✦

"Ezra!" Lena gasped when she opened the door to find me standing there, arms laden with as many dishes as I could safely carry. Hansen and Dad weren't far behind me, each holding what they could as well.

I was pretty sure there was still more in the car.

Maybe I *had* gone overboard.

"Hi, Lena," I said, shooting her a wide grin.

"What is all of this?" she asked as she stepped aside to let me and my family in.

"Men cook for Christmas, right?"

"Well, yes..." She trailed off as the three of us formed a procession toward their dining room. "But, you know, you cook for us all day every day. You didn't need to go through all this trouble."

Carefully sliding the dishes onto the long buffet table set up under the windows that looked out over the water, I turned to Lena.

"I don't mind, truly. Plus..." I started, moving closer and

dropping my voice. The commotion of our arrival had drawn a crowd, and the Delatou women and their significant others began to filter into the room. "You don't really want to eat anything Leon cooked, right?"

Lena tipped her head back and barked out a laugh, and I grinned alongside her. Leon approached, eyes narrowed in suspicion, sliding his arm possessively around his wife's waist.

"No one but me should be making my wife laugh like that, Wendt," he groused.

"Sorry, sir."

Leon chuckled and settled his free hand on my shoulder. "I'm just messing with you, son." He glanced over my shoulder. "I see you came bearing gifts."

I shrugged. "It is Christmas, right?"

Leon nodded and said, "And because of you, we won't starve."

Lena turned to him, the smooth skin of her forehead scrunching in confusion, and I bit back a laugh. Looked like someone was in trouble.

"You spent all day in the kitchen," Lena said. "What were you doing in there if not cooking?"

"Ahh, well...you see—" Leon started, but Lena held up a hand.

"Save it." She turned away from him and rolled her eyes. The laugh I'd been holding back broke free, and Leon's frown deepened. "You were probably watching fishing videos or something equally ridiculous."

"Fishing videos are not ridiculous!" Leon protested.

Sensing an argument brewing, I slipped away, my eyes scanning the crowd of brunette heads for one in particular. Like the water parting on the Red Sea, Brie's family shifted out of the way until I had a clear line of sight to her.

"Fuck," I breathed.

She was...exquisite. A goddamn dark-haired angel sent from above and gliding toward me on bright red satin pumps. My eyes trailed slowly up her legs, covered in black tights, meeting the indecently high hem of her little red dress. The skirt was full and structured, a white sash tied around her trim waist, the corset top suctioned to her full tits, the tops of which bounced with every one of her steps. The long sleeves were sheer and billowy before they cinched at her wrists. A delicate diamond pendant the size of my thumbnail and shaped like a heart rested against her chest, and matching studs twinkled in her ears through the cloud of her curled hair.

But the rest of it faded away when those blood-red lips parted in a wide smile, her green eyes twinkling under the warm white lights and candles Lena had decorated with.

"Fuck," I said again when she at last stopped in front of me. "You are..."

"Do you like it?" she asked almost shyly, dropping her eyes to the floor.

I tucked a finger under her chin and raised her gaze back to mine. "'Like' isn't even close to strong enough to describe my feelings about it," I said, using my free hand to smooth down her side, the material soft beneath my touch. "You're stunning, Brie. But you already knew that."

"Still nice to hear," she said, that gorgeous blush blooming in her cheeks.

"I'll tell you every day if you want."

Brie winked. "I'll take it under advisement."

I groaned quietly, and her laugh was music to my ears. Truthfully, I liked that she was making me work for it. I'd hurt her, and I understood she had to guard her heart against the possibility of that happening again—especially after what she'd gone through in the aftermath.

The chase would make the reunion that much sweeter, and I couldn't wait for the day she finally gave in.

"So what sorts of treats did you whip up for us?" I asked, trailing behind her as she skirted the table, eyeing the evening's offerings.

"Nothing."

I looped my fingers around her wrist and pulled her to a stop as we reached the end of the table and the tiered trays of sweets.

"You mean to tell me you didn't prepare any of this?" I asked.

"Nope," she said happily. "Boys cook, remember?"

"Of course I remember," I growled, hooking my thumb over my shoulder. "I slaved over that shit for hours."

Brie giggled. "I'm sure your hard work will be rewarded."

I raised a brow, not missing the seductive tone to her words. "By you?"

"Maybe if you're a really good boy."

Instantly, my cock thickened, and I hissed a curse as I angled myself away from her family and adjusted myself. Brie laughed, the sound more carefree and joyful than anything I'd heard from her in ages. I couldn't help but grin in response.

"I missed that laugh."

I missed you, I wanted to add.

She leaned closer, her sugary scent wrapping around me as she dropped her voice and said, "I think it might be back for good."

I pulled back to study her face, finding nothing but contentment and...happiness. Was I somehow responsible for it?

Awkwardly, I cleared my throat. "So if you didn't bake, who did?"

Brie turned toward her family and pointed at Logan and Cal. "Those two."

"You let *Logan* into the kitchen?"

Brie blinked at me, confused. "What's wrong with that?"

I'd gotten to know Logan Daniels fairly well during my time in Apple Blossom Bay, simply thanks to proximity to this family and the fact that he was married to the eldest daughter. He was...energetic, a classic Golden Retriever personality, which made it even more fitting that he owned one. He was exuberant and helpful, always down to throw himself into whatever task was asked of him with more enthusiasm than I think I'd ever shown for anything in my entire life. The fact that he was an attorney had done nothing short of blowing my mind when I found out. Rectifying the carefree, energetic man I knew with someone who possessed any sort of gravitas for court proceedings had been difficult.

In short, he was kind of a goof, if one of the best guys I'd ever met, and I couldn't imagine him slaving away in the kitchen over baked goods.

Cal, on the other hand, was a numbers guy, a perfectionist. He'd follow a recipe to the letter to ensure it yielded the correct results, so picturing him whipping up the treats was a far easier task.

Those two together, though? Oil and water. Yet, somehow,

they were great friends.

The only explanation was the women they'd chosen to share their lives with forced a connection that wouldn't have happened otherwise.

And adding Owen Lawless into the fold? Who was already Cal's best friend but had easily ingratiated himself into the Delatou family—even before he and Delia had figured their shit out, which they finally had around Thanksgiving.

Brie's sisters had found themselves some truly impressive partners, and I wanted so badly to be a part of it myself. Did I find myself all that impressive? Of course not. I simply wanted to consider myself an extension of this family unit. I wanted to call Brie mine, wanted to truly have Leon and Lena be like parents to me instead of only considering them as such inside my head.

And I'd never had siblings, so I couldn't think of anything better than suddenly calling the Delatou women my sisters and their significant others my brothers.

I'd never really stopped to consider it before—what exactly I wanted out of life. I had Hansen and my dad, and for a long time, that was enough. They'd always be my true family, but I didn't think there was anything wrong with wanting to expand that family to include these people too.

"Ez?" Brie asked, pulling me from my thoughts.

I shook my head to clear them and said, "What were we talking about?"

She giggled and said, "You were concerned that I let Logan in the kitchen."

"Right," I said, snapping my fingers as I picked up the thread of our conversation. "I guess I'm just shocked you didn't take control of all this."

Brie shrugged. "If it makes you feel better, I *did* supervise. But you know the rules. Women cook at Thanksgiving, and men cook—"

"Christmas," I finished for her. "Yeah, I got it. Why do you think I brought enough food to feed a small army?"

"Because cooking for people is your love language," she said matter-of-factly.

I stilled, dumbfounded, remembering my earlier comment to Hansen. Sometimes, I forgot how truly well this woman knew me. How we'd spent months of phone calls getting to know one another. I was deeply pleased to discover she hadn't forgotten everything in our time apart.

Maybe she hadn't forgotten *anything* and, like me, had simply chosen to keep her memories locked away to protect herself.

After everything had gone down with Shannon, after the judge had granted our divorce and I washed my hands of her, I hadn't handled it well. I guess maybe I thought it was safe to fall apart because she wasn't around to witness it, and Hansen was too young to know the difference. When I'd pulled the plug on me and Brie, well...Hansen had still been too young to know anything was wrong, but I had done a much better job at keeping it together, mostly because I knew I'd still have to see her regularly, and I refused to let her see me hurting.

But somewhere along the way the last few years, I'd cracked the lid on that box, and everything about Brie and our time together that I'd carefully stowed away was leaking out into my mind, my emotions and our memories prying the box open wider, freeing themselves at last.

I was surprised to find I wasn't afraid to face them. In fact, I relished those feelings. I *wanted* to remember—and wanted to make new ones with her and my boy by my side.

"Ezra?" Lena called, pulling me from my thoughts. I looked at her, and she asked, "Would you be a dear and go grab a few bottles of wine for dinner? Whatever you think will go best with all of this."

"Sure," I said happily. Wine selection was one of my favorite parts of being a chef. The component that could make or break a meal.

"I'll go with you," Brie offered.

I held out my arm, gesturing for her to go ahead of me. "Lead the way."

The second we were out of sight of her family, she reached back for my hand, threading our fingers together.

"We're doing this now?" I asked, glancing pointedly at where we connected as she pulled me through the house.

Brie shrugged. "This feels...safe."

I snorted, and Brie shot me a glare. There was nothing safe about this woman. Not about her body, her mind, her tinkling laugh and soft moans that grew in volume the closer she got to her climax. Everything about her screamed *danger*, the kind of warning that urged you to turn back before you fell under her spell.

Unfortunately for me, that ship had already sailed. I was fully entranced by Brie Delatou, had been since the moment I met her.

We didn't speak further as we descended a staircase into the wine cellar, and goosebumps erupted on Brie's skin as the cool, dry air washed over us. She let go of my hand to wrap her arms around herself.

"Hurry before I freeze."

"You don't want to help?" I asked as I approached the wall of wines.

"N-no," she said, teeth chattering. "Just w-wanted to be a-alone with you."

"All you had to do was ask," I said, not facing her as I perused the selection, ultimately deciding on Pinot Noir. In deference to Brie, I knew to stay far away from Cabernet, but the sweeter Pinot Noir grape was safe territory. I shot her a wink as I turned back to her. "I'll happily be alone with you anytime you want."

Brie rolled her eyes, a small smile playing on her red lips. "We're not there yet, Ez."

"I know, I know," I said. "Hand holding only for now."

She nodded, and I chuckled. Gripping the bottle necks between the fingers of one hand, I reached for Brie's with the other and tugged us back upstairs. She breathed a deep sigh when the warm air greeted us, her pebbled flesh once again smoothing out.

I wasn't sure where she stood on wanting her family to know something was happening between us, so I dropped her hand before we crossed the threshold into the dining room.

"Wait!" someone shouted as we were about to enter the room.

Brie and I skidded to a halt, glancing confusedly at each other.

"What's wrong?" Brie asked.

Lena jerked her chin, and the rest of the family snickered behind their hands as they all looked at something over our heads.

Oh, no...

Slowly, I raised my gaze to the arched entrance, somehow

already knowing what I'd find. The Delatou women were the queens of meddling, and I should've known we wouldn't be safe from their handiwork.

My heart dropped then kicked up speed until it was pumping almost uncomfortably against my sternum when I took in what hung above our heads.

A sprig of mistletoe.

chapter 29
Brie

Stricken by panic at the sight of the mistletoe, knowing what it meant to find myself beneath it with Ezra at my side, I looked at my mom, who wore a massive, self-satisfied grin.

"Mom!" I shouted. "What are you doing?"

"Forcing you two to figure your shit out."

"Lena…" my father warned in a low voice.

"What?" she asked him, feigning innocence.

"You're meddling."

Mom waved a hand, dismissing him. "She's my baby, and I want her to be happy."

"Stop talking about me like I'm not right here!"

"If it makes you feel better," Rik said, "I warned them this was a bad idea."

"Thanks, Dad," Ezra muttered.

Poking his head out from behind his grandfather, Hansen said, "Papa, what's happening?"

Rik rested his palm atop Hansen's messy curls and said, "Nothing you need to concern yourself with, *Älskling*."

Ignoring them, Mom said to me, her expression softening, "It's time, my sweets." Then, she pointedly turned and left the room through an arch on the other side, the rest of my family following behind her.

"Time for what?" I yelled after her, but everyone ignored me. Exasperated, I turned to Ezra and buried my face in his chest. "That little—"

"Brie," Ezra warned.

"She's manipulating us!"

"It only works if you want to be manipulated."

My gaze flew to his, dazzled by the honest-to-god twinkle in his eyes. A small smirk played on his lips, drawing my attention there. To the plump bottom one and thinner top one. Remembering how they felt against mine—against my entire body, electrifying my synapses with each new connection, wringing endless pleasure from me with them.

Did I want to be manipulated? Did I want to let my mother shove me into participating in this tradition?

"What do you say, honey?" Ezra asked, the old nickname sliding over my skin like the sweet, sticky substance. "You gonna let me kiss you?"

"Do you *want* to kiss me?"

"More than I want my next breath."

Who was I to deny this man air?

Tentatively, I stepped closer, trying to take things slowly.

Ezra, apparently, was done waiting, because the second I moved, he was on me. His arms slid around my waist, palms warm, spanning my back, pressing me closer.

Then his lips were on mine, and everything in me went lax, a sigh escaping me as we came together. I'd missed this, more than I wanted to admit, which was wild given we'd really only kissed a handful of times. But that first time, the caving to our most carnal desires, that morphed into those months of phone calls. Getting to know him over that distance and span of time...I knew Ezra better than I knew anyone in the world save my family, and I think he knew me better than even my sisters did.

I found my way home in his kiss, and I couldn't remember why I'd deprived us of it for so long.

I opened for Ezra, and he swept his tongue into my mouth. I sank further into him, reacquainting myself with his scent and his taste and the way it felt to be wrapped in his arms.

But I pulled away before we could get too deep, before his hands could wander lower than the small of my back. Before I lost myself entirely to him.

Ezra made a noise of protest when I extricated myself from his grip.

"Where are you going?"

"I don't want to do this here," I said, and he bent to rest his forehead against mine.

"So let's go back to my place," he whispered, angling his head to nip at my ear.

With a giggle, I shoved him away, needing some air to breathe, but I gripped his hands in mine.

I squeezed his fingers. "There's no reason to rush."

He guided one of my hands to his lap, pressing it against the thick length of his cock straining against his fly. "This seems like a pretty good reason to me."

I hissed at the contact, at the reminder that I turned him on this way. That something as simple as a thirty second kiss had him hard as stone.

Quickly, before a member of my family could walk in on

something so private and intimate, I snatched my hand away, but I soothed Ezra's frown by rising onto my tiptoes and giving him a light kiss.

"I promise it'll be worth it," I said before shooting him a wink and striding away.

I only had to hope he didn't decide I wasn't worth the wait.

The bell over the door to the bakery chimed, and since it was slow enough during these colder winter months that I was the only one running the shop, I moved from the kitchen and behind the counter, ready to greet my latest customer.

I pulled up short when I found Ezra waiting for me with a massive bouquet of flowers.

"What're these?" I asked when he held them out.

"My way of asking you to go on a date. I even asked Ella what your favorite is."

I couldn't help the startled laugh that burst from my mouth.

Ella hadn't steered him wrong, and I lifted the fragrant tulips to my nose, inhaling deeply.

It was five days after Christmas. Five days since my mother had forced us into kissing under the mistletoe. Unbidden, my hand went to my mouth, lips still tingling all this time after, the memory lingering.

"Are you sure that's a good idea?"

Ezra groaned. "I've been giving you your space and time to sort your feelings out, but yes, I think it's the best idea I've ever had. I want to see where this thing goes, honey. Badly."

"What about Hansen?"

"What about him?" he asked, stepping closer. "He's not going anywhere, obviously. He's my son, and my world will always revolve around him, but it's a world that's significantly darker if it doesn't include you too."

"What happened to being just friends?"

"Fuck 'just friends.'" He moved around the counter and took the blooms from my hand, setting them aside so he could wind his arms around my waist. "Can't you see now that 'just friends' was never going to work for us? We've always been destined for more. Let me show you how good it can be."

Awfully pretty words that settled deep into my bones and suffused my body with heat.

So I replied, "Yes, Ezra Wendt. I'd be happy to go on a date with you."

The grin that broke out across his face could've melted all the snow on the streets outside with its warmth.

"Thank you," he said, leaning close and dropping a kiss on my cheek. "Meet me at the winery tomorrow night at seven."

"See you then."

With a wink, he was gone, and before the door fully closed behind him, I was already tapping out an SOS text to my sisters. I needed their help figuring out what to wear, so I planned on inviting them over tonight to plan.

As I pressed send, another message appeared in the group chat.

Three letters. The same three that started my own.

Ella: SOS

I didn't think before throwing myself into action. The beauty of being a business owner was making my own hours, and it was slow enough right now that I didn't feel an ounce of guilt for potential lost business as I clicked off the neon OPEN sign and rushed onto the slush-covered sidewalk, locking the door behind me.

I power-walked three storefronts down to the flower shop, the bell jingling above my head as I pushed inside.

"Ella?" I called. The show room was empty, but after my greeting, footsteps scuffed along the worn hardwood floor from the back.

"Brie?"

"Fanny," I said as the woman came into view, too concerned for my sister to worry about pleasantries. "Where is Ella?"

"She called in sick," Fanny said, eyes rolling briefly toward the ceiling and the apartment above where my sister lived. "She wasn't supposed to work today in the first place, but we had several funeral orders come in last night, so she offered to come down and help me this evening." Fanny held her hands up, knuckles swollen with age. "I'm not as spry as I used to be."

"She sent us an SOS text," I explained. "Is there something I should be aware of before I go up there?"

"Well...it's not really my place to pry," Fanny started. "But you know these walls are thin. I heard some arguing up there a bit ago. One of the voices was male. Then a door slammed, and footsteps pounded down the back stairs. I didn't get a good look at who it was, but..."

"Alfie," I breathed.

Fanny nodded solemnly. "You better get up there."

I reached for her and pulled her into a brief hug. The woman was an institution in Apple Blossom Bay, sort of a community grandmother, and had taken great care of my sister both as a boss and a friend. I was certain if Ella hadn't contacted us herself, Fanny would've done it eventually.

"Thank you," I said, squeezing her hands before letting her go, moving into the back of the shop and out the door then rounding through another and up the stairs to Ella's apartment.

I found Delia at the top, waiting.

"Ella," my middle sister said, following it up with a light knock. "It's Delia and Brie. Open up, please."

There was an extended silence, then a hoarse voice said, "It's unlocked."

With a shared look of concern, Delia twisted the knob and admitted us into Ella's space. Everything appeared normal. The kitchen was spotless, a vase of winter irises decorating the otherwise-bare countertop to the right. The TV was off on the left side, a blanket strewn over the back of the couch.

But beyond that came the unmistakable sounds of muffled sobs, and Delia and I crossed the small room in a heartbeat, finding Ella curled into a ball on the floor in the narrow space between her couch and coffee table.

Instantly, we shifted her upright and wrapped our arms around her. The moment we enveloped her, she cried harder, her entire body shaking. The panic in Delia's eyes surely mirrored my own, but we could do nothing except hold her, rubbing soothing circles across her back and smoothing our hands down her hair as she purged whatever emotional distress she was experiencing.

After a while, her sobs quieted to intermittent sniffles, and that's when Chloe and Amara arrived.

"What is going on?" Chloe asked, both of them waddling over to us as quickly as they could in their advanced pregnancies.

"We don't know," Delia whispered. "She hasn't said a word."

"I'm sitting right here," Ella groused, and my shoulders relaxed fractionally at the irritation in her voice. If she was scolding us, she wasn't totally lost to her pain.

"We've been here for a half hour, El," I told her softly, "and that's the first thing you've said."

"I'm sorry," she breathed, straightening so my and Delia's arms fell away from her. "I...fuck, I've been so stupid."

"What's going on?" Chloe asked, dropping herself onto the couch behind Ella, who then leaned on Chloe's legs.

"Alf—" Ella seemed to choke on the word, eyes once again welling with tears. She squeezed them shut enough to expel the liquid and gave herself a little shake, clearing her throat. Her voice was flat when she spoke again. "Alfie dumped me."

I gasped, Chloe and Amara both cursed softly, and Delia jumped to her feet, moving toward the door.

"I'll kill him," she said, her hand reaching for the knob.

"No!" Ella said, expression turning pleading. "Please, Lia. Just...let it go."

"He hurt you," our middle sister said, venom in her tone and anger flashing in her whiskey-colored eyes. "He at least deserves to have his dick cut off."

Ella snorted a laugh. "I'm not gonna argue that," she said.

Delia's eyes narrowed, and Chloe and Amara straightened, as if they'd all come to a realization that had gone right over my head.

"How many?" Amara asked softly.

"At least three that I know of," Ella said.

"That little fucking weasel," Delia spat.

"Now *I'm* ready to kill him," Chloe said, rubbing a hand over her womb. "Mama Bear is pissed."

"This one too," Amara said, mimicking Chloe.

God, it was still so strange to see not one, but two of my sisters pregnant and due so close together. Roughly five weeks separated their due dates, and all of us were so excited to be welcoming two little peanuts into the family at once.

But circling back to the matter at hand, I said, "Someone tell me what I'm missing here."

Ella turned to me, her green eyes vibrant with pain. "He cheated on me, Bee. Repeatedly."

I gasped again. "How did you find out?"

"Got a few 'hey girlie' Instagram DMs. When I confronted him about it, he flew off the handle, saying I didn't trust him and just spewing all kinds of bullshit. Then, he told me he couldn't be with me anymore and left."

"Fuck, El," Delia said, moving back into the small living room and sitting on the floor beside her. "I'm so sorry."

Ella gave her a sad smile. "I'm sad, of course," she said. "But I'm more pissed off than anything. I gave that man—no, that *child*—so much of myself. For three years, I suffered through strained relationships with all of you, put up with him repeatedly talking shit about Mom and Dad and the family business, let him belittle me and make me feel horrible about myself. And for what? For this?" She gestured to herself, to the ratty, oversized band tee and black, threadbare sweatpants hanging off her frame.

"I fucking hate that I wasted so much time on him. Time I'll never get back."

I was struck then by the contrasts of our situations. Ella had spent three years with a piece of garbage who had dimmed the natural, free-spirited light she'd exhibited all her life to the point where we hardly saw it anymore. Meanwhile, I'd been running from the man who wanted nothing more than to foster my own light, to be by my side and support me in whatever I wanted to do.

Going from the high of Ezra asking me on a date, finally putting into motion this relationship we'd once tasted and now wanted more of, to sitting here with my sister as she fell apart was jarring to say the least.

"That's definitely a tough pill to swallow," Chloe said. "But look at it this way: you're still young, you're hot, and now you've got all the freedom in the world to find a man who will worship the ground you walk on, exactly as you deserve."

Ella gave her a weak smile. "I just don't know if I'm cut out for dating."

Delia rolled her eyes. "We didn't mean right now," she said. "You only just got rid of that douchebag. But when you're ready...there will be someone out there for you."

"You really think so?"

"I know so," Delia confirmed with a confident nod. "In fact...I have an idea."

She trailed off, and me and my other sisters groaned.

Ella held up a hand. "I love you, Lia, but...no."

"No, what?"

"Whatever you're thinking, the answer is no. I just got out of a three-year relationship that left me shredded emotionally. I need time before you decide you want to meddle."

"Me? Meddle?" Delia asked, placing her hand over her heart in mock affront. "Well, I never..."

"You literally do it all the time," I said. "And now you've rubbed off on Mom!"

Delia's gaze swung to me, mischief dancing in her eyes as always. "How'd that work out for you, Baby Bee? You and Ezra get your smooch on?"

I folded my arms over my chest. "I don't kiss and tell."

"Except for the times you *have* kissed him and told us," Amara pointed out.

I glared at my second oldest sister. "No one asked you."

"The mistletoe clearly worked its magic," Delia crowed gleefully. "You can't mess with that kind of karma."

I knew I wasn't getting out of this without giving them something, but before I opened my mouth, Chloe piped up. "Oh, something happened alright. Did you guys see the text she sent us?"

I winced, hoping they'd missed it. I should've known better than to think anything would get past Chloe. She was a romance novelist, for crying out loud. She lived for stuff like this.

Each of my sisters withdrew their phones and read the text I'd sent at the same time Ella had.

Amara looked up at me, mouth open in surprise. "He asked you out?"

I nodded, unable to fight off the grin that overtook my face. "Tomorrow night for NYE."

"Ugh," Ella groaned. "Thanks for reminding me. Alfie and I

were supposed to go to a party, and instead, I'm going to sit here crying and marathoning Anne Hathaway."

I couldn't help but choke on a laugh, and all four of my sisters glared daggers at me.

"I'm sorry!" I said, raising my hands in surrender. "It's just... When did we decide Anne Hathaway was the cure for a broken heart?"

There was a beat of silence before we all burst out laughing, and though Ella didn't stop crying, it morphed from sad to mirthful quickly.

"Anne Hathaway is a national treasure," Ella said, wiping the tears from her face.

"You're not wrong," I agreed, my sisters nodding with me. "But that's not the point. Now that this happened"—I gestured to Ella—"I'm not even sure I should go."

My sisters' dissension was instantaneous.

Ella wagged her finger in my face. "Don't use me as an excuse." With something other than her pain to focus on, color returned to her face, and I supposed I could be grateful for that at least.

"You need us," I replied lamely.

Ella rolled her eyes. "You came when I called and reminded me that Alfie is a jackass who doesn't deserve my tears. Am I still going to cry? Yes. But truthfully, he and I have been done for a while. He was just the one brave enough to set us free."

I couldn't argue with her, not as each of my sisters and I shared knowing glances. We'd all noticed that Alfie hadn't been around as much the last month or so, and for that, we'd all been grateful. We wanted to support Ella in any and everything, but her relationship with him was something we'd struggled to get behind.

I hadn't forgotten the night we'd gone to Birdie's and he'd fought with my father *and* Owen, who owned the place. Then afterward, after all the drama had gone down with that crazed fan at Lawless, the way he'd shown up and thrown a fit until Ella had left with him... It hadn't sat right with me or Delia. He'd made her cry more often than not, and I never understood what she saw in him.

Now wasn't the time to ask—in fact, I'd be happy never to discuss the rat again.

"You guys really think I should go?" I asked softly.

They all chorused their agreement, and Ella reached out for my hand.

"Just because I'm unhappy right now doesn't mean you have to live down in the dumps with me. This is your chance, Bee. You've been gone for that man since the moment you laid eyes on him. I think it's time to let yourself be happy."

Chloe, Amara, and Delia made gestures and sounds of agreement, and tears sprang to my eyes as I studied each of them in turn. I was more grateful than ever for them. We'd had our ups and downs as teenagers and in our early twenties, but they were my best friends and I wouldn't trade them for the world.

"Then what do you say we head over to my place so you guys can help me pick out something to wear?"

I grinned as they squealed and tackled me, the five of us landing in a heap on the floor.

chapter 30
Brie

"Ezra?" I called when I unlocked the door to the winery and stepped inside.

Instantly, I was cocooned in the coziness of the building. Outside, a storm was brewing, and I was grateful for my all-wheel drive keeping me from sliding into the ditch on the slick roads on my way up. In fact, the snow was coming down so thickly, I'd almost called Ezra and cancelled.

Thankfully, not because of Ella, who had been adamant I keep the date, but because travel conditions were growing treacherous.

But I wanted to see him, so I braved the blizzard.

Despite the fact that no Def Leppard greeted me from the direction of the kitchen this time, the sense of déjà vu was as forceful as a gut punch.

On this same day three years before, I'd arrived here for what was supposed to be a simple afternoon of cooking with the super-hot new chef.

What I ended up with was so much more than that.

"In here!" he responded, and I followed his voice to the dining room.

I gasped when I turned the corner and the scene unfolded

before me.

The house lights were dimmed, and what seemed like hundreds of candles glowed around the space, atop each of the tables and along the mantle, above the crackling fire lit in the hearth. In the center stood Ezra, alongside a table topped with two domed dishes and a bottle of white wine.

"How is it possible you've gotten more beautiful since yesterday?" he asked.

My cheeks heated, and I was grateful for the low lights hiding the worst of it. My outfit wasn't anything fancy—a simple black wool sweater and velvet skirt set I paired with tights and black satin pumps, minimal makeup, and a loose fishtail braid in my hair. I felt impossibly sexy, and by the way Ezra's gaze raked over my body from head to foot, I knew he thought the same.

"You're just saying that."

"I'm actually not," he assured me. "You're the most stunning, most astonishing woman I've ever laid eyes on, Brie."

"Well, you're not so bad yourself, Chef."

He crossed the room to greet me with a peck on the cheek then grabbed my hand and led me to my chair.

"What is all this?" I asked.

Once we were seated, he said, "It didn't make sense for us to go to some fancy restaurant when I'm the best chef I know."

I grinned, not bothering to refute him. His food was without a doubt the best I'd ever tasted, and I found his confidence in himself sexy as hell.

"So what did you make for me?"

Ezra leaned across the table and, with a flourish, lifted the cover from my plate.

"Your meatballs!" I exclaimed with a laugh. "Finally!"

"You did demand I feed them to you one day," he reminded me. "So your wish is my command."

"And I'm assuming these are your infamous glazed dill butter potatoes?" I asked, pointing at the thinly sliced spuds fanned out on one side of my dish.

"And roasted veggies," he confirmed. "So dig in."

Excitedly, I picked up my fork and sliced a meatball in half, dragging it through a bit of the gravy he'd drizzled on top before bringing it to my lips. The scent of fragrant herbs and seasonings invaded my senses, and I popped the bite into my mouth. The second I closed my lips around it, I moaned.

Something so simple had no right being that delicious. As I chewed, the flavors exploded on my tongue, and I closed my eyes as I savored the complexity. The firmness of the meatball combined with the creaminess of the gravy was the most perfect pairing, and I wanted to eat these every day for the rest of my life.

"Well?" Ezra asked when I opened my eyes, his own plate still untouched.

"That's the best meatball I've ever had."

I'd offered Ezra plenty of compliments over the years, and I knew thousands of other people had as well, but I'd never seen him blush with the praise like he did then. The knowledge that I was responsible had pride and satisfaction rising in my chest.

God, he was beautiful. I thought so every time I looked at him. With his brown hair that was longer on top and swept over his head in waves, brown eyes like pools of melted chocolate, square jaw, straight nose, and high cheekbones—well, he was downright pretty. Though he shaved daily, dark facial hair constantly shaded his cheeks and chin, the promise of the beard I was certain he could grow but had never seen. It gave him a slight air of ruggedness that truthfully had my panties wet from a simple cursory glance in his direction.

Assured that I was enjoying myself, Ezra dove into his own food, and we chatted about nothing and everything—but mostly, we talked about my plans for the bakery for the next four months while business slowed to a glacial crawl.

"Well, thankfully," I started, licking the final bit of gravy off my fork in a way that had Ezra's eyes darkening, the chocolate depths almost wholly overtaken by his darker pupils. "I don't *need* the shop revenue to survive, but my online store will stay open, so I'll still be making an income from that. I was actually approached by the community center to host a few baking classes, so I'll have that to fill my time as well."

"Will you host those at the bakery?" he asked, his voice a low rasp that had goosebumps skittering across my skin. We weren't talking about anything intimate, and yet, his entire demeanor had shifted.

Clearly, he was hoping the evening would head in that direction, and when he shifted his leg out and brushed my calf with the toe of his shoe, I was hard pressed to find a reason why it shouldn't.

"Yes," I breathed, and my heart rate kicked up. "There's plenty of room in the kitchen to host ten or fifteen people."

"That's great," he said absently. "Will you share a recipe from Granny's cookbook?"

"Of course. Gotta keep those family traditions alive." I gnawed on my bottom lip, holding back my deepest desire, unsure if speaking it into the world would somehow bite me in the ass later.

"What aren't you saying?" he asked, narrowing his eyes on my mouth.

I sighed, hating and loving how well he knew me in equal measure.

"I have this dream…" I trailed off. I dropped my voice to barely above a whisper. "I want to write a cookbook."

Ezra blinked, surprised, but then his face broke into a broad grin. "You'd write the best damn cookbook out there," he said firmly.

"You think?"

"I *know*."

"I just…have all these ideas running around." I tapped my temple. "And I've implemented some of them at the bakery, but… Is it greedy of me to want to expand?"

"Of course not. You've worked your ass off to make that bakery a success in this small town, and the take-and-bake mixes were a truly ingenious idea. I know the people across the world who have purchased them would love the chance to own a full book of your recipes."

"And Granny's. I couldn't do it without her."

"Well, of course not," he agreed, reaching across the table for my hand. "And I love that she's been able to give you something so special even though she's no longer here."

"Me too." I gave him a watery smile, my nose stinging with emotion at how easily he accepted this was something I was going to do, how quick he was to support me.

This man—I didn't deserve him, but I'd spend forever proving my worth anyway.

"What would you call it?"

I grinned, loving that he knew me well enough to understand I'd already had that figured out.

"'The Granny Smith Collection: Traditional Recipes with Modern Flair,'" I said proudly. "Or something like that. But I know I want Granny to be the headline."

"Even though you're doing all the work?" Ezra asked.

"But I didn't do all the work. Probably seventy-five percent of my recipes are ones I've taken from her cookbook and updated. Honoring her is the only way I'll do it."

"Fair enough."

I dropped my gaze to the table and added, "We could...work on it together. Make it a full-fledged cookbook instead of just pastry recipes."

He was silent for so long, I eventually hazarded a glance, bracing myself for his reaction.

His mouth popped open comically in shock. "You mean that?"

"Of course I do. You're the best chef I know, and people everywhere would love your recipes as much as mine."

"I've never given it much thought," he said. "But maybe that was because I had too much other shit going on that kept me from pursuing that sort of dream." He squeezed my fingers. "Can I think about it?"

"Of course you can. Take all the time you need."

Ezra grinned. "I don't deserve you."

"Funny," I said, matching his expression, "I was just thinking the same about you."

Ezra hummed in response, his tongue darting out to trace across his bottom lip, distracting me. But I wasn't ready to pop this bubble—though I was practically vibrating in anticipation of where I knew the night would lead. Still, I wanted more time to enjoy this moment, reminiscent of us chatting on the phone but being able to reach out and touch him if I felt like it.

"What do *you* plan to do with your time off?" I asked.

"A little of this, a little of that," he said noncommittally, and I groaned.

"C'mon, Chef. You can do better than that."

His eyes met mine then, their chocolatey depths turning molten in the candlelight. "You promise you won't laugh?"

"I would never laugh at you."

"I want to start a community garden."

I blinked in surprise, which quickly morphed into genuine excitement. "Ezra, I *love* that idea."

"Yeah?" he asked, still unsure.

"*Yeah*," I promised. "The community would love that, and it'd be a great way to teach kids about the benefits of growing their own food, as well as the hard work that goes into it."

"That's exactly what I've been thinking!" he exclaimed. "At Thanksgiving, I mentioned to Liam about setting up an appointment with him and Amara, and that'll be happening sometime after the new year. We can't exactly move on construction until the snow melts and the ground thaws, but I want to get a jump on design and ordering seeds and starters. Dad and Jay are excited to contribute to the project as well."

"Sounds like you've got it all figured out, but...you should ask Ella for help."

"I should?"

"She's...Alfie dumped her." I knew Ella wouldn't want me to blast her business to everyone, but this was Ezra. I knew my secrets were safe with him. "So she's struggling right now. And it's slow at the flower shop in the winter too, so I bet she'd love to help. Plants are kind of her thing, after all."

"What if I wanted you to help me?"

I shrugged, my insides warming at the thought of working on such a project with him. It would be a great addition to the community, and I fully planned on leaving my mark on it. I envisioned strawberry and rhubarb plants, chives and mint, but I wanted my sister to have something to distract her from her heartache, and there was nothing that girl loved more than having her hands covered in dirt.

"I'd be happy to assist, but you should also ask Ella."

"Consider it done," he said, and I grinned.

"Thank you."

"I hated that Alfie tool anyway."

I snorted. "We all did. I'm sad she's hurting, but I know this is for the best."

Ezra only hummed in response, his thumb drawing lazy circles along the back of my hand.

"So...my dad is watching Hansen tonight," he said softly. "I mean, he lives with us, so that's a nightly thing, but what I'm saying is, he's not expecting me home."

"Do you want to get out of here?" I blurted, ready to follow the path this night was headed down right until the very end.

Before Ezra could respond, my phone let out a loud alert—the one from my weather app. I withdrew it from my coat pocket and read the message on the screen, then glanced up at Ezra with wide eyes.

"What?" he asked, brow creasing. "Is everything okay?"

"Everything is fine, but apparently, the storm is pretty bad."

Ezra frowned as I rose from the table and made my way toward the doors that led out to the patio. On the wall to the left was a switch that controlled the exterior lights, and when I flipped it, Ezra let out a low curse.

While we'd been wrapped up in our delicious meal and good conversation, the snow had continued to fall. In addition to what we'd already gotten, a few feet more had fallen, the mountain of powder now reaching about halfway up the doors. I didn't need to look out in the parking lot to know both my Bronco and Ezra's Subaru were buried.

I gave him a sheepish smile. "I don't think we're going anywhere tonight."

Ezra reached for my hand, lacing our fingers together and squeezing reassuringly. I wasn't scared or concerned that I had to spend the night here, but I *was* pleased I wouldn't have to do it alone.

"Where are we going to sleep?" he asked then waggled his eyebrows suggestively. "Or not."

I let out a girlish giggle at his ridiculousness. "I have an idea," I said, pulling him out of the dining room and back toward the lobby.

All evening, I'd been giddy, basking in the glow of Ezra's attention. But that effervescence in my chest increased, as though a host of butterflies had taken up residence in my stomach and their little wing beats made my heart pump faster as I led him toward my favorite family secret. Very few people were granted access to the knowledge, and I couldn't wait to share it with Ezra.

"The offices?" he asked in confusion.

I merely smiled and shook my head. Since the door that led to the Delatou, Inc. corporate offices was off the lobby, it wasn't a bad guess, but it wasn't where I was headed. Instead, I beelined for a door on the opposite side. The keypad to access what lay beyond was carefully concealed behind a panel flush with the wall. Someone would have to be paying extremely close attention to discover it, and even then, without the code, they'd never make it through.

I flicked the panel out of the way and punched in the code less than ten people in the world knew. When the lock clicked free, I pulled the door open.

"After you," I said to Ezra.

His expression was dubious as he asked, "You're not taking me down here to kill me, are you?"

"Absolutely not," I promised him. "If I wanted to kill you, I would've done it years ago."

He barked out a laugh and reached for me, pulling me flush against his body and pressing one hard kiss to my mouth. Then he pulled away and descended the staircase into the darkness.

chapter 31
Ezra

"WHAT IS THIS PLACE?" I asked Brie quietly, afraid to raise my voice and rouse any creepy crawly things potentially lurking in the darkness at the foot of the stairs. Not to mention, the temperature dropped the lower I went, which didn't help quell my anxiety that she was about to attempt murder.

It seemed like the perfect place to hide a body until the ground on the vineyard thawed and she could bury me out there, where no one would ever locate my remains.

Instead of answering, Brie pressed against my back and reached past me. A moment later, the space illuminated, and I audibly gasped.

Moving deeper into the cellar, I spun in a slow circle until I once again faced Brie. "How have I been working here for nearly four years and never knew this place existed?"

"It's a family secret," she said. "Well...and Cal knows about it, but that's a story for a different time."

"And now me," I said, stabbing a finger into my chest. "Now I know about it too."

Brie grinned. "You do. I trust you to keep it between us, or we'll be forced to change the code again."

"Again?" I asked, raising a brow.

"Delia brought a high school boy she'd been...*seeing* down here once. They'd been drunk and young and stupid, and he'd shattered one of the bottles from Great-Grandpa Delatou's first ever batch of wine. So Daddy forbade her from seeing him again, banned him permanently from Delatou property, and immediately changed the code."

I whistled low. I understood being an overprotective parent—my sole purpose in life was to shield Hansen from the worst of human nature, to ensure he wasn't exposed to the darkest parts of people—but I also thought it was different with a father and son. The father-daughter relationship wasn't one I'd ever understand.

"Your dad is terrifying."

Brie snorted, turning her back to me as she paced along the shelves, running her hands over the bottles displayed there like trophies, some of the labels yellowed and curling at the edges with age.

"You think that's bad? I lost my virginity in the backseat of the limo at my senior prom. Ella, the only one of my sisters still living at home at the time, spilled my plans for the evening to my parents."

I grimaced, already sensing what was coming. "He didn't."

"Oh, he did. Showed up at the Villa, pulled my date from the backseat by his hair, and threatened to beat him with the baseball bat he was brandishing if he ever touched me again."

"Oh my god," I said, hand flying to my mouth. "That's...extreme."

She simply nodded. "I was so embarrassed, I didn't show my face at school for the rest of the year. It was the first and only time I let my dad throw our family name and money around to influence the school into letting me complete my last few weeks of high school remotely."

I shook my head, a chuckle escaping me.

"I asked him for his blessing, you know," I told her.

"You *what*?" Brie exclaimed, whirling toward me, her fists coming to rest on the gentle swells of her hips.

I hitched a shoulder up in a half shrug. "At Thanksgiving. The guys got to talking about fixing up Christmas dinner, and your dad mentioned how happy he was to have help for once. One thing led to another, Cal opened his big mouth—"

"He does that sometimes," Brie said with a chuckle.

"—and I told your dad I'm crazy about you and wanted the chance to pursue it."

"What did he say?"

"Told me we're both adults and don't need his permission but that I had his blessing anyway."

Brie sighed, a blissful smile spreading across her face. "I love that man."

"He loves you too," I assured her. "That's why he gets a little crazy."

"I guess as a parent yourself, you'd know firsthand."

I nodded. "I'm going to do everything I can to make sure Hansen grows up without knowing the pain I've endured. I hate more than anything that he already understands what it's like to lose a parent, exactly like I did, but luckily for him, he gets to grow up with the same role model and teacher I had. Between me and my dad, we shouldn't screw him up too badly."

Brie stepped closer to me, sliding her arms around my waist

and tipping her head back to look up at me. "That little boy is lucky to have you as a father, Ez. You're doing amazing with him."

I took a deep breath and exhaled slowly, trying to fight off the emotion suddenly clogging my throat.

"I try," I croaked eventually, and she rose onto her tiptoes to press a kiss to the underside of my jaw.

She grabbed my hand and pulled me deeper into the cellar. The walls were exposed brick, and though the space was dry and cool, a slight scent of softly decaying earthiness hung in the air.

"Did you know my great-grandpa opened this place during Prohibition?" Brie asked as she led us through another doorway and down a hallway. No modern updates had been made beyond the installation of electricity, and sconces dotted the walls at regular intervals. Beneath our feet, the floor was hard, packed dirt, loose bits floating upward with every step, turning the air around us hazy.

"I did not," I replied, curious where she was going. She didn't actually expect us to sleep down here, did she?

Before I could ask, we reached the end of the line, where our path was blocked by a solid brick wall.

Brie turned to me with a wicked, mischievous grin. "He had to get creative with storing his products. Prohibition ended seven years after this place became operational, so for nearly the first decade of business, my family smuggled wine from right here to much of the Midwest."

My eyes widened in shock.

"Yep," Brie said proudly. "Chateau Delatou was built on a foundation of criminal activity. We may be on the right side of the law these days, but I like to think some of that recklessness still lives on in me and my sisters."

From what I'd seen in my years around the family, it definitely did.

"I don't understand. How did they operate as a winery without being able to...sell wine?"

"Great-Grandpa ran it as one of those old-fashioned soda shoppes. Though, I guess back then, it wouldn't have been old-fashioned," she added with a giggle.

"Well, while that's an interesting piece of Delatou family history, it doesn't explain what we're doing down here."

Wordlessly, Brie reached for the final sconce on the wall, gripped its base, and pulled.

A moment later, after a loud *thunk* and much lower, ominous creaking, a crack appeared in the brick wall before us.

"Smuggler tunnels," I breathed.

"Smuggler tunnels," she confirmed with a smirk. "You wouldn't believe the trouble my sisters and I got into down here as kids. We'd climb on each other's shoulders to reach the sconce and go crazy."

"Oh, I'm sure I can imagine," I said with a laugh. "Where does it lead?"

Brie pressed a palm flat on the door and pushed it further open. "Follow me and find out."

Then she disappeared beyond the door, the darkness swallowing up her body almost instantly.

I could do nothing but trail after her, curiosity dragging me forward.

Emboldened by the darkness that descended once I crossed the threshold and the door shut behind me, I reached out blindly for Brie. As my hand connected with what I assumed was her arm, she stilled, and I used that moment to locate her hips and latch on.

I pushed her backward until her body collided with something hard.

"Sorry," I whispered.

"What are you doing?"

"This," I said, then dropped my mouth to hers.

Without the ability to see, I relied on sound and sensation to guide me as I moved my lips against hers. The soft mewling that came from her throat, which had a chuckle rumbling through my chest. The way her hands moved into my hair, tugging, dragging me impossibly closer. I moved my hands off her hips and groped around on the thing behind her, pleased to discover it was a wine barrel sitting upright. Gripping her around the backs of her thighs, I lifted her onto it, putting her at the perfect height to press my hard angles against her soft curves, my aching cock coming to rest perfectly against her stomach.

The pressure had sparks bursting behind my closed eyelids.

"Fuck," I growled, moving from her lips to trail a path of open-mouthed kisses across her jaw and neck. "I need to get you naked immediately."

Through heavy breaths, Brie said, "Let's get out of here. Then I'm yours all night."

Without another word, I reluctantly pulled my hands from her body, though I grabbed one of hers instead. Hopping off the barrel, she retrieved her phone from the ground and directed the flashlight ahead, navigating us toward our destination.

Less than two minutes later, we came to another hidden door, and when we stepped out, we found ourselves standing in an unfinished basement.

"Where are we?" I asked. "Is this someone's house?"

"Not anymore," Brie said, not offering anything else as she pulled me toward an ascending staircase. At the top, she punched in yet another code, and we emerged into a large, modern foyer. To my left was a heavy oak door, the wind howling beyond. To my right was a hallway. Brie moved to the wall and pressed a rocker switch, flipping on the can lights in the ceiling.

Stepping to the center of the room, she held out her arms and said, "Welcome to the Villa."

chapter 32
Brie

"HOLY SHIT," EZRA BREATHED. "There's a fucking smuggler's tunnel from the winery to *here*?"

I grinned, pleased I'd managed to surprise him. The tunnels—and the fact that my family had been smugglers—was a well-kept Delatou secret. I wasn't even sure if any of my sisters had told their significant others.

Well, okay, that was a lie. I *knew* Ella hadn't told Alfie, mostly because Dad threatened to disown her if she did.

"Smugglers had to get creative back in those days, you know?" I said, starting the story the same way my dad had when he'd passed it along to me and my sisters. I moved to one of the walls and turned the heat up, grateful my parents hadn't yet gotten around to winterizing the house. "To anyone paying close attention, particularly law enforcement watching for these types of things, it would've been strange for Great-Grandpa Andreas and his buddies to be seen entering and leaving the winery grounds at all hours.

"But having guests come over for a party and covertly sneaking cases of wine out that were then driven off when the guest left with no one the wiser?" I grinned. "Genius. So that's how the tunnels came to be, and when Prohibition ended, though they

309

weren't necessary anymore, my ancestors decided to keep them open and operational."

Ezra crossed the room and scooped me into his arms.

"Worked pretty damn well for us tonight," he said against my lips.

"That it did. Now what do you say, Chef? Wanna take me upstairs to my old room and ravish me?"

"Fuck yeah." He didn't even set me on my feet before spinning toward the staircase and taking the steps two at a time to the second-floor landing.

"Which one?" he asked, groaning when I bent and nipped at his earlobe.

"Second on the left."

My sisters and I had spent every summer growing up in this house. Once school was out for the year, Mom and Dad would pack us up and haul us up here, getting away from the city life and letting us run rampant through the vineyards for three months while they tackled tourist season. When they'd built the new house on the point, selling the one in Traverse City and leaving this one behind for good, we turned it into an Airbnb for guests. It was within walking distance to the winery and the grounds, and we offered a shuttle that drove people into town and the city for meals and shopping.

But the room Ezra walked us into, with its white walls, grey-toned hardwood floors, and massive bed topped with a fluffy, white down comforter, would always be mine. No matter how different it looked or how many strangers called it their home away from home for a few days.

"You ever kiss a boy in this room?" Ezra asked as he dumped

me on the bed.

"Never," I promised him, and he knelt on the mattress, shuffling until he was between my thighs. "How about you change that?"

Ezra folded himself over me, capturing my mouth in a blistering kiss that I felt in every single cell of my body. My nerve endings hummed when I was near him, like my particles were all charged with energy. I wanted him to keep touching me forever, to permanently keep me in that place of bliss.

He broke the kiss only long enough to reach behind his neck and tug his sweater and the tee over his head, revealing his smooth, pale skin and the lean muscles beneath. My hands reached for him, roaming his flesh, and I grinned when goosebumps rose in my wake.

"Your touch," Ezra whispered. "Fuck, I've missed it, honey."

"I've missed *you*," I responded, punctuating my words by curling my palm around his nape and tugging his lips back to mine. We lost ourselves in that kiss for untold moments, in our tongues sliding together, in teeth against lips and errant hums of pleasure.

"Too many clothes," he said absently when he skated his palms down my sides, over my own sweater.

Even in the dimness, the room only illuminated from the massive full moon and the lights filtering in from the foyer, I could clearly see every plane and hollow of his face. His beautiful chocolate eyes had gone as dark as the night sky flecked with stars. Sparkling and glowing just for me.

I sat up so he could free me of the wool, and since I hadn't worn a bra, a moment later, I was entirely topless, my nipples pebbling in the chilly room. Then he bent and captured one of those tight peaks with his lips, laving one with his tongue before moving onto the other. He chased his mouth with his thumb, brushing it over my flesh until I was writhing, my pulse thrumming incessantly in my clit.

"Need you now," I murmured as he moved north, trailing kisses up the column of my throat until he was once again a breath away.

"You have me."

His hand reached to my hair, toying with the end of my braid. With a gentleness that made my heart ache, he unwound the tie from the end, slipping it onto his wrist, then slowly unweaving the strands. When it was fully unraveled, he dove his fingers in and massaged my scalp. I moaned at how good his strong fingers felt against my roots.

He was always taking care of me, always making me feel cherished and wanted and desired in a way I'd never experienced before.

And god, I half loved him for it.

"Need you inside," I whined, trying to distract myself from *that* dangerous thought by reaching for his belt and deftly undoing it and his pants, tugging them down his hips. He backed away from the bed to kick out of them while I stripped out of my skirt, tights, and panties.

Once again, Ezra stilled, watching me. Despite the low temperature in the room, my skin heated with his perusal, his eyes branding my skin, warming me from the inside.

"You are so fucking beautiful, it almost hurts to look at you."

"I love the way you look at me," I said, reclining on my elbows and dropping my legs wide, more brazen than I'd ever been before. Well, more so than I'd ever been with anyone but Ezra. This man—he made me unhinged. Bold. Out of my mind with need.

"How do I look at you?"

"Like you're a man starved and I'm your favorite meal."

Ezra grinned, his teeth flashing in the dark room. "I've dreamed about this," he said as he climbed back onto the bed. But he didn't move over me. Instead, he stopped a few feet shy and flopped onto his stomach.

Putting him eye level with my pussy.

"About what, exactly?" I asked, reclining once again, a surprised exhale leaving me when he reached out and trailed a finger through my slit.

"About having you again. About tasting this honey sweet cunt. About your perfect pussy wrapped around my cock." His hand came up to cup one of my breasts, and I grabbed the other, both of us rolling my nipples between our fingers. The pressure and touch was woefully inadequate and too far away from where I needed it. I squirmed, trying to bring myself closer to him, to get his mouth on me, and he chuckled darkly.

"So fucking needy," he said.

"Touch me, Ez."

"What's the magic word?"

"Please."

"Please, *what*?"

Realization dawned, and my toes curled against the sheets as I said, "Please, Chef."

Ezra rewarded me with a long, slow lick from back to front, his flattened tongue hitting all the sweet spots along the way. God, it was too good. Too perfect. Too much of everything I'd been missing, of everything we'd denied ourselves.

I gripped a handful of his hair, holding him to me.

"You taste so fucking good, honey. Like your namesake. I want to fucking drown in you."

"More, Ez."

"You want my fingers? My cock?"

"All of it."

"All in good time, baby." He shifted so he could smooth his hands up my thighs, pressing them back, opening me wider. I was more vulnerable than I'd ever been in my life, but I'd never felt safer. With this man, it was okay for me to fall apart. I was encouraged, even, to be my truest, most confident self—not the youngest of five sisters who often got babied or lost in the shuffle, but a desirable adult woman who knew what she wanted and asked for it.

He only stared at me, studying me. Revered me like I was a deity and he was simply worshiping at my altar.

Then, at last, he dove into his feast.

I expected him to take his time after all his teasing and pretty words, but Ezra surprised me by eating me with gusto, by lapping at my pussy like it was ice cream melting on a hot day. By unceremoniously shoving two fingers in me, his chuckle vibrating against my swollen, sensitive flesh in the most delicious way when I let out a yelp of surprise.

He drove me higher and higher, his fingers pumping in and out, curling against that innermost spot as his tongue flicked relentlessly against my clit.

And when he sealed his lips around that bundle of nerves and sucked, then added a third finger—I blew apart with a scream, my entire body quaking endlessly as we rode it out together.

At last, I stitched myself back together and opened my eyes, finding Ezra hovering over me, a self-satisfied smirk on his face.

"You are so fucking sexy when you come."

"You should make me do it again."

Ezra barked out a laugh and sat back on his heels, his hands on my inner thighs, absently smoothing his palms against my skin, deliciously abraded by his stubble. I sat up to watch him, my eyes straying right to his cock, thick, impossibly hard, the tip leaking precum. It seemed to pulse under my gaze, and I reached for him. He hissed sharply through his teeth as I closed my fist around him, pumping him slowly, mesmerized by his silken feel over the impossibly hard flesh beneath.

"You gonna take a taste?" he asked.

"I actually have a confession to make," I said as I stroked him.

"What's that?"

"I've never actually given head."

"Brie," he groaned. "You're killing me."

I shrugged and giggled. "I just want all our cards on the table here." I paused, and my voice had dropped to barely above a whisper when I spoke again. "What if I'm bad at it?"

The idea thrilled me, of having his cock in my mouth, of letting him pump into my throat and spill down it. But it worried me too. What if I hurt him? What if I sucked at sucking?

Gripping my waist, he lifted me and settled me so I straddled his lap. Cupping my face in his hands, he forced me to look at him as he said, "There is *nothing* you could do to me that I won't like. I could get off watching you run around your kitchen, baking all your delectable treats. Tell me you understand that."

"Really?" I asked as I continued to explore his flesh.

"*Really*," he assured me, then gritted out, "You keep doing that, and I'm going to come before I ever get inside you."

I didn't let go but brushed a kiss to the underside of his jaw. "And we can't have that."

Ezra shifted me slightly so his broad head slipped through lips, my orgasm coating him, and he reached between us to spread it down his length.

"I haven't been with…" I croaked out, my words dying in my mouth, unsure what prompted the outburst. I cleared my throat noisily before I tried again. "I haven't been with anyone since you."

I expected him to, at the very least, show some level of shock or surprise. Instead, his arms banded tighter around me, and with one of his lopsided grins, he said, "You been saving yourself for me, honey?"

"So what if I was?" I shot back, the words braver than I felt with heat rising to my face.

"Lucky for you," Ezra said, swiping his thumb along my cheekbone, "I haven't been with anyone since you either."

"There's just one problem."

Ezra stilled, eyes wide with panic. "Yeah?"

"I'm not currently on birth control, so we're going to have to use a condom."

"Why?" he blurted then slapped a hand over his mouth, clearly not having meant to ask. If there was one thing I knew about Ezra, it was that he believed women's bodies were theirs to do with as they wished. It was my decision not to be on birth control, and I knew he wasn't questioning that.

"I never went back on it after the miscarriage, knowing I wouldn't be having sex with anyone again for a good, long while. I was terrified of intimacy, of giving anyone that kind of access to me again.

"Except you," I continued, pressing my lips lightly to his. "You make me feel safe in a way I never thought I'd find. There's no one but you who gets me like this."

"Ever?"

"*Forever*," I corrected.

Ezra simply stared at me, wide-eyed. "I am in awe of you, Brie Delatou. You're the strongest woman I know, and I promise I'm going to work my ass off every day to prove I'm worthy of the trust you've given me."

He captured my mouth again, and against his lips I said, "I know you will."

With kisses to my eyelids, the tip of my nose, my cheeks, jaw, everywhere he could reach, he asked, "Are there condoms here?"

I giggled as I crawled off his lap and over to the bedside table. As I pulled the drawer open, Ezra's palm landed on one of my cheeks in a playful smack, and I arched my back, a surprised moan leaving me. I hadn't expected to...enjoy that so much.

"You like that?" he asked, sounding as surprised as I felt.

I glanced over my shoulder at him as I felt around in the dark for the box of condoms I knew the housekeeping staff stocked every guest room with. "Do it again and find out."

Ezra reached for me, settling both palms on my ass and massaging the cheeks before lifting one and bringing it down, harder than the first time. I moaned again. The contact stung, a handprint surely blooming on my skin, and my pussy clenched, needing to be filled by him.

"Fuck, Brie. That's so hot. Who knew my girl liked to be spanked?"

At last, I found what I was looking for and crawled back to him, once again straddling his thighs, his cock jutting between us.

"I like trying new things with you," I told him before ripping the condom wrapper open. I withdrew the rubber and pinched the tip then slowly rolled it down Ezra's length.

When I finished, his breath left him in a *whoosh*, and I giggled.

"Lift up," he said, scooping his palms around the backs of my thighs and lifting me slightly. "Put it in."

I grabbed his cock, unable to resist toying with him as I slid the tip through my lips, coating the condom in my desire. Then I fit it against my entrance and sank down.

"Too big." I dropped my head to Ezra's shoulder as I met resistance on the way down, bracing my knees alongside his thighs. He was massive, and it had been so long.

"It'll fit, honey. Just go slow."

"Fuck," I breathed as I took him a few more inches.

"Goddamn, woman. I love when you swear."

I inhaled sharply through my nose and took him a bit deeper, then further until I impaled myself fully, giving myself a moment to adjust to the way he stretched me, waiting for the moment that pain relaxed to pleasure.

"You okay?" he asked.

"Took you too fast," I mumbled. "Been too long. But god, it

feels good to be full of you again."

"Not as good as your pussy feels. I was made for this pussy, Brie." His hands rubbed soothing circles up my back. "Probably better for me you didn't start moving right away anyway. Your pussy feels like heaven, and I was about to erupt. Fuck, baby," he whispered, wrapping the length of my hair around his fist and tugging my head back. "How did we go so long?"

With a kiss to my mouth, he let go, and my hair became a curtain around us, cocooning us in this space where only we existed. And with the snow piling up and blanketing the world outside, with miles of vineyard and forest between us and the rest of civilization, it truly felt like we were the only two people in the world. Like we were trapped in a snow globe where everything was good and real and *right*.

I KNEW THE INSTANT Brie fully relaxed around me, the tension in her entire body as she adjusted to my size soothing away like wiping fog off a window.

"That's it, honey. Told you it would fit. I'm so proud of you."

"I'm gonna move now," she said, shifting on her knees to raise herself off me a bit, only an inch or two, before sinking back down. Without the resistance in her pussy, I sank even deeper into her body, and we both groaned.

"Fuck, you take my cock so perfectly."

"So deep, Ez," she gasped, her hands coming to my shoulders, head dropping forward as she once again lifted—this time, until barely the tip remained inside—then impaled herself once again.

"Take what you need, honey. Use me. My cock, my body—all of it is yours."

Her movements were stilted at first, her hips undulating until she found the perfect rhythm and angle. But when she did, my girl used my body like her own personal sex doll, like I was only there to help her seek her pleasure and nothing else.

"You like that, Chef?" she asked as she bounced on my cock, those perfectly full, round tits swaying in my face, her dusty pink nipples begging for my mouth. "You like me on top?"

I groaned, grasping her hips and digging my fingers into her flesh. "You have no idea how sexy you are. All my wildest dreams brought to life in the perfect fantasy."

"Your cock feels so good," she said, her breath sawing in and out of her as she picked up her pace. Each time she sank onto me, her pussy clamped around me, the pressure like a vise, slowly squeezing my release to the surface. Already, it built at the base of my spine, my balls tingling, drawing up, preparing to blow.

My hands dug in harder, and Brie moaned. "That's it, Ez. Mark me. I want your handprints on my hips and thighs tomorrow."

"How about my teeth marks on these tits?" I asked, bringing one hand up to cup a breast, laving the tip with my tongue before suctioning my lips around it, scraping my teeth over the tight bud. Then I moved to the swell, sinking my teeth deeper into her smooth, delicate flesh, sucking. She released a long, low moan, telling me how much she liked it. I pulled away, grinning at a job well done. Her skin was marred by the perfect indentation of my teeth, a red mark blooming between, and I knew she'd have a hickey in the morning. I loved it so much, I gave the other side the same treatment. Fuck, I was already hard as a statue, but the idea of seeing those crescents from my teeth on her smooth skin tomorrow made me *feral*.

I wanted marks like that all over her body—her neck, shoulders, tits, stomach, that impossibly soft skin between her thighs.

Brie writhed faster, her clit rubbing against my happy trail. From the way her pussy clenched me, I knew she was close, and when I reached between us, one brush of my thumb over that bundle of nerves had her coming with a cry. I fucking loved the way her inner walls fluttered around me, how she threw her head back and screamed my name at the ceiling as I gripped her hips tightly and bucked up into her with punishing, jerky thrusts, forcing her to feel every single second of her climax.

"That's it, my beautiful girl," I hissed through my teeth, my jaw clenched as I continued to fuck her, racing toward my own release. "You scream my name as loud as you want to. Let the whole fucking world know who fucks you this good. That I'm the *only* one who gets you like this."

Brie only nodded, her chest heaving as she continued to move with me, letting me seek my own pleasure.

At last, that pressure at my spine released, my cock pulsing as I called her name, spilling into the condom. Like a chain reaction, she whimpered and broke apart again, head falling to my shoulder as she spasmed and shook.

When we came down, Brie lifted her head to look at me. Those green eyes blazed in the dimness of the room, and the blissed-out smile on her face had the caveman in my chest roaring in satisfaction.

"I want to do this every day."

I grinned. "My cock is yours whenever you want it. I'll never get tired of your pussy."

Brie's gaze flared but quickly softened. "I don't just want that, though. I want...everything, Ez. Whatever you're willing to give me."

"It's all yours, Brie," I assured her. "*Everything.*"

She pressed a kiss to my nose. "Me too."

As much as I didn't want to pop this perfect bubble and ruin the moment, I said, "Do you think we should talk about...before?"

Brie shook her head emphatically. "No. I don't want to rehash the past except to say…I can't go back there, Ez. We're either all in on this, or we're not in this at all."

I brushed errant strands of hair out of her face and pressed a kiss to her forehead.

"I was an idiot for a long time, Brie, thinking I had to sacrifice my own happiness for the sake of Hansen. But I've come to realize that Hansen is happiest when I'm happy too. And *I'm* happiest with you. So yeah, we're all in on this."

"Forever?" she asked tentatively.

I nodded emphatically, capturing her lips in a searing kiss, branding her taste on my very soul. When I pulled away, I told her, "If you want forever, then I'm yours until the end of our days."

"I love you," she blurted.

"I love you more."

Brie giggled. "Not possible."

Somehow, though I'd gone soft, I was still buried inside her, and her words had my cock perking up again, rapidly hardening against the tight squeeze of her pussy. "I'll prove it to you," I said before I flipped her on her back.

With the confessions of love hanging between us, our joining was nothing short of magical lovemaking.

I rested one hand on the mattress by her head, lifting the other to cup her cheek as I began a slow rocking of my hips in and out of her, languid strokes designed to drive us both insane, so at odds with our frantic fucking the last time. Brie's eyes fluttered closed, her hips rolling to meet every single one of my thrusts.

"Open your eyes, honey," I said, and those vibrant greens popped open. "Be here with me."

"I'm always with you." She snaked her arms around my neck, pulling me into her, connecting us from chest to groin. Her legs tangled around my back, squeezing me tightly, cocooning me in her embrace.

I buried my face in her neck as I increased the pulse of my hips, working us faster, breathing her in and imprinting every single sensation of this moment on my memory.

"Have I ever told you that you smell like cake batter?" I asked, darting my tongue out to lick a path up her throat. "And taste just as fucking sweet."

"Ez," she whined as her legs started to shake.

"Watch me, baby," I said, shifting to finger her clit. "Watch me as we unravel."

"I'm here." Her eyes, though heavily-lidded, locked on mine. They widened slightly as I brushed my thumb against her nub then pumped into her roughly, harder, as I pressed down.

She detonated with a cry, her entire body arching off the bed to meet mine where I hovered above her. I followed her down, the tight squeeze of her pussy milking my own release.

Time warped and stilled, and my heart expanded almost painfully in my chest. This woman was mine, and this round of sex wasn't simply our first time making love.

It was a claiming, Brie imprinting herself on my soul in a way I knew I'd never be rid of. Hell, I never wanted to be rid of it, of her. Of how tightly she held me, comforted me, brought me back to life. Of her beautiful body and even more impressive mind. Of her laughter, how her green eyes sparkled, shifting from emerald to pine depending on her mood.

I felt like I lived entire lifetimes in the span of seconds, and clear as day, I could see our life together stretch out before us. This was only the beginning.

As we came apart together, as Brie quivered beneath me and my cock pulsed deep inside her, draining me dry, our gazes remained locked, and tears slowly leaked from Brie's eyes.

I'd barely come down before I rocked back on my heels and gathered her in my arms, holding her tightly to me.

"What's wrong? Did I hurt you?"

"Not this time," she said with a wet chuckle, and I lightly pinched her side in retaliation. When she pulled away, she wore the biggest smile I'd ever seen on her face. "Haven't you ever seen happy tears?"

Warmth spread through me as I grinned in response.

"I promise, honey. Happy tears are the only kind I'll ever make you cry."

"I'm counting on it," she said, then captured my mouth with hers.

She tasted salty and sweet.

Like forever.

Like *mine*.

chapter 34
Ezra

Near-blinding sunlight streaming through the open curtains pulled me from sleep the next morning. Sometime in the night, the storm had broken, but Brie and I had been too wrapped up in talking and trading orgasms to notice. Still asleep, she sprawled across me—her head on my chest, arm slung over my middle, leg hooked over mine. My hand was buried in her hair, and I'd forever marvel at the silky strands, obsessed with the way they slipped so easily through my fingers. Her mouth was parted slightly, adorable puffs of air leaving her and fanning over my chest. Sighing contentedly, I wrapped my arms tighter around her, and she whimpered in her sleep before settling again, a small smile on her lips.

Fuck, I loved her so much it hurt.

This strong, selfless, gorgeous, insanely talented woman; a woman I had no right calling mine, but one I'd wake up to on thousands of mornings just like this. I vowed to be the best man for her. She deserved nothing less than my everything.

"Good morning."

I turned toward her sleepy voice, grinning down at her as she blinked slowly, rubbing her eyes.

"Good morning, gorgeous. How're you feeling?"

She stretched next to me, rolling onto her back and offering me a full view of her perfect fucking body. I couldn't help bending over her and cupping her breasts as I dropped my mouth to hers.

"Sore," she said when I pulled away. "In the best way."

"How about we head back to the winery, and I'll make you breakfast?"

"Mm," she moaned, arching her back like a cat and pushing those gorgeous tits up against my chest. "Can we take a bath first? I'm not ready to face the world yet."

"A bath sounds perfect." I gave her one more kiss before moving away and rising from the bed. I bit back a groan, biting down on my fist at the image she presented. Her olive skin and dark hair were a sharp contrast to the crisp white sheets, and her curvy body posed just so made her look like a sexy, naked pinup from some old-timey photoshoot.

"What're you looking at?" she asked, the delicate skin between her brows creasing.

"You."

"What about me?"

"Just...everything." I shuffled around to her side of the bend and folded over her, once again capturing her mouth with mine. "You're the most beautiful woman I've ever laid eyes on, and I'll never understand what I did to deserve you."

She reached up to cup my cheek, her thumb brushing back and forth, the rasp of my stubble filling the space between us. "You didn't do anything but be yourself, Ez. That's exactly what I need."

I grinned and pressed a kiss to her palm, my heart growing

three sizes in my chest. Then I backed away and headed down the hall to the bathroom, with its freestanding tub and assortment of luxury soaps and scrubs.

Spinning the taps, water gushed into the deep basin, and I tested the temp before pouring a healthy portion of the eucalyptus-scented bubble bath, watching for a moment as the water frothed.

Then I went back to Brie.

She sat up in bed, sheet pulled up under her armpits, her phone in her hand. She shook it in my direction and said, "Just letting the fam know I'm okay."

"Shit," I breathed, stalking across the room for my pants. "I should tell my dad what happened and that I'll be home in…a few hours?" I quirked a brow at her in question.

Brie giggled. "I think a few hours is safe."

"Actually," I said, scooping her up from the bed and cradling her against my chest, "a few hours will never be enough."

"Enough for what?" she asked as we entered the bathroom. Instead of setting her down and letting her get in the tub herself, I stepped over the ledge and sank us both into the hot water. Brie hissed as we settled in.

I nuzzled her neck and said, "A few hours will never be enough to satiate me, not where you're concerned."

Brie shifted in the water so she was nestled between my thighs, her head dropping against my chest as she said, "I never thought I had much of a sexual appetite. Turns out, I just didn't have much of one for anyone who isn't you."

"I'll feed your pussy my cock all day, every day," I promised, pressing a kiss to the side of her neck.

"What about my mouth?"

"Definitely."

Brie reached below the surface of the water and located my dick, squeezing it and sweeping her thumb across the slit, her tongue darting out to drag along her lower lip in an approximation of what she'd do to me much lower.

"Sit on the edge," she directed, floating out of my arms and turning to face me.

"Why?"

"I want a taste," she said pointedly, staring at my cock.

Morning head? She didn't have to ask me twice before I was rising from the water and perching on the lip of the tub. I stroked myself a few times as Brie drifted closer, her eyes widening and darkening.

"You want this cock?"

"Badly."

"You want to choke on it? Want me to spill my cum down your throat?"

"Please, Chef. Feed me."

"Jesus Christ," I breathed. "You are so goddamn sexy. I'm gonna fuck that pretty little mouth."

Brie turned only to turn the water off. The bubbles nipped at the bottom curves of her tits as she knelt before me, hands on her thighs below the surface, pushing those gorgeous breasts together.

"A goddamn wet dream," I mumbled as she opened her mouth and stuck out her tongue, waiting for my cock.

So I fed my girl.

The tip barely touched her tongue before she closed her lips around me and sucked, pulling me in deeper. I groaned, my hand finding its way into her hair, guiding her.

"This mouth," I said, reaching down with my free hand to trace her lips around my shaft. "Almost as good as that pussy."

Brie pulled off with a *pop*, glancing up at me through her eyelashes. Her cheeks were rosy, eyes bright. "Am I doing okay?"

"You're doing amazing. Keep going."

"Can I use my hands?"

"You can use whatever the fuck you want on me. Just keep sucking that cock like a good girl."

Her chest flushed with my praise as she lifted a hand from the water and gripped my cock at its base, holding me still as she lowered her mouth to me once again.

I dropped my head back as she closed her lips around me, swirling her tongue over my head, like I was a lollipop she was desperate to get to the center of. I gripped the edge of the tub painfully hard to keep myself upright as Brie sucked hard, my orgasm rising to the surface.

"You sure you've never done this before?" I asked through gritted teeth.

Brie only hummed around me, bobbing her head both in affirmation and to take me deeper. The little gag she made when my tip branded the back of her throat was the sexiest fucking thing I'd ever heard, and I couldn't help bucking into her just to hear it again.

"So sexy choking on my cock, honey."

"Wanna make you come like this," she said when she popped off, a thin trail of saliva connecting her mouth to my crown. Her hand continued to work me, squeezing tightly, handling me recklessly. I glanced down at her when I heard splashes and found her clearly pleasuring herself as she worked me over.

And that was enough for me.

"My turn," I told her, slipping back into the water, her delicate hand remaining wrapped around my shaft.

"I think I'm too sore for all this," she said as she tugged on me, cheeks flushing bright pink with embarrassment.

"How about my fingers, then? I'll take it easy."

I wasn't above pleading, because damnit, I wanted her too. I wanted to take care of her, to make her feel good more than I wanted to seek out my own release.

Brie swung around and rested her back against my chest.

"Just relax, honey," I said, slipping my palm down over her chest, flicking her nipples before traveling further south, over the taut skin of her abdomen and bare skin at her pubic bone. My fingers slipped between her lips, my middle one circling her clit slowly.

Brie released a breath and sank further into me. I lifted her thighs and spread them, flattening my feet on the bottom of the tub, holding her open for me by pinning her legs to the sides.

I glanced down her body and groaned.

With her skin flushed from the warmth and my touch, droplets of water sluicing down her body, her gorgeous sex just barely above the surface—fuck, I'd never seen anything hotter in my life. And with the imprints of my teeth bruising the delicate skin of her tits? The caveman within me was positively feral.

"Look at you," I said, once again settling my hand between her thighs, lightly running my finger around her entrance but not dipping in. "You're so fucking sexy all spread out for me like this.

Now, do me a favor."

"Anything," she breathed, her chest already heaving as her pulse kicked up. I could see it in the way the skin thrummed right over her heart.

"Lift your arms and wrap them around my neck."

She did as I asked, her hands curving around the back of my neck, fingers toying with the hair at my nape. "Now what?"

"Keep them there. I told you I'd take care of you, honey, and I will, but only if you don't move your arms. Good girls get rewarded, and you're going to be a good girl, aren't you?"

"The best," she promised.

"That's my girl," I said, lightly slapping her pussy, grinning when a small whimper slipped free from her lips.

"Please," she whined, her nails scraping against my scalp.

"Please, *what*?"

"*Please, Chef.*"

"Since you asked so nicely."

I eased a finger into her slowly, not wanting to hurt her, wanting to give her time to adjust. I'd worked her hard last night, and my girl had taken my cock like a fucking champ every time, but this wasn't the time for roughness. This was a slow, sensual torture, and I lazily pumped that single digit in and out.

"I'm fucking obsessed with the way you clench around me. I wish you could feel how tight you are."

"More," she begged.

"You sure?"

"More."

I withdrew and slipped another finger in, and Brie cursed softly under her breath.

"So sexy when you're all undone and begging for me," I murmured, bending to press soft kisses to her shoulder and neck. With my other hand, I cupped a breast, tweaking her nipple in a way that had her clenching tighter around me. "And so fucking responsive."

I loved learning her body, relished in the knowledge that I was the one who got to discover her like this, to run my hands and mouth over every single inch of gorgeous skin and discover exactly what unraveled her. What she liked and didn't like. What made her moan and scream. What made her come all over my cock and fingers.

With my free hand, I collected the mass of her hair and wrapped it around my fist, tugging her head to the side to expose her neck.

"Look at that," I said, running my nose over her throat, inhaling deeply. Even after a night of sweaty fucking and the time spent in this tub, she still smelled of pastries, the scent enough to get me high. "All this smooth, unblemished skin. What do you think, honey? Should I mark you here too?"

"Yes."

"You gonna cover it up later?"

"Never."

The answer surprised me as much as it thrilled me. "Why not?" I asked, continuing the lazy thrust of my fingers inside her, scissoring them, massaging her inner walls in a way that had her hips undulating in my lap.

"Want everyone to see," she said breathily, her eyes falling closed in bliss. "Let them all know I'm taken now."

"That's right, baby," I said, nipping at her earlobe. "You're mine. I claimed you, and we're going to make sure the world knows it."

I took a moment to explore her neck, working my lips and tongue up and down, searching out that perfect spot that drove her absolutely wild. I found it right below her ear, where the edge of her jaw curved away. She twitched against me, moaning.

Without a word, I picked up the pace of my hand, using my thumb to roughly circle her clit as I pumped faster, fucking her harder.

And when I scraped my teeth over that spot on her neck and sucked the skin into my mouth, soothing the sting away with my tongue, she detonated.

All spread out, her legs forced wide by mine, my hand in her hair holding her steady and her hands wrapped around my neck, fingernails pressing almost painfully into my skull, she was a fucking sight to behold as I took her apart. Her pussy clamped down hard on my fingers, pulsing against them, her legs and arms shaking, entire torso bowing as her climax claimed her.

I slowly worked her through it until she was begging me to stop, but I did only once she ceased quivering, her body falling limp against me.

She twitched as I withdrew my fingers from her and angled her head slightly to watch me bring them to my mouth as I licked them clean.

I wrapped my arms tightly around her, tucking her head under my chin. She let go of my neck at last and settled her arms atop mine.

"I think we should start every day like this," she said happily.

And who was I to argue with that?

chapter 35

Brie

"How do you feel about a family dinner?"

I stilled at the stove in my bakery kitchen, where I was slowly stirring a cinnamon roll glaze, waiting for the moment it started to bubble before I removed it from the heat. The rolls themselves were nearly ready to come out of the oven, and the entire kitchen smelled of cinnamon and sugar.

It was two weeks into the new year, and Ezra and I were at the bakery, where he was helping me with my online shop orders by measuring out dry ingredients for the scone and muffin kits I needed to mail out by the end of the week. He may not have been the more talented pastry chef of us two, but I trusted him to at least correctly measure ingredients.

Even if he'd once told me he "measures with the heart."

"I have dinner with my family every week," I reminded him.

"Okay, fair. What I mean is, like...both of our families. A special dinner. A...coming out of sorts."

"A coming out with what?"

"Our relationship?"

"Oh!" I said, smacking myself on the forehead. "You want to do a fancy dinner for that?"

Ezra shrugged, feigning nonchalance, but I could tell my

question and confusion bugged him. "I just thought it might be a good idea to get everyone together and tell them all at once."

I moved around the island so I could wrap my arms around his waist and pull our bodies together. I relished the fact that I could do this now—that I could touch him freely and without consequence.

"Will you be cooking?"

Ezra rolled his eyes. "Duh."

"What're you thinking of making?" I asked, tilting my head to press a kiss to the underside of his jaw. A grumble emanated from his chest.

"Pizza," he rasped, lowering his face to my neck and inhaling deeply, then licking my skin like I was an ice cream cone. "God, your scent drives me insane. How do you always smell so sweet?"

I pushed away from him before we could get carried away, having far too much work to get done for what would happen if I remained tangled in his embrace.

"I come by it naturally," I said cheekily as I returned to my glaze.

Ezra snorted. "Right."

"Hey!" I protested, spinning and throwing an errant piece of dough across the room at him. "I'll have you know, I'm very sweet. Everyone says so."

"That's because they've never heard the filthy shit you say in bed."

My cheeks heated, still not entirely used to the seductress persona I adopted behind closed doors, though I grinned widely at Ezra anyway. I loved the side he brought out of me when we were pressed skin-to-skin. I may have spent all day, every day dealing with customers, surrounded by baked goods, and showing the world I was as sweet as my treats, but I was anything but at night, when Ezra played with my body. My thoughts were sinful, scorching enough to set the sheets on fire.

But to the rest of the world, I was simply reserved, demure Baker Brie.

That was fine by me. I wanted to keep Ezra and our explosive connection all to myself.

"I think a family dinner is a wonderful idea," I said at last. "Especially if you're making pizza. You know how much I love your Margherita."

"Not as much as you love my meatballs," he said with a wink, and a laugh burst free from me.

God, being with him was so *easy*.

Admittedly, we were still very much in the honeymoon phase, but even when we hadn't been as serious about our connection, when we were just trading orgasms and swapping stories over the phone, I'd still never fallen so effortlessly into a relationship with someone. It was why I hardly dated—I often found it difficult to connect with people when my whole life revolved around food, my family, and this small town I called home.

But Ezra understood me better than anyone, because those things were all things he deeply valued as well. He was my equal in so many ways but different enough that we never ran out of things to discuss or discover about each other.

I hoped we never grew out of it.

"Why is Ezra Wendt using my kitchen to make pizza?" Dad asked Saturday evening when he walked into the house. He, Cal, Owen, and Logan had been out ice fishing in the bay, his cheeks bright red over the edges of his dark beard. The scent of fish layered over the fresh, cold air that clung to him. Even Rik and Hansen had gone, and Hansen rushed through the door with a brief greeting to me before beelining for the kitchen and his father. The rest of the guys followed, heading straight for the blend of pizza sauce and baking crust wafting from that direction.

"Because he wanted to do something nice for the family to show his appreciation."

"Right," my dad snorted. "It has nothing to do with the fact that you guys have been seeing each other and he's trying to get into my good graces."

My mouth gaped as I stared at my father. "How do you know?"

My dad pursed his lips. "Please, Brie," he said, waving a hand. "I know everything that happens on this peninsula."

"Not everything," I mumbled under my breath. If he did—if he had any idea of all the ways the men we'd welcomed into our family had used his daughters' bodies... Well, they'd already be dead.

"And you're forgetting he told me he wanted the chance to pursue something with you."

"Well, he did," I confirmed.

"And is he treating you well?"

"The best."

Dad squeezed my shoulder then hauled me in and dropped a kiss atop my head. "That's all I can ask for."

Male laughter echoed from the kitchen, and a moment later, the cavalry of my sisters appeared from the den, heading for the sound.

I hooked a thumb over my shoulder. "Guess I better go see what all the fuss is about."

My parents' house had always been full of noise. With five girls, one opinionated mother, and one larger-than-life father, there was always plenty of conversation and laughter.

But to walk into the kitchen and find not only my sisters, but our significant others as well, to be presented with the physical portrait of our growing families... My heart swelled almost painfully in my chest. Inexplicably, tears pricked my eyes. I loved my sisters, and I loved their husbands and boyfriends for loving them.

I loved Ezra most of all.

And Hansen—god, I adored that little boy. He was whip smart, hilarious in that kid way of his, and had a heart three times the size of his little body. He wove himself so seamlessly into the family. My mother fawned over him, my dad was obviously excited to have a little boy running around, and my sisters were patient and attentive when he wanted to share some rambling story about a project he was working on in school or talk all about action figures and superheroes.

In addition, Rik got along great with my parents, which made it that much easier when everyone converged on their house for occasions like this.

My sisters and I were finding our people and slowly knitting our lives together, weaving our significant others into the tapestry of the Delatou legacy.

"I caught a fish that was this big!" Hansen exclaimed, spreading his arms as wide as they would go. "Papa had to help me haul it out of the water."

Ezra's brows rose as he said, "Wow, bud! That's amazing!" Over Hansen's head, Ezra glanced at his dad, who held his hands apart in a more accurate and modest approximation of the fish Hansen caught.

"He's quite the perch whisperer," Logan said with a chuckle, ruffling Hansen's hair.

"I want to be a professional fisherman when I grow up," Hansen said, beaming at Logan's compliment.

Rik approached his grandson and squeezed his shoulder. "You can be whatever you want, *Älskling*."

Hansen only grinned wider, and my heart expanded with it.

These Wendt men were my family now, and I was made for days like this, when the people I loved most were gathered around me, happy and healthy.

At last, I wove my way through the men until I reached Ezra's side. He paused, placing toppings on one pizza before tugging me into his embrace, planting a kiss atop my head.

"I talked to my dad," I said conversationally.

"And?"

I shrugged. "He already gave you his blessing. He's happy for us." I let my eyes sweep the room then looked up at him. "Everyone is happy for us."

"Me too," he said, capturing my lips in a quick, searing kiss that ended way too soon. I must've made a noise of protest, because he chuckled and said, "Don't worry, honey. There's more where that came from. Later. When we're alone."

"My three favorite words."

"Is it time to eat yet?" Hansen asked, squeezing between my and Ezra's legs, his little face scrunched in distress. "I'm starving."

With a chuckle, I stepped away from his father.

Ezra only rolled his eyes and settled a hand on Hansen's shoulder, turning him toward the entrance to the kitchen.

"Go round everyone up, kiddo," he said. "Pizza is coming out now."

"Yes!" Hansen cheered, pumping his fist in the air and racing from the room, careening around the corner so fast, I gasped, thinking he'd slip and slide right into the opposite wall. Thankfully, he remained on his feet and disappeared deeper into the house, chanting that it was pizza time. The group followed him out, laughing at his exuberance.

As Ezra began removing the pizzas from the oven, I picked up one of his homemade garlic knots and shoved it in my mouth, desperate to quell the hunger pains. Like Hansen, I, too, was starving, the scents of tomato and melty cheese mingling in the air, creating an enticing aroma and driving me insane while I waited for Ezra to finish.

"Hey, honey?" he asked, and I focused my attention on him instead of the pies on the counter.

"Yeah?"

"Will you bring those out to the dining room before you eat

them all?" he asked, gesturing to the garlic knots.

I stuck my tongue out but did as he asked, his murmured "brat" following me out.

My family had gathered at the table around Hansen, who sat at the head—in the seat typically reserved for my dad—a fork in one hand, butter knife in the other, napkin tucked into the collar of his shirt like a bib.

"Someone is excited for pizza," I said, ruffling his hair after setting the garlic bread down.

"It's my absolute favorite," Hansen reminded me.

"I know," I told him. "Hey, remember the first time we met? When you, your dad, and I ate grilled cheese together at the winery?"

Hansen's eyes squeezed shut, face scrunched up in thought. "Not really," he said, glancing at me. "I feel like I've always known you. You've always just been part of our family."

A chorus of *aww*s rose from my sisters and mom, and tears pricked my eyes.

This kid. I'd never understand what I did to not only find a love like what I had with Ezra, but to get Hansen out of the deal as well. He was truly the best kid I could've imagined. Smart, curious, funny, a total goofball—he kept everyone on their toes with the stuff that came out of his mouth. But he also had the biggest heart out of anyone I knew, which was saying something, given he was barely six years old. It was heartening to see that, despite what he'd gone through as a toddler and having to grow up without a mother, he'd still turned into the sweetest boy who hadn't let that deter him in the slightest from finding joy in every day.

In short, I loved Hansen.

But he wasn't *mine*, and I hated that small part of my brain that refused to shut up about it, the one that liked to remind me I could've had my own baby and lost it.

The one begging me to take another shot.

As Ezra appeared in the doorway with the first of the pizzas, I realized with a start that we hadn't discussed that. We hadn't discussed much about the future beyond wanting to face it together. I needed to tell him.

Soon.

Tonight.

I gave him a broad smile as he slid the pie to the center of the table, hoping it masked the worst of my anxiety. I opened my mouth to thank him, my family rising from their seats to reach for slices.

Mom had just laid one on Hansen's plate when Chloe appeared behind Ezra, face pale.

"Coco?" I asked, rushing to her side. "Are you okay?"

"Uhh...Logan?" she said to her husband, ignoring me.

"Yeah, babe?" Logan asked, not lifting his eyes from the food in front of him.

"My water just broke."

Eyes wide, I glanced down to see Chloe's jeans were in fact wet, like she'd peed herself.

"Holy shit," I breathed.

And that seemed to be the catalyst that sent the rest of the room into action. Before, where you could hear a pin drop, there was now a flurry of activity. My mother stood at the table, openly sobbing. Dad, stoic as ever, remained seated, grinning widely around a mouthful of pizza. Next to him, Hansen ignored the adults as he dove into his own slice. Ezra backed to the edge of the room as Logan rushed to my sister, scooping her into his arms as best as he could with her bump between them, murmuring low words of comfort and affirmation to her before setting her down and hustling them both out of the room without a word to anyone else.

This was their moment, and I knew he'd keep us updated. I watched them go, excitement for my sister and the arrival of my niece tinged by the worry that I'd never have the opportunity to experience such a thing myself.

chapter 36
Brie

WHEN I WOKE THE next morning, I found the bed next to me empty, the sheets cool enough to mean Ezra had been up for a while.

After Chloe had gone into labor the night before and the excitement had worn off, we'd settled into a bit of a tense family meal, not wanting to let Ezra's hard work go to waste. Still, the entire affair was tinged with melancholy. People had babies every day without any issues, but it was different when someone you cared about deeply was giving birth. Logically, I knew something going wrong was a high improbability, but it did nothing to quell the anxiety I had over the whole thing.

Once we finished dinner, Ezra, Hansen, Rik, and I had returned to the Wendts' house, and Ezra did his level best to distract me with his tongue and hands and cock.

And once he'd wrung every possible ounce of pleasure from me, I drifted off into a dreamless sleep with his arms wrapped tightly around me.

Waking in his bed was disconcerting to say the least, since we'd only spent the night together a few times, and it had always been on my turf.

I loved his house, though. He'd shown me endless before-and-after photos of all the updates they'd done a few years ago, and Rik's penchant for carpentry and other aspects of home remodeling was evident in how gorgeous the house looked now. Ezra's room was masculine, with slate grey walls balanced by light oak floors that ran through the entire house, plus his massive king bed with its matte black metal frame. Windows flanked each side, though they were covered with blackout curtains. There was a thick black and white Moroccan-inspired rug on the floor, a matching runner covering the white marble in the en suite bathroom, though the floors were heated, which did wonders for my frozen toes as I padded in to relieve myself before going in search of my boyfriend.

After putting on a pair of sweatpants—which happened to be his—I trotted out into the kitchen to find the three Wendt men in various stages of their morning routine.

Rik sat at the circular table nestled into the bay window, the paper propped up in front of him, his half-moon glasses perched on the tip of his nose. Hansen was at the island, his knees tucked under him on the stool as he bent over what appeared to be a drawing pad. Ezra was at the stove, something sizzling in the pan before him.

"Baker Brie!" Hansen shouted happily when I appeared.

I approached the island and gave him a side hug, pressing a kiss to the top of his head. "Morning, kiddo."

Then I approached his father and repeated the process, though my kiss landed on Ezra's lips.

"Good morning, honey."

"What're you making?"

"Denver omelets," he said then dropped his voice. "It's a good way to get Hansen to eat vegetables without knowing it."

I inhaled deeply. I loved Denver omelets, and truthfully, I was starving.

After filling a mug with coffee, I turned to Ezra and asked, "Do you have creamer?"

He nodded at the fridge. "In the door."

I opened the stainless-steel monstrosity and found a bottle of my favorite caramel non-dairy creamer waiting in the door.

"You drink Planet Oat creamer?" I asked, arching a brow.

Ezra chuckled and shook his head, padding over to me to place a quick kiss on my forehead before returning to the stove. "I bought it for you."

My heart swelled in my chest, and I was certain I had hearts in my eyes as I stared at him. "Thank you," I whispered.

Ezra winked and pointed his spatula at the stool next to Hansen. "Sit."

"Yes, Chef."

A grumble emanated from his chest, and I giggled as I moved to sit next to Hansen. To keep him occupied while he cooked, Ezra had given him a pad of paper and a box of colored pencils. I studied the drawing as I sipped my coffee, and Hansen hummed some indistinct tune as he colored in the head of a surprisingly detailed dragon he'd drawn.

"What's his name?" I asked.

"Balthazar the Bloody," Hansen said matter-of-factly, and I couldn't help the startled laugh that left me.

"He's cool."

Hansen looked up at me, eyes narrowed. God, he looked so much like his father when he did that. Ezra made the same face when confused about something. "You mean it?" Hansen asked.

"Of course," I assured him. "I would never joke about dragons."

His face brightened. "Thanks! I have a whole book full of different ones. Dragons are so awesome." His expression fell a little as he added, "I wish they were real."

I reached up and brushed a curly lock of his chocolate brown hair off his face then tapped his temple. "They are real," I told him. "They just live in here."

He grinned. "I like that. You're smart, Baker Brie."

I smiled in response. "Thanks, kiddo. You're pretty smart too."

And the only one I'd let get away with calling me Baker Brie. It was how Ezra had introduced me all those years ago, and while he may not remember the details of that meeting, it had been important enough—*I* had been important enough—that he hadn't forgotten who I was.

"Did you know Dad has been reading me this super cool book series about dragons?"

"Really?" I asked, surprised. I hadn't known that, but it was just like Ezra to do something so sweet for his boy. I knew Hansen was quickly learning how to read, but the fact that Ezra wanted to keep him close and do something so special for him made my heart melt. "Which series is that?"

"It's called *Eragon*," Hansen said proudly. "It's about this poor farm boy who discovers a dragon egg, and when it hatches, he realizes he was meant to be a dragon rider, and she belongs to him."

"Wow. That sounds amazing."

"Have you heard of it?" he asked me.

"In fact, I have," I told him, easily picturing the blue dragon on the cover of the first book. "The dragon is blue, right?"

"Yes!" Hansen cheered excitedly. "My favorite color."

It cracked me up that this kid was barely six years old and knew his favorite color so matter-of-factly. I loved his zest for life, how everything around him was magical and full of possibilities. I sincerely hoped he never grew out of it, and while I was around, I'd do everything in my power to ensure every day was filled with things that would make him smile like he was right now.

"Her name is Saphira, right?"

"Yep!" he said, coloring the dragon on his sheet of paper the same as Saphira's scales.

"Did you know there's a reason for that? A deeper meaning behind her name?"

Hansen canted his head to the side, considering. Then he looked at his dad and said, "You never told me that."

"It's good for other people to teach you things," Ezra said, plating a perfectly constructed omelet and walking it across the room to Rik.

"So what does it mean?" Hansen asked me.

"Well, a sapphire is a type of gemstone," I said. "Can you guess what color it is?"

"Blue!"

"Exactly," I told him, grinning widely. "So *Saphira* is just a play on that."

"That's so cool," he breathed, glancing down at his drawing and studying the blue scales he'd given the dragon. He glanced back up at his dad and said, "I want a whole room full of sapphires, please."

He said it so calmly, so confidently, that Ezra and I shared a look before bursting into laughter. From across the room, even Rik chuckled softly as he shoveled his food into his mouth. Hansen's forehead creased in confusion.

"What's so funny?" he asked. "Did I do something wrong?"

"Oh, of course not, bud," I said, pulling him into my side and dropping a kiss atop his head. "It's just that sapphires are very precious gemstones, which means they're pretty expensive. But how about this? I'll search online to see if I can find you some imitation gems that are as big as baseballs? You can keep them in your room and pretend they're the real thing."

"You'd do that for me?" Hansen asked, voice full of awe.

I softened. "Of course. I'd do anything for you."

"Are you my new mommy?" he blurted.

Ezra was so startled by Hansen's question that he dropped his spatula, and it clattered loudly to the floor in the now-silent room. Slowly, he spun to his son, moving around the island to set a plate of breakfast in front of Hansen then turning him and settling his hands on Hansen's shoulders.

I was stunned stupid, my mouth gaping like a fish as I tried to find something to say. But there wasn't anything I *could* say. I would never delude myself into thinking I could replace Shannon, and truthfully, I didn't want to. That woman had caused this family untold amounts of pain, but for all her faults, she was still Hansen's mother. Without her, he wouldn't exist. I knew I'd never meet her, and while I wanted to hate her for the way she treated my man and his boy, I couldn't, because without her, they wouldn't be here with me now.

"Do you like Brie?" Ezra asked Hansen.

His eyes darted to me then back to his dad. "I love my Baker Brie," he said quietly, and my heart squeezed painfully.

"I love you too, kiddo."

"And I love you both," Ezra said. "I know your mom's not here anymore, and it's okay if that makes you sad. But I think, if you're okay with it, we'll keep Brie around for a while?"

"A while?" I asked, quirking a brow.

Ezra shushed me, though he winked before refocusing on Hansen.

"I want her around all the time," Hansen said with a shrug.

Ezra reached out for me, and I laced our fingers together. "I think we can make that happen. What do you say, honey?"

"All the time works for me."

Ezra swallowed audibly, his eyes going a little glassy as we sat there, hands clasped, the three of us connected. Such a quiet, early morning moment, and I knew it would become one I looked back on fondly and frequently.

Though the spell was quickly broken by Rik clearing his throat from the breakfast nook.

"Don't I get a say in this?" he asked, rising from his seat to bring his empty plate to the sink, rinsing it then loading it in the dishwasher.

"I guess," Ezra said with an overly dramatic sigh, letting go of me and Hansen to return to cooking.

Rik looked at me, grinning, a mischievous glint in his eyes. "You know I adore you, Brie, and I'm happy to have you become a part of this family."

"Thank you—"

"But…"

Ezra groaned, and my cheeks heated. I should've known it wouldn't be that simple.

"Dad," Ezra warned. "Brie is our guest and my girlfriend. Tread carefully."

It was the first time he'd called me such, and I flushed with pleasure under my anxiety over whatever Rik was about to say.

"It's nothing bad," Rik said, waving a hand to dismiss his son's protests. "I was just going to say that if you're going to engage in…*adult playtime*…maybe you could be a little quieter about it? Or do it somewhere else."

I felt all the blood drain from my face as I slapped a hand over my mouth.

"Fuck," Ezra breathed.

"Dad, you said a bad word!" Hansen piped up. "Swear jar!"

My blood roared in my ears as I thought back to last night, to the hours Ezra and I had spent tangled around each other in his sheets, of the ways he'd played with my body, strumming on my clit and pounding into me with his fingers and cock until I was boneless with pleasure and completely spent. Being with him had always unlocked something in me, a confidence and inhibition I'd never found with anyone before. And while I'd tried to be quiet, there was no guarantee I'd succeeded…

What could Rik have heard?

"I love you, boy," Rik said to his son. "But there are some things a father just doesn't need to know about his son. I let it slide those months you guys were doing…whatever on those late-night phone calls, but I draw the line at having to hear both of you under the roof I'm trying to sleep under."

"Oh my god," I whispered, burying my face in my hands. I'd never been more mortified in my entire life. In that moment, I wanted nothing more than to crawl into a hole and pretend I didn't exist.

Reasonably, I understood Rik knew Ezra had sex. Obviously, Hansen's existence was proof of that. But he was right—there were certain things a father shouldn't know about his son, and the way he sounded when he came, or the noises he elicited from his girlfriend while he drove her to climax, were definitely on that list.

"Wait a minute," Ezra said, his face pale, eyes comically wide. "*Months?*"

Rik chuckled in disbelief. "The walls in this place were paper thin before we renovated."

Ezra covered Hansen's ears as he said, "Fucking hell. Do you think *he* heard?"

"Daaaaad!" Hansen wailed, attempting to shove Ezra away.

"Nah," Rik said. "His room is on the opposite side of the house. I'm the one unfortunate enough to share a wall with you."

"Jesus," Ezra breathed. "I'm...so sorry."

"It's fine," Rik said. "We all have urges."

"Gross. Don't say urges." Ezra sounded like such a petulant teenager with that comment, I couldn't help but laugh.

"Just...keep it down," Rik continued, unperturbed, before he winked at me and disappeared from the room.

When he'd gone, Ezra looked at me and let out a disbelieving snort. "What the hell?"

"I can never show my face in this house again," I said into his chest as Ezra gathered me into his arms.

"You think I'm ever letting you leave?" he asked, pulling away and placing a kiss on the tip of my nose.

"You really want this?" I asked quietly.

"You? Always, in all the ways you'll let me."

I grinned as he captured my mouth with his, but before the kiss could get too deep, Hansen said, almost conversationally, "What's adult playtime?"

We broke apart as we devolved into a fit of laughter, and Ezra moved away from me, ruffling Hansen's hair on his way back to the stove.

"Something you'll learn about when you're older."

Hansen harrumphed but didn't press the issue as he continued forking eggs into his mouth.

Ezra set my meal in front of me, and as I lifted a bite to my lips, my phone pinged.

My heart rate kicked up when I realized it was a text from Logan to my entire family.

Logan Daniels: Aleah Iris Daniels made her debut at 6:22 this morning. She's 7 pounds, 4 ounces, 21 inches long. Chloe is doing well and said you guys can come down and meet her whenever you want.

Mama: Such a beautiful name for a beautiful little girl! Grammy and Papa can't wait to meet her!

Delia: God she's gorgeous! Congratulations, you two. QB and I will be down in

a few hours. We love you <3
  Ella: Omg look at all that hair!
  Amara: Well now I'm ready to kick my little tenant out. Can't wait to meet her!
  Me: I'm coming down ASAP. Congratulations, guys! Love you!!!!!

I looked up at Ezra and grinned. "I have a niece."

"Chloe had the baby?"

"Yes!" I cried happily, flipping the phone around to show him the picture Logan had attached to his message.

Aleah was cuddled up to Chloe's chest. My sister looked exhausted but wore the most blissed-out smile I'd ever seen on her face. My niece was a tiny bundle in her arms, wrapped in one of those standard white hospital blankets with teddy bears and balloons on it. She had a full head of Delatou dark hair, and I loved her so much already.

"When are you going to go see her?"

"As soon as I run home and change," I said with a laugh, already moving off my stool.

"Not so fast, missy," Ezra said, coming around to block my path before I could get further than a few steps. "Eat first. Then I'll take you into the city."

"Oh, you don't have to come with me."

"Your sister just had a baby," he said, sliding his arms around my waist and bending to nuzzle my neck. Goosebumps erupted across my skin, and I sucked in a sharp breath as he nipped at my earlobe. "And your family is my family now, right?"

I was having difficulty thinking straight with his hands on my body like this, and I shoved him in the chest until he yielded a step, not wanting to get carried away with Hansen right next to us.

"Yes, my family is your family." I angled my head and glanced over my shoulder at Hansen, who was licking the leftover syrup off his plate. I couldn't help but giggle. "And yours is mine?"

Ezra pulled me back in to plant a chaste kiss on my forehead. "It's all yours, honey."

A few hours later, we walked into my sister's hospital room to find my entire family already there. Amara, who was nearing her own due date, and Cal, who looked both terrified and awestruck at the idea that he'd have his own little bundle of joy soon. Ella, who was looking better than I'd seen her in weeks—basically since the breakup. The dark circles under her eyes had all but disappeared, and she was smiling widely and cooing at baby Aleah in her arms. Delia and Owen stood at Chloe's bedside, chatting with her and Logan, and Mom and Dad hovered over Ella's shoulders, already completely enraptured with their first grandbaby.

I didn't know where to begin, so I settled for giving Ezra's hand a squeeze and moving to Chloe's side.

"Baby Bee," she said softly as I approached, her expression wary but content in equal measure.

I leaned over her to give her a hug, careful of the tube still snaking from her right arm.

"Hi, sissy," I said when I pulled away, my eyes filling with tears.

"Or should I start calling you 'Mama' now?"

"Nah," Chloe said, her gaze going misty. "We'll save that for the little one. I'll always be *your* big sister." She pulled me close to whisper in my ear. "I'm sure this isn't easy for you, but just know I'm happy you're here. We love you so much, and I understand if you need to take a minute."

My heart melted into my stomach at the care she was showing me, this woman who had just given birth and had a tiny, helpless baby to worry about.

In truth, I had been nervous coming here. I loved my sisters so much, and I was so excited that Chloe and Amara were starting their own families, but I'd be lying if I said it wasn't bittersweet. I should've brought the first Delatou grandchild into the world, and it gutted me to know that baby never got to live, that I never got to meet him or her.

So while I was ecstatic for my sisters, seeing baby Aleah was also incredibly bittersweet.

"I love you," I told her. "And I appreciate you thinking of me. Now that you mention it...I think I will take a second."

Chloe gave my hand a squeeze and nodded in understanding. "Take all the time you need."

I turned from her side and crossed the room to Ezra, grabbing his hand and pulling him into the corridor.

Chloe was right—I did need a minute, but not for the reasons she thought. Being here, in this place, surrounded by my family and the new life Chloe and Logan had brought into the world, reminded me that Ezra and I needed to have a serious conversation.

One I wasn't sure how he'd handle, but a desire I needed to get off my chest nonetheless.

"What's going on?" he asked when I led us away from the room and into a quiet alcove. "Are you okay? I know this can't be easy—"

"I want kids, Ez."

I would've laughed at the way his face slackened in shock had I not been dead serious. Blurting it out probably hadn't been the way to go, but the only way I was going to get this out was by ripping off the bandage.

"Okay..."

"I lost our baby," I said matter-of-factly. "And it's killed me inside ever since. I was so young when it all happened, but I've always wanted to be a mother, and the last few years hasn't changed that. If anything, the fact that I'd been so close to making that dream a reality only reinforced the desire. I'm telling you this because, while I know we're just getting started, you also deserve complete honesty from me. You've already got Hansen, and I love that little boy. But I want my own children, Ezra. I want to experience being pregnant and bringing life into this world. I want to take on that adventure with you, but if that's not something *you* want, I need to know now. Otherwise, we're just wasting our time here."

The last sentence gutted me to speak, but Ezra needed all the facts. He deserved to know where I stood, and while it would kill me if he wasn't interested in having more children and chose to walk away, I'd understand. His last baby mama hadn't exactly been in it for the long haul.

But I wasn't Shannon, and I could only hope he loved me enough to realize that, and that maybe our desires for the future lined up in a way so I could have my cake and eat it too.

When I finished, I was breathing heavily, having used all my air to get the words out before he could interrupt me or I lost my nerve. But my gaze stayed locked on his face; I forced myself to resist the urge to look away in case I didn't like what I'd see in his chocolate eyes.

A thousand emotions I couldn't name flitted across his face until finally, his gaze softened, and a small grin graced his perfect mouth.

Backing me against the wall, his hands came up to cup my cheeks. His touch was gentle, reverent, as though I was a treasure that needed to be handled with care. I appreciated him—loved him—so much more in that moment. Because I *was* fragile in that moment, and that he understood that and comforted me instead of running spoke volumes about the kind of man he was.

"Listen to me very carefully, Brie Anne Delatou," he said slowly, punctuating each of my names with a light kiss to my lips. "Shannon and I didn't work out for a number of reasons, the least of which being she just wasn't cut out to be a mom. But *you* are going to make an amazing mother one day, and the fact that you're choosing me to be the man to give you those babies? I'm fucking *honored*. I love you more than anything in this world except for Hansen, and I'll get you pregnant as many times as you want."

My eyes watered and spilled over, and I let free a sound that was something between a laugh and a sob. I settled my hands over Ezra's on my face. "You mean it?"

He nodded emphatically. "I'd give you the world if I could. Whatever you want, honey. All you have to do is ask."

I was full on sobbing now, and he pulled me into his chest to muffle the worst of it. They were tears of joy, sure, but also of relief—and a little bit of mourning. Mourning the loss of the child we could've had together, but relief and joy over the fact that he was willing to try again with me. Exactly as we'd given our love story a second chance, we'd give ourselves a second chance to be parents together.

He pulled away and swiped the tears from my cheeks. Then his mouth kicked up at the corner in a little smirk. "You wanna start trying right now?"

I barked out a laugh and shoved him away, lifting the hem of my shirt to dry my face before we went back into Chloe's room.

"Not yet," I said, and he hooked his arm around my shoulders, pressing a kiss to my hair as he led me back down the corridor. "But soon."

chapter 37
Brie

THE RINGING OF AN outgoing call filled the bakery kitchen as I waited for my sister to pick up. I moved around the island, tidying up the mess I'd made putting together more take and bake mixes and prepping for the next day. Though tomorrow was Valentine's Day, I was operating at shortened hours because I had a special surprise planned for Ezra, and I wanted to make sure I had enough time to execute it.

"Hey, Bee," Amara said when she answered at last, sounding a little out of breath.

"Hey, Mar. You okay?"

"I'm fine," she said, sucking in some air. "Just disgustingly pregnant. My phone was downstairs, and I was up in the nursery."

"How's that going?" I asked.

"It's pretty much set up," she said. "But I wanted to make sure the furniture was put together before the baby shower next weekend so I have places to put all that shit."

I chuckled. Thanks to my insider knowledge, Amara wasn't prepared for all the "shit" Mom, my sisters, and I had bought for that baby. It was a good thing the nursery had plenty of space, because she and Cal were going to need it for the baby.

"Are you nervous?"

"A little bit," she admitted. "Seeing Chloe and Logan with Aleah... It's hard to imagine something that size has to come out of my body, but they're so tiny and fragile. And then we're just going to leave the hospital with them? And be responsible for keeping them alive forever? That's...daunting, to say the least."

"You and Cal are going to be amazing parents, Mar. And you've got the whole family to help you."

"I know," Amara said, sniffling a bit. "The baby isn't even here yet, but I already know we couldn't do it without you all."

"Auntie Brie will happily come over for snuggles whenever you want."

I could hear the smile in Amara's voice as she said, "Love you, Bee."

"Love you more."

"Now, there's a reason you called?" my sister asked, suddenly all business.

I chuckled and said, "Yeah, actually. I was wondering if it'd be okay for me and Ez to stay at the Villa tomorrow night."

"For what exactly?"

"I...have a surprise planned for him to celebrate, but my apartment is too small, and his house is too full of other people."

"Ahh, so a *kinky* surprise," my sister said knowingly, and I was grateful she couldn't see my blush.

"Yes, a kinky surprise," I said, surprised by the evenness of my tone.

My sisters and I didn't shy away from discussing our sex lives, but I'd never really had much to contribute before. After New Year's Eve, they'd hounded me until we had a movie night, when

I told them everything. It felt good to get it all off my chest, to have my sisters squeal and fan themselves over my stories instead of being the one gassing them up for their own escapades.

Ezra didn't know I told them all about the stuff we got up to behind closed doors, but what he didn't know wouldn't hurt him. My sisters were my best friends, and we didn't keep secrets.

"In that case, be my guest," my sister said, chuckling at her pun. Technically, the title to the Villa was jointly held by the seven of us, but the company managed bookings and advertising. "It's not like anyone else is using it right now anyway."

I was suddenly very grateful for the snow and lack of winter tourists that precipitated closing the winery—and its connected businesses—for the first three months of every year.

"Thanks, sissy," I said, gearing up to end the call.

Before I could, she said, "Wait! Question."

"What's up?"

"Any idea why I've got a meeting with him on the schedule for next week? We don't typically start menu planning for the spring until March. But maybe because I'll be off on leave, he wants to get a head start..."

She trailed off, waiting for me to fill in the blanks, but I wasn't about to ruin this for Ezra. Since New Year's Eve, he'd been busy doing research and making plans for the community garden he wanted to open. I was wildly excited for him—and for the project itself. It was a passion of both of ours, to give back to the community in any way we could and teach people the merits of growing their own produce whenever possible.

"That's not my secret to tell," I said. "But I think you'll like the idea."

My sister growled, a sound that legitimately sounded like a bear or some other feral creature on the other end of the line.

"I'm too pregnant for this shit," she said then unceremoniously hung up.

I couldn't help but laugh. The deeper she got into her pregnancy, the stronger her mood swings. Where Chloe had basically been sunshine and rainbows, Amara wasn't having as easy of an experience. Her morning sickness had lasted deep into her second trimester, and once she'd gotten that under control, she was diagnosed with gestational diabetes. For Chloe, pregnancy had been smooth sailing. Unfortunately, Amara had a much bumpier road.

Idly, I wondered which category I'd fall into when I got pregnant—or if I'd land somewhere in between.

All I knew was I couldn't wait to find out.

❧❧❧❧❧ ❧❧❧❧❧

After an all-too-brief phone call with Ezra the day before to tell him I'd be MIA and to meet me at the Villa tonight, I'd been running around like a mad woman, both in prep for bakery hours and getting all the supplies I needed to execute my plan.

It had been a long time since I'd attempted to mold my own chocolate, but I was more than a little pleased with the final product—and I hoped Ezra would be too.

When I finally finished and stowed the chocolates in the fridge to make sure they wouldn't melt before I had time to get set up, I dashed upstairs and rushed through an everything shower. I lathered my body in coconut-scented edible body butter, left my hair to air dry in long, soft waves, and wrapped myself in a red silk robe before heading back downstairs.

The plan was simple: lay out on the dining room table and decorate my naked flesh in the chocolate I'd painstakingly made for Ezra...then let him consume it off me before he consumed me.

I'd briefly considered asking one of my sisters to come help me, but even though we were close, we weren't close enough to be all up in each other's privates. This was an intimate thing for only me and Ezra. He'd be the only person—*ever*—who got me like that.

After putting the confections I'd need on a small paper plate, I moved into the dining room, dropped my robe, and climbed onto the table. The surface was frigid beneath my overheated flesh, but it helped soothe some of my nerves.

Sitting up and bending in half, I first placed a trail of chocolate-covered cherries on my ankles, knees, and thighs. Then I reclined to add a square of dark chocolate over my smooth pubic bone, drizzling a little of the liquid chocolate over it for good measure before adding some to my belly button. I removed the remaining treats from the plate and unceremoniously tossed it across the room, making a mental note to pick it up tomorrow.

Next, I laid flat and put heart-shaped chocolates filled with caramel over my nipples, taking shallow breaths to ensure the rise and fall of my chest didn't send them falling to the table.

The final touch was a chocolate-covered strawberry I held between my lips.

I couldn't move, meaning I couldn't check the time, so I had no idea how long I waited until I heard the keypad on the front door beep, Ezra's "hello?" proceeding him inside.

I hadn't really thought this through, hadn't considered he wouldn't know where to find me. Since I'd been here most of the day and it was the middle of winter, I'd turned just about every light in the house on to combat the early onset darkness that blanketed our state this time of year.

He continued to call for me, and my body hummed with anticipation as he moved closer until finally, from the corner of my eye, I saw him appear at the threshold to the dining room.

"Well, well," he said, his grin obvious in his voice, "what do we have here?"

He approached my side, smirking down at me.

"Hey, honey. This all for me?"

I blinked twice, hoping it conveyed to him that, yes, this was all his—the treats and my body.

His gaze raked over my body, my blood heating in its wake as he rubbed his hands together like a man presented with too many choices, trying to decide which option to select first.

"Where do I begin?" he said softly, reaching out and trailing a finger along the underside of my breast, dragging it down my side, over my hip, and along the line of my quad.

"How about I start with these cherries and work my way up? Does that sound good?"

I blinked again in response, and he grinned wickedly as he bent over my ankle, his tongue darting out to scoop the cherry into his mouth, his lips lingering, a soft moan emanating from his throat as the sweetness coated his tongue.

He repeated the process on the other side, then my knees and thighs, driving me insane with his glancing touches and the wet press of his lips against my flesh.

I wasn't aware I had so many erogenous zones on my body; leave it to Ezra to find and exploit each and every one of them.

By the time his mouth hovered over my pussy, I was a puddle of unspent desire. A can of soda shaken and desperate for release.

"You taste like coconut."

"Lotion," I attempted to say around the strawberry, but it came out as more of a random mumble.

"Shh, baby. You keep quiet and let me work."

I moaned as he pressed his mouth to my skin and dragged his tongue from hip bone to hip bone, close but still too far from where I needed him most. I could feel my arousal pooling at my entrance and slipping free to coat my thighs. I wanted Ezra to clean it all up, to lick every inch of me until I was a writhing mess.

And then, I wanted him to fuck me until I saw stars.

He leaned into my pussy and scooped up the chocolate without warning, his tongue dipping briefly into my slit before he pulled away, and I whimpered.

I needed more, and he rewarded me by following his tongue with a finger, tracing around my clit without applying any pressure, only to remove it. The tip was coated in more chocolate, and Ezra sucked it into his mouth, eyes fluttering closed.

"I'll never be able to eat chocolate another way," he said when they popped open.

Then he turned and headed across the room, and I made a sound of protest.

"Patience, baby," he said, coming back with the bowl of strawberries I'd cleaned and cut the tops off earlier. "I need to make sure I clean you up. Can't let any of your hard work go to waste."

He lifted one of the strawberries from the bowl and brought it to my pussy, sliding it between my lips and using it to clean up the remaining liquid chocolate from the sensitive flesh. I resisted the urge to squirm, setting my feet on the table and dropping my knees wide to give him better access.

I was rapt on his mouth as he lifted the fruit to his lips and took a sinful bite.

I loved watching him savor the treat, knowing it was something I'd created for him, something he was clearly deriving great pleasure from.

When he swallowed, he said, "Best chocolate-covered strawberries I've ever had. Although I had a feeling the one on your lips will be my undoing."

I didn't dare move, could barely breathe for fear of upsetting the heart-shaped chocolates I'd settled over my nipples. Ezra dropped more of the chocolate sauce on my stomach, drawing a path from my navel to the valley between my breasts, adding to the bit already pooled in my belly button, then topped it with a line of whipped cream.

His eyes were nearly black, his expression ravenous as he pulled back to study his work.

"I have no idea what I did to deserve you," he said as he lowered his mouth to my flesh, his tongue wet and hot as it licked up the mess he'd made.

It was too much. The best of his tongue combined with the cool texture of the whipped cream against my skin was a contrast that had goosebumps erupting all over. All that was left were the chocolates on my nipples and the chocolate-covered strawberry I held against my lips. It had started to melt while I waited, some of the taste coating my tongue. I had to admit, I'd done a damn good job.

Ezra pressed kisses to the curves of my breasts, circling around the peaks but never going for that sweet spot I needed him to touch.

I made a noise of protest when he bypassed my chest entirely to lick a path up my throat, and he chuckled darkly.

"Needy little girl," he said. "I like that you can't talk. Can't tell me what you want. You're entirely at my mercy, aren't you, honey? I could torture you for hours, and you'd lay there and take it like the good girl you are."

I moaned low as heat pooled between my thighs with his words.

"But I'm not going to torture you, baby. Not tonight. Everything about you right now is too delicious, too fucking tempting. I need to sample it all."

At last, he shifted his head and closed his mouth around my nipple, his teeth softly scraping my sensitive flesh as he cleaned up every bit of the chocolate coating my skin.

He pulled back and licked his lips, though they were coated in melted candy. "Fuck, you're sweet."

After repeating the process on the other side, biting at me in a way that had my back arching, desperate to get closer to him, for him to give my core some friction, he at last hovered his face over mine.

"I love you," he said before he bent and captured the final strawberry and my lips with his. I opened for him, letting the chocolate-covered fruit mingle between us, loving that I could taste it and every other sweet treat he'd collected from my body on his tongue.

"Need you now," I breathed when he pulled away.

"Right here?" he asked.

"Right here," I confirmed, clawing at his shirt. He obliged me, pulling it over his head before stepping out of his pants. Then, he reached for me, dragging me to the edge of the table and off before spinning me and bending my front over its cool surface.

"Gonna fuck you just like this," he mumbled, smacking my backside. "Wanna watch this gorgeous ass ripple with every thrust."

"*Ezra*." The word was part whine, part moan, and entirely frustrated.

"My greedy fucking girl."

"Only yours," I agreed. I wasn't even sure I was making sense, so horny I was seconds away from coming apart.

"I didn't bring any condoms, honey, and I really don't feel like running upstairs."

"Don't. I need you now."

"Bare?" he asked, pressing a kiss between my shoulder blades. I turned my head to look at him. "If I take you bare, honey...I'm not pulling out."

"Don't."

"You're not on birth control."

"Put a baby in me, Ez."

"Fucking hell, woman," he said, brushing his head through my slit then lining up with my entrance. "You have ruined me."

I gasped as he roughly pushed inside, and he gave me a beat to adjust before setting a punishing pace that had my thighs slamming uncomfortably into the edge of the table. But the pain was secondary to the pleasure he wrung from my body, from the high I got just being connected to him like this. The slapping sounds of our thighs and the wet sounds of him pumping in and out of me echoed through the otherwise quiet room, and I braced my feet to better greet him, to drive him deeper each time.

He drove me higher and higher until my climax shimmered before me, the pressure on my clit nearly unbearable as I clenched my walls tighter around him and reached between us to thumb that bundle of nerves. A few brushes of my fingers was all it took to set me off into space, the edges of my vision darkening as stars danced in front of them.

Distantly, I heard Ezra say, "Last chance to back out," through gritted teeth.

"Never. I want your babies. No time like the present to start trying."

His grip on my hips tightened as he pistoned faster, prolonging my orgasm as he found his own. With a rough, almost strangled cry, he spilled, hot and long, inside me.

He quickly withdrew and flipped me onto my back, lifting my hips and holding me there. I hooked my heels on the edge of the table to keep myself upright.

"Can't waste any of my cum, can we, baby?" Ezra asked, reaching a hand between my thighs when I was steady so he could shove anything that leaked out back in.

It hit me then that we were really doing this.

The life together.

The family.

The babies.

Everything.

I grinned at him as I came down from my high, our entire future stretching out in front of me in my mind.

"I love you so much," I said, tears springing to my eyes and flowing freely.

"I love you more, honey."

chapter 38

Ezra

"You ready?" Brie asked, gripping my hand tightly as we walked into the winery.

"As ready as I'll ever be."

Today was the day of my big meeting with Amara and Liam, and in true Brie fashion, she'd made it a family affair. We'd moved it from the offices to the restaurant, which was still closed, to accommodate the entire Delatou gang. Since I'd been the one to call this meeting, I was, for once, not cooking lunch. We'd talked Tanya from Granny Smith's Tavern into feeding us, and as long as I got to stuff my face with one of her signature mushroom and Swiss burgers when this was all over, I could survive this meeting.

"It's going to be great," she said as we made our way through the lobby. Chatter from her family greeted us, and I hated the lead weight that settled in my stomach.

For some reason, I felt like a lot was riding on this. My livelihood wouldn't suffer if the community garden didn't pan out, but I genuinely felt as if the community's would. There was all kinds of undeveloped land on the peninsula, all of which was owned by the Delatou family. All I wanted to do was to carve a little piece out for myself and the rest of the residents of Apple Blossom Bay to enjoy.

Truthfully, I didn't think that was asking too much.

"Ezra, my boy!" Leon boomed as Brie and I crossed the threshold, and I couldn't explain why, but I instantly relaxed. This man had been a number of things to me over the years: friend, confidant when my world was falling apart, boss, caretaker of my child, friend again when he'd ultimately stepped aside as CEO.

But now that Brie and I were committed to each other, our dynamic had yet again shifted, and I found myself bracing for the moment when he'd pull me into one of his signature back slapping hugs...and strangle me to death instead of releasing me.

"Relax," Brie whispered and let go of my hand as her dad dragged me into an embrace.

I sighed deeply when he let me go.

Maybe one day, I'd grow out of that terror, but...Leon Delatou was an imposing man, and nothing in the world was more important to him than his girls.

As a parent myself, I knew the feeling, but I also understood it was different between a father and son than between a father and daughter. Would I retaliate against anyone who dared hurt Hansen? Of course.

But Leon was the kind of man who would go scorched earth for his daughters.

With a hand on my shoulder, he directed me away from Brie and toward the head of the table, pausing at a chair beside Liam. Across the table from him sat Amara, Cal next to her, their hands clasped together.

"You taking good care of my girl?" Leon asked before letting me go.

"Always," I promised him.

Leon nodded and moved around to sit on Calvin's side, and Brie took the seat next to Liam.

But I needed her next to me, and even two feet apart was too much.

"Trade with her," I told Liam, glancing between them.

"Oh, Ez, it's fine," Brie said, waving her hand.

"I don't mind," Liam said, already rising to move.

"C'mon, honey." I patted the chair next to me. "Sit."

"Possessive and demanding," Amara said with a twinkle in her eye.

"I'll take that as a compliment," I told her.

"Don't worry," she said, sharing a quick look with her boyfriend. "It was one."

I felt a little bad forcing Liam out of his seat, but he didn't seem too bothered by it. In fact, the man had more excitement shining on his face than I'd ever seen from him as he slid into the seat next to Ella and immediately drew her into conversation, their heads bent low together.

I hadn't realized they'd known each other that well. Obviously, the entire Delatou, Inc. and Chateau Delatou staff knew the family, but Ella wasn't all that connected to the winery, and from my understanding, Liam rarely ventured into town, save for supplies.

Interesting.

My gaze swept across the rest of the people gathered; over Chloe and Logan, Delia and Owen, Leon and Lena, Liam and Ella, Amara and Cal, finally settling on my girl.

She gave me a reassuring smile, and with a cleared throat to garner everyone's attention, I launched into my speech.

In truth, I barely remembered what I said, seeming to black out in my desire to get it all out as quickly as possible. I hated being the center of attention like this. I liked my food to do the talking for me. But it was obvious to me from my time spent around them that, in this family, we didn't shy away from the hard conversations or asking for what we wanted.

When I finished explaining how I planned to use it as a learning tool for our youth, to allow adults the opportunity to put fresh produce on their tables, to give the community a fun project to work on year-round, I closed my eyes, mentally bracing myself for the onslaught of questions and backlash.

But it never came.

Instead, a loud clap broke the quiet, and Leon said, "That's a wonderful idea, Ez."

My eyes popped open and connected with his. "You really think so?"

"I absolutely do." He turned to his wife and reached for her hand. "We'll help you however we can."

A chorus of agreements rose from the table, and I relaxed further. Convincing these people that this was a good idea—and something the community needed—was more than half the battle.

I was feeling good; great, even.

Until I realized Amara and Liam appeared to be having a silent conversation with hand gestures and meaningful looks.

And I knew when Amara opened her mouth that I wasn't going to like what she had to say.

"It's a great idea, Ez. It's just...we don't really have winery land to allocate for it."

The bottom dropped out of my stomach, and my heart sank to the floor.

Fuck, I hadn't even considered that. I'd been so sure my idea was sound, that I'd done all my research, that Amara and Liam would jump at the chance to make it work.

How could I have been so naïve? They were running a business here, one that couldn't cater to my little hopes and dreams.

"I'm sorry, man," Liam said with a wince, though at least he had the decency to meet my gaze head on. "We're looking to expand our white grape production, and the only undeveloped land we have at the moment is that hillside where we'll start planting those in a few weeks."

Shit, I'd forgotten all about that. And speaking of...

"Weren't you supposed to go out west to pick those new plants up?"

Liam chuckled, and Amara huffed out a sigh.

"I was, but with Amara's pregnancy, we didn't really have the few weeks it would take to spare, so we just shipped them in."

That made a lot of sense. In truth, I never understood why Amara wanted him to drive out there in the first place. I knew she trusted his judgement above all others when it came to these things, save her father's, but that was a long way to travel knowing he might not approve the purchase.

Then another thought occurred to me.

"But you're still going on a road trip."

"I am," Liam said, and I didn't miss the way Ella almost imperceptibly stiffened next to him. "At the end of April, once planting season is over and we have a lull before tourist season picks up."

"Where are you headed?"

"Out west," he said with a laugh. "I figure I'll venture through South Dakota, Wyoming, and Idaho on my way to Portland for my brother's wedding."

"That sounds like a hell of adventure," I said.

"I've never done anything like it, but I've always wanted to."

"I imagine it'll be the trip of a lifetime," I said. "I did a backpacking and cooking trip through Europe right after I graduated high school, and it was the best thing I've ever done." On my right, Brie cleared her throat, and I glanced down at her, smiling softly. "Except for you, of course."

"And Hansen," she added.

"And my boy."

"Hey!" Owen said suddenly from the other end of the table. "If you're heading through Idaho, you should swing through Dusk Valley. My brothers are in charge of the ranch these days, and West runs a dude ranch. I'm sure he'd be happy to put you up for a few nights."

"I just might take you up on that," Liam said, taking a breath to continue, but Brie cut him off.

"Sorry to break up this little bromance brewing here," she said, gesturing between Liam and Owen, "but can we please get back to the matter at hand?"

"Right," I said, mentally smacking myself.

"I'm not sure there's much more to discuss," Amara said. "We can't offer up any Delatou land, and I'm not sure where else on the peninsula you'll find a plot big enough."

"We can use mine," Brie piped up.

I glanced down at her, brows drawing together. "Yours?"

"I've never told you?" she asked.

"Told me what?"

"When we turned eighteen, Mom and Dad deeded us each a forty-acre plot of land on the north end of the peninsula, surrounding their house. Chloe built a house on hers—which Amara and Cal now live in. Delia broke a chunk off hers to use for the distillery. As of right now, my, Amara's, and Ella's sit empty, so we can use a split of mine for the garden."

I blinked in shock, unable to believe what I was hearing. Between the five Delatou daughters sat nearly two hundred acres of undeveloped land. I'd known from my time working for the family that their roots in the area ran deep, that Leon's grandfather had once owned roughly ninety percent of the peninsula, but this...

I couldn't let Brie do this for me. Could I?

"That land isn't meant for you to just give away, honey," I told her.

Brie scoffed. "It's my land, *honey*. I can do with it what I want."

"And you want to help me with this community garden."

It wasn't a question, just a flat statement that I was having difficulty believing. Brie had so much of her own shit going on, between getting started on the cookbook and expanding her online store, plus keeping the townspeople of Apple Blossom Bay fed with her delectable treats, that I wasn't sure where she'd find the time.

"Of course I do," she said, like me questioning her sincerity was the dumbest thing in the world. Ignoring the other people in the room with us, she turned and crawled into my lap, cupping my cheeks in her hands and moving so her lips were a breath from mine. "I know this is your passion project, and I fully support that, but you can let me help you—and you will. Just like you're helping me with the cookbook. This is just another thing we can do together."

I didn't answer verbally, only nodded and pressed my lips to hers quickly.

"I don't know what I did to deserve you," I whispered.

She tapped my nose before climbing off me and said, "You got really lucky."

"So...you're going to use Brie's land?"

"Yes," my girl answered her sister before I could. "I've been meaning to develop it anyway. I think it's time."

"You don't mean..." Amara trailed off, eyes wide, dancing between me and her sister.

"Yep," Brie said happily. "I'm building a house too."

"*What*?" I exploded. "For what?"

Brie turned a quizzical look at me. "For us."

She said it like it was the most obvious thing in the world, but to me, it wasn't. We'd briefly discussed living conditions, knowing we wanted to be together always, but I'd been under the impression we'd start looking in the spring, when more houses started going on the market.

I hadn't planned on her choosing to build us an entire fucking house.

"I can't let you do that," I told her.

Sensing another argument brewing, a number of our party rose from their chairs and peeled off, including Cal, Owen, and Logan. What did surprise me was that Ella also disappeared, and the second she did, Liam, who'd had his eyes glued to her retreating form, awkwardly rose from his chair.

"I'm gonna take a walk," he said, discomfort obvious in every line of his body. "Go see if Ella needs help."

When he'd gone, the only people who remained were Brie's other three sisters and parents.

Fuck. There was a time and place for conversations like these, and honestly? This wasn't it. But I could see it in the straight, firm line of Brie's shoulders, ramrod spine, and clenched jaw that we were hashing this out here and now.

"Sweets," her dad said softly. "Are you sure this is what you want to do?"

Still sitting on my lap, she turned to face her parents and sisters. "Of course I'm sure."

"But are you really?" I asked, unable to stop myself from pressing the issue.

This was a huge decision. Building a house, first and foremost, wasn't going to be cheap. And second, well...I supposed I was having a hard time wrapping my brain around the fact that this was something she wanted to do with *me*. *For* me, Hansen, and my dad—because we all knew wherever his grandson went, Papa would follow.

"Stop it," Brie said, rising to her feet. "All of you just *stop*."

The six of us stilled at her words, tone more commanding than I'd ever heard from her before.

"I know you all care about me, and that's why you're pressing this issue, but I'm not a little girl anymore. I'm twenty-five, and I've been making my own decisions for a long time. I get that you want to protect me, but..." She glanced down at me, and everything in her softened. "Being with Ezra is the first thing I've done right in a long time." I squeezed her hand, and she faced her family again. "I'm building our forever home on my land, and we're building the community garden on it as well. End of story."

Pride surged within me, and it took everything I had not to go full caveman, throw her over my shoulder, and take her somewhere we could be alone.

But that would undermine her authority here, and I wasn't about to take this moment away from her just because I couldn't control myself when she was near.

Her family loved her, and I knew they'd get on board eventually, but those moments where they sat still and silent were some of the longest of my life. Brie practically strangled my hand with how hard she gripped it, clearly willing herself not to react further, not to push for a response.

At last, Delia rose from her chair, rounded the table, and pulled her baby sister in for such a tight hug, I heard Brie's back crack.

"I'm so fucking proud of you," Delia said when she pulled away.

After that, the rest of the Delatou women and Leon followed suit, and I soon found myself engulfed in a tangle of limbs.

When we broke apart, Brie's family resumed their seats and chattered about nonsense while I pulled Brie to the side.

"Are you sure about this?"

I earned a glare and a defensive stance as she narrowed her eyes and crossed her arms over her chest.

"Do I need to repeat what I told my family?" she asked.

With a grin, I hauled her against me, settling for the first time in over an hour now that I had her wrapped in my arms. "Of course not," I said into her hair. "I just wish you would've talked to me about this before blurting it out in front of your whole family."

Brie leaned back so I could see her face, and her mouth turned down into a frown. "I wanted it to be a surprise."

I prodded the corner of her lips until she giggled. "But we're in this together, honey. You can't go making life altering decisions without me. What were you planning on doing? Building the house and surprising me with it when it was finished?"

"Well...yeah."

I chuckled and cupped her cheeks, bending to press a light kiss to her lips. "You're unbelievable."

"But you love me."

"More than anything except Hansen," I confirmed.

"As it should be."

"We'll build the house together," I said. "We'll find a contractor and start planning, just as long as you don't mind my dad being involved?"

"I have forty acres," she reminded me. "Even carving out some of it for the community garden, we'll still have plenty of space. I was actually thinking he could build his own place on the property."

"Like a little in-law suite of sorts?"

"Exactly."

I sighed, hugging her tightly to my chest, wishing I could meld our bodies together so I could always feel her against me like this, could always have her heart beating in time with mine.

"I'm not sure what I—no, what *we* did to deserve you, but my god, are we lucky to have you."

"Nah." Lifting her head, she offered her mouth up to me. When I met her halfway, she murmured against my lips, "I'm the lucky one."

FIVE WEEKS LATER

"Come on, honey! Hurry up, or we're going to be late!"

"It's not possible to be late to your own celebration," she grumbled. "At my family's winery, no less."

At last, my girl appeared at the top of the stairs, and my mouth went dry.

Over the years, I'd seen Brie in numerous situations. Dressy casual for family dinners. Covered in flour and fruit sauces, hair a mess, apron covering her leggings and tee at the bakery. Naked and writhing beneath me.

But somehow, this was my favorite: in one of her cute little sundresses, a long sleeved top and leggings underneath to ward against the cold, and black combat boots. She was equal parts feminine and edgy, a walking contradiction, and I loved every single side of her she gave me.

The five weeks since the meeting about the community garden had come and gone in a flash of constant activity. The fact that it was slow season for tourists proved to be a blessing, because Brie and I could focus all of our efforts on our upcoming projects.

First, we'd sat down with Jay Daniels—who happened to be Logan's father—about construction on our home and my dad's guest cottage, which would really be a thousand square-foot home designed to his exact specifications. Our place would be over twice the size of that, with a large master and en suite that included a massive freestanding tub, Hansen's room, which we were letting him decorate himself, and plenty of spare rooms to grow our family. True to form, the kitchen would be the focal point of the living space. Brie and I were taking our time choosing appliances and finishes, wanting it to be the space of our dreams where we could both create as well as teach Hansen and any future children the tools of our respective trades.

And now that the worst of the winter storms had passed and more temperate weather was on the horizon, Jay and his team would begin digging the foundation the first week of April—which was only a week away.

Next, once we'd decided on the best spot for the community garden, the entire Delatou clan, all their significant others, and I began planning the layout and how exactly we'd operate it. The point, for me, was to give back to this town while also using it as a place of learning. It would survive entirely on donations, and thanks to Brie's family, including Logan, Cal, and Owen, we had enough to operate for probably a decade before we'd even begin to see the bottom of our coffers.

I supposed it paid to be connected to the rich and famous. Even Logan's brother-in-law, Brent Jean, who was a star professional hockey player, had donated a significant sum, as had a few of his teammates and a few of Owen's from his NFL days.

Everything was coming together better than I ever dreamed,

and I was impatiently waiting for the last of the snow to melt and the ground to thaw so we could get to working the soil and readying it for plants.

Thankfully, the family had allowed us to use the garage at the Villa as a sort of makeshift greenhouse, and we'd been keeping some starters there in preparation. Did I think we'd have it all figured out in our first year? Of course not, but I knew we'd have fun figuring it all out. With Brie by my side, even the bad days were good.

With those two projects, we were arguably busier than we had time for, given Hansen's school and activity schedule and Brie's burgeoning online business. But somehow, we were gluttons, because we began work on the cookbook as well.

Those were honestly some of my favorite days, when Brie and I spent endless hours in the kitchen while Dad was working and Hansen was at school, honing recipes and playing around with old favorites. Learning from each other was fun too, and I was never mad about the times that ended with us naked and tangled with each other.

For the past few years, I'd spent my birthday wallowing.

This year, though, I had so fucking much to be thankful for, so much to celebrate, that I found myself getting a little misty-eyed as Brie and I drove down to the winery for my party.

"You seem nervous," I said to Brie as I drove. She'd been un-characteristically quiet, not talking my ear off about the cook-book or garden like she usually would.

"I'm not nervous," she scoffed. "Just a lot on my mind."

I reached over the console and grabbed her hand, giving it a reassuring squeeze. "Talk to me, honey."

Our gazes connected briefly before I had to return my attention to the road, but she said, "Just wondering how we're going to do it all. Maybe we bit off more than we could chew."

We'd reached the drive to the winery, so I didn't answer her until I pulled into a parking space and turned the car off. Then I turned to her and said, "We can do this, Brie. *You* can do this. But no one is going to think any less of you if you decide to take a step back from some of it."

She nodded sadly, her shoulders slumping, like I hadn't told her what she wanted to hear. But we weren't in the habit of lying to each other, and I meant every word.

This woman... She was so young still, only twenty-five. She had her whole life to realize her dream of publishing a cookbook or of doing any of the other thousand things she'd set her mind to.

"I'm proud of you always, honey. You know that, right?"

"Of course," she said softly, giving me a half-smile that was edged with an emotion I couldn't name. Instantly, an oily, unsettled feeling sloshed in my gut, but Brie was withdrawing her hand from mine and pushing out of the car before I could press her on what was really bothering her.

If something was truly wrong, she'd tell me. Right?

Shaking it off and making a mental note to bring it up later when we were home, I once again captured her hand with mine, and we walked inside together.

As usual, the whole crew was gathered. Beer and wine flowed, tables pushed against the perimeter of the room and laden with food—that I didn't cook for once—that guests could enjoy buffet-style.

The moment we appeared, we were both swept off in opposite directions. Liam approached me first, a move that surprised me, given his propensity for hanging out on the fringes of these types of gatherings, wanting to fill me in on how our starter plants were going. Immediately, I lost sight of Brie in the surprisingly large crowd, but I tried my best to fight my concern that maybe she was avoiding me.

After all, it was my birthday, and whatever was going on with her had nothing to do with us, so I did my very best to enjoy myself.

Soon, Leon and Lena joined my conversation with Liam, and we veered off plants in favor of discussing how the plans for my and Brie's house were coming along. Jay had also been responsible for building Leon and Lena's and Chloe's homes, as well as constructing the distillery Owen and Delia had built the previous fall. He'd also done all the contracting work on Brie's bakery, and I was excited to see the vision for our home come to life under his experience and watchful eye.

The most special part, though, was that because my dad worked for Jay as a foreman, he'd also be helping spearhead the project, and Delia would be in charge of interior design.

So much had changed in four years, and it truly amazed me. If you'd told me back when everything had gone down with Shannon that I'd move to a small town in Michigan, meet the love of my life, and settle down here, I'd have said you were crazy. While I'd grown up with only my dad as my family and had spent a few years with just him and Hansen, I found my heart expanding as the realization dawned that I'd found all of these people who welcomed me and mine into the fold with open arms. I'd created the family I'd longed for my entire life, and I couldn't have done it without Brie.

Which was why, the second it didn't feel rude to do so, I offered hasty goodbyes to her family and pulled her out of the winery to head home.

I'd been on pins and needles all day, waiting for the moment when I could get her alone so we could finally hash out whatever was eating at her.

Dad and Hansen had gone to Detroit for the weekend, and I was grateful Brie and I had the house to ourselves for once. We could lay it all out there, and then I could fuck her into oblivion afterward.

Before she could get too far away from me as we walked into the house, I directed Brie into the kitchen and turned her to face me.

"What's going on?"

She wouldn't meet my eyes as she said, "What do you mean?"

"I mean, you've been distant and acting weird all day. Are you...mad at me? Having second thoughts about us?"

The words were razor blades in my throat, but I pushed them out past the pain. Truthfully, Brie leaving me on my birthday would really be par for the course, but I forced myself to relax, to wait her out before I went jumping to conclusions.

Instead of answering me, she moved to the pantry and rifled around behind some canisters until she withdrew a long, rectangular Tupperware container.

"What's this?" I asked as she approached and set it on the island in front of me.

"Happy birthday," she said simply, removing the top.

Inside were a dozen cupcakes, each decorated differently, indicating their different flavor combinations.

The exact same cupcakes she'd made for my birthday and shipped to me from Chicago three years ago.

"You remembered," I said, looking at her in awe.

Brie rolled her eyes with a little laugh. "Of course I remembered." At last, she came to me, wrapping her arms around my waist and tipping her head back for a kiss.

I wasted no time giving her what she wanted, sighing deeply in relief as we connected. Kissing her was coming home, and even the few hours I'd gone without her lips on mine, when I'd fully spiraled and wondered what the hell I'd do without her, had been too goddamn long. Her tongue darted out against my lips, seeking entry, and I let her have it. Her flavor coated my tongue as she swept hers in, a combination that was entirely her own—all honeyed sweetness.

I spun us and hooked my hands behind her thighs to lift her onto the counter. Then I notched my thumb under her chin and tilted her head where I wanted her, trailing open-mouthed kisses down the column of her throat.

One of Brie's hands fisted in my hair while the other gripped my shirt, and before I could get too deep into my exploration of her body, before I could strip her out of her dress and eat her for dessert instead, she said, "I've got one more gift for you."

I pulled back, eyes sweeping over her face as my forehead scrunched in confusion.

"All I need is you."

Brie smiled softly. "That's sweet, but I think you're going to like this one."

"Okay..."

"Before I give it to you, I have a question to ask you."

"Anything."

"Marry me?"

She moved her hands to the nape of her neck and unclasped her necklace, pulling it free from the collar of her dress and sliding something off it before holding whatever it was out to me.

In her palm rested a small silver circle.

With a start, I realized it was a ring.

"Shouldn't I be the one asking you this?"

Brie waved me off. "Who gives a fuck about tradition?"

I grinned. Damn, did I love it when my girl swore.

"I was going to, you know. Ask, I mean. And soon."

She shrugged. "I'm just beating you to the punch. I want to marry you. As soon as possible."

"What's the rush?"

"I love you," she said. "More than I ever thought I could love someone. You're everything I ever dreamed of, and I'd endure every moment of heartache and disappointment and years without you again if it brought us to this moment."

"Me too," I whispered.

My loveless marriage, Shannon's infidelity, substance abuse problems, the accident. For her—and for Hansen—I'd happily live it all again.

"So I want you to be my husband. I want the whole thing with you, Ez. The big house on the bluff overlooking the water. The kids running around. Growing old right here on this peninsula with my family—*our* family—surrounding us."

"And I'll give you all of it."

"You already are," she said, and silver lined her eyes as she grinned at me. "You already *have.*" She dipped her hand down the front of her shirt and withdrew a folded piece of paper. "I've been carrying this around all day, waiting for the perfect opportunity to give it to you. There's nothing that says we have to get married right away, but..."

She handed me the paper, and I unfolded it, my brain taking several beats to process what my eyes were seeing.

A sonogram.

"...I want us all to have the same last name when our baby comes," Brie finished.

When I looked up, awestruck, and met her gaze, those beautiful green eyes more vibrant than ever with unshed tears, I was surprised to find my own vision blurry as well.

I'd done this once before. Had a woman come to me and tell me she was having my child. Had stood with another partner in a different city halfway across the country and held a different sonogram of a different baby.

And this experience was worlds away from that one.

With Shannon, I'd been scared to death, both by the infancy of our relationship, which, at the time, hadn't been much more than fuck buddies, and by the thought of bringing a child into the world.

Hansen had been the best thing that ever happened to me...until Brie came along. All I felt in that moment, presented with the proof of our child growing in her womb, was a deeply rooted sense of peace. Of rightness. Of the realization that Brie and I were endgame, and our baby would never have to endure what Hansen had.

That, with her, Hansen and I finally found the family I'd always longed for.

Unintelligible words left my lips as I struggled to verbalize my thoughts into something that fully encapsulated everything I was feeling.

At last, I settled on, "I love you," and drew her in for a deep kiss.

When we broke apart again, both breathing hard, Brie said, "I love you too."

"I can't accept this, though," I said, closing her fingers around the ring.

"You don't want to marry me?" she asked, expression stricken.

"Oh, I fully plan on marrying you," I told her. "But you're going to be the one wearing a ring until that day."

With a wicked grin, I lifted her off the counter and walked us to my room, dumping her unceremoniously on the bed before moving to my dresser and withdrawing the ring box that had sat there for nearly two months.

"I bought this after Valentine's Day," I said, turning to her again. She sat on the edge of the mattress, and I knelt before her, popping the box open. I'd gone for something unique, something that represented Brie and what I felt for her. The stones sparkled under the overhead lighting, exactly like Brie's face.

"A baguette?" she said with a little chuckle.

"Seemed appropriate," I told her.

The rectangular sapphire glinted on a simple rose gold band, two tiny diamonds flanking it. I removed it from the cushion and held it out to Brie. Her hand shook as she lifted it, and I slipped it on her finger, pressing a kiss to her knuckles.

She clasped my face in her hands and bent to kiss me, but a breath away, she said, "Thank you for making me the luckiest girl in the world."

"Nah, honey," I said. "I'm the lucky one."

acknowledgements

As always, the first people I have to thank are my family. My parents, who don't balk when I wax poetic about all the stories I want to write, who are the most supportive of my dreams and have been from day one. To my sister, who lets me hang out with my babies when I'm having a rough day (which is basically every day of the week) and who lets me complain about how badly I just want to be writing full time. Who loves books as much as I do, and who shouts about my stories online to anyone who will listen like she's not related to me. My grandparents—particularly Granny J, who always texts me her thoughts when she's finished each new book, and who my love of books comes from. To Grammy and Grumpy who aren't here but I feel with me every step of the way anyway. To my aunts, uncles, and cousins, who constantly ask about how writing is going, or are buying, reading, and recommending my books to other family and friends. I couldn't do this without y'all.

To Mer, who continues to show up for me day after day. Who gets me better than just about anyone and knows exactly what to say to bring me back to earth when I'm spinning out, pull me back from a cliff when I'm ready to throw myself off it, or pick me up when I'm having a bad brain day. Best friends like you are one in a million, and I'm so fucking thankful you're mine.

To all the author friends who supported me, ran ideas with me, and genuinely were just there for me when I was in the trenches with this one. For being a text or a DM away, for reminding me I'm not alone in the struggle, and for uplifting me when I'm feeling down. I love y'all forever, and I'm so thankful for you. And to the ones who have overall given me a soft place to land and been there to cheer me on. I'll never be able to thank you all enough.

To Sarah, for blowing this cover out of the water. The sky, the colors, the vineyard? It's all perfection. I love working with you, and I can't wait to keep doing it for years to come.

To Meg Jones, the creator of the "dicktionary," for letting me include one in the back of this book, and to Hailey Dickert for the "spread your" pages wording. Appreciate you both so much!

Lastly, to my readers. Every page read, post, reel, DM, and recommendation to a friend—it all makes a difference, and it's the difference between me not doing this and me being one step closer to my dream of making writing my full-time gig. There aren't words for how grateful I am for you, whether you've read one page of one of my books, or all six of them cover to cover. THANK YOU.

about the author

Amanda Chaperon realized her passion for books, and for writing, at a young age. Growing up, she was rarely found without a book in her hands, a hobby she carried into adulthood. Now, she writes what she loves to read: messy, relatable characters, lots of steam, and always a happily ever after.

She currently lives in Michigan's Upper Peninsula with Gryffin, her Golden Retriever. She loves all things romance, fantasy, young adult, and thrillers that keep her up at night. You can follow her on Instagram, Threads, and TikTok at @achaperonwrites.

Dicktionary

My dear sweet reader, please use this guide to avoid (or seek out) the spicy scenes, which can be found in the following chapters:

Chapter 9
Chapter 13
Chapter 18
Chapter 32
Chapter 33
Chapter 34
Chapter 37

Spread those pages, my friend.

www.ingramcontent.com/pod-product-compliance
Lightning Source LLC
Chambersburg PA
CBHW031829310726
48972CB00005B/1217